Tom Johnson's Submarine

And How He Met Napoleon

By

M P Middleton

 New Generation Publishing

My thanks to:

Andy Eskelson
who advised on Mechanical and Nautical technicalities

and

John Middleton
who helped with research and editing

Pen to Print

Real People, Real Stories

This book has been produced with assistance from
The London Borough of Barking and Dagenham
Library Service
Pen to Print: Real People, Real Stories Creative Writing
Project 2016
with funding from The Arts Council, England Grants
for the Arts.

CHAPTER ONE

Small and wiry, with a head of curly brown hair, Able Seaman Jimmy Young got on with all his shipmates. It may have been because of the twinkle in his bright-blue eyes, or perhaps his cheeky smile, but everyone liked him.

He entered The George Inn in Southwark on Monday evening in hope of meeting some of his old seafaring friends. Few people were there. He called for a tankard of ale, and sat by the door nursing his drink, and pondering on his situation.

Now that the war with Napoleon was over, the Navy had no need of him nor a lot of other sailors. He had tried daily to find a berth on a ship. Although he was a man of experience, employment was given more readily to younger men. His friend, Paddy Gaskin, had invited him to join him in free trading. Despondent, he toyed with the idea.

Jimmy was not averse to setting his hand to petty pilfering, but engaging in smuggling was going a bit too far. The problem with smuggling was, if caught, it would mean imprisonment or execution. Although tempted, he had declined Paddy's invitation.

Now he sat gazing into his ale and calculating how long it would be before his money ran out.

Soon the inn received another visitor.

Having walked across London Bridge, Tom Johnson made his way to The George, where he would meet the gentleman who had requested a rendezvous with him at an inconspicuous location. Tom had made the appointment at The George for old times' sake.

It's been a while, he thought as he entered.

Stopping inside the door, he looked around the familiar taproom. It had changed little in the ten years since he had last visited. The same smells hung in the air. The whiff of tobacco, smoked over countless years; The musty woodiness of sawdust on the floor; the tang of smoke from the fire burning on the hearth of the big Inglenook fireplace; The warm scent of candles, whose light gave the room a warm and friendly glow, and the bitter savour of ale. Tankards stood on shelves behind three huge barrels. A wide plank of polished wood placed across them formed a bar.

Above the tankards were small barrels and bottles holding various types of liquor.

I don't suppose my tankard is still here, Tom mused.

Tom's eyes wandered away from the shelves as he caught a faint aroma of cooking floating from the entrance to the kitchen. He recognised familiar kitchen sounds, too. Was that the same faded brocade curtain covering the archway?

And there, beside the fire, was Tom's favourite seat, at the far end of a high-backed settle facing the door. Tom had appreciated the spot for its proximity to the fire and its view of the room—a good vantage point. It was far enough away from the door to avoid drafts, yet not so close to the fire as to be uncomfortably hot.

Tom ran his hands over the worn surface of the table in front of the settle, feeling for an old mark. Looking down at the table top, there, dark and mellowed, he saw his initials, carved some twenty years before.

He smiled, remembering. It was after the first time he had escaped from the Fleet Prison. In an act of sheer defiance, he had sat at the table, bold as a Maltese monkey, bent over the task of cutting his initials into the wood, while the runners searched The George—a place Tom was known to frequent—and left without him.

He put a hand to his forehead and chuckled. It was not the first or last time he had escaped prison.

His Irish parents, his sister, Maura and his brothers, Jack and Liam, had died of a fever when he was ten. He alone in his family had survived the illness. Afterwards, he lived by his wits on the streets, avoiding capture and the workhouse. His life of crime truly began at the age of twelve when he fell in with a gang of smugglers. Working with them had put money in his pocket.

For fourteen years, he had sailed to France and Spain, carrying contraband—well-hidden below— dodging blockades and excise men. The crews of the ships on which he sailed were made up of outcasts from assorted nations. Tom had learnt to speak French and Spanish fluently. He also picked up a smattering of Italian and Greek.

Tom loved the sea. He loved living on ships, being part of the crew. His particular liking was for soft, dark summer nights, the only light from the myriad stars scattered in the endless deep black skies.

Tom had risen to captaining legitimate ships, but, since Napoleon's defeat, that had recently come to a halt. If all went well with this meeting tonight, he could soon be back on the ocean.

'Tom Johnson, as I live and breathe!' a serving maid said as she moved towards him from the kitchen.

Tom looked up. He frowned for a moment, not knowing her.

'Nancy!' he exclaimed as he recognised her features, now past their youthful freshness. Many a time had he lain with her in the attic room she occupied at the top of the building. Warm and plump, she had been. Her dark hair, undone, contrasted with her creamy, soft skin. He remembered her eyes shining at him after they had coupled. When she got up to put on her shift, the sight of her had filled him with a longing for more. He had lain with many women over the years, but none as satisfying as Nancy. The way he felt about Nancy was the closest he ever came to love.

'How are you, Nancy?' He asked.

Her face seemed thinner, her bosoms bigger. He wondered whether the shape of her behind had the same sweet roundness he had known.

I wonder if she'd lie with me again? Tom thought. *Ah, but I have this business going on. Maybe when I've done with it, I'll come back and try my luck.*

'I'm fine, Tom. How are you? You've not been in The George for a long time. Where have you been?'

'Well, Nancy, would you believe I've been earning an honest living?'

'Not you, Tom Johnson. I don't believe it!' Nancy said, pushing teasingly on his shoulder.

'It's true. I've been piloting Naval expeditions. Covert expeditions, I might add. But I've been at a loose end since Bonaparte's capture.'

Nancy's eyes widened in disbelief.

'The Navy hired *you*? With *your* record? You're joking!' she said, sitting down beside him.

Tom felt an old thrill as Nancy moved close. Without thinking, he placed a hand on her thigh. She allowed it to linger there.

Maybe, if there's time, she might like to renew our acquaintance tonight, Tom thought.

The door opened. A well-dressed gentleman entered. Tom's attention moved from Nancy to his rendezvous.

The Gentleman removed his hat from his stylishly upswept hair and looked around. There were only three other men, apart from Tom, in the room. Two lolled on a bench by a window, drunk on gin. Another sat idly by the door. The gentleman's eyes swept over and past them before meeting Tom's gaze. Tom nodded faintly. The elegant gentleman strode to where Tom sat.

'Go, Nancy. This is business,' Tom murmured.

Nancy slid from the settle, casting Tom a promising smile before going towards the kitchen. Glancing back, she saw the gentleman sit opposite Tom.

'Are you Johnson?' the gentleman asked, his voice spiced with a hint of a French accent.

'I am,' Tom replied, his voice low. 'You must be

4

Colonel Corbeau.'

Corbeau inclined his head in assent and placed his hat and gloves beside him.

'You have been apprised of the business I wish to discuss?' Corbeau asked.

When Jimmy heard the French note in the gentleman's voice, he sat up, instantly alert. The war had taught him to be wary of anything French. *What's a Frenchie doing in London?* he thought.

He moved nearer the fire, making a play of warming his hands and surreptitiously cocking an ear to the men's conversation.

Tom sat back in his seat, eyeing Corbeau speculatively.

'I am aware you wish to gain liberty for a certain party,' Tom replied, shifting his position.

'Just so. I am informed of your inventing a craft you claim can proceed under water,' Corbeau said, scrutinising Tom with equal speculation.

'I do not claim it, Monsieur. I have created it. It is called a submarine. I, and my associate demonstrated the craft in the Seine. Although impressed with the vessel, Napoleon's minions found the cost of constructing it too high. It was to our mutual regret we parted company,' Tom explained.

'Ah,' Corbeau said, nodding his dark head.

Nancy appeared through the curtain, curiosity driving her to Tom's table.

'Do either of you gentlemen require refreshment?' she asked.

Corbeau's languid, white hand impatiently waved her away.

'A tankard of ale, please, Nancy,' Tom said, watching her hips sway as she moved towards the barrels.

'The cost of your Submarine is of no consequence. Its effectiveness is,' Corbeau said, his eyes on Nancy as she came back to the table with Tom's tankard.

Corbeau waited until she had returned to the kitchen before he continued. Leaning forward, he spoke rapidly in a low tone.

'We mean to sail to St Helena with your submarine. When we arrive, we will crave an audience with the Emperor. You and I will meet with Napoleon. A footman will be with us. This man will resemble Napoleon. The Emperor will don the footman's livery. Three men will go in, and three men will come out. Your submarine will aid in his removal from the island. That is the plan in a nutshell.'

Jimmy listened to what they discussed and couldn't believe what he overheard. *Are they truly planning to rescue Napoleon from St Helena?*

Jimmy hated the French with a passion and loved England with equal fervour. He considered it his patriotic duty to do all he could to foil the two men's plans. However, not only was he driven by a sense of responsibility, he was sure his loyalty would gain him a reward.

Tom sat forward, steepling his fingers before his mouth as he listened to the plan. He paused before responding.

'A simple sounding proposal,' Tom observed.

Corbeau smiled, inclining his head.

'I see several problems, however,' Tom said. 'How is the double to make his escape, for example? He is bound to be recognised eventually. Surely this man will be imprisoned, at the very least.'

Corbeau's smile waned. He casually turned up his palms, shrugging his shoulders.

'I leave that to you, Mr Johnson. I hear you have escaped incarceration many times. I am sure you can think of something. Our safety is of no consequence. The Emperor's liberty is all that concerns me.'

'My liberty *is* of consequence, Corbeau. My

freedom is very precious to me. I am now a respectable sea captain. I do not wish to go back to my old life. Danger was exhilarating in my youth. It beckons me no longer. Why, we could be shot or hanged for such a venture if caught,' Tom said, his usual affable expression replaced by glowering brows.

Corbeau rose, picking up his hat and gloves.

'All the more reason to devise something effective, Johnson. I shall leave you now to think on my proposal. I assure you, we will reward you handsomely for your pains. I shall return here tomorrow at noon. Good day to you, Sir,' Corbeau said, inclining his head again before moving to the door.

When Jimmy saw the French gentleman rising from the table and leaving the tavern, he decided to follow. He trailed the man along Borough High Street until he hailed a hackney cab, which carried him out of sight. Jimmy continued walking, thinking how he should proceed. He felt sure if he presented himself at The Admiralty, no one would take notice of him. An idea flashed into his mind. He decided Captain Crenshaw would be the very person to tell. It wasn't all that far to Poland Street where his former Captain lived. He would visit him and tell him of the treason about to be committed.

It's a bit late to be payin' calls, and besides, I'd need to clean meself up a bit, he thought, feeling his stubbly chin, and regarding his run-down appearance.

He quickened his pace, his step lighter, his mood brighter as he made his way back to his lodgings.

I'll sort meself out and go and see him first thing in the mornin', he thought.

Unaware of Jimmy, Tom leant back on the settle. He stretched his legs out before him under the table and folded his arms across his chest. Resting his gaze on the ceiling for a while after Corbeau left, he let out a long breath.

It will not be an easy task finding a man who looks like Napoleon. The plan needs a lot of refining, Tom mused.

Nancy had been observing Tom and the Frenchman from behind the kitchen curtain. She moved back into the taproom and hurried to Tom.

'Who the bleedin' hell was he?' she asked, wiping the table with a threadbare cloth.

'Someone with an interesting proposition, Nancy,' Tom said.

Leaning forward, he picked up his tankard. Some of his ale sloshed onto the table as he sat back with a jolt. 'Good God! Nancy! This is my old tankard. You've kept it all this time!' Tom exclaimed, staring at it.

'I couldn't bear to part with it, Tom. I hoped you'd come back one day,' Nancy said, hiding the unaccustomed shyness overtaking her as she mopped up the spilt ale with her cloth.

'Well I'm damned,' Tom said, his white teeth gleaming in a broad smile.

He took a long draft and wiped his mouth with the back of his hand.

'Are you going to take him up on his proposition?' Nancy asked.

'I don't know. It's dangerous if it goes wrong,' Tom mused.

'You used to thrive on danger, Tom,' Nancy remarked, putting an arm around his shoulder.

Tom felt the swell of her bosom against his arm. Slowly, he turned his head to look up into her eyes. There he saw the sparkle he remembered.

'He's coming back tomorrow at noon. I might lie here tonight if there's a room free,' Tom said, his voice husky.

'No, Tom, there's no room free. But you're welcome to share my bed if you like,' Nancy said, catching her lower lip between her teeth.

'I was hoping you'd say that, Nancy,' Tom said, patting her behind with a practised hand.

'I finish in half an hour. You can go and wait for me if you want,' Nancy said, her head tilted to one side as she gave him a saucy grin.

'I'll do that, Nancy,' Tom said, rising, and swilling back the rest of his ale.

'My room is …'

Tom interrupted her, bending his head near her ear.

'the same room as before, Nancy?' he whispered.

'Yes, Tom.'

Tom leaned closer and kissed her neck.

When Tom woke on Tuesday morning, he felt good; better than he had in a long time. He glanced around the familiar room. Remembering his night with Nancy, Tom smiled and stretched languidly. He thought of her voluptuous body as it yielded to his passion. He recalled the familiar smell of her, the sound of her, and the feeling of having returned home.

He had moved slowly, savouring every exquisite moment, pleasuring her as well as himself. They had reached the height of their ardour together, just as they always had in the past, and had fallen asleep, entwined in each other's arms.

Rolling over, he reached for her.

She wasn't there.

He swung himself out of the bed to find a pitcher of hot water and clean towels on the washstand. A bright fire burning in the grate took the chill off the room. He washed and dried himself. A clean shirt lay over a chair, beside it a pair of clean drawers.

As he put them on, he recognised them as his. Like his tankard, she had kept the clothes he had left behind. After dressing, he ran his fingers through his coarse, springy hair. Smiling, he took a long look around the room before clattering down the rickety stairs.

When he arrived in the taproom, Nancy was there. A

glow of a glance passed between them.

Nancy disappeared into the kitchen. Tom took his usual seat. Nancy returned moments later with cold mutton and a hunk of bread on a plate.

'Good morning, Tom,' she said as she put the plate before him. Tom looked up at her, a smile lighting his eyes.

'Good morning, Nancy-love,' Tom said, catching her hand, and kissing it.

'Not here,' Nancy said under her breath, put a knife and fork beside his plate and moved away.

She came back and placed Tom's tankard before his plate. Sitting opposite him, she watched him eat.

'You slept a long time, Tom. Your gentleman will be here soon,' she said.

As Tom finished his breakfast, Corbeau arrived. Nancy removed the plates and took herself back to the kitchen. Corbeau seated himself in her place.

'Well, Johnson, what have you decided?' Corbeau asked, without preamble.

'I have decided to aid you, Corbeau,' Tom replied.

The tension in Corbeau's face relaxed.

'Good,' he said with a hint of a smile. 'Where is your submarine now?'

'It's under cover at Blackwall Reach.'

'Good,' Corbeau said again. 'My associate and I will meet you with a coach at the Mint tomorrow at nine. From there you will take us to your craft. We will have further discussion then.'

Rising, swiftly, without another word, Corbeau left The George.

Nancy moved to Tom's side.

'What's happening, Tom?' she asked.

'I'm to meet him tomorrow, Nancy. After today, I might not see you till the business is completed. When it is, I'll return, I promise,' Tom said, giving her a warm look.

Nancy met his gaze with a roguish smile.

'Then we'd better make the most of tonight, Tom Johnson,' Nancy said.

CHAPTER TWO

On Tuesday morning, after overhearing Tom's conversation with Corbeau the night before, Jimmy went to Captain Crenshaw's lodgings at number ten Poland Street. Opening the iron gate, he walked up the path. He straightened his coat and adjusted the stock at his throat before he knocked at the door.

A plump maid in a lace-trimmed cap opened the door and peered at him. As she smoothed a hand over her crisp, white apron, worn over a light-grey dress, she looked him up and down.

'Can I help you?' the maid asked, giving Jimmy an appraising stare.

'I'd like to speak to Captain Crenshaw if you please,' Jimmy said returning the maid's look with one of feigned authority. 'It's a very important matter, about treasonous activity.'

The maid eyed him with suspicion.

'Treasonous activity? What's that then?'

'Well, me dear, I can't tell you, 'cos it's secret. Is your master at home or not?' Jimmy asked.

'Why should I tell you?' she asked.

'Because, if you don't tell him I'm here, and the activity comes to light, you'll be in trouble, me girl,' Jimmy said, making to turn away and go back to the gate.

'Wait a minute,' the maid called. 'I'll ask the Captain whether he wants to speak to you. What name shall I give him?'

'Able Seaman Jimmy Young. I served under him on *Ignatius,*' Jimmy said.

'You'd better come in and wait,' she said, holding the door open.

Jimmy stepped into the spacious hall.

The maid shut the door and gestured to a wooden hall chair set against the wall.

'Sit there,' she said and disappeared up the sweep of the stairs, which rose to the side of where the chair stood.

Jimmy sat down on the hard hall-chair. He took off his cap and fiddled with the brim, looking about the cool, dim, hall. The light from the stained-glass fanlight over the front door cast dappled patches of colour on the patterned floor tiles. Five doors led off the square shaped hall. Jimmy smelled polish and, wafting up from the kitchen, the unmistakable aroma of cooking cabbage. He heard the murmur of voices coming from upstairs, then the sound of the maid's footsteps, plodding in her heavy shoes. As she came down the stairs, Jimmy looked up to see Captain Crenshaw's head peering over the upper bannister.

'What's all this, Jimmy? Come up, come up,' he called.

Jimmy rose from his seat and walked towards the stairs.

'I didn't know who else to tell, Cap'n,' Jimmy called back as he ascended.

Jimmy had always seen his captain dressed in his uniform, his appearance meticulously well-groomed. Today, although his straight, light-brown hair was neat, there was stubble on his chin, and he was in his shirt sleeves with no neckcloth, his black trousers somewhat creased.

'Milly mentioned something about treason,' Crenshaw said with a frown as he took Jimmy's arm and led him to his set of rooms at the back of the house.

'Yes, Cap'n. They want to rescue Boney,' Jimmy said.

Crenshaw's eyes rounded. His mouth opened in a gasp.

'Good God,' he said as he ushered Jimmy into his study.

The smell of beeswax polish, books, and ink greeted Jimmy as he entered the neat, bright, airy room.

'Jimmy, are you sure?' Crenshaw asked after firmly closing the door.

'Sure as I'm standing here, Sir. I overheard this conversation, see, in The George, in Borough High Street.'

Crenshaw perched himself on the edge of his desk, gesturing to an upholstered chair behind it.

'Sit down, man, and tell me exactly what you heard.'

Jimmy sat and recounted in detail what Corbeau and Johnson had discussed.

Crenshaw listened, a frown on his face, his lips pursed. His intelligent brown eyes looked intently at Jimmy as he talked. When Jimmy had finished, Crenshaw blew his breath out slowly.

'Jimmy, would you be willing to say all this again to someone at The Admiralty?'

'Course I would, Cap'n if they'd listen to me,' Jimmy said sitting up straight.

'I shall go with you. I know a few men there. We can't sit around and do nothing. We must act on this, and swiftly.'

'Do you mean we're going now, Cap'n, Sir?'

'I do, Jimmy. No time like the present,' Captain Crenshaw said, flashing Jimmy a beaming smile as he pulled a bell cord in the corner of the room.

The sound of the maid's heavy shoes sounded again on the stairs, and Milly appeared at the door.

'Did you ring, Captain?' she asked.

'Yes, Milly. Ask Dick to get me a Hackney, if you please.'

Milly nodded. She left the room, and they heard her shoes sounding on the stairs again.

'Excuse me, Jimmy, I'll try not to be long. I must clean myself up. Do my best to look the gentleman, y'know,' he said with a grin.

When Crenshaw returned, he looked more like the Captain Jimmy knew. Clean-shaven, his shirt's crisp, high collar and the neatly tied cream-coloured cravat spoke of elegance. His fawn trousers tapered fashionably at the ankle, and his polished black boots shone. His dark-brown coat, too, was of fashionable cut; double-breasted with a shawl collar and wide shoulders. He carried his hat and his tan gloves. Jimmy was impressed.

'Sorry for the wait, Jimmy. All set now?' Crenshaw said.

'Aye-Aye, Cap'n,' Jimmy answered, putting two knuckles to his forehead.

As Jimmy followed Crenshaw down the stairs, he wondered whether someone *would* reward him for what he was doing.

Downstairs, Dick, the houseboy, waited for them.

'The cab's out the front, Captain,' he said.

'Thank you, Dick,' Crenshaw said, flipping a penny in Dick's direction.

Dick caught it and smiled as he opened the front door.

Crenshaw and Jimmy made their way down the path and out through the iron gate to where the cab awaited them.

Catching sight of them, the driver tipped his hat.

'Where to, guvnor?' he called.

'Ripley Building, please, Jarvey,' Crenshaw said and entered the Hackney cab.

'Up you come, Jimmy,' he said, holding out a hand to help Jimmy up.

As the cab moved off at a smart trot, Crenshaw turned to Jimmy.

'You're a good man, Jimmy. If Bonaparte were to escape again, all hell would break loose. I'm glad you came to see me,' he said.

'Well, Cap'n, I couldn't hear such a thing and do nothin', could I?'

'No, indeed,' Crenshaw said.

The roads were busy at this time of day;

stagecoaches vied with carts piled high with goods for delivery to businesses and shops. Other cabs stopped to let passengers down and take up those hailing them. Important occupants of private carriages expected the right of way. A lot of abuse went back and forth.

'Nearly there now, Jimmy,' Crenshaw remarked as they passed the statue of King Charles I at Charing Cross.

When they arrived, Captain Crenshaw alighted and paid the fare. Jimmy looked up at the impressive building as he got down from the cab.

They passed into the busy courtyard and made their way to the entrance. In the vestibule, Crenshaw spoke to Jimmy in an under voice.

'We might have difficulty getting to see someone with authority enough to deal with what you overheard. I shall stress the importance of our being seen, but it might take some time to get anyone to listen.'

A uniformed lieutenant approached them.

'Captain Crenshaw? Why it *is* you, Sir. Lieutenant Dodson. We served together on *Hotspur*.'

'Indeed, we did, Dodson. How are you?' Crenshaw said holding out his hand.

Dodson shook it.

'Longing to be back at sea, Sir. What's the nature of your business?'

'It's a delicate matter, Dodson. I am not sure what department I should go to or whom I need to see. It is of vital importance I see someone immediately. You see, Able Seaman Young, here, has overheard a plot to rescue Napoleon.'

Dodson blinked several times and jutted his chin. He looked about the vestibule, a hand to his throat.

'I am not sure who would deal with this, Captain. Come with me to my office, I shall make enquiries,' he said and led the way down a long corridor.

Crenshaw and Jimmy followed.

Over a period of several hours, Captain Crenshaw and Jimmy passed from one office to the next. No one seemed to know what to do with them.

Finally, they were set to wait in a draughty hall on the second floor. Crenshaw's patience was beginning to wear thin. He looked at his pocket watch for the umpteenth time and let out an impatient grunt.

'One would think such an important matter would draw *someone's* attention. Do they not realise how serious this is?' he said to no one in particular.

He stood up and began pacing, a thunderous expression on his reddening face.

'What is this serious matter you speak of, Sir,' a portly old man said from out of the shadows at the end of the hall.

Crenshaw turned to see an elderly, stout man, dressed in dark clothes, leaning on a walking cane. His expression mild, his thinning, white hair framed his face. Old, intelligent eyes gave Crenshaw a concentrated stare.

The man was familiar to Crenshaw. It was a moment before recognition came to him. He was Admiral John Jervis, Earl St Vincent, the most competent First Lord of the Admiralty that had ever held the office.

'My Lord,' Crenshaw said, bowing to the Earl.

St Vincent acknowledged the bow with an inclination of his head.

'Who are you, Sir, and what is your business here?' he asked, his voice slow and calm.

'I am Captain Crenshaw, Sir, late of *Ignatius*. I had the pleasure of serving under you once, Sir, as a midshipman on *Boyne*, under Captain Grey.'

'Did you now? Well, well. That was a while ago, to be sure. So, what brings you here, Crenshaw?'

Crenshaw briefly told the Earl of what Jimmy had overheard in The George.

St Vincent listened quietly, his head bowed, a

knuckle to his mouth.

When Crenshaw finished, St Vincent, frowning, took a long breath through his nose. He looked at Jimmy, who had come to stand by his captain, cap in hand, eagerness filling his eyes.

'What do you hope to gain from this tale, Young?' St Vincent said at length.

'Well, me Lord, firstly, the satisfaction of knowing I've done me duty. But I won't lie to you, me Lord. I had hoped to gain *some* reward,' he said, lowering his eyes and glancing up at the great man.

'Hmm,' St Vincent said looking at Jimmy with narrowed eyes. 'Well, at least you're honest. I will give you that,' he said chuckling gently.

'You may leave this with me, Crenshaw. If you will wait here a little while longer, I shall send my secretary to you. You may give him your details, and I shall contact you with further instructions. Rest assured, you did the right thing in coming here. I am only glad I happened to alight on you; otherwise, you might have been left kicking your heels here till midnight.'

'Thank you, my Lord,' Crenshaw said, much relieved.

St Vincent nodded and made to leave. But he turned back to Jimmy.

'Oh, and by the by, Young, I shall personally see that you are indeed rewarded for doing your duty.' He nodded and turned away from them to continue at a leisurely pace down the hall, disappearing around the corner at the end.

Jimmy scratched his head, glancing at Crenshaw.

'Do you think he'll do what he said, Sir?' Jimmy asked.

'Oh yes. Most certainly,' Captain Crenshaw replied.

Within five minutes, a dapper man moved quickly towards them. Dressed all in black, his linen, pristine white, he carried a ledger under his arm.

'You are Captain Crenshaw, Sir, I assume?' he said.

'I am,' Crenshaw said with a gracious nod.

'And you are Able Seaman Young?'

'Yes, that's me,' Jimmy replied, his eyes twinkling.

'I am Sir William Farringdon, Earl St Vincent's secretary. Follow me, if you please. My office is below.'

Jimmy and Crenshaw followed Farringdon, who led them downstairs and through a maze of corridors, until they arrived at a large office, stuffed to the roof with books and ledgers. A huge desk stood in front of the window; several chairs arranged before it.

'Be seated if you please,' Farringdon said as he went around the desk to take his own seat. He selected a sheet of paper from a desk drawer and picked up his pen.

'First, may I have your rank, your full name, and your addresses so we may contact you when we decide what is to be done.'

The two men gave Farringdon the information.

'Now, Able Seaman Young, will you please tell me exactly where you were and what you overheard. I shall take it down as you speak,' Farringdon said, dipping his quill in the inkwell before him.

Farringdon stopped Jimmy from time to time to ascertain the exact meaning of what he was saying, then, nodding, he resumed writing.

'… And after I lost the Frenchie, I went home to think on it. The next morning, I decided to go and tell Captain Crenshaw, and he said we had to come here, so here we are.'

Jimmy finished, and sat back in his chair, blowing out his cheeks in relief.

His quill nib scratched as Farringdon continued writing in the silence that followed. Putting down his quill, he looked up at the two men before him.

'What do you make of this, Captain Crenshaw?'

Crenshaw frowned and rubbed his chin.

'If you are asking me whether I believe Able

Seaman Young, the answer is, yes, I do.'

'You misunderstand me, Crenshaw. I do not disbelieve that Able Seaman Young overheard *something*. The question is, what did he overhear? In a crowded tavern, it is hard to hear one's companions talking, let alone other people's conversations,' Farringdon said, looking from Crenshaw to Young and back again, a tight little smile on his thin lips.

'Oh, it weren't crowded, Sir. It were as quiet as the grave, it bein' well past ten o'clock at night. There was only two other men there, and they was three sheets to the wind, not a peep outa them,' Jimmy said, nodding vigorously.

'Hmm,' Farringdon said glancing at Crenshaw.

'Indeed, Sir William, I have always found Jimmy to be an honest and intelligent man. He is hardworking and trustworthy. I believe he did hear some kind of plot.'

'Hmm,' Farringdon said again, stroking his sparse moustache.

Jimmy was beginning to feel uncomfortable.

Am I bein' accused o' somethin'? he thought.

He glanced furtively at Crenshaw.

Crenshaw, catching the glance, gave Jimmy a reassuring nod.

'I think you must leave this with me. It is a delicate matter which we must approach with caution. I shall tell Earl St Vincent and no doubt he will discuss it with the appropriate people. We shall probably call upon you to recount your story again, Young. Hold yourself in readiness.'

Farringdon turned to Crenshaw.

'Perhaps you could accompany him once again, Captain Crenshaw?'

'Of course, Sir William. I am at the Navy's disposal,' Crenshaw replied, rising from his seat.

Jimmy rose too. Being nervous, he began to fiddle with his cap again.

Farringdon bowed his head slightly, first towards Crenshaw and then towards Jimmy.

'Your servant, Sir,' Crenshaw said, with a slight bow of his own.

Jimmy nodded several times.

'Good day, Sir,' he muttered as he touched his forehead.

Jimmy followed Crenshaw from the room and stood in the hall, breathing heavily.

Crenshaw, who had begun walking along the corridor, turned back to Jimmy.

'What ails you, man?' he asked.

'That were fearful, Sir. I never did speak to anyone so high up in me life afore,' Jimmy said, taking out his handkerchief to wipe his brow.

Crenshaw laughed.

'But you did very well, Jimmy. Very well indeed.'

'Did I, Sir? It's kind of you to say so,' Jimmy said, with his irrepressible grin.

Crenshaw laughed again.

'Come on, Jimmy, let's leave this place. I've had enough for one day,' he said.

Looking about to get his bearings, he found the way to the vestibule behind the front door.

'Will you get a cab for me, if you please,' the Captain said to the porter on the door.

'At once, Sir,' the porter replied, sending a hall boy out into the street.

While they waited for the Hackney, Captain Crenshaw turned to Jimmy.

'I want to pay a visit to The George myself Jimmy so that I can get an idea of the lay of the land,' he said. 'Will you come with me tomorrow? Come to Poland Street in the morning at about Ten Thirty. We shall then go together to The George.'

'Aye-aye, Cap'n,' Jimmy said, recovering his usual ebullience, now he was not in such exalted company.

When the cab pulled up, Captain Crenshaw and

Jimmy climbed into it. Leaning back in his seat, excitement grew in Jimmy. As the cab moved off, he voiced his anticipation.

'I'm lookin' forward to visiting The George tomorrow, Cap'n. You never know, we might overhear them at it again.'

CHAPTER THREE

On Wednesday morning, Tom, lying on his stomach, woke again in Nancy's bed.

I could get used to this, he thought, inhaling the scent of Nancy's hair on the pillow. He turned over, then swung himself out of the bed.

He saw his clothes, cleaned, and pressed, lying over the chair.

Nancy must have seen to them.

Tom went to the basin. Pouring the water Nancy had left for him again, he washed with her soap.

Almond scented. Ha, I'll smell good all day.

When dressed, following the aroma of cooking, he went down to the kitchen.

The George was a galleried coaching inn. Three days a week many coaches took off early on long journeys to as far afield as Dover or Cornwall.

The travellers often stayed overnight before embarking on their coach trip the following day. They needed a good breakfast to sustain them on their long journeys. Other customers would come for a meal well in advance of their coaches taking off. Tom knew the six maids, including Nancy, would be kept busy waiting on the guests.

The kitchen was alive with activity; Gem, the cook, master of his domain. Having produced dozens of breakfasts three times a week for many a year, his technique was equal to none. Sausages, bacon, black pudding, mutton, and whatever other meat the butcher could supply he expertly prepared on the enormous range at the back of the kitchen. Pots bubbled, pans sizzled, and the oven baked, filling the large room with tempting smells. A sideboard holding stacks of plates rested against one wall. The cook's assistant, Billy, a boy of about thirteen, took from the stacks and put the plates on trays resting on a long table in the middle of the room. He then filled the plates with the guest's orders. In between times, he sliced bread, piling it on platters at the end of the table.

The serving maids picked up the trays and platters and took them to the dining room. They returned with a constant stream of dirty dishes and deposited them in the scullery which led off the kitchen. Today it was Betty's turn to wash them. A petite, curly-headed blonde girl, Betty was Nancy's cousin.

The little scullery had a stone floor and two big sinks. A large copper hung over the black-leaded range where hot water continually bubbled. A door led to a courtyard where the laundress hung out her washing to dry. A window on either side of this door let in light. Another door opposite them led to a passage with access to stairs up to the gallery.

Betty was kept busy washing not only the dishes but also cooking pots, cutlery, and tankards.

As Tom entered the warm, steamy kitchen, he saw Nancy return from the dining room and go to the scullery to deposit more dirty dishes. He waited for her by the scullery door, and, catching her around the waist from behind, he planted a kiss in the curve of her neck.

Nancy leant her head back against him for a moment, breathing a sigh, as a delicious thrill ran through her.

But, however much she enjoyed his attentions, she was busy.

'Stop, Tom, love. I'm working,' she said, straightening her back and smoothing her apron.

She turned around in his arms, which still held her.

'Do you want something to eat before you go?'

'That porridge smells good. Is there cream in it?' he asked, reluctantly letting her go.

Betty came out of the scullery wiping her hands on her apron.

'We always put cream in it, Tom. Shall I dish you up some?' she said.

Tom winked at her.

'Yes please, Betty,' he said.

She took a bowl and filled it from a large, black pot simmering on the hob.

'Thanks, Betty,' Tom said and turned back to Nancy.

'Can I eat it here, Nancy-love? I don't want to be seen in the Taproom. If there's any trouble about what I'm doing, I don't want anyone to know I've been staying here.'

'Do you expect trouble, Tom?' Nancy asked, tweaking a fold of his neckcloth into place.

She trusted there would *not* be trouble. Nancy hoped Tom would come back to her when he had finished this business with the Frenchman. She'd always had a tenderness for Tom. After their intimacy of the past two nights, she didn't want him to disappear from her life again.

'If I'm careful, there won't be trouble. I'm not the tearaway I was when I was young,' Tom said.

A fleeting memory of the handsome, young, black-haired rogue she had known, made Nancy smile.

'I still can't believe you're going straight, Tom,' she said.

'Well, Nancy-love, what I'm doing isn't exactly straight. But if it comes off, I can afford to be honest the rest of my life.'

Nancy frowned.

Loud sizzling and the smell of fish overrode the other cooking smells.

Billy dished up kippers and mushrooms, putting them on the next set of plates.

'Ready, Nancy!' he called.

She shook her head at Tom then took the tray of steaming breakfasts from the table.

'I'll be back in a minute, Tom,' she said and left with the tray for the dining room.

Betty, having added several spoons of honey to

Tom's porridge, put it before him on the table.

'Can I get you anything else, Tom?' Betty asked.

'No thanks, Betty. I'm fine,' Tom said, with a nod, and scooped up a spoon of hot, sweet, creamy porridge.

Betty went back to the scullery to carry on washing the dishes.

As Tom sat at the kitchen table eating his breakfast, he watched the girls bustling about him, going back and forth with trays of breakfasts. All the girls were attractive, but Tom's senses quickened each time he saw Nancy come back to the kitchen.

By God, she was a pretty girl when she was young, he mused, *but now, she's a fine woman, like a good wine, bold, warm, and mellow.*

Tom finished the porridge and sat back in his chair as Nancy came back with another tray of dirty dishes. She went with it to the scullery and came back to wait for another tray. It was hot work hurrying in and out of the kitchen; Nancy passed the back of her wrist over her forehead.

Blue smoke and the smell of lamb chops rose from the range.

While Nancy waited, she moved to stand beside Tom.

'Do you think your business with the Frenchman will take long, Tom?' she asked putting a hand on his shoulder.

'A good few months, I'd say, Nancy,' he said.

Glancing up into Nancy's face, her disappointed expression tugged at his heart. He moved around in his chair and pulled her onto his knee.

'Don't look so down, Nancy. When it's over, I'll come back to you, I promise,' he said kissing her cheek.

'Will you, Tom?' Nancy asked, questions in her sad eyes.

Betty came out from the scullery. Seeing Nancy occupied, she took up the next tray and left the kitchen, smiling to herself.

Tom adjusted his hold on Nancy, bringing their bodies closer. He gazed at the swell of her breasts peeping over the top of her bodice. Moving the tip of his finger over her skin, he shifted his gaze to her eyes.

'Nancy, after the past two nights, I'm happier than I've been for a long time. I know a good thing when I see it. I want you for my woman, so I *will* be back.'

A blissful glow filled Tom, seeing the excited wonder on Nancy's face.

'Do you really mean it, Tom?' she asked.

Her eyes narrowed.

'Don't mock me, now, Tom. Don't say it just to please me and then not come back at all.'

Tom came to a decision and took a deep breath.

'I swear it, Nancy, listen. I've never said this to any woman, but I say it to you now. I love you, girl. I'll even marry you if you like,' he said, and, to his surprise, he meant it.

Nancy's jaw dropped, and her eyes opened wide.

'Marry me, Tom? Ah, you can't be serious!'

'Don't you want to marry me, Nancy?' Tom asked trying not to laugh.

Nancy shook her head and let out a deep, accentuated sigh.

'Tom Johnson, when I first knew you, I used to dream of being your wife. But I gave up hoping a long time ago,' Nancy said, her heart beating fast.

'Will you wait for me, Nancy?'

'I've waited this long; I can wait another few months,' she said the sparkle coming to her eyes.

'Well, I suppose that makes us engaged, like gentry,' Tom said, hugging Nancy closer to him.

Forgetting where they were, they sat for a moment, enjoying each other's nearness, contemplating the enormity of their intentions.

'I wish I had a ring to give you. But I'll get one when I come back,' Tom said.

Molly, one of the other serving maids, came into the kitchen and stood looking at the two, her hands on her hips.

Tom noticed her and put Nancy off his knee.

Nancy glared at Molly, who sniffed and picked up the next full tray.

Tom stood up.

'Now, Sweetheart, I'd better be off. I don't want to be late for this meeting with the Frenchies,' he said.

Tom took Nancy in his arms and kissed her soundly. Letting her go, he smiled broadly before turning to a door at the back of the kitchen and passing through to the stable yard. Nancy was left breathless in the kitchen, mesmerised. Her dreams of marriage were fleeting these days. She had almost given up hope of ever seeing Tom Johnson again. Now she was to marry him. After all these years, she was going to be Tom Johnson's wife!

Oh God, let it be true. Let him come back to me.

CHAPTER FOUR

Tom stepped out into the noisy inn yard, whistling a love song. Through his whole life, he had rarely made plans for his future, living on his wits.

And here I am, engaged, just like a gentleman, to the greatest lover I have ever had, he thought.

He picked his way along the cobbled yard of The George. It smelled of horses. He had to move carefully to avoid their slurry. Being a coaching inn, it had dozens of stalls for patrons' horses and for the teams which pulled the coaches. This was a busy time for the stable lads as they prepared the coaches standing in the inn yard. They carefully checked the harnesses, the wheels, and the breaks on the coaches going on their long journeys. They inspected the interiors, calling a pot boy to clean them if necessary. When the coaches were ready, the ostlers put the horses to harness.

When Tom reached the arched entrance to the yard, he turned onto Borough High Street. At eight-thirty in the morning, the pavements thronged with people. Sounds of coaches and carts, the clip-clop of horses' hooves and jingling harness mingled with street sellers' cries. The smell of their wares blended in the morning air. Eels, pea soup, steaming coffee, hot Chocolate, and a host of other tempting aromas, made Tom wish he had eaten more than just a bowl of porridge.

As a scrawny kid, petty thievery had been Tom's occupation. It was the only way he could survive after his family had died and he must fend for himself. He had become expert at dodging his way through crowds on pavements. He developed a knack for picking rich men's pockets or pinching the odd morsel of food from the sellers' stalls. He thought of those days as he strode along, comparing his youth with his manhood. Now he was a respectable sea Captain, albeit without a vessel.

A shame to turn to dishonest activities again, he

thought. *But needs must.*

He came to St Saviour's Church at the end of Borough High Street and crossed the road, walking towards London Bridge.

Reaching the other side of the bridge, Tom turned right into Lower Thames Street.

The crowds became thinner as Tom walked past the Custom House and the Tower Stairs, which led up from the river. Here, he remembered when he had joined the ranks of the mudlarks for a while. He had used these stairs to reach the banks of the Thames at low tide to scavenge in the mud, with a group of sociable boys, for anything that could be sold. Mudlarking was a dirty, smelly occupation. Although it had not lasted long with him, he smiled, remembering his comrades by the Thames.

Those were the days, he thought.

His scavenging ended when he took ship on a smuggling vessel, meeting new comrades and growing up fast.

He continued reminiscing as he turned left to make his way up Tower Hill.

Skirting the Tower itself via Little Tower Hill, he turned left and stood before the Mint where he was to meet Colonel Corbeau.

A coach approached from Cable Street moments later, carrying Corbeau and another man.

They were both dressed in understated style.

Corbeau wore a woollen, bottle green, frock coat, reaching his knees. Straps, fastened under his highly-polished square-toed shoes, held his light grey trousers smoothly in place. The collar of his white linen shirt stood tall. About his throat, he wore a wide cravat, tied in a soft bow. He carried the same high, silk-covered hat Tom had previously seen him wearing.

His companion's clothes were similar in style, his coat made of midnight blue velvet and his trousers a soft light-brown twill.

As the coach stopped, Tom moved forward to greet them.

'Good morning, gentlemen,' he said.

A groom climbed down from the box and opened the coach door. Letting down the folding steps, he stood to one side. He held out his arm for Corbeau to lean on as he alighted.

'Good morning, Johnson. May I introduce my associate, Count Mollien,' Corbeau said.

The elderly, imperious Count, peered at Tom, with contempt. The expression on his face suggested an unpleasant smell hovered beneath his nose.

Tom didn't like the man looking at him in this way—even if he was lowly born. He took on a careless pose.

'Pleased to meet you, Mollien,' he said, with a broad grin.

Mollien leant away from Tom. In French, he addressed Corbeau.

'Is it necessary to rely on this upstart?'

Tom, whose knowledge of the language was as good as any Frenchman's, gave Mollien a hard look. If there was one thing Tom hated, it was someone regarding him as beneath notice.

Annoyance filled him.

'It's not necessary to have dealings with me at all, Mollien. Good day to you, Messieurs,' Tom said in perfect French, before walking briskly away from them.

Corbeau gave Mollien an impatient glance. Mollien had achieved high status in the Ministry of Finance. However, as the son of a shopkeeper, he was, in truth, not much better than Tom and somewhat inferior to Corbeau.

Corbeau set off in pursuit of Tom. Catching up with him, he took Tom by the arm.

'Monsieur Johnson, do not take umbrage, I beg. I also find Mollien insufferable. But he has access to Napoleon's elder brother, Joseph, who is financing this endeavour. We need him. I apologise on his behalf, Monsieur,' he said, his manner far less arrogant than the day before.

Tom listened to Corbeau in silence, keeping his expression indecipherable. He turned to view Mollien before returning his gaze to Corbeau. Tom was several inches taller than Corbeau and the years had added bulk to his once lean physique. He presented an imposing figure. Corbeau raised his eyes to Tom's face. Tom took a long breath before he spoke.

'I appreciate your apology, Corbeau, but I want it understood, I will be treated with respect if I am to provide my services. Is that clear?' Tom said.

'It is. Come, now, Johnson. Please, take us to your craft,' Corbeau said, gesturing towards the coach.

With a grunt, Tom walked back to the coach where Mollien had remained. Corbeau entered it and seated himself next to Mollien.

Tom gave directions to the coachman for Blackwall Reach. He climbed in, seating himself opposite Corbeau, as far away from Mollien as he could get.

The three remained silent in the dim coach; their faces turned towards the windows.

Low tide in the Thames exposed the thick oozing mud on the river's banks. The sharp, salty smell of wet decay and the high stink of sewage wafted into the coach. Tom leant over to pull up the windows, reducing the bothersome odour.

Mollien produced his handkerchief and pressed it to his nose. Although the smell of the river receded, the sickly-sweet scent from Mollien's handkerchief, sprinkled liberally with violet cologne, replaced it. After several minutes, Mollien removed it from his nose to address Tom.

'Mr Johnson, when I was First Minister of the Treasury, a certain Mr Robert Fulton—an American, as I recall—made overtures to the Emperor regarding the use of a submersible vessel, which could be used to deliver explosives to blow up enemy ships,' he said, folding his hands in his lap.

'That's right, Monsieur. Mr Fulton invented the prototype of the vessel, *Nautilus*. I was his associate,' Tom said, giving Mollien a hard stare.

'Then why is it that you, and not Mr Fulton, comes to us with this proposition?'

'Because, Monsieur Mollien, I am sorry to tell you, Mr Fulton is now dead. And, might I point out to you, it was Corbeau who came to me, not me who approached him,' Tom said, trying to curb the irritation rising in him at Mollien's haughty attitude.

He continued. 'Although Napoleon and the French Navy were impressed when we demonstrated our prototype, you rejected it, and vetoed the building of a full-sized submarine.'

Mollien looked down his nose at Tom.

'I remember the incident, Johnson. When Fulton's proposal came to my notice, I could not sanction the exorbitant sum he required. The financial situation was not healthy, you must understand. However, His Majesty, King Joseph, wants to help his brother escape his intolerable incarceration. He is, therefore, willing to finance any means by which this may be brought to pass.'

'I am gratified to hear it, Monsieur,' Tom said.

He paused, giving Mollien narrow-eyed scrutiny.

'Of course, initially, I shall need monies in advance. For expenses, *you* must understand. Ten thousand should do it,' Tom said and held his breath.

'It will, of course, be an advance on the forty thousand agreed upon, Mr Johnson,' Mollien said.

Tom had no recollection of having agreed on any sum, but forty thousand sounded highly acceptable. It was with difficulty he kept his face straight.

'But of course, Monsieur,' he said.

Silence took hold again in the swaying, stuffy coach. The men, avoiding eye contact, turned their faces once more towards the windows. They watched the streets go by, seeing an occasional glimpse of the Thames between the soot-begrimed buildings.

On arriving at Blackwall Reach, the coach halted. The footman jumped down from the box and came to the window.

Tom leant forward, opening the window to stick his head out.

'What is it, lad?' Tom asked.

'John Coachman wants to know where you want to be set down,' he said, tipping his hat.

'The north end, if you please, where the dry docks are situated,' Tom said.

The boy looked puzzled.

Tom opened the door. Jumping down, he moved to look up at the driver, calling out a series of directions to him.

'Right you are, Sir,' the driver said.

As the groom took his seat, Tom climbed back into the coach. He sat back, leaving the window open.

The coach took off again, manoeuvring along the intricate passages between quays, and docks. It stopped outside the high, wide doors of Tom's covered-in dry dock.

The footman alighted, again performing the same ritual with the door, the steps, and his arm.

Tom and the two Frenchmen alighted and stood before the doors to the dry dock. A brisk wind lifted their coat tails and caught at their hats. The Frenchmen held on to their brims to keep their hats from blowing away. Nearing a smaller door set into the larger one, Tom produced a key from his coat pocket. He unlocked the smaller door, swinging it open, causing a shaft of light to pour into the darkness within.

The shadow of a vessel appeared, supported beneath on keel blocks along the centre line fore and aft and bilge blocks to the side. Shafts of wood rose at an angle to support the sides of the craft.

Tom lit a taper attached to a long pole. Turning a tap protruding from a pipe fixed to the wall, one by one, he ignited the gas lights hanging from the ceiling.

'Gentlemen, may I present to you the submarine, *Eagle*.'

All ships look bigger out of water. She was an awe-inspiring sight with her masts rising majestically from the deck

Corbeau gazed up at the ninety-foot vessel, overawed.

'I did not expect anything so big, Johnson,' he said, walking around to the prow.

'The original, *Nautilus*, is a lot smaller,' Tom told him.

'Tell me, Johnson,' Mollien said, 'if this is an underwater vessel, why does it have masts?'

'Monsieur, it is not possible for the crew of *Eagle* to stay beneath the waves for more than a few hours at a time. When she is moving from place to place, she sails like any other ship. When she submerges, the masts are struck. Eh… that means they are folded down on the deck.'

'Is it possible for us to enter it, Johnson?' Corbeau asked.

'It is, Monsieur. Follow me.'

Tom led Corbeau to a flight of steps at the side of the dock. They ascended to a platform which overhung the ship's deck. Tom climbed down onto *Eagle*. Corbeau followed him, and together he and Tom helped Mollien down.

Lifting a hatch that lay flush with the deck, Tom descended a set of steep steps into the interior, followed by Corbeau and Mollien.

In the near darkness, Tom took a lamp from a shelf and lit it, raising it to illuminate the main cabin.

There was just enough headroom for the men to stand upright.

Corbeau looked about him, intrigued by all the

polished-brass switches and dials.

'What do all these instruments mean, Johnson?' he asked.

'Corbeau, it would take a long time to explain them to you, and even then, without a knowledge of engineering and navigation, it would still be meaningless,' Tom said.

Corbeau frowned.

'It seems small and cramped in here,' he said, putting a hand up to touch the ceiling.

'This compartment is eighteen feet by twelve. There are other compartments fore and aft, and steam engines fore and abaft them. If necessary, the vessel can hold up to fifteen crew and two engineers.'

'I, for one, am glad I shall not be sailing in it,' Mollien said.

With difficulty, Tom managed a civil answer.

'Throughout the voyage to St Helena, she will be tethered to your ship, Monsieur. There will be a small crew aboard manning *Eagle*. But we may discuss these things as you ready your vessel. I infer you have a ship?' Tom asked Corbeau.

'We have, Johnson, *La Miséricorde*, anchored in the Thames near the London docks,' Corbeau said.

'Most convenient,' Tom said. 'It would be best if you set sail a day or two before me. We may meet up in the channel. But again, we will discuss these things when we make our plans. When and where shall we meet again?'

'Perhaps The George would be a convenient rendezvous since it is where we had our first meeting. Can you hire a private parlour?'

Tom rubbed his chin.

'Probably. I'll talk to Nancy. Doubtless, she can arrange it for me,' Tom replied, his heart dancing as he realised he hadn't said his last goodbye to her before he went a-venturing.

'Here is my card, Johnson. If I do not hear from

you, I shall meet you in The George, at noon, on Saturday,' Corbeau said as he moved towards the ladder.

When Tom had extinguished the lamp, they made their way out of *Eagle*. Standing beside her, Tom turned to Corbeau.

'I have a smaller vessel also, Corbeau. She is *Nautilus,* the prototype submersible designed and built by Mr Fulton, with my help. I am of a mind to ready her for sailing, too.'

'Why is that necessary, Mr Johnson?' Corbeau asked.

'She is more manoeuvrable. If we run into difficulties with *Eagle*, we will have *Nautilus* to fall back on. Humour me, Corbeau. I like to cover all eventualities.'

Corbeau shrugged a shoulder. 'Very well, Mr Johnson. You are more experienced in these matters than I.'

Corbeau waited for him as Tom put out the gas lights with a long snuffer.

Outside, a light drizzle moistened the air.

'Please hurry, Corbeau. My coat will suffer if it gets wet,' Mollien said.

Corbeau stifled his impatience and opened the coach door himself for the elderly man.

Tom finished locking up, and joined them, swiftly mounting into the coach.

Mollien glared at him.

Tom got the impression that the old devil intended to leave him to make his own way out of the dock. He hoped most of his dealings would be with Corbeau.

I'm not too keen on Corbeau either, but he's preferable to that whey faced old picksome, Tom thought as the coach took off.

Retracing the route they had taken, they travelled in uncomfortable silence. This time, Tom didn't close the window, thinking, *Let the puffed-up swine suffer the smell.*

Arriving outside the Mint, Tom alighted and looked up at the men in the coach.

'Au revoir, Messieurs,' Tom said, tipping his hat as the footman closed the door.

Corbeau inclined his head in reply.

Mollien did not look at Tom but with his nose in the air, stared straight ahead.

As the coach drove off, Tom spat.

'Arrogant bleedin' stuck up Frenchie bastard,' he said under his breath.

And then, he remembered Nancy.

Wait till I tell her I'll be around a bit longer, he thought, and he chuckled.

CHAPTER FIVE

Having watched Corbeau's coach move out of sight, Tom began walking back to The George. On the corner of Borough High Street, he came across a scruffy looking lad calling out to passers-by to buy a broadsheet from him. Tom gave the lad a penny and took the paper. Folding it, he slipped it into his pocket and continued on his way to see Nancy.

In the tap room of The George, he sat in his usual seat, waiting for her to appear. It was half-past one, and the staff in The George were busy serving dinner to a variety of customers. Some were tradesmen, who closed their shops at one o'clock for an hour to have their meal. Others were dandified gentlemen, late risers who, having slept off their revels of the night before, were about to embark on a new day. The George was, for some, a fashionable spot where they might meet their cronies for coffee in the private rooms on the first floor. With boisterous voices, they called to each other from the open galleries overlooking the courtyard below.

Nancy came down the stairs, out of breath, her face red, after serving a group of young bucks in the Green Parlour. She didn't see Tom, who caught her arm as she walked past him.

'Get off me, you misbegotten lout,' she said, her voice shrill and angry.

'Nancy?' Tom said, rising from his seat.

'Tom! I thought you were one of the ruffians from upstairs. Dirty rotten pack of lechers that they are. Sorry for the sharp word. What are you doing here? You said you wouldn't be seeing me for a long time.'

'Well, Nancy-love, I thought I wouldn't. But nothing's planned yet. It'll be a couple of weeks before we're ready to take ship for … where we're going,' Tom said putting an arm around her waist.

Nancy favoured him with a broad smile.

'Sit down, Tom, and I'll get you a drink. Do you want food, too?'

'Yes, please, Nancy. I think I can smell stewed mutton.'

'You can, Tom. I'll get some for you,' Nancy said, disappearing into the kitchen.

She was back in a short while with a dish of mutton stew and a plate of bread. She placed them on the table before him and went to draw a tankard of ale.

'I haven't time to sit with you, Tom,' she said, setting the tankard by his right hand. 'It'll be the best part of an hour before all the dinners are served and done with.'

'That's fine, Nancy, I picked up a broadsheet on my way here. I'll amuse myself with that while I wait for you to finish. I need to speak to you about hiring a parlour.'

Nancy gave him a quizzical look before going to the kitchen again.

Tom set to eating his stew, satisfying his growling stomach. When he had finished, he picked up his tankard and took a long draft. Sitting back, replete, he wiped his mouth with the back of his hand. Looking about, and seeing no sign of Nancy, he fished the broadsheet out of his pocket, unfolded it and began to read.

Tom was not especially interested in politics, satisfied with a general understanding. This broadsheet, *The Weekly Trumpet*, seemed to focus on tedious minutia. Scanning the paper, he snorted a chuckle at a cartoon of the prime minister, Robert Jenkinson, 2nd Earl of Liverpool. Reading further about the latest taxation and the new legislation regarding vagrant veterans of the war, he became angry and threw the paper down.

He sat pinching his lower lip, gazing into space, wondering how much longer Nancy would be.

He didn't notice the two men who appeared at the door.

Able Seaman James Young and Post Captain Richard Crenshaw entered The George. They sat by the window to the right of the door, facing the room. Crenshaw removed his hat and placed it beside him. Jimmy pulled his cap from his head and stuffed it in his pocket.

Betty came into the taproom from the kitchen and, seeing the new customers, made her way to the table where Jimmy and Captain Crenshaw sat.

'What's your fancy, gentlemen?' she asked.

'I shall have a tankard of ale if you please,' Crenshaw said, smiling at the pretty serving maid. 'What's your pleasure, Jimmy?'

Jimmy wondered whether he should make so bold as to ask for brandy.

Hang it all, he thought. *I think I deserve it, after all the worry I've had.*

'I'll have a glass of brandy, if I may, Sir. To settle me nerves, like,' Jimmy said, feeling brave.

Captain Crenshaw raised an eyebrow at the request but turned with a nod of approval to Betty, who moved off to get their drinks.

'So, Jimmy, you are partial to a glass of brandy, are you?' Crenshaw said, taking out his pipe and filling it from his tobacco pouch.

'Just to settle me nerves, Cap'n, like I said,' Jimmy replied, giving his captain a sheepish look.

'You deserve it, Jimmy, after yesterday,' he said as he stood up.

Crenshaw went to the fireplace, took a spill from a spill vase on the mantelpiece and put it into a flame in the fire till it glowed red. He touched the tobacco with the glowing spill, drawing on his pipe till smoke rose from the bowl. Replacing the spill on the mantle, he returned to his seat.

Meanwhile, Jimmy looked about the room. He sat

up straight when he caught sight of Tom. When Crenshaw sat beside him again, Jimmy plucked at his sleeve.

'Cap'n, Sir, it's him,' he whispered.

'Him? You mean one of the men you heard discussing our delicate matter?' Crenshaw asked.

'Yes, Cap'n. I swear, it's him,' Jimmy said, excitedly pulling on his captain's sleeve.

'All right, Jimmy, keep calm. We shall sit here and see what he does,' Crenshaw said.

'Look, Sir, here comes the serving maid he were making up to.'

As he spoke, Nancy came out of the kitchen and sat opposite Tom.

'She is of no interest to us, Jimmy. We shall wait for a half an hour, and see whether anyone else turns up. If they do not, we shall leave and come back tomorrow.'

Betty came towards them with a tankard and a glass. She placed them on the table and took the coin Crenshaw withdrew from his pocket.

'You may keep the change, my dear,' he said with a sweet smile.

Betty bobbed a curtsey.

'Thank you, Sir. Is there anything else I can do for you, Sir?'

'Well, my dear, there is,' he said. 'That gentleman sitting on the end of the settle. I have a fancy I know him. Can you tell me who he is?'

Betty looked over her shoulder, following Crenshaw's gaze. Immediately seeing that the man in question was Tom, she turned back to Crenshaw.

'That's Tom Johnson. He hadn't been here for years and just turned up out of the blue a couple of days ago.'

'Ah ... no, he is not who I thought he was. Thank you,' he said and took a sip from his tankard. Betty went back to the kitchen.

Jimmy noticed Tom speaking quietly to Nancy.

'Will I go and have another listen, Cap'n?' he asked.

Crenshaw gave a nod, and Jimmy performed the same manoeuvre as he had before, stealthily going to the fire to warm his hands.

'I am to meet the Frenchman here on Saturday, Nancy,' Tom said. 'He wants me to book a private parlour in which we may discuss our business. Can you see to that for me?'

'The little parlour next to the dining room is free, Tom,' Nancy said.

'Ah, that's a bit small. What about the Blue Parlour off the gallery?'

'Oh, it *is* for hire, but it would cost you a lot of money, Tom. It's the best room in the place.'

'I ain't paying for it, Nancy; the Frenchie is. Can I book it for this Saturday and onwards for, say, three weeks?'

Nancy put her hands flat on the table in front of her. Her mouth dropped open as her eyes widened in surprise.

'That'll cost a fortune, Tom,' she whispered in awe.

Tom put his hand over hers.

'It's all right, Nancy. As I say, I ain't paying for it. Will you book it for me?'

Nancy shrugged.

'All right. But why do you need such a big room?'

'There'll be more men apart from the Frenchie and me. I'll need a large table in the room, too. We will be perusing nautical charts and such,' Tom said.

'Perusing? That sounds very grand.'

Tom leant over and chucked Nancy under the chin.

'What we are dealing with is something *very* grand, Nancy. And if it comes off, and they pay me for my part in it, we'll be made for life.'

Nancy gave him a sceptical look.

'Anything like that sounds dangerous, Tom.'

Tom gave her a knowing smile.

'I remember you always used to say I live a

charmed life,' Tom said, rising from his seat.

'Where are you going, now, Tom?'

'I have a lot of equipment to buy. I'll be back before nightfall. Can I share your bed again tonight?' he asked.

Nancy's heart leapt, and her cheeks turned pink. Her eyes shone.

'You know you can, Tom,' she breathed.

Tom leant over and kissed her cheek.

'Later, then,' he said. And picking up his hat, he made for the door.

When Tom left, Jimmy went to sit next to Captain Crenshaw again. He recounted everything he heard.

Crenshaw leant his head towards Jimmy as he listened intently.

When Jimmy had finished, Crenshaw nodded.

'Well, Jimmy, we must report this. However, we will only do so when Farringdon contacts us. We have 'til Saturday.'

'What will we do in the meantime, Cap'n?'

Crenshaw frowned, thinking. He fished in his pocket and took out five silver shillings.

'Jimmy, do you think you could stay here for a few days? Take a room and have your meals here. That way, you can keep a weather eye on what's happening. If anyone questions you, tell them you're em ... you're waiting for your sister to arrive, but you don't know exactly when that will be. Can you do that, Jimmy?' Crenshaw asked, putting the shillings in Jimmy's hand.

Jimmy looked down at the shillings and then looked at Crenshaw.

'Of course, I can, Cap'n.'

'If you need more money, send me a note.'

'I'm sure that'll be enough, Sir,' Jimmy said, jingling the coins in his fist.

'I'll come to see you on Saturday afternoon,' Crenshaw said, picking up his hat and preparing to leave.

'If you get into any trouble, come straight to me, yes?'

'Yes, Cap'n, I will. I doubt there'll be any trouble, though,' Jimmy said.

Crenshaw nodded as he rose from his seat. He put on his hat, gave Jimmy's shoulder a squeeze, and left The George.

Jimmy sat where he was for a long while, wondering how he had got himself into such an adventure. He looked down at his glass. There was still a mouthful of brandy left. He picked it up and poured the liquor into his mouth. Rolling it around, he savoured it on his tongue; who knew when he would taste expensive brandy again. He swallowed, and felt the warmth all the way down to his stomach. Licking his lips appreciatively, he put the glass down.

Glancing over at Jimmy, Betty noticed he had finished his drink and came over to him. Wiping the table, she picked up Crenshaw's tankard and Jimmy's glass.

'Can I get you anything else?' she asked.

'Yes, me girl, you can. I need a room for a few nights. Can you fix that for me?'

'I think there's one free. I'll have a word with Nancy. She sees to the booking of the rooms,' Betty said and went to the kitchen.

In a few moments, Nancy moved from the kitchen and came to Jimmy's table.

'Betty says you need a room. The only one I have is an attic over the galleried rooms. All the rest are booked,' Nancy said.

'Oh, that's all right. If there's a comfortable bed, I'll be happy,' Jimmy said, and gave Nancy his famous twinkling smile.

Nancy smiled back at him.

'How long will you be staying?'

'Well, that's the problem, Miss Nancy. You see, I'm

waiting for me sister, Mary, to arrive from Ireland. I don't know exactly when she'll get here. But I fancy it'll be before the end of the week,' Jimmy said, thinking he shouldn't mention Saturday in case he gave the game away, somehow.

'Is your sister looking for work?' Nancy asked, sitting down opposite him.

'She is. The gentleman who was sittin' with me wants a maid, and I suggested me sister. I have to send him a note when she arrives,' Jimmy said.

Nancy rose from her seat, her attention drawn to several men entering the taproom to sit at a vacant table.

'I hope she gets the job,' she said, before moving to serve the men.

Jimmy inwardly smiled, pleased with himself for thinking up the story.

An official-looking letter, addressed to Captain Crenshaw awaited him on the hall table at his lodgings. Grasping it firmly in his hand, he ascended the stairs two at a time. He entered his room and locked the door before opening the letter. Sitting at his desk, he swiftly read the short note:

To Captain Richard Crenshaw.

Sir,

Following our meeting yesterday, I have discussed the matter with the relevant ministers. They are of the opinion that this delicate affair must be handled with the utmost care and secrecy. His Lordship, Earl St Vincent, has therefore suggested you present yourself at the Foreign Office in Fludyer Street on Thursday morning at ten o'clock. A preliminary meeting is arranged with Sir George Hetherington, Lord Castlereagh's secretary,

I remain

Sir William Farringdon.

Crenshaw folded the letter. Sliding it into his inside pocket, he leant back in his chair, rubbing his chin as he contemplated.

He had not expected his own involvement in the matter. He had merely brought Jimmy along to The Admiralty to tell them what he had overheard.

I would prefer not to be involved, he thought.

And then an idea struck him.

Ah, but at least if they employ me in dealing with it, I should no longer be on half pay.

Allowing his imagination to run into the realms of fantasy, he mused further.

I could find better lodgings. Maybe employ a servant.

Smiling to himself, he changed into evening dress and went out to have dinner at his club.

CHAPTER SIX

Three months before Tom Johnson's first meeting with Corbeau, Capitaine Adrien Babineaux sailed from Le Havre on a clipper containing supplies bound for St Helena. By the grace of fair winds, the journey took only eight weeks.

His official mission was to deliver correspondence to Napoleon from his friends and family. His unofficial, secret mission was to carry messages to his General from those who were planning his escape from captivity.

Aged twenty-eight, Babineaux was a good-looking young man. A tall man, his body was well muscled. He wore his blond hair cut short, in the fashionable Brutus style, which well suited his handsome face. Babineaux was quiet and observant by nature. His reserve had featured in his military accomplishments. His dedication to assignments, along with his intelligent and creative approach, had earned him an array of military honours.

Because of these qualities, Corbeau had chosen his cousin, Babineaux, to assist him with his undertaking. His own flamboyant personality would not suit the delicate mission. Babineaux would blend with any group of men without attracting notice.

A stiff breeze blew on them as Babineaux, and the other disembarking passengers walked down the gangplank at Jamestown, St Helena's main port. British soldiers guided them to the Port Office, located in a long low building near the dock. There, the elderly, care-worn Captain Stapleton examined their papers.

When he came to Babineaux, seeing from his papers that he was French, he glanced up swiftly.

'What is your business here Monsieur, er...' he checked the name on his papers again.

'Monsieur Babin ...?'

Unperturbed, Babineaux smiled.

'Your pardon, Sir, it is pronounced Babino. I am here to deliver correspondence to…' he paused a moment, not wishing to offend a British officer's sensibilities by calling the Général by his official title. 'Monsieur Bonaparte.'

Babineaux's English was excellent, his accent slight.

'Sergeant Morgan,' the captain called.

The man came into the office to stand inside the door.

'May I see this correspondence, Monsieur Babineaux?' Captain Stapleton asked.

'Of course, Captain.'

Removing a package of letters from his inner pocket, Babineaux placed it on the Captain's desk.

'Thank you, Monsieur Babineaux. We shall return them to you when we have checked them,' the captain said and turned to the sergeant.

'Sergeant Morgan, take Monsieur Babineaux next door and search him thoroughly if you please.'

'Yes Sir,' Sergeant Morgan said and gave Babineaux a push.

'Gently, Morgan. This man is not a criminal. We are simply observing the formalities, are we not?'

'Yes, Sir,' the sergeant said and glared at Babineaux.

'This way,' he growled.

In the little room next door, the sergeant's considerable bulk took up a lot of space. His eyes were small in his fat red face; his black hair stood up in spikes; his uniform strained to contain him.

He was not an attractive man. He gave Babineaux another push.

'Remove your coat, waistcoat, boots and trousers,' he said, a scornful twist to his lips.

Babineaux inclined his head graciously. He removed his clothes and handed them, one by one, to the sergeant.

Morgan felt in every pocket of the coat, ran his hand down it and, giving Babineaux a sneering smile, inspected the hem. He performed the same scrutiny on his waistcoat and trousers and then slid his hand into Babineaux's boots, after that he examined the heels.

'Put your hands up,' he rumbled.

Babineaux obeyed, and Morgan felt him all over with his fat, damp hands.

Satisfied he had nothing hidden about his person Morgan stood back.

Babineaux lowered his hands.

'Where's your luggage?' Morgan asked.

'It is in your Captain's office, Sergeant,' Babineaux said. Although his voice was calm, his irritation was growing.

Morgan viewed him, eyes narrowed, chin jutting.

He left the room and returned moments later with Babineaux's portmanteau.

'Where's the rest of your luggage?'

'There is no more. My stay is a short one. I am merely a courier,' Babineaux said, his smile wearing thin.

'Oh, I'm sure you are!'

Morgan rummaged through Babineaux's shirts, cravats, and underwear. He found Babineaux's shaving gear and rummaged through that as well. Reaching the bottom of the portmanteau, he let out a triumphant cry.

'Ha! What have we here, then?' Morgan said, pulling out Babineaux's dress uniform from the depths of the portmanteau.

'Please, Sergeant Morgan, be careful. It is my dress uniform. I may need to wear it when I visit Longwood House.'

Morgan gave him another narrow-eyed look and proceeded to inspect the precious uniform.

Finding nothing, he turned his attention to the portmanteau. Feeling in a pocket to one side, he pulled out a notebook. Frowning, he leafed through it, found it blank, and cast it aside. Morgan dipped into the pocket again and produced a hussiff. Being a soldier, he was familiar with its purpose as a compendium of mending equipment from thread and needles to scissors and pins. He unrolled it, inspected it, and put it on top of the notebook.

'Put your clothes back on and pack your stuff in your bag,' Morgan snarled, lips tight.

Babineaux returned the notebook and hussiff to the pocket. He carefully refolded his uniform and placed it back in the portmanteau, adding his underwear, cravats, shirts and shaving gear. He put on his clothes and turned to Morgan.

'Is there anything else?'

'Not unless you can think of something yourself. You may go,' Morgan said.

Babineaux wanted to ask directions to Longwood House but knew he would get no help from Morgan. He opened the door and stepped into the Captain's office. The last of the passengers had gone. Captain Stapleton sat back in his chair, gazing out of the window. He turned when Babineaux appeared.

Sergeant Morgan came into the office behind him.

'Will that be all, Captain?' he asked.

'Hmm? Oh, yes, Sergeant, you may go.'

Morgan saluted and lumbered out of the office.

Captain Stapleton, with a sigh, watched him out of sight, then looked up at Babineaux.

'I am sorry if he mistreated you, Mr Babineaux. Many veteran soldiers have a hatred for the French.'

Babineaux chuckled.

'Many French have an equal hatred of the English,' he said with a wry smile. 'I wonder whether you could tell me the way to Longwood House, Captain?'

'I infer you wish to see Napoleon, Sir?' the captain said.

'I do, Captain, as soon as I may.'

'I am sorry to tell you, Babineaux, you may not. Not before the governor, Sir Hudson Lowe, approves you. He insists on examining all who seek audience with Napoleon, before personally issuing a pass.'

'Where is Sir Hudson Lowe? May I see him?' Babineaux asked.

Captain Stapleton rubbed his chin and frowned. He let out a sigh.

'Ah, I might as well accompany you. I must deliver these letters of yours to Plantation House, anyway,' he said.

Stapleton rose from his seat behind the desk to open the office door.

'Corporal,' he called.

A man standing with three others at intervals outside the building marched up to his Captain.

'Sir,' the corporal said, saluting.

'Have my horse saddled, and another horse for Mr Babineaux, here. Bring them round as soon as possible.'

'Sir,' the corporal said again, hurrying off to the other end of the building before rounding the corner out of sight.

'Will your stay be long, Babineaux?' Captain Stapleton asked.

'No, Sir. I am to deliver the correspondence, wait to see whether there is a reply and then take the next ship for Le Havre.'

'The next ship is in a week's time. Perhaps if you have nothing better to do, you might like to have dinner with my wife and me one evening. It is not often she has pleasant company,' the captain said. 'In fact, you may find yourself inundated with invitations. This is a most boring posting. Without seeming to insult you, Sir, any visitor serves to relieve our boredom, even a Frenchman.'

Babineaux laughed.

'I am not insulted, Sir. I am amused.'

The corporal returned leading two chestnut horses. Babineaux noticed their immaculate turnout. Their coats brushed to a fine gloss, their mains and tails neatly braided, the tack polished, leather gleaming and brass shining, all indicative of the exacting army discipline on St Helena.

The corporal handed Captain Stapleton's bridle to him. He took it and patted his horse's neck before mounting. Babineaux took his bridle from the corporal and mounted also.

Standing back, the corporal saluted. Captain Stapleton returned the salute, and as they rode off, out of habit, Babineaux saluted, too.

'Is it far, Captain?' Babineaux asked as they passed through Jamestown.

'Nothing is very far on St Helena, Babineaux. The Island is only about forty-seven square miles, and a lot of that is cliffs. It's a godforsaken place, to be sure.'

They had left Jamestown behind and now rode towards Plantation House on a track through lush green vegetation.

'The place was chosen well to imprison Bonaparte. Escape from this island would be nigh on impossible,' Captain Stapleton remarked.

'Indeed,' Babineaux replied, recognising the truth in the statement, but undeterred from the endeavour.

Stapleton continued, 'Even so, there have been attempts to free Bonaparte. This is why the Governor is harsh. He is without pity, but his stringency is necessary.'

'I quite see that, Captain. However, I served under the Général, and it is hard for me to see him thus,' Babineaux said.

They rode in silence for a while.

'You know, sometimes I have sympathy for Bonaparte,' Captain Stapleton mused. 'I am aware of his greatness, a formidable enemy. Incarcerated as he is, it must irk him sorely—ah, Babineaux, I would not talk as I do to anyone else. If the Governor should know of my sentiments, I would probably be court-martialled,' Captain Stapleton said with a rueful smile.

Babineaux chuckled. 'Your secret is safe with me, Captain.'

Plantation House came into view. Surrounded by trees, a white, two-story, square mansion with wings either side, shone on a rise before them. A large portico at the front provided shelter for coaches in inclement weather.

Riding around to the stables at the back of the house, Stapleton and Babineaux dismounted. An orderly appeared and took charge of the horses, while the two men made their way to the front door.

At their approach, a footman opened the door.

'May I help you, Captain Stapleton?' he asked.

'Yes, Smith. This gentleman needs to see the Governor.'

Smith took a glance at Babineaux.

'Can you tell me what it is about, Sir?'

'Indeed. He wants to visit Napoleon and is here to gain permission to do so,' Stapleton said.

'I see. Come in, Sir,' Smith said, holding open the door.

'If you would care to wait, Sir, I shall find the governor's secretary.'

'In that case, Smith, will you take possession of these letters which Mr Babineaux has brought for Napoleon. They must be approved,' Stapleton said, handing the correspondence to the footman.

Smith took them. He acknowledged the Captain with a nod and left the hall.

'Take a seat, Mr Babineaux. We might have to wait a while.'

Babineaux sat, but the wait was not long. Within ten minutes, Smith returned.

'The Governor will see you, Mr Babineaux.'

'Good luck to you, Sir,' Stapleton said, offering his

hand.

Babineaux smiled and shook hands with him.

'Thank you, Captain,' he said and followed the footman down a corridor to a door facing them at the end. Smith knocked gently.

'Enter,' came the command from inside the room. Opening the door, Smith stood just inside the threshold.

'Monsieur Babineaux, Your Excellency,' he announced before moving aside to allow Babineaux to enter. Babineaux stepped into the room. Smith left, closing the door behind him.

Sir Hudson Lowe's rigid stance, his straight back and his erectly-held head spoke of a military man. He looked to be in his fifties. Lean-faced with a long narrow nose, thin lips, and gaunt cheeks, he wore his sparse grey hair brushed forward. Tall and lean, he observed Babineaux with piercing dark eyes under forbidding bushy brows.

'Good day to you, Monsieur Babineaux. I hear you wish to see Général Bonaparte,' the governor said, his voice deep and cultured.

Babineaux cleared his throat as he glanced at Napoleon's letters resting on the governor's desk. No time was lost delivering them to the Governor, who would not have had opportunity to read them yet.

'I do, Your Excellency,' he said. 'I am to wait to see whether he wishes to reply to any of the letters before you.'

The Governor moved behind his desk and sat. He looked Babineaux up and down, rubbing his chin as he considered Babineaux's response.

'Have you been searched?' he asked.

'I have, Your Excellency, quite thoroughly; so was my portmanteau. I assure you, I have nothing to hide,' Babineaux said softly.

The Governor looked directly at Babineaux, tapping his fingers on his desk as he thought.

Babineaux quietly met the Governor's gaze.

Sir Hudson reached for a sheet of paper, sliding it in front of him. Dipping his quill in the inkwell on his desk, he wrote several lines. He carefully blotted it and handed it to Babineaux.

'You may go to see him tomorrow, Mr Babineaux. Where are you staying?'

'I do not know, yet, your Excellency. I would be obliged if you could recommend suitable accommodation.'

'Yes, Mr Babineaux; you may stay here where we can keep an eye on you. You will be escorted to Longwood House and back again tomorrow.'

Babineaux gave a slight frown and nodded.

'No doubt you think I am overcautious. When I tell you, we have had information regarding Bonaparte's brother, Joseph, arranging for the General's release from captivity, I am sure you will appreciate our position. We are all on high alert. I hope you understand you are not under particular suspicion. But measures must be taken to combat any attempts to spirit Bonaparte away.'

Babineaux gave Sir Hudson an understanding smile.

'Of course, Your Excellency. I do see your dilemma. I would be happy to stay here if that is your wish.'

The governor gave a curt nod and rang a bell on his desk.

A small man wearing the neat black suit of clothes and white wig of a clerk appeared from the room next door.

'Your Excellency?'

'Yes, Williams, will you see to it that Mr Babineaux is accommodated here tonight? He is to visit Bonaparte tomorrow. Send word to Longwood to that effect. Arrange for Sir Gordon to escort him there at ten o'clock.'

He turned to Babineaux. 'Will that suit you, Sir?'

'Indeed, Your Excellency. Thank you,' Babineaux

replied.

'Come with me, if you please, Mr Babineaux,' Williams said, going to the door, and holding it open for him.

Before Babineaux followed Williams to the door, he bowed to the Governor.

'Good day to you, Your Excellency,' he said.

Sir Hudson had picked up one of the letters addressed to Napoleon. At Babineaux's words, he looked up.

'Hmm? Oh, yes, yes, good day,' he said, too preoccupied with the letters to give further response.

CHAPTER SEVEN

The weather, for once, was clement on the island of St Helena. This was good, as today Napoleon looked forward to meeting his visitor. He intended to have time alone with him in Geranium Valley, a secluded place where no one would observe them.

Sir Hudson Lowe gave Napoleon little leeway, imposing rules and keeping him well guarded. However, he permitted Napoleon to walk a short distance from Longwood House, his residence, without guards. Lowe also allowed him the occasional visitor, provided they were thoroughly searched before the visit.

The following morning, when Captain Babineaux rose from his excellent breakfast and moved to the hall of Plantation House, one of the Governor's aides greeted him.

The man's black hair was slicked back from his unusually high forehead. Of pale complexion, his hands were white and smooth, his slender figure graceful. He bowed his head formally.

'Good morning, Mr Babineaux. May I introduce myself? I am Sir Gordon Atherton.'

Babineaux returned the formal bow.

'Good morning, Sir.'

'The Governor sends his compliments and returns Napoleon's correspondence,' Sir Gordon said, handing the letters to Babineaux.

'Thank you, Sir Gordon,' Babineaux replied, placing the letters in the inner pocket of his coat.

'I have been appointed to accompany you to Longwood House,' Sir Gordon said, his voice as smooth as his hair oil.

Although Babineaux could find nothing specific in the man to which he could take exception, he found him repellent; reminiscent of a snake.

Bestowing his sweetest smile on him, Babineaux said, 'How considerate of the Governor to supply me with an escort. I know I should not find my way without you.'

'Just so,' Sir Gordon replied, returning the smile coldly.

Babineaux knew insincerity when he saw it and was at once on his guard.

'Our horses await us outside. Shall we?' Sir Gordon said, opening the door, and holding it for Babineaux.

Sir Gordon's large bay stallion stood beside the horse Babineaux recognised as the one he had ridden the day before.

Sir Gordon's horse was restive. He mounted it and pulled sharply on the reins to gain control. Babineaux's horse sidled from the bay. Before mounting, Babineaux gently smoothed the horse's neck till it quietened.

They rode east, the journey being similar in distance to that of the day before.

After riding some way in silence, Sir Gordon turned his head towards Babineaux.

'Tell me, Mr Babineaux, are you part of this latest conspiracy to free Napoleon?' he asked.

Babineaux's heart leapt. Even so, he managed to hold the reins lightly in his grasp, not disturbing the horse. He turned his head slowly to look at Sir Gordon.

'Surely, you jest, Sir?' he said quietly.

'No, I do not. Every Frenchman who visits Napoleon is under suspicion. Why should you be an exception?' Sir Gordon said, raising an eyebrow.

'Have there been many attempted escapes?'

'Enough talked of to initiate caution. Our information that another is imminent makes us more so,' Sir Gordon said, taking his eyes off the road to bring his gaze onto Babineaux.

Babineaux noticed how pale the man's blue eyes were as they coolly scrutinised him.

'Even if I was a conspirator, which I am not, do you think I would admit it to you?' he said breathing evenly to quell his unease.

'Undoubtedly you would not. However, I am a good judge. You did not flinch when I accused you. It may be that you are not,' Sir Gordon said.

Babineaux wanted to laugh. He kept his breathing steady.

'Truly, Sir Gordon, you *are* a good judge. You have my measure, indeed. All I want is to deliver these letters, wait for a reply and go home to France to my sweetheart.'

Babineaux caught a look of disdain in Sir Gordon's eyes before he turned his attention back to the road. Babineaux felt safe. Not for the first time his calm exterior had come to his aid.

At ten-thirty, they arrived at Longwood House.

'I am sure you will not be long, Babineaux. I shall wait to accompany you back to Plantation House,' Sir Gordon said as they arrived at the stables.

Babineaux thought a moment as he dismounted.

He had hoped to spend time alone with Napoleon to give him his other letters. He did not want the possibility of Sir Gordon breaking in on their privacy.

Yet would it not look suspicious if I try to dismiss him, as if I had something to hide, he thought.

'I am glad of your escort, Sir Gordon. I would not wish to lose my way,' Babineaux replied. 'Will you not join me in my visit, Sir?'

Sir Gordon laughed.

'Why would I want to spend time with him? I think not,' he replied.

'As you wish, Sir. However, I may be some time with the Général. What will you do with yourself in the meantime?'

'Oh, do not concern yourself with me. I am sure I shall find plenty with which to occupy myself. In fact, I think I will take my horse for a gallop; he needs exercise,' Sir Gordon replied, masking a sly smirk as he thought of his mistress who lived a short ride away.

Babineaux smiled, breathing an inward sigh of relief. He passed his bridle to a groom and watched Sir Gordon ride off.

Babineaux ascended the steps at the front of Longwood house and was about to knock when the door opened to him. He recognised The Marquis de Montholon, one of Napoleon's companions, who had come to the door.

'You are Capitaine Adrien Babineaux?'

'I am, Monseigneur. I come with letters for Général Bonaparte,' Babineaux said, giving the Marquis a courtly bow.

'He awaits you, Capitaine. Follow me,' Montholon said as he led the way to the Salon.

Napoleon stood with his back to the room, staring out of the French windows, his hands behind his back.

Babineaux noticed that Napoleon had put on weight since he last saw him after Waterloo. Yet his back was as straight as ever.

'Capitaine Adrien Babineaux, Mon Général,' Montholon Announced.

Napoleon turned to look at the young officer. His regal pose was the same as Babineaux remembered; his blue-grey eyes as piercingly observant as ever.

Babineaux swallowed the lump that came to his throat. He held the ex-emperor in such reverence, impulsively, he took several steps forward and went down on one knee, bowing his head, he took Napoleon's hand and kissed it.

Napoleon, moved by this exhibition of respect, was taken aback. The harsh lines on his face softened as he put his hand on Babineaux's shoulder.

'Get up, Capitaine. If you are seen paying homage to me, we will both be in trouble. You may leave us, Montholon.'

Babineaux stood up, tears filling his eyes.

'Your pardon, Mon Général. I have so very much looked forward to meeting you; I could not help myself.'

Napoleon, his hand still on Babineaux's shoulder, kissed him on both cheeks before holding him at arm's length.

'Ah, Adrien. If there were more like you, I would not be in the condition in which you find me. But you have letters for me, have you not?' he said, letting him go.

Babineaux nodded. Taking the official correspondence from his inner pocket, he handed them to his Général. He took the liberty of moving closer to Napoleon to murmur in his ear.

'I have others about my person, Mon Général.'

Napoleon stiffened, his eyes alert.

'Perhaps you would like to take a walk with me, Adrien?'

Smiling, Babineaux slowly nodded.

Leaving Longwood House through the French window, Napoleon, at a leisurely pace, led Babineaux down a well-trodden path. Within twenty minutes they arrived in Geranium Valley, a beautiful, peaceful spot with a stream running through it. Willow trees dipped down over the stream, creating a screen. Napoleon drew Babineaux beneath it.

Without a word, Babineaux took his penknife from his pocket, removed his coat, and turned his right sleeve inside out. He pulled down the cuff and, with the penknife, undid the stitching in the lining to reveal a carefully folded paper, which he handed to Napoleon.

Napoleon took it from him with reverent hands.

Under one willow Napoleon's servants had placed a bench. Napoleon sat on it and carefully unfolded the note, smoothing it on his knee.

Babineaux stood watching the former Emperor, his

attitude one of quiet admiration. He could not believe he was in the presence of one so exalted, yet fallen into such distressing circumstances. His heart brimmed with love and sympathy. He had served in the Grenadiers, beloved of Napoleon, and learnt to admire the great leader.

The tranquillity was only broken by a bird singing high up in the willow tree, and by the stream's murmuring as it flowed beside them. The scent of summer flowers wafted on a soft breeze.

Napoleon took his time reading and rereading the note. When he had finished, he let out a long breath and raised his eyes to Babineaux's.

'How did you get here, Babineaux?' Napoleon asked.

'On a clipper out of Le Havre, carrying supplies here, Mon Général.'

'Were you searched?'

'Indeed, I was, Sir,' Babineaux said with a sardonic grimace.

'And they did not find this?' Napoleon said, tapping the letter. 'Ha!'

Babineaux shook his head and gave a shy smile.

'There are three more, Sir. They did not find them either.'

'Ha,' Napoleon said again, derisively. Rising from the bench, he patted Babineaux's back.

'Do you know what this letter contains?' he asked.

'I do, Sir. They told me, in case it should be lost.'

'Oh, then, you may give me your opinion. I am not above taking advisement.'

'I think it is an excellent plan. My only concern is how they will find someone who resembles you enough to replace you.'

Napoleon shook his head, turning down the corners of his mouth.

'I do not think my looks are so remarkable that one cannot be found,' Napoleon said with a quizzical smile.

Babineaux gave a soft laugh and continued.

'Pardon my boldness, Sir, but does your brother have access to funds to finance the enterprise?'

'Your care for me moves me, Adrien. I invited your opinion, and you have given it. There is nothing bold in what you say. To answer you, yes, King Joseph has the funds,' Napoleon said, warming to the young man's unassuming manner.

Babineaux had heard Napoleon was imperious and difficult. So far, he had seen nothing of this in him.

Who would not be difficult to deal with in his position? Babineaux thought.

He used the penknife again to undo his left cuff and produced the other three letters, together less bulky than the one sent by Corbeau.

Napoleon took them and carefully placed them inside his waistcoat. Before coming out from under the willow tree, Babineaux put his coat back on.

'I shall read them later, Babineaux. Give me your arm while we return to Longwood.' Babineaux proffered his arm. Napoleon leant on it.

They walked in silence until Napoleon spoke again.

'If I relate to you what I wish to say to Corbeau, will you remember it? I dare not write a letter for fear of it being found.'

'I can, Sir. I have an excellent memory. That is why they entrusted me with the letters.'

'Good. I shall tell you as we walk.'

Babineaux attentively listened as Napoleon told him all he wanted to say to Corbeau, finishing as they reached the lawn before Longwood house.

Napoleon stopped and turned to Babineaux.

'Will you dine with me this evening?' he asked.

'Oh, Mon Général, I would be most honoured. Thank you,' Babineaux said, his heart beating high with joy.

'Present yourself here at seven o'clock. I shall now go for a nap. All this intrigue has made me tired. Till this evening,' Napoleon said, with a slight inclination of his head.

Babineaux bowed deeply and watched as Napoleon walked up the steps to the door, which a servant opened before he reached it.

Babineaux heaved a relieved sigh. The meeting had gone well. Napoleon was happy to go along with the plans Corbeau had presented.

Babineaux found Sir Gordon waiting for him a little way from the steps of Longwood house, leaning against a tree, smoking a cheroot. Seeing Babineaux, he flicked the cheroot away and strolled towards him.

'Was your meeting successful, Babineaux?' he drawled.

'I gave him his letters, if that's what you mean, Sir Gordon. Before I take ship again, I must return to pick up his replies.'

'Had a nice little tête-à-tête with him, did you?' Sir Gordon sneered.

'Yes, Sir, I did. You will, no doubt, be interested to know, I enquired whether he knew of plans afoot regarding his escape. He did not,' Babineaux said, amused by the flash of interest in Sir Gordon's mocking eyes.

'But then,' Babineaux continued, 'I doubt if he would confide in such a lowly creature as I if he knew.'

Babineaux saw a muscle moving in Sir Gordon's cheek and wondered what emotion was causing him to grind his teeth.

Sir Gordon fixed a pleasant expression on his face and gave Babineaux a smile.

'Come, let us find our horses and ride back to Plantation House. I will show you some interesting botanical specimens on the way. Isolated as it is, the island holds unique plants. And unique animals, too. But perhaps you are not interested in such things?'

The change from an attitude of hostility to one of bonhomie did not fool Babineaux. He realised Sir

Gordon's motive was to lead him into a false sense of security.

He probably thinks I am a fool, Babineaux thought. *He may do so. He will be less troublesome if I appear in that role.*

'Why on the contrary, Sir Gordon. Although I am no expert, biological science fascinates me.'

Sir Gordon proved to be most knowledgeable about botany. Although Babineaux knew little of what Sir Gordon was saying, he showed great interest.

After half an hour's peering at plants in the hot sun, to Babineaux's great relief, Sir Gordon said he had an engagement. They resumed their ride and were soon approaching Plantation House. When they arrived, Babineaux thanked Sir Gordon and went in search of Williams.

'Bonaparte has invited me to dine with him this evening. Is it permitted?' he asked.

'It is,' Williams said. 'The pass the governor gave you allows it.'

'Am I permitted some small exploration of the Island?'

'Yes, you are. Your only restriction is your association with Napoleon without permission.'

'Thank you, Sir,' Babineaux replied.

He went to his room.

Babineaux took the notebook from the pocket in his portmanteau. Sitting at an escritoire beneath the window, he took up a pen and wrote all that Napoleon had dictated.

When he finished, he cut the sheets of paper from his notebook with his penknife and folded them up tightly. He took off his coat. Turning his cuff down again, he tucked the note into it and folded it back into place. He returned the notebook to the pocket and took from it the hussiff. Removing the needle and thread, he carefully replaced the stitching on the lining of his cuffs.

Part of his brief from Corbeau was to reconnoitre the island. In case of anything going wrong with the current proposal, he wanted to have an alternative plan in place; therefore, he needed detailed maps of the area. Having a whole week to wait for his ship, Babineaux could make valuable notes to present to Corbeau.

He left the house and walked about for several hours. On his return, he took to his room. Locking the door, he sat before the escritoire again with his notebook and carefully crafted a map of the area he had visited.

When he had finished, he leant back in his chair. Tired, he stretched and yawned.

He lay on his bed thinking about his morning and fell asleep.

On waking, he washed and put on a clean shirt. While donning his dress uniform, he thought about the invitation.

Imagine, me, dining with the Emperor. Who would have thought I would ever do that?

CHAPTER EIGHT

On Saturday morning, Tom, sitting in his usual place on the settle, was finishing his breakfast of bacon, eggs, and black pudding. He smiled as he saw Nancy coming towards him. Stopping beside Tom, she put a hand on his shoulder.

'Tom, there's a man here says he wants to speak to you,' she said.

Tom looked up at her, putting his hand on hers.

'Did he give you his name?' Tom asked.

'He's French. He says he's Adrien Babineaux,' Nancy said, glancing at the handsome young man standing by the door watching them.

When Tom looked at him, Adrien lowered his gaze. Tom was unimpressed. A man who could not look another man in the eye was not to be trusted, in Tom's opinion.

'Tell him to come over, Nancy,' Tom said. 'And bring him a tankard of ale.'

Nancy moved back to the door where Adrien waited. He stepped forward.

'Is the man you were talking to Tom Johnson?' Adrien asked.

'Yes, he is. He says you're to go over, and I am to bring you a tankard of ale,' Nancy replied.

Adrien smiled.

'Thank you, Miss,' he said, moving towards the settle as Tom watched him approach.

'Good morning, Mr Johnson. May I sit with you?' Adrien asked.

Tom extended his hand, palm up, indicating the seat opposite him.

Adrien slid into the seat, giving Tom an appraising look.

'My cousin suggested I make myself known to you,' Adrien said.

Jimmy Young, having by this time made the seat by the fire his own, cocked an ear when he heard Adrien's accent. He expected Captain Crenshaw today and hoped he would arrive soon.

'Your cousin, Mr Babineaux? Who is your cousin?' Tom asked, narrowing his eyes.

'He is Colonel Paul Corbeau,' Adrien replied, amused by the flicker of recognition he saw pass over Tom's face.

'Ah …. So, you are the one who travelled to St Helena to contact "Our Friend",' Tom said, still not sure about the suitability of the man before him.

'Correct. I delivered a message and obtained a reply.'

'You had no difficulty getting to see "Our Friend"?' Tom asked, frowning.

Adrien gave a shrug.

'None at all, Sir.'

'You intrigue me, Monsieur. I have heard it is hard for a Frenchman to gain an audience with this particular gentleman,' Tom said, drawing his brows together.

Adrien gave Tom a mischievous smile.

'I am a quiet man. People tend to trust me. My humble manner puts them at their ease.'

His soft voice gave credence to what he said.

'Most times,' he added as he remembered Sergeant Morgan.

Tom chuckled. The man went up a notch in his estimation.

Nancy came to the table with two tankards of ale. She placed them before the men, looking with suspicion at Babineaux, who glanced up at her.

Nancy gave Tom a questioning frown.

'It's all right, Nancy. Mr Babineaux will be working with me,' he said before turning to Babineaux.

'May I introduce you to my fiancée, Mr Babineaux. This is Nancy.'

Babineaux rose.

Enchantée, Mam'selle,' he said with a courtly inclination of his head.

Nancy glanced at Tom, rolling her eyes. She turned to Adrien and sketched a curtsey.

'Likewise,' she replied, placing a possessive hand on Tom's shoulder.

Adrien resumed his seat.

Two men entered the Taproom and went to sit in a corner near the bar, some distance from Tom.

Tom noticed them out of the corner of his eye and sensed something odd about them.

Nancy smoothed her apron.

'I suppose you have business to discuss. Just call if you want anything,' Nancy said and, with a glance and shining smile for Tom, she bustled off to serve the two men.

Adrien watched her go.

'How much does she know?' he asked, and sipped at his ale.

'Very little. I trust her, but she'd be uneasy if she knew the full extent of our activities,'

Adrien smiled and nodded.

Tom leant forward a little.

'Corbeau told me little of his plans. Perhaps you could enlighten me further?'

Babineaux took a mouthful of ale. He put his tankard down and regarded it a moment before he spoke in a low voice.

'Our first intention was that our friend should swap clothes with a "servant", ride with me to the dock and then simply walk on to our ship.'

'That sounds an excellent plan. I have always been an advocate of hiding in plain sight. But you wouldn't need me if you were to do that,' Tom said.

'No, Mr Johnson, we would not. However, we had to abandon that proposal.'

'Why was that?' Tom asked.

'Because, Mr Johnson, on my visit to St Helena, I came up against the governor's aide, Sir Gordon Atherton. He is an unpleasant, watchful, and suspicious creature. A man perfectly suited to supervise British security. A man who also bodes ill for our endeavour.

'He escorted me when I visited the Général at Longwood. On the way, he asked me, outright, whether I was involved in an attempt to rescue Napoleon. I managed to convince him I was not.'

'Why did this make you change your original plans?' Tom asked.

Babineaux glanced at Tom. Corbeau had not wanted to give Tom much information. Babineaux thought they should trust Tom more.

'When I returned to London, Paul and I discussed what the presence of this man might mean to us. I believe Atherton would have been suspicious if he caught sight of the disguised Général with me as he escorted us to the ship. He might have searched him. We could not take that risk. We decided to devise a new plan and employ you to help us with it.'

'I see,' Tom said, pursing his lips, and nodding thoughtfully.

'In what way would I be involved?'

'The Général would still be in disguise. However, I would climb with him to the top of a cliff not far from Longwood, lower the Général down to the bottom of the cliff, and from there onto your submarine. We would pass beneath the waves, avoiding the British patrols. You would then rendezvous with our ship and sail away.'

Tom frowned.

'In principal, your plan sounds workable, but it needs refinement. Do we have reliable maps of the terrain?' Tom asked.

'I had time to reconnoitre and make notes. From these I have drawn maps. Not the whole island, you understand. I did not have time for that. But I have the parts that are relevant to our endeavour. I have included more detail than current maps contain.'

'A promising idea. It is good to be prepared for all eventualities,' Tom said.

He put the last of his bacon in his mouth before pushing his plate away. Taking a swig of ale, Tom glanced at Adrien over the rim of his tankard. He remained dubious about him and unconvinced of his ability.

'Have you got the maps with you?' Tom asked.

'No, Mr Johnson. I gave them to Paul. He will show them to you when he arrives,' Adrien replied.

He sensed Tom's uncertainty and looked him directly in the eye.

'I perceive you do not have confidence in my ability, Mr Johnson.'

'To be honest, Babineaux, I do not,' Tom said, rubbing his chin.

'I assure you, I am an able map-maker. I had much experience in the army, reconnoitring, and so forth. But you may judge my work when you see it, Sir,' Adrien said.

'I look forward to it,' Tom said, raising his tankard in salute before quaffing the rest of his drink.

'Before my cousin arrives, Mr Johnson, will you show me the parlour you have booked for our use?' Babineaux asked as he stood up.

'Of course. Follow me,' Tom said, and made for the door leading to the passage.

Adrien swiftly downed the rest of his ale. Taking a handkerchief from his pocket, he wiped his mouth as he followed Tom.

Jimmy Young rose from his seat and went cautiously after them.

Tom led the way along the passage to the stairs up to the gallery. He took a key from his pocket and walked to a door at the end.

Jimmy arrived at the other end of the gallery and

moved towards them.

'Mornin', Cap'n,' he said and, going past them, made for the stairs leading up to his little room.

'Good morning, Jimmy,' Tom said. 'Any sign of your sister?'

'No, Sir,' Jimmy said drawing down the corners of his mouth.

'Ah, there are squalls in the Irish Sea,' Tom said.

'Isn't there always? She'll get here soon enough,' Jimmy said and touched his forehead before continuing on his way to the stairs.

Adrien watched him and frowned.

'Who was that?' he murmured.

'He's a sailor. He's taken the attic room above the gallery. He's harmless,' Tom replied as he opened the door to the Blue Parlour.

Adrien watched as Jimmy slowly scaled the stairs.

'Harmless? I'm not so sure. There is something not right about him,' Adrien said.

He continued looking in Jimmy's direction then turned and walked into the Blue Parlour.

'A pleasant room,' he remarked as he looked around him.

Adrien's eyes took in the long low room, made bright by four high, sash windows gracing one wall, their weighty wooden shutters folded back. Heavy, blue silk brocade curtains hung on either side of them, held back by tasselled ropes. Between the windows high pier glasses rose to the ceiling. Along the opposite wall were a series of polished oak sideboards, punctuated by chairs upholstered in the same material as the curtains. A dark blue carpet ran along the middle of the floor. A lighter shade of blue covered the plastered walls. Two chandeliers hung from the white ceiling, their crystal pendants twinkling in the sunlight streaming through the windows.

Thick logs burned in the steel grate of a carved limestone fireplace at one end of the room. On either side, at right angles to the fireplace, stood two Chesterfield couches upholstered in blue-dyed leather.

An enormous table stood at the other end of the room, more chairs placed around it. On the table, Adrien saw many rolled-up maps and charts.

'This is where our meetings will take place,' Tom said, indicating the large room with a wave of his arm.

Adrien frowned.

'It seems rather grand for a group of conspirators. One pictures clandestine meetings in dark cellars,' he said, his amber eyes sparkling.

Tom laughed.

'As I said before, Babineaux, I have always found hiding in plain sight works best.'

Babineaux tilted his chin.

'How so?' he asked.

Tom shifted his stance and took a breath.

'In my younger days, I was a smuggler. The authorities rarely caught me, passing me by as I sat watching them searching for me. I am famed as one whom no prison can hold.'

'And do you still embrace this life?' Adrien asked, amused by Tom's frank admission.

'Not at all. I was given a pardon and, for six years, I worked for the government, piloting ships in enemy territory. The Americans and your countrymen were the enemy,' Tom said giving Adrien a roguish smile.

Adrien chuckled as he went to the big table to inspect the maps. He unfolded one and then another, casting a practised eye over them.

Astonished, he looked at Tom.

'These are valuable maps, Mr Johnson,' he said.

'Yes, they are. I believe it is foolish not to have the best equipment when so much depends on getting to St Helena and back without problems.'

'I agree, and I am impressed by your efficiency,' Adrien said, inclining his head.

When his cousin initially told him about Tom,

Adrien was hesitant. He disliked the idea of trusting what sounded like an unreliable villain. He had decided to visit The George before the appointed time to sound Tom out prior to the meeting.

He realised now that although Tom was rough around the edges, he was intelligent and meticulous. Adrien revised his opinion.

He took out his pocket watch to check the time.

'It wants but ten minutes to the hour. They will arrive soon,' he said replacing the watch in his waistcoat pocket.

Tom sighed. 'I had better go down to await them. I am sure the high and mighty Mollien will expect an escort,' he said, wrinkling his nose.

Adrien laughed.

'I heard you and he got off to a bad start. I admit, he is a man always on his dignity. But he is old, Mr Johnson. Swallow your pride and treat him with respect. Remember, we shall be at sea for many weeks. Unpleasantness between us will make our voyage more uncomfortable than it needs to be.'

'What a good-natured soul you are, Babineaux,' Tom murmured. 'Agh,' he snorted, 'I know you're right. I'll do my best to curb my vanity. But I warn you; I may not succeed,' Tom said as he left the room.

As he descended the stairs, he thought about Babineaux.

He's a pleasant young man, but soft. Not the stuff conspirators are made of.

In his little room above the Blue Parlour, Jimmy had done his best to listen to what was going on below him. He rolled back the carpet and put his ear to the floor, but all he could hear was muffled voices.

If I had a brace and bit, he thought, *I could drill a hole.*

He stood up and looked around his room, frowning. His frown disappeared when he caught sight of a glass on the stool beside his bed. He snatched it up and put it upside down on the floor.

I've used a glass to listen on walls before now, he thought. *It should work on a floor, too.*

Lying down beside it, he pressed his ear to the glass.

Jimmy held his breath. The voices sounded louder but still muffled. And then the voices stopped. He heard a door close and nothing more. Jimmy rose swiftly from the floor and, opening his own door, passed through onto the small landing leading to the stairs. Creeping downward, he was in time to see Tom descending the stairs to the passage leading to the taproom.

Straightening his coat and running his fingers through the front of his hair, Jimmy followed.

Tom entered the taproom and went to his usual seat.

Jimmy came in after him and looked about. He saw Betty polishing tables. He thought quickly. He had to find an excuse to stay in the taproom.

'Miss Betty,' he called.

Betty hummed quietly to herself as she worked. She turned at the sound of Jimmy's voice and smiled when she saw him.

'Can I get you something Jimmy?' she asked, wiping her hands on her apron.

'I woke late, Miss Betty. Am I too late for breakfast?' he asked, congratulating himself on his ingenuity.

'You *are* a bit late, Jimmy. But I think there's some black pudding left over. I'll fetch it for you,' she said as she picked up her cloth and polish and went to the kitchen.

Jimmy hesitated a moment before sitting at the other end of Tom's settle. Tom glanced up from the pamphlet he had found on his table. He nodded to Jimmy and continued reading.

Betty came to Jimmy with the black pudding and bread on a plate, plus a tankard of ale.

'Thank you, Betty, me dear,' Jimmy said, his eyes twinkling.

Betty grinned and nodded before going back to her polishing.

Tom's lip curled in disdain as he threw down the pamphlet. It dealt with parliamentary reform and a call to those who supported the conspirators of Cato Street, all condemned to hang. Tom frowned, wondering what would become of him if the plot he was engaged in was discovered.

'Bah,' he said under his breath.

He heard the door open and looked up. Seeing Corbeau standing in the doorway, Tom dismissed his thoughts. Corbeau hesitated a moment before ushering in three other men, one of whom was Mollien.

Tom rose from his seat, frustration twisting in his chest at sight of Mollien. Remembering Adrien's words, he took a deep breath and stepped forward.

'Bonjour, Mon Seigneur,' he said to Mollien, inclining his head graciously.

'Good day, Mr Johnson,' Mollien replied, urbanely accepting Tom's courtesy.

Corbeau glanced at the two of them, surprised by Tom's changed attitude to the Count.

'Will you show us to the room you have hired, if you please, Mr Johnson,' Corbeau asked.

'With pleasure, Corbeau. Be so good as to follow me, if you please,' Tom said, wondering how long he could keep up his new-found civility.

Tom led the way to the door to the passage, followed by the four Frenchmen. From the passage they moved towards the stairs, and ascended, their boots making a din in the late morning quiet.

Tom opened the door to the Blue Parlour and stood back to allow the men to enter.

Mollien crossed the threshold first and saw Adrien step forward. Clicking his heels, he bowed his head before the Count, who gave a grandiose nod, acknowledging the greeting as his due.

Observing Mollien's acceptance of the salutation, Tom laughed inwardly.

Corbeau ushered Mollien and the other two men towards the fire. With a wave of his hand, he gestured towards the couches.

'Be seated, Messieurs,' he said.

As the men took their seats, Mollien glanced at Tom keenly.

Adrien, understanding Mollien's expectation, moved to Tom's side.

'I think they await your offer of refreshment, Mr Johnson,' Adrien said in a hushed voice.

'Uh?' Tom uttered. 'I am not a hired lackey. I don't know where they keep the liquor, anyway.'

'I know where it is. I did some reconnoitring while I waited. Your dignity will be your undoing, Mr Johnson. Do not trouble yourself, Sir. I shall do it,' Adrien said and went to one of the sideboards opposite the windows.

He produced six glasses and placed them on a tray. Next came a bottle of Sack. Adrien poured the liquor into the glasses and took the tray to the men by the fire where Corbeau and Mollien were engaged in conversation. The other two men sat in silence listening to them. Each took a glass, nodding their thanks to Adrien.

Adrien put his tray down on a small table between the couches and took up the other two glasses, handing one to Tom.

'Santé,' Adrien said, raising his glass to Tom.

'Santé,' Tom replied and took a sip, his ire dissipating.

Corbeau put his glass down and rose from his seat to speak.

'Monsieur Renoudin, you have not met our English associate, Mr Tom Johnson, who is to provide us with the submersible vessel in which we shall transport

Notre Ami to safety. Mr Johnson, may I introduce Count Mollien's aide, Monsieur Émile Renoudin.'

Renoudin stood to bow graciously to Tom, who returned a nod.

All this bowing and scraping is making my head hurt, Tom thought.

'And now, Gentlemen, I am sure you all wish to know whom I have brought to you. He does not speak English, Mr Johnson, you must forgive me when I continue in his native French.'

'Not a bit, Corbeau. You know I speak good French,' Tom said, glancing at the men in turn.

'Stand up, if you please, Laroche,' Corbeau said.

The man stood. He was somewhat smaller than average height. He moved out from the couches and a little towards the door so that all the men could see him. He wore an enormous dark blue great coat, too big for him. Between his black beard, his dark-brown hat pulled down over his forehead, his oversized cravat, and his fashionably high shirt points, little could be seen of his face.

Laroche took off his enveloping greatcoat followed by the cravat. He folded down his collar and removed his hat. Lastly, he peeled off his false beard and removed a wig.

Gasps of astonishment broke the silence.

The man put his hands on his hips, threw his head back and gave a throaty laugh.

'Who do I remind you of, Messieurs?' he said.

The men all spoke at once, incredulity and excitement filling them.

Corbeau raised his hand for silence. The hubbub died away.

'This, Messieurs, is Christophe Laroche, a farmer from Corsica. My brother, Henri, came across him while passing through his village a month ago, and noticed a resemblance to a person we all know. Henri travelled to England with him and presented him to me on Thursday. With his hair cut just so and his beard shaved, he looks the part. Do you not agree?'

Tom Johnson stared, dumbfounded. He had seen caricatures in newspapers and pamphlets, and once he had seen a portrait in an exhibition. Laroche looked exactly how he imagined Napoleon would look.

Renoudin and Mollien, eyes wide, raised their hands in astonishment. Adrien stood apart from them, his lips pressed together as he enjoyed their wonder. He alone had shared the secret with Corbeau.

'If you remember, Gentlemen, I suggested replacing our Général with a double. I intimated as much in my letter to him. Everyone thought it could not be done. Just as I had begun to despair of finding someone, Henri wrote to me and told me of Christophe. Henri explained things to him. He told Christophe that life on St Helena was boring, with little to do. Christophe asked whether he would have servants, and sleep in a comfortable bed. Henri told him he would and …'

'And I could think of no better life, not working my fingers to the bone for a crust, being waited on, my every whim gratified, so I agreed,' Laroche said.

'Why even his voice sounds like the Général, with his Corsican accent,' Renoudin said.

'His voice is indeed like that of Napoleon. His turn of phrase is not. He is a farmer, and he sounds like a farmer,' Mollien said.

'Oh, don't worry about that, Mon Seigneur. On the voyage, Adrien will teach me how to say things properly, will you not, Sir?' Christophe said giving them a beaming smile.

Adrien nodded his assent.

'He's certainly a good-humoured sort of fellow,' Tom said quietly to Adrien as he picked up the bottle to replenish their glasses.

'Indeed, he is,' Adrien agreed, his eyes twinkling as he sipped the excellent Sack.

'So, Gentlemen, to business,' Corbeau said,

indicating the table on which Tom had placed the plans of his submarine and the maps. 'We must organise our departure from London, order provisions, and chart our course.'

Taking a small leather case from his pocket, Corbeau handed it to Tom.

'These are the maps of the area where Napoleon is held. Adrien drew them for us,' he said.

After taking the maps from their case and poring over them for some moments, Tom straightened his back, inhaled deeply, and turned to Adrien.

'Mr Babineaux, I owe you an apology. I must confess I did not think your mapmaking would be of such a high standard. They are perfect, Sir,' he said.

'Thank you,' Babineaux said with a smile, inclining his head.

The rest of the men moved to the table to look at the Maps. Renoudin took up a set of drawings.

'What is this, Mr Johnson?' he asked.

Tom glanced over Renoudin's shoulder.

'They are the plans for the submersible *Eagle,* Sir,'

Renoudin spent some minutes studying them, frowning, and running his finger here and there.

'Hmm,' he said. Putting them down, he turned to Corbeau.

'Where is your crew, Corbeau?' he asked.

'They are lying low aboard my ship, *La Miséricorde,* which is moored near London Dock,' Corbeau replied. 'We will sail in a week to ten days, depending how our plans progress and on the weather and the tides.'

Jimmy didn't follow the group of men, thinking he had stretched his luck far enough. Instead, he sat where he was to wait for Captain Crenshaw.

He did not wait long. Captain Crenshaw spotted Jimmy as soon as he entered The George.

He noticed Jimmy's agitation.

'What's the matter, Jimmy? You look worried,' Crenshaw asked as he sat opposite him.

Jimmy was breathless with excitement.

'Cap'n, there's a load of Frenchies gone up to the Blue Salon with Tom Johnson. I tried rollin' back the carpet in me room and listenin' with a glass, but I couldn't hear nothin'. If I could make a hole in the ceiling, I would easily hear what they're sayin',' Jimmy said, eager to thwart whatever was going on.

Betty, busy polishing the table near where Jimmy and Crenshaw sat, heard their conversation and paused in her work to listen.

'I don't think a hole in the ceiling would go unnoticed, Jimmy. And anyway, they will probably speak in French.'

Jimmy wrinkled his nose. 'Ah, I never thought o' that. What are we goin' to do, then, Cap'n, Sir?'

Captain Crenshaw leant forward towards Jimmy.

'I received a letter from Sir William Farringdon. Do you remember him, Jimmy, Lord St Vincent's secretary?'

'Yes, Cap'n,' Jimmy said with an eager nod.

'Sir William arranged an appointment for me with Lord Castlereagh's secretary.'

'Lord Castlereagh, Cap'n? Ain't he high up in the Government, Sir?'

'He is, Jimmy. He is the Foreign Secretary,' Crenshaw said.

'God a' mighty, Cap'n, we're goin' right to the top, ain't we?' Jimmy said, rubbing his palms together.

'My first interview on Thursday was with his secretary. Yesterday, I met the man himself,' Crenshaw said.

'An' what happened, Cap'n?'

'He wants us to keep observing them, Jimmy. He will send professional covert agents to watch them. He also mentioned a reward for you,' Crenshaw said, sitting back and smiling at the expression on Jimmy's face.

'Well, I'm blessed!' was all Jimmy could say.

'Can I get you anything, Gentlemen?' Betty asked, her usual pleasant smile a little tarnished.

'Would you like another brandy, Jimmy?' Crenshaw asked.

'No Cap'n. I'll have ale if I may, Sir. I gotta keep me wits about me,' Jimmy replied, winking.

'Two tankards, then?' Betty said before she scurried to the kitchen.

'Nancy?' Betty called when she was safely there.

Nancy came out of the scullery.

'What do you want, Betty. I'm busy,' Nancy said.

Betty took Nancy by the arm and pulled her back into the scullery, closing the door.

'It's Jimmy, and the man with him,' Betty whispered. 'Nancy, is Tom up to something? I know he's hired the Blue Parlour, and he's there now with a group of Frenchies.'

Nancy turned pale.

'He *is* up to something with the Frenchies, Betty. But he won't let me know what it is. What's Jimmy got to do with anything?'

'I was polishing a table near them and I overheard him and his friend talking. They said some men are coming to watch what's going on,' Betty whispered urgently.

Nancy put her hands to her mouth.

'Oh, God! No! Not now!' she said.

CHAPTER NINE

Betty felt helpless as she watched Nancy wring her hands while pacing back and forth in the small space of the scullery. Nancy suddenly stopped, her eyes darting from left to right. She grabbed Betty's shoulders, startling her. Their eyes locked as Betty felt Nancy's grip tighten on her shoulders.

'We have to warn Tom,' Nancy said, breathing fast.

Betty bit her lip, clutching her hands together on her chest.

'I could go to the Blue Parlour and tell him he is needed down here,' Betty suggested, eager to help in any way she could.

Nancy shook her head.

'No, don't do that. Some of them Frenchies seem high-born. They wouldn't like being disturbed. No, we'll wait till Tom comes down. You go and keep a watch for him, and keep an eye on that little weasel, Jimmy, as well—and his friend,' Nancy said, her eyes narrowed, her mouth bitter at mention of those who might cause Tom's downfall.

Betty's frown deepened.

'I liked Jimmy. He has a merry way about him,' she said, shaking her head. 'He told me his friend used to be his captain. He seemed pleasant, too. Just goes to show, you never know, do you?'

'Yea,' Nancy said, preoccupied, trying to think.

Betty looked intently into Nancy's face.

'Have you got an idea, Nancy?' she asked.

'Sort of,' Nancy mused, her mouth pursed.

She stood still for a moment before turning to Betty.

'You go and wait for Tom to come down from the Blue Parlour, Betty. Try and get him on his own. Tell him I want to see him urgently,' Nancy said.

'Right,' Betty said. 'I'll go and keep an eye out for him.'

A smile dawned on her face as she had a thought.

'Ah! I know. So as I don't miss him, I'll stay by the door to the passage and give it a polishing,' she said, nodding decisively.

'Good idea, Betty. I'll stay behind the bar and serve any customers who come in.'

Betty gasped and put a hand to her mouth.

'Nancy, I forgot. Jimmy and his captain ordered ale.'

'I'll see to them, Betty,' Nancy said.

As they left the scullery, Betty picked up a fresh cloth and polish. She moved to the door leading to the passage.

Nancy left the kitchen for the taproom and went to the bar.

Once there, Nancy pulled two tankards of ale and took them to Jimmy and Crenshaw. She forced herself to smile at them as she put the tankards on the table before the men. She took the coin Crenshaw gave her and went back to the bar. Picking up a cloth, she began taking tankards from their shelf, polishing them one by one, all the while carefully observing Jimmy and Crenshaw.

Usually, Betty would give the door a quick dusting. Today she concentrated meticulously on every inch of it, rubbing the wood to a high shine. After fifteen minutes, the door was immaculate. Still, there was no sign of Tom.

Betty wondered where next she could apply her polish and decided the bannister on the stairs leading up to the gallery was the perfect spot. She certainly would not miss Tom if she were there.

She began with the newel post and had polished the handrail and spindles halfway up the stairway when the door to the Blue Parlour opened. Adrien came out, holding the door for Corbeau, Mollien and Renoudin. Laroche followed, now with his beard and his clothing in place again, hiding his face.

Betty removed herself from the stairs and went down to the passage, standing aside to let the men pass.

Tom was the last to leave the Blue Parlour. He took the key from his pocket and locked the door.

As Tom came down after the men, Betty caught his sleeve. She glanced at the Frenchmen as they made their way to the door of the taproom.

Tom looked at Betty's hand holding his sleeve. He switched his gaze to her face and saw her concerned expression.

'What's wrong, Betty?' he asked, frowning.

'Nancy wants to see you urgently. Go to the kitchen and wait for her,' Betty whispered.

'I can't, Betty. I have to go with these men,' Tom replied, trying to shake Betty's hand from his sleeve.

Betty tightened her grip.

'No, Tom! It's urgent. You *have* to see Nancy,' Betty hissed.

Tom tried to protest.

'But …'

'Tom!' Betty snapped, 'It's *very* important. Go!'

'Agh! … all right, I'll go. But it had better be truly important.'

Tom caught up with the group of men who were waiting for him in the taproom. Putting on a pleasant expression, Tom took Adrien to one side.

'My apologies, Babineaux. There is something I must see to. I will not be long. Did you come by carriage?'

'We did, Mr Johnson. We came in two carriages; I shared with La Roche,' Adrien replied.

'Good, then I will be with you by the time the horses are put to. I am sorry, but it seems the matter is urgent,' Tom said.

He turned from Adrien and marched purposefully towards Nancy. Stepping behind the bar, he took her by the arm and propelled her to the kitchen.

Arriving in the kitchen, Nancy shook her arm free.

She bundled Tom into the scullery, closed the door and stood with her back to it.

Much annoyed, but becoming curious, Tom demanded answers.

'What's going on, Nancy? What's so urgent? Don't you know I'm in the middle of addressing business matters?'

Nancy swallowed. Her eyes stared. Her breathing quickened as she steeled herself to tell him. She took a step forward to face him.

'They're on to you, Tom,' she said.

Tom's jaw dropped. He drew back, his eyes narrowing.

'On to me? On to what? Who's on to me?' he demanded.

'The sailor, Jimmy. Betty overheard him and his captain-friend talking. She told me they said the Government plans to have you watched,' Nancy said, rendered breathless by the enormity of the situation.

Tom's voice deepened with anger, and his nostrils flared.

'Hell's Teeth! Damn the little bastard's eyes!' he uttered between gritted teeth.

Deliberately breathing slowly, he gained a little composure.

'What exactly did they say?' he asked.

Nancy shook her head.

'I don't know, Tom. It was Betty who overheard them. You'll have to ask her,' Nancy said.

She caught Tom's hand in hers and looked up into his eyes.

'Tom, in the name of God, give up this thing. Whatever it is, give it up. I don't want to lose you.'

Tom exhaled slowly as he cupped her chin in his hand.

'You're not going to lose me, Nancy-love,' Tom said.

Leaning forward, he gave her a gentle kiss.

'What is it you're mixed up in, Tom?' Nancy asked.

Tom shook his head.

'I can't tell you, Nancy,' he said, a hand at his throat.

Unseeing, he gazed into the distance while his mind turned cartwheels.

'Be easy, Nancy. It'll be alright,' he said at last. 'I'll tell the Frenchies what's happened, and we'll arrange to meet somewhere else. Meanwhile, I'll have to put Jimmy, and whoever they send to spy on us, off the scent. It's a mercy o' God Betty overheard.'

Tom lowered his head, his fingers at his temples as he thought. He looked up.

'I might need your help, and Betty's, to dupe them all into thinking I'm on legitimate business,' he said looking deeply into Nancy's eyes, trying to gauge her mood.

He knew she loved him as much as he loved her. He could see how agitated she was and hated himself for causing her pain.

'Will you help me, Nancy?' he asked gently.

'Of course, I will, Tom, if it stops you from getting into trouble. But you're still going to go through with whatever you're doing with the Frenchies, aren't you?'

Tom's eyes darkened as he nodded.

'And I don't suppose anything I say will make you change your mind?'

Tom shook his head.

'I've put in too much time and effort, not to mention money, to give up now, Nancy. I'm sorry, Love. I must go through with it. I'm very nearly sold on the rightness of it if truth be told.'

Nancy sighed.

'All right, Tom. If it means so much to you, I'll help you. But you've got to tell me all about it. I'm not going blindfold into such a dangerous scheme. Do you hear me?'

It was Tom's turn to sigh.

'You'll only be unsettled, Nancy,' he said.

'And what do you think I am now? At least if you tell me I won't be imagining all sorts of horrible things,' she replied, a petulant look on her face.

'Oh, Nancy, what a woman you are!' Tom said.

He took her in his arms and kissed her.

Nancy didn't struggle but kissed him back.

Moving her cheek to his, she whispered in his ear.

'I can't lose you, Tom. I can't.'

Tom took her by the shoulders.

'I told you, Nancy. You won't lose me. If the worst comes to the worst, I can say I infiltrated the group of Frenchies so that I could thwart their schemes.'

Nancy leant back from him a little.

'You would *do* that, Tom?' Nancy asked.

'In a flash, sweetheart. When have you ever known me to have a conscience in such matters?'

Nancy stood back from him. She tilted her head as she placed her hands on her hips.

'You are a rogue, Tom Johnson!' she said, trying not to smile.

'Yes, Nancy, I am. Always have been and always will be. I'll tell you everything when it's all straight in my mind,' he said, giving her behind a pat before he left the scullery.

Hurrying through the kitchen to the taproom, he saw a coach and horses standing outside the door. Exiting, he found Adrien and Laroche sitting in the coach as they waited for him.

Jimmy and Captain Crenshaw, oblivious to their being under suspicion, sat talking and watching for the Frenchmen to come down from the Blue Parlour. They saw Betty polishing the door and noticed her disappear into the passage.

'Should I go up to my room and keep a watch from there?' Jimmy asked. 'Sittin' doin' nothin' for so long is killin' me.'

'No, Jimmy. We will bide our time here till the group reappears. Have patience,' Crenshaw said.

'I've never been a patient man, Cap'n. I always have to be a doin',' Jimmy said, nervously fiddling with the handle of his tankard.

After a moment, he spoke again.

'Have you any idea when the covert men will come to keep watch, Cap'n?' he asked.

'No, I haven't. I would guess that we will not be told. Covert means covert. Why, they could even be those two men sitting near the bar,' Crenshaw said.

Jimmy's eyes opened wide.

'Do you think that's them, Sir?' Jimmy asked glancing furtively at the two men.

'I don't know, Jimmy. All I'm saying is they could be,' Crenshaw said, trying not to let Jimmy's impatience annoy him.

Jimmy sat up straight when he saw the five Frenchmen leave The George.

'Johnson ain't with 'em, Cap'n,' Jimmy observed.

Captain Crenshaw took a sip of his ale. Over the rim of his tankard, he saw Johnson stride towards Nancy and practically drag her into the kitchen.

'I wonder what that's all about,' Jimmy said, pressing his lips together.

'All's not well, Jimmy,' Crenshaw observed.

Betty appeared again from the passage, carrying her polish and cloth. She walked straight past Jimmy and Crenshaw, making her way to the bar.

In a few moments, Tom came from the kitchen and left by the door.

'There's a lot o' comings and goings, Cap'n. What do you make of it?' Jimmy asked.

'I've no idea, Jimmy,' Crenshaw said, as puzzled as Jimmy. 'But something seems to have upset all three of them. It's probably nothing. Perhaps a lover's tiff. Who knows what they are all up to.'

Crenshaw was quite right. The two men sitting quietly near the bar, drinking their ale, and saying not a word, were indeed the covert agents put in place to observe The George's occupants and report anything untoward.

And Tom had been right to sense something odd about them.

The two men had noted Jimmy sitting at Tom Johnson's table. One had twitched an eyebrow when the five Frenchmen had entered, and Tom Johnson led them upstairs. One had glanced at the other again when the five men left. And both had watched with interest when Tom had stridden up to Nancy and rushed her to the kitchen. They had also seen Betty busying herself with her polishing cloth. By an infinitesimal nod, they had agreed that Jimmy and Crenshaw were the two who had informed about the activity in The George.

'I do not think anything more will happen today, Jimmy,' Crenshaw said.

'Are you sure, Cap'n?' Jimmy asked, disappointed that, apart from the Frenchmen's coming and going, and Nancy, Tom and Betty rushing in and out, nothing notable had taken place.

'I am pretty sure. Come, I will give you dinner. I hope you like mutton. The cook always serves mutton on Saturday for dinner.'

'That's very good of you, Cap'n. I like a bit o' mutton,' Jimmy said rising from his seat.

Crenshaw also rose, easing his stiff shoulders before he and Jimmy left The George.

The two men rose when Jimmy and Crenshaw had gone.

'I believe our information is not unfounded, Mr Sweet,' the taller of the two men said under his breath.

Mr Sweet swilled the last dregs of his ale.

'I think you are right, Mr Brooking,' he replied quietly, dragging the back of his hand across his mouth.

They left The George together and made their way to the Foreign Office in Fludyer Street to give their report and recommend that a full-scale operation should be set in motion.

CHAPTER TEN

Tom climbed into the coach to sit opposite Adrien and Laroche. At first glance, Adrien noticed Tom's brooding expression.

'Is all well, Mr Johnson?' he enquired.

Tom focused his eyes on Adrien, blowing out his cheeks with a long breath.

'No, Babineaux, it is not,' Tom said, his mouth hard.

Tom's dark look sent a chill along Adrien's spine.

'Are you sure he can't understand English?' Tom asked, shifting his gaze towards Laroche.

'Not a word, Sir. Tell me, what has happened?' Adrien asked.

Tom looked out of the window gathering his thoughts. In a moment, he turned back to face Adrien and delivered the blow.

'It may be that we are discovered,' he said.

Adrien gasped as his eyes rounded in dismay.

'What?' he exclaimed, sitting back in his seat, staring at Tom in disbelief.

Adrien took a quick look at Laroche, who was too preoccupied with looking out of the carriage window at the London streets to take notice of anything else.

'How so?' Adrien queried, his voice low and urgent.

'Do you recall the sailor we encountered in the Gallery?'

Adrien nodded.

'It seems you were right about him. One of the serving maids, Betty, overheard him discussing us with an acquaintance. Apparently, the Government are sending spies to watch our activities,' Tom explained.

Adrien felt his chest tighten. He clenched a fist.

'I don't believe it! Why, we have hardly started. How did they find out?' he asked.

Tom's lip curled in disgust.

'I don't know. The sailor has been hovering around

for the past week. I reckon it must be down to him.'

'I wonder how much they know?' Adrien mused, his eyes darkening.

'I can't tell. Corbeau and I discussed the matter at length last Monday. I don't remember whether the sailor was there then, or not. If he was and listened to us, he knows about the submarine and may have heard mention of St Helena. In any case, we must not meet in The George again. And somehow, we must put the misbegotten cur off the scent.'

Adrien nodded. His eyes narrowed as he deliberated.

'I do not relish the thought of telling the others,' he said a sardonic twist to his mouth.

'No, neither do I,' Tom said, irritation filling him at the thought. 'I would like to get my hands on that little swine and choke the life out of him.'

'No doubt he considers himself a patriot,' Adrien murmured.

'Hmm,' Tom grunted.

Tom spent the rest of the journey looking out of the window in company with Laroche, his quick mind assessing all aspects of the situation.

Several weeks before Corbeau had contacted Tom Johnson, he had arranged to rent a large house in Aldeburgh Street, number fifty-two. Situated on the outskirts of the fashionable part of London, the address was unremarkable, but the three-story building's aspect was handsome and respectable.

Corbeau lived there himself. When Mollien arrived from France with Renoudin, they had stayed in a hotel. However, Corbeau suggested they come to take up residence in Aldeburgh Street. They had recently relocated and now shared a suite of rooms to the back of the house.

Adrien Babineaux, when he returned from his visit to St Helena, was also allocated rooms. They were not as grand as that of Mollien, nevertheless, comfortable.

When Henri had brought Laroche to England Corbeau had established Laroche in two rooms at the top of the house, keeping him out of sight. Henri had rested there one night before returning to France.

A lane at the side of Aldeburgh Street led to Aldeburgh Mews, which ran parallel to the back of the house, where Corbeau kept three coaches and ten horses.

The six conspirators alighted, and Tom found himself in the stable yard. It reminded him of the brief time he had spent working as a groom in a place such as this. He inhaled the familiar smells of horse, hay, and leather. Hearing the stable boy's banter, he smiled to himself.

The work was hard, but comradery between the grooms was high. Not so high, though, that when the opportunity arose, Tom did not turn down the prospect of returning to the smuggler's band.

'Come, Mr Johnson,' Adrien called, bringing him back from his reverie.

'This way, Sir,' he said holding open a door for Tom to enter the back of the house.

A cool, shadowy vestibule lay behind the door, the floor laid with dark, patterned tiles. Its enfolding quietness did nothing to calm Tom's agitation. He followed Adrien and the other four men to a wide staircase, which they climbed to the first floor.

'Follow me,' Corbeau said as he led them through a hall, doors to unknown rooms leading off it. Opening one door, he ushered them into a sober drawing room at the front of the house. Sunlight fought its way through the heavily curtained windows, shedding a modicum of light over the antiquated furniture. A bright fire burned in the grate, alleviating the sombre atmosphere.

As the men filed into the room, Corbeau motioned them towards the old-fashioned plush chairs and couches, before stepping to the side of the fireplace to pull a bell rope.

Tom crossed the room to stand at the window, adopting a familiar stance from his days on the deck of a ship. Legs planted wide, hands behind his back, he looked out on the quiet street below. Tuning out the buzz of French conversation behind him, he composed himself to relate the news of their discovery.

A footman and a maid entered, placing trays on the sideboard to one side of the fireplace, their movements noiseless and unobtrusive. The French maid quietly asked each man what beverage they would prefer. Going back to the sideboard, she spooned tea and poured hot water into a teapot for Adrien and Corbeau. While waiting for it to brew, she poured coffee and served it to Mollien, Renoudin and Laroche. The footman offered them little cakes from a tiered stand, while the maid went to Tom.

'Would you like refreshment, Sir?' she asked.

Tom glanced at her with a frown.

'Ah, thank you, no,' he said, with a hint of a smile before returning his gaze to the window. When the servants left the room, Tom turned to face the group. He cleared his throat.

'Your pardon, gentlemen, I have something to tell you,' he said.

All talk ceased as the five men turned to listen to what Tom had to say.

Tom's eyes wandered over them, noting Adrien's uncomfortable expression, Corbeau's impatience, Mollien's indolent unconcern, Renoudin's affected servility towards his master and Laroche's innocence. Tom took a deep breath before he spoke.

'We have a complication to our plans, Messieurs. Corbeau and I were overheard talking in The George. I don't know how much was heard, but they informed the Government of our activities, and The George is no longer a safe place to meet.'

Stunned silence met his words. The men stared at Tom and then at each other.

Corbeau broke the silence.

'Who overheard?' he asked.

'I believe it was a sailor who has taken a room in The George. I have seen him sitting with a man, whom, I am told, was his captain. What they have heard and who they told, I do not know. But I believe I have a way of finding out,' Tom replied.

Adrien caught his cousin's eye.

'Paul, is there a room big enough in this house where we may meet?' he asked.

Corbeau frowned as he pondered.

'The billiard room. It is not as large as the Blue Parlour at The George, nor so opulent. However, in the circumstances, it would be adequate. It is in a sorry state; nevertheless, I will instruct the servants to make it ready for use.'

'Does the billiard table have a cover?' Tom asked. 'Could it accommodate maps and charts?'

'I think so, yes,' Corbeau said. 'But tell me, Mr Johnson, how do you propose to find out what the sailor knows?'

Tom shifted his position.

'I mean to contact an old associate. I will ask him to impersonate a Government official and visit the sailor. He will interrogate him and find out what the man knows, and then *we* will know.'

'Excellent, Mr Johnson. Who have you in mind?' Adrien asked.

'His name is Peter Marriot. He used to be an excise man. But seeing the lucrative nature of my trade, he joined me in my smuggling enterprises. His current occupation is as a cartographer. It was from his establishment I purchased our maps and charts. I choose him because he can be impressively officious when necessary,' Tom said, grinning.

Corbeau put down his cup as he surveyed the reaction of the other men.

'How long will it take to contact him?' he asked.

'If you agree to my involving him, I will go and speak to him this afternoon. His establishment is in Rathbone Place,' Tom replied.

'In the absence of any other option, Mr Johnson, I think that is where we should start,' Adrien said.

'If they know about the submarine, we may have to sacrifice it to throw them off the scent,' Tom stated.

'But our endeavour hinges on the submarine. Without it we cannot safely remove the Emperor from St Helena without him being seen,' Corbeau said, a tight frown marring his smooth brow.

'You forget, Corbeau. I told you, I have the original vessel, *Nautilus*. It is smaller, but that is a good thing. We can hide her more easily. Although she cannot stay submerged as long as *Eagle*, I assure you, she can do the job.'

Corbeau turned to Mollien.

'What say you, Mon Seigneur?'

Mollien fished a stylish silver snuffbox from his coat pocket and took a delicate pinch of snuff between finger and thumb. He gave Tom a long stare before speaking.

'At first, I would have said we should abandon this plan and think of some other way to rescue The Emperor. Now, however, I feel if something can be salvaged from this wreckage, we should consider it and proceed,' he said and applied the snuff to his nose.

'Bravo, Sir,' Adrien cried.

'Do any of you have further suggestions?' Tom asked.

The men glanced at each other, murmuring, and shaking their heads.

'Well, if that is all, Messieurs, I will now go to Rathbone Place to speak with Peter Marriot,' Tom said breathing an inward sigh of relief.

'Would you oblige me, Mollien, and ask your hall boy to find me a Hackney cab? After I have spoken with Mr Marriot, I will return and inform you of the outcome.'

Half an hour later, at number fifty-five Rathbone Place, Tom alighted from the cab and paid the jarvey. He paused before walking up the steps to the front door.

He had renewed his acquaintance with Marriot some days earlier. Although they had not seen each other for some years, it was not long before they slipped into their old association. Both were intelligent men. Both, at one time, cruised on the wrong side of the law. Both were now not so reformed as not to dabble in shady activities.

Tom rapped on the black, lion's head knocker.

As he waited, Tom looked about him. Rathbone Place was a busy street, attracting both tradesmen's traps and gentlemen's carriages. Looking at the pedestrians, he could not help comparing them with those in Borough High Street where work-a-day clothes were the norm.

Here there were many artisans dressed flamboyantly, other people arrayed in genteel style, yet others in sober clothes.

Tom Turned towards the door as it opened. A young lad, wearing an apron stained with ink—as were his fingers—gave Tom an enquiring look.

'Is Mr Marriot available?' Tom asked.

'Are you not the man who came to see him the other day?'

'I am. Is he here?' Tom asked.

'Yes, Sir. Go straight up,' the lad said, sweeping a hand in the direction of the stairs. Tom ascended and knocked on the door of the room where he had previously met Marriot.

In a moment, Marriot came to the door.

'Tom, me old shipmate! Come in. Come in! I didn't think I'd see you again so soon.'

Tom removed his hat. Marriott took it from him and placed it on a small table inside the door.

'Is there something I can help you with?' Marriot asked, indicating a chair beside his desk.

Tom sat.

'Yes, Peter, there is,' he said, 'I've run into a bit of trouble.'

Peter sat at his desk as Tom proceeded to tell him all that had occurred.

'That's a bit of a rum go,' Peter said after hearing the story. 'What is it you want me to do?' he asked.

'Well, Peter,' Tom began, drawing a breath. 'You were always good at putting on an act. What I want you to do, is to dress up as an official government clerk.'

Peter's eyebrows flew up, and he blinked.

Tom smiled at his expression and continued.

'Go to The George tomorrow, and pay a visit to the sailor who is staying there. I want you to say the Foreign Office has sent you to interview him and learn exactly what he overheard,' Tom explained.

'I infer you want to know whether he knows about your submarine,' Peter said.

Going to a sideboard, Peter poured two generous measures of brandy into glasses and handed one to Tom.

'Exactly,' Tom said. He accepted the brandy and took a sip.

Holding the glass up to the light, he inspected the amber liquor.

'Damn it, Peter! Where did you get this?'

Peter tapped the side of his nose with his finger.

'I still have connections, Tom,' Peter confessed. 'What time do you want me to visit him?'

'Early morning, if you can. I want to get this whole matter out of the way. Will you assist me?' Tom asked.

'I will, Tom. I haven't had a bit of fun in a long time.'

Tom grinned. Standing up, he slapped Peter on the back.

'We must find out the sailor's full name. I'll ask

Betty; then I shall return to you. If you come early Peter, hopefully, you may find the little swine still abed. Nancy or Betty can show you the back way to his room in case there are spies in the taproom. I knew I could rely on you, Peter.'

Tom sighed with satisfaction, pleased to have Peter helping him out of his difficulty.

He smiled broadly at Peter

'To your health,' Tom said, raising his glass.

'To your success, Tom,' said Peter raising his glass in turn,

When they finished the rest of their brandy, Peter picked up the bottle.

'More?' he asked.

'I would like to, but I should not,' Tom said, picking up his hat.

'I must go now. Goodbye, Peter; I will see you later,' Tom said.

Peter saw Tom out of his room and, turning back in, he realised he still had the bottle in his hand. He looked at it, frowning.

'Ah, why not,' he said to himself and, picking up his glass, he poured another measure.

When Tom left, he walked a little way along Rathbone Place and was fortunate enough to find a vacant Hackney cab. He climbed into it and gave the driver the direction to Aldeburgh Street.

When shown up to the drawing room, Tom found Babineaux alone.

'Be seated, Mr Johnson. Is all well?' Babineaux asked.

'I cannot stay long, Babineaux. I must get back to The George. I came only to tell you that Peter Marriot is willing to interview Jimmy and will call on him early tomorrow to do so.'

Babineaux smiled and nodded.

'So, then we will know exactly what *he* knows. That

is good, Mr Johnson,'

'Indeed,' Tom said, adding, 'There is something I want you to do, Monsieur.'

Babineaux gave Tom an enquiring look.

'Will you come to The George on Sunday afternoon and meet me in the Blue Parlour? By that time, I will have formulated my plans more precisely. I will explain them to you, and you may relate them to Corbeau. You must enter The George by the scullery.'

'How will I find it?' Babineaux asked.

'You may have noticed that the entrance to the inn yard is to the side, before you come to the front door,' Tom said.

'Yes, I have seen it,' Babineaux said.

Tom nodded, 'Good. You must walk along the yard to the end. Turn left and you will find yourself in a courtyard. Pass through it and you will see the door to the scullery before you,' Tom explained.

Babineaux nodded.

Tom continued, 'I will warn Nancy and Betty to be on the lookout for you. From there, they will show you to the passage leading to the stairs that go up to the gallery.'

'Do you think we may still go forward?' Babineaux asked.

'I am determined we should, Babineaux. And once I am determined, I always accomplish my task.'

Babineaux smiled and showed Tom out.

He watched him from the window as Tom hailed a cab.

'I hope you are right, Tom Johnson,' he murmured to himself.

Mr Sweet and Mr Brooking entered The George. They made their way to the same seats they had occupied before. Mr Sweet caught Betty's eye and lifted his chin to beckon her over.

Betty was cleaning the top of the bar. She wiped her

hands and smoothed her apron before moving to their table.

'What's your pleasure, Gentlemen?' she asked, giving them her usual friendly smile.

'Two tankards of ale, my dear,' Mr Sweet said, putting a coin on the table.

Betty smiled again and went to the bar. As she came back with the ale, she heard the door open. Having delivered the tankards to the men, Betty turned and saw Tom come in. He looked about and, seeing Betty, he strode to where she stood.

'I need to speak to you, Betty,' he said. 'Will you come with me to the kitchen?'

Without waiting for an answer, he marched to the kitchen and held back the curtain for Betty to enter.

Once inside, Betty looked up at Tom's determined jaw and stormy eyes.

'What do you want, Tom?' she asked.

'Betty, I need your help. I want to know the sailor's full name. He must have written it in the register when he hired the room,' Tom said.

'I remember it, Tom. He is Able Seaman James Young. Why do you want to know?'

Tom inhaled deeply.

'Because, Betty, Peter Marriot, my old compatriot, has agreed to come and question him tomorrow to find out what he knows about my business.'

'But why should Jimmy tell him anything?' Betty asked, puzzled.

'Because, my dear, Peter will be dressed as a clerk and will say he was sent by the authorities to find out what Jimmy knows,' Tom explained.

Betty glanced at Tom, one eyebrow raised. The affair was beginning to add a little spice to her day.

'Do you think Jimmy will believe that?' she asked.

'Oh yes. I have seen Peter in action. He can play a part as good as any actor on a stage. He will get Jimmy to tell him everything,' Tom said, with a knowing smile. 'Now, Betty, I need you to be ready to let him in at the scullery door. Then, if there is anyone spying, they won't see him going up to Jimmy's room. What time does Jimmy usually wake?'

Betty thought a moment, enjoying being part of the conspiracy.

'He generally appears for his breakfast at about nine o'clock. If your friend Peter is at the door at about half-past eight, I can let him in and show him up.'

'Thank you, Betty. Between us all, we will scotch any government agents from disrupting our enterprise,' Tom said, giving Betty's shoulder a squeeze.

'What is your enterprise, Tom?' Betty asked.

'Ah, Betty, I haven't even told Nancy that—although I have promised her I will,' Tom replied.

'Is it something very bad, Tom? Is it dangerous?'

'It's somewhat dangerous,' Tom said, wrinkling his nose. 'As to being bad, that depends on your point of view. The Government certainly would not approve of what we are doing. Others with different political views would think otherwise. Enough now. I must go to Peter again and tell him Jimmy's name and what time he must arrive tomorrow. I'll go out through the scullery courtyard. The spies might already be in place,' Tom said, giving Betty a peck on her cheek before he went on his way.

Tom returned to Rathbone place. The apprentice boy raised his brows at his returning so soon and bade Tom go up.

'So, did you find out his name?' Peter asked when he opened the door to Tom.

'Yes, I did. He is called Able Seaman James Young,' Tom said, placing his hat on the table.

'Betty said he rises at nine, so, if you are there at half-past eight, she will show you straight up.'

'I'll be there, Tom. I'm looking forward to it,' Peter said, rubbing his hands together.

'There is something else you can do for me, Peter,' Tom said.

'What's that, Tom?' Peter asked.

'You know my dry dock in Blackwall reach?'

'Of course, but it's been a while since I was there,' Peter replied. 'what is it you want me to do?'

'I want you to contact the old crew, as quick as you can, and tell them to rendezvous there tomorrow night,' Tom said.

'I know where a few of them lodge, Tom. I'll contact them and tell them to spread the word. But what do you want them for?'

'I need them to ready *Eagle* and *Nautilus.* I will wait till you find out exactly what our little sailor boy knows before I finalise my plans. I shall return tomorrow afternoon, and you can tell me how went your interview with Jimmy,' Tom said as he picked up his hat and went to the door.

'Till tomorrow then, Tom,' Peter said as he showed him out.

After his busy Saturday, as he had promised, Tom called again at Rathbone Place at noon on Sunday. The same printer's apprentice let him in. Tom swiftly made his way to Peter's room, knocked, and entered.

Peter sat at his desk preparing a map for printing. He looked up when Tom came in.

'How did it go, Peter?' Tom asked.

'Like clockwork, Tom,' Peter replied, putting down his pen.

'He wouldn't stop till he ran out of puff. In fact, I couldn't shut him up, so eager was he to "do his duty" and make the conspiracy known. He hates the French and recommended we hang all those involved.'

Tom grimaced. Thinking how easily Peter managed to prise information from Jimmy, his expression changed to a smile as he chuckled.

'So, he fell for it. How did you persuade him to

talk?' Tom asked, sitting on a seat beside Peter's desk.

Peter stroked his chin and laughed softly.

'I produced a letter from Lord Castlereagh giving me authority to investigate the matter.'

Tom laughed.

'How did you manage to get hold of that?'

'Ah, well now, Tom, you know I am a skilled mapmaker, do you not? Did you know I am also adept at forgery?'

Tom chortled and shook his head.

'If I had a copy of Castlereagh's signature, I could have forged it. But I didn't need to, as our friend Jimmy would not know it from that of a cabin boy.'

Tom snorted. 'Stupid little bastard. How much does he know?'

'A lot,' Peter said pressing his lips together.

'Damn his eyes,' Tom said clenching his teeth. 'Does he know about the submarine?'

'He does, Tom, I'm sorry to say,' Peter said, pressing his lips together again as he shook his head.

'Does he know about the plan to rescue Napoleon?' Tom asked, hoping the answer would be no.

Peter Nodded. 'He does, Tom.'

Tom pounded his palm with his fist. 'God blast and damn it,' he uttered.

'Will this mean you must abandon the whole thing?' Peter asked.

Tom's eyes blazed.

'It most certainly does not. I had an idea when I first knew our plan might have been discovered. That's why I wanted you to get the old crew together. Any luck with that?'

'Yes, I wrote notes to those whose address I know and sent young Nate, the apprentice, to deliver them. I told them to spread the word and meet up tonight at Blackwall. But why do you want *Eagle* made ready in such a hurry? Do you want them to sail her?' Peter asked.

'No, I'll get Jimmy Young and his shipmates to do that. Our lads needn't be too particular, just make sure she can sail far enough to run aground,' Tom said, a smile hovering on his mouth.

'Good God, why, Tom?'

'I want to put the authorities off the scent. I'll explain it all to you and the men when we meet tonight.'

Peter shrugged. 'Seems a shame,' he said.

'The other thing is, I want *Nautilus* made ready, too,' Tom said.

'You're not going to scupper her as well?'

'No, Peter. But I want her to look like a steam yacht.'

Peter's eyebrows flew up.

Tom laughed.

'I'll explain that part to you as well tonight, Peter, when it's all straight in my mind.'

Tom pursed his lips looking thoughtfully at Peter.

'I wonder, Peter …' he said, rubbing his chin.

Peter watched Tom's face. He knew that look. Tom was hatching something.

'Go on,' Peter urged.

Tom gave Peter a sidelong look.

'I wonder whether you would consider accompanying me on the voyage to St Helena?'

Peter straightened his shoulders; his eyes brightened.

'I would consider it, yes. I haven't been at sea for a long time. Why would you want me with you?' Peter asked, returning a sidelong look of his own.

'Because, my friend, if you truly are an adept forger, your skills could be useful. For example, we will need passes to get us onto the island. There will be at least six sets of papers for you to produce. The journey will take up to nine weeks. You can work on them as we sail. And you might even pose as a British official, giving credence to the legitimacy of our arrival. What say you?'

A slow smile dawned on Peter's face. He took a long breath, and let it out on a soft laugh.

'By God, Tom, I'll do it. It's a while since I went a-venturing.'

'Good man, Peter! However, I don't want just you with me on the voyage. I want Pedro as well. When we remove Napoleon from St Helena, we must transport him in *Nautilus* out farther than the Naval patrols. It will take at least two of us to monitor the controls, and you might be otherwise occupied. Will you ask him?'

'Very well, Tom. I suppose you know what you're doing. Ah, but it will be good to be with the old lads again,' Peter said, slapping Tom on the back.

'Aye, it will. That's one of the best parts of the whole thing. Working with me mates again,' Tom said.

CHAPTER ELEVEN

When Tom left Peter, he hailed a Hackney to take him to The George.

Over the past week, he had become so enmeshed in Corbeau's plans. A deep sense of disappointment filled him at the thought of the whole thing falling apart.

When he heard the scheme to liberate Napoleon had been discovered, the bones of a plan to impede the Government in bringing the enterprise to an end had formed in his mind. It would mean sacrificing his beloved *Eagle*. But then, he would be compensated when he received his forty-thousand-pounds.

Sitting back in his seat, he smiled. Already his plan was taking shape.

Arriving at The George, Tom paid the driver and entered the door to the taproom with a flourish.

Noticing Jimmy sitting by the fire, Tom decided to start on his course of action right away.

Before sitting down, he went to the kitchen to find Billy, the cook's young assistant. He saw Gem, the cook, busy making bread.

'Gem, where's Billy?' Tom asked.

'I dunno, Tom,' Gem said,' and, taking a lungful of air, he bellowed. 'Billy!'

In a moment, they heard a clattering on the staff stairway, and Billy appeared.

'What ya want, Gem?'

'Nothin—it's Tom as wants you,' Gem replied and turned his attention back to his bread.

'What ya want, Tom?' Billy said, tilting his chin.

'Do you know who Jimmy Young is, Billy?' Tom asked.

'That's the short, sailor cove, ain't it?' Billy said.

'Yes, Billy. Does he know you?'

'I don't reckon so. I'm never in the taproom or the dining room. I've seen him skulkin' around in the gallery, though,' Billy replied.

'Good,' Tom said fishing half-a-crown from his pocket and holding it in front of Billy. Never having seen one before, Billy's eyes glinted at the sight.

'I am about to talk to Jimmy, and then I shall leave the Taproom. I fully expect Jimmy to go out after that. I want you to follow him. And then I want you to find out who lives in the house where he goes. Take this half-a-crown and if you do what I ask, you shall have another,' Tom said, taking Billy's hand and placing the coin in it.

To Billy, half-a-crown was a good few month's pay. A huge grin covered Billy's face as he looked at the coin and then at Tom.

'Right, y'are, Tom. I'll wait outside the front door and follow him like you want,' Billy said, pocketing the coin and removing his apron.

'Thank you, Billy,' Tom said, ruffling the young lad's unruly hair.

Tom returned to the taproom from the kitchen and went to his seat.

He turned towards Jimmy.

'Good afternoon, Sir. Jimmy, is it not?' Tom called to him.

Jimmy jumped in alarm. His head came sharply round, hardly believing Tom was addressing him.

He nodded.

'That's me, Cap'n Johnson. Good afternoon, Sir,' Jimmy replied, his startled eyes furtively moving here and there.

'Will you join me?' Tom asked, patting the seat next to him.

'Er … yes, Sir. It'd be a pleasure, Sir,' Jimmy said as he got up and moved to sit beside Tom.

'Would you like a drink, me Lad?' Tom asked.

'That'd be a kindness, Sir. I'll have a tankard of ale, if it may please you, Sir,' Jimmy said, rubbing a clammy hand on his trousers.

Tom put a finger up to call Nancy to his table. She had noticed the unusual flair Tom displayed as he entered the taproom and as he spoke to Jimmy. She couldn't understand why he was even talking to the traitor. Putting down the tankard she was polishing, she tossed her cloth beneath the bar before moving to Tom's table.

'Good afternoon, Nancy. A tankard of ale for my friend, Jimmy, and another for me, if you please,' he said in a loud voice.

Nancy gave Tom a questioning look.

He winked at her.

She forced a smile and went to draw the two tankards of ale.

Out of the corner of his eye, Tom watched the two men sitting by the bar. One flicked his eyes in Tom's direction. The other frowned slightly in reply.

Oh, yes, Tom thought, *I have the measure of you, me lads. You're the spies, alright.*

He turned his attention back to Jimmy.

'Now, Jimmy, I hear you are a sailor and are looking for work.'

'Yes, Cap'n, that's right. I ain't had a job in months and me money's runnin' out,' Jimmy replied, warming to Tom, but still a little wary.

'I might be able to help you, lad. I'm gathering a crew together to sail the Atlantic,' Tom said, smiling at Nancy, who put their tankards down with a snap.

Tom has some explaining to do, she thought.

'Oh, aye, Cap'n?' Jimmy said, a worried frown appearing on his face. 'What's your cargo, Sir? I won't have any doins with nothing illegal, mind. I'm an honest man.'

Jimmy, proud of his statement, concentrated on the tankard in his hand a moment before he took a gulp.

'Ah, Jimmy, you've heard of my former reputation, I think. I am no longer a smuggler. I am a respectable captain of an honest ship. Why, did you know, during

111

the recent war I was given a pardon and hired by the Government to pilot their ships in dangerous waters? Does that not speak of my honesty?' Tom asked.

Jimmy choked on his ale and coughed.

'Is that a fact, Cap'n Johnson?' Jimmy said when he had recovered. 'I didn't know, Sir. I heard different. It just shows you, don't it? You can't believe all you hear, can you?'

Tom nodded sagely.

'You're right, Jimmy. When you hear only half a story, it's easy to jump to the wrong conclusion. Now, can I count on you to be part of my crew? I hear you are a capable man at sea—or have *I* heard wrong?' Tom said, fingering his chin.

'I *am* a hard worker, Cap'n. You can ask anyone who's served with me. But you haven't told me. What's your cargo?'

'I can't tell you that, Jimmy, as I don't precisely know what it is myself,' Tom replied.

He glanced furtively about him and leant closer to Jimmy.

'It's government business. But don't breathe a word to a soul. It's a state secret,' he said in a low voice.

Jimmy slowly turned his head to look at Tom, his eyes wide and his mouth open.

Tom looked at him sidelong.

'I can trust you, can't I, Jimmy?'

Jimmy swallowed.

'Of course, you can, Cap'n. Abserlutely,' Jimmy said, captivated by the thought of being involved in something so important.

'Good. Well, man, are you in?' Tom asked.

'In, Sir?'

'Yes, Jimmy. In, as a trusted member of my crew,' Tom answered.

Jimmy laughed nervously.

'Oh, yes, Cap'n. I'm in all right.'

Tom gave Jimmy a wide, gleaming grin.

'Good. Now, *as* a trusted member of my crew, may I rely on you to find another ten or twelve men to help man my ship?'

Jimmy scratched his head and frowned.

'I suppose I can, Cap'n. I knows a good few sailors out o' work. They'd be glad of a job, I reckon.'

'Excellent, Jimmy! I knew I could rely on you,' Tom said rising from his seat.

Picking up his tankard, he swallowed the rest of the ale in one go and passed his hand over his mouth.

'I'll speak to you further on the matter a little later. We should sail within a week.'

Tom patted Jimmy's shoulder while stealthily glancing at the two men. They gave little away. Still, Tom could see their unease.

Let them put that in their pipe and smoke it, he thought.

Tom made for the kitchen, smiling at Nancy on his way.

Nancy, her eyes narrowed, flung down her cloth again. With a savage tug, she straightened her apron and followed him. When she reached the kitchen, she found him standing by the scullery door, waiting for her.

Breathing heavily, she moved towards him and put her hands on her hips.

'Tom Johnson, what the bleedin' hell are you doing?' she hissed at him.

Tom smiled and shrugged.

'What do you mean, Love?'

'Don't you give me *what do I mean*. Why are you talking to Jimmy?'

'Oh, *that*.' Tom said, with a laugh. 'It's a ruse to put the Government men off the scent. If they see me being friendly with Jimmy and offering him a job, and they hear Jimmy agreeing to work for me, well, what will they think of our little friend? Will they still trust his information?'

Nancy shook her head and stamped her foot, tears of frustration coming to her eyes.

'Why can't you tell me what you're up to?' she said, glowering at him.

Noticing her tears, Tom drew back.

'Aw, Nancy, don't start crying on me,' he said. He never knew what to do when women cried.

'I'm not crying, I'm cross,' Nancy said frowning. 'Because you don't trust me enough to tell me what's going on.'

Relieved that his Nancy was not turning soft, he took her by the shoulders and looked into her angry face.

'I do trust you, Nancy-love. I'll tell you everything tonight, I promise. Till then you'll just have to trust me,' he said as he stroked her cheek.

Nancy realised she couldn't win. With a resigned sigh, she gave up trying.

Women, Tom thought and continued with the business in hand.

'Now listen, Nancy, Monsieur Babineaux is coming here later. I've told him to come in by the Scullery. Can you and Betty keep an eye out for him? When he comes, will you show him up the back way to the Blue Parlour? I'll wait for him there.'

Nancy pressed her lips together and nodded.

'Good girl,' Tom said, as he bent his head to kiss her.

He left the kitchen by the scullery. In the passage, he looked around to make sure no one was there to see him as he made for the stairs. Arriving in the gallery, he strode to the door of the Blue Parlour, key in hand.

Once inside, he locked the door. Going to the table, he unrolled maps and charts and began working.

Tom pored over his work, absorbed in plotting a course along the Thames. Next, he studied the sandbars along the coast, charting the best passage for *La Miséricorde* to take.

After some time, a knock sounded on the door. Tom rose from his seat and stretched, easing the stiffness in his shoulders. His eyes stung from so much concentration. He rubbed his lids with his knuckles before going to the door.

Nancy had led Babineaux by the back way up to the Blue Parlour. When Tom opened the door, he found them standing before him.

'Come in, Babineaux,' Tom said, holding the door open.

'Good Evening, Mr Johnson,' Adrien said as he walked into the room. Seeing Tom's work on the table, he moved to inspect it.

Tom turned to Nancy standing on the threshold.

'Thank you, Nancy,' Tom said.

Nancy lingered. Her curiosity aroused, she tried to see inside the room.

'I'll talk to you later, Nancy-love,' Tom said, giving her arm quick squeeze.

Nancy turned away and walked back to the stairs, glancing behind her before she descended.

Tom, still standing in the doorway, nodded, and closed the door.

He came to stand by Adrien, who looked up from the charts.

'You have been busy, Tom,' he said. 'You certainly know what you are doing.'

Tom smiled, accepting the compliment with unaccustomed reserve.

'It is merely a sketch of what would be the best course, Babineaux. It needs refining,' Tom said, modestly.

Adrien turned back to the charts and followed a line with his finger.

'From what I see here, Tom, your plans are remarkably thorough,' Adrien said as he straightened his back. 'But I am sure this is not what you asked me here to discuss,' he said, turning from the table.

'No, just part of it,' Tom replied as he stood with his back to the fire. 'I have an idea about what must be done to put the authorities on the wrong track. How far ahead is Corbeau with his preparations of *La Miséricorde*?'

'His crew is up to full compliment. Most of his provisions are stowed on board. He has checked the tides, employed a pilot...'

Tom interrupted him.

'Ah yes, the tides. They are crucial to my plan. Let me explain. I want to sail *Eagle* down the Thames and run her aground.'

Adrien leant his head back, eyebrows raised, eyes wide.

'What? Are you mad? Why would you want to do that?'

'To make the authorities think the escape plan abandoned,' Tom replied.

'How can you be sure she will run aground?' Babineaux asked.

'There are many locations along the Thames where one has to beware of sandbars. Strictly speaking, they do not consist of sand, more of silt. They are extremely unpredictable; with tides moving in and out continually, they shift. That is why charts must be kept up to date. The idea came to me when I remembered seeing a boat run aground just before Woolwich some time ago. The bar wasn't charted. I have checked on the current chart and it is still not marked,' Tom Explained.

Babineaux looked puzzled. 'Have you any idea why it is not marked?'

'Probably because it is close to land. Most ships stay in the middle of the channel where the water is deepest. But if traffic on the river is crowded, a ship may be forced farther in towards the bank. This is what happened to the ship I saw foundering.'

'So, you mean to run *Eagle* aground on that spot?'

'I do, yes,' Tom said with a confident smile. 'The authorities are sure to question me. I am used to that. I have a story ready to tell them. I shall explain that the crew and I are innocent dupes in a conspiracy or something like that. When I am released—for I know I shall be—I shall wait a few days, showing myself about the place, telling people I have been left a legacy in my Irish uncle's will, and I mean to sail there shortly to claim it. I shall then sail *Nautilus,* disguised as a steam yacht, to rendezvous with *La Misericord.* Do you think Corbeau would be ready to sail on Tuesday? I intend to run *Eagle* aground on Thursday, and I want you French out of the way before I do.'

'I am sure we will be able to do that. When I tell Corbeau of your plans, I am certain he will do all he can to comply,' Adrien said, a glint in his eye at the thought of getting underway at last.

Tom moved to the table where he had been working. He picked up a large sheet and rolled it up.

'This is the chart for the coast around the estuary near Margate. I have mapped a course for *La Miséricorde.* If you follow it carefully, you will be safe. From Margate, you must navigate to the Straits of Dover. I have marked a spot on the map where she may anchor safely and where we may rendezvous,' Tom said, handing the rolled-up paper to Adrien.

'Thank you. I shall pass it on to our navigator,' Adrien said, taking it from Tom. 'Why do we rendezvous at the Straits of Dover?'

Tom smiled. 'I know the coastal waters surrounding Britain like the back of my hand. There are sandbanks all around there. Those in that particular location are dangerous. It is safe to anchor in the spot I have marked. When *Nautilus* meets up with her, we shall sail together. The Navy charts are not always accurate. If by chance the authorities are alerted, I can make sure they follow me and run aground.'

'Is there danger for you in doing that?' Babineaux

asked.

'No. I have done such a thing in the past. Do not concern yourself, Babineaux.'

'Do you think we may run into trouble at Portsmouth? It is a Naval base, is it not?' Babineaux asked.

'It is. If someone who knew of my activities in the Thames saw me, they might smell a rat. Therefore, I shall stay below at that point. If we are careful, all will be well. Once we are through the Channel, it will be plain sailing to Plymouth and then to St Helena.'

'You seem confident of our success, Mr Johnson,' Adrien remarked admiring Tom's optimism.

'I am, Babineaux,' Tom said with a carefree smile.

'I hope you will not have too much difficulty convincing the authorities of your innocence when you run aground.'

Tom gave him a quizzical look.

'My Nancy says I lead a charmed life. The Navy gave me a pardon when they hired me as a pilot and navigator. I must simply convince my interrogators that I am still an honest man.'

Adrien raised his eyebrows and shook his head.

'You seem to know what you are doing. I trust you are right. Who will man *Nautilus?*'

'I shall, with my friends Peter Marriot, and Pedro Morales. She needs very few crewmen. I have asked Peter Marriot to contact the men who helped me to build *Eagle.* They will ready her for sailing. They must also disguise *Nautilus* as a yacht. Peter and Pedro know how to handle her. Peter is already committed to sailing with us to St Helena. I have asked him to enlist Pedro to do the same,' Tom explained.

Adrien looked dubious. 'Can they be trusted?' he queried.

'Oh, yes. I have known them most of my life. They do not care for politics or owe allegiance to any authority. If anything, being my comrades, they have some allegiance to me. And I shall pay them well. They can be trusted.'

Adrien drew a resigned sigh.

'I shall report all this back to Paul and leave it to him how much he tells Mollien. As it is the only plan we have, I doubt he will discard it.'

'Whether he does or not, I shall need compensation for my efforts so far,' Tom said, pursing his lips.

Adrien laughed.

'You are a mercenary, Mr Johnson. In company with your friends, you owe allegiance to no one.'

'Political allegiance can change like the wind. Mine is constant. Mine is to myself,' Tom said with a cynical smile.

CHAPTER TWELVE

After Tom left him, Jimmy Young sat thinking on what had just taken place. He knew his suspicions had not been wrong. He knew what he had heard Tom Johnson and the Frenchman talking about was to do with aiding Napoleon's escape from St Helena.

Going over their conversation in his mind, he remembered hearing Tom Johnson say, "*I am aware you wish to gain liberty for a certain party*". He had also heard the Frenchman's words, "*we mean to sail to St Helena with your submarine.*"

He had heard them mention "*the Emperor*".

And the Frenchman had said, "*The Emperor will enter the submarine.*"

How else was he to interpret such words other than as treason?

But now Johnson had said he was on government business. Surely the Government was not hiring Tom Johnson to help Napoleon escape? Were they using Johnson to scupper the Frenchmen's plans?

It was all too much for Jimmy. The idea of being a patriot and helping the Government appealed to him. That was why he had gone to Captain Crenshaw with his story. That was why he had agreed to go with Crenshaw to The Admiralty. And that was why, now, he had agreed to throw in his lot with Tom Johnson.

I promised Cap'n Johnson I wouldn't breathe a word of this, but I can't understand it. Surely, tellin' Cap'n Crenshaw wouldn't be breakin' me promise? After all, if I'm to believe Johnson, we're all on the same side, Jimmy thought.

With a decisive nod, Jimmy made up his mind. He finished the last dregs of his ale and went out of The George, determined to ask Captain Crenshaw's opinion.

Billy, lounging by the door to the tap room, saw

Jimmy come out and walk along Borough High Street. Keeping a reasonable distance between them, Billy followed Jimmy.

Jimmy walked the now-familiar route to Poland Street. He knocked at the door and waited for Milly to open it.

'Do you want to see Captain Crenshaw again, Jimmy?' She asked.

'Yes Milly, is he in?' Jimmy said, pulling off his cap.

'He is. Come in. I'll tell him you're here,' Milly said, her attitude to him somewhat softened as, over the past two weeks he had become a frequent visitor.

Jimmy heard Milly, in her heavy shoes, trudge up the stairs to Captain Crenshaw's room. The mumble of voices travelled down into the hall and, moments later, she descended again.

'He says you can go up,' she announced.

She clumped to the back of the hall, the noise of her footsteps receded as she disappeared down the back stairs, which lead to the kitchen.

As Jimmy climbed the stairs to Crenshaw's rooms, he wondered whether cabbage was always on the menu in the house.

'Good evening, Jimmy. How are things?' Captain Crenshaw asked, holding open the door to his sitting room.

'I don't know how things are, Cap'n, an' that's the truth. I'm confused. That's what I am, confused,' Jimmy fretted.

Alarm filled Captain Crenshaw when he saw Jimmy's agitated state.

'Be calm, Jimmy. Sit down. Tell me what has happened,' Crenshaw said as he led Jimmy to a couch near the window.

Jimmy sat on the edge of the seat, gripping one hand with the other.

Crenshaw took a seat opposite him.

'Now, Jimmy. Try to explain why you are so worked up,' Crenshaw said, leaning forward.

'Well, Cap'n, it's Tom Johnson. He wants me to get a crew together to sail with him,' Jimmy began, then told Crenshaw the whole story.

When Jimmy had finished, Crenshaw sat still, a frown wrinkling his forehead.

'Hmm, I wonder what he's up to?' Captain Crenshaw said at last.

'I dunno, Cap'n. But I don't like it. I don't like it at all,' Jimmy complained.

Captain Crenshaw's eyes wandered around the room as he massaged his chin while musing on the problem. His narrow-eyed gaze came to rest on Jimmy as he pursed his lips and nodded.

'I think you must go along with it, Jimmy. Find him his crew, and anything else he wants you to do.'

'Are you sure, Cap'n? I don't want to get meself had up for corroborinatin in something that might mean me endin' up incarsimerated, or worse,' Jimmy said, his eyes wild with worry.

'It won't come to that, Jimmy,' Crenshaw said, getting up to pace slowly about the room.

'Not if I go to the authorities and tell them the situation. I shall inform them that you are not involved in their scheme but are merely going along with what Johnson has suggested with the intention of keeping them informed.'

Jimmy took a deep breath.

'All right, Cap'n I'll do it,' Jimmy agreed. 'But I don't like it,' he said, screwing up his nose and shaking his head.

'Don't be anxious, Jimmy,' Crenshaw said, smiling. 'I shall go again to Lord Castlereagh's office to inform them of this development.'

Although he didn't know it, Crenshaw was doing exactly what Tom had hoped he would do.

CHAPTER THIRTEEN

After Babineaux left, Tom continued working until he heard a scrabbling outside his door. He rose from his seat and went to open it. Billy stood outside.

'I didn't know if I was to knock,' Billy said, eyeing Tom.

'Come in, Billy,' Tom said.

Billy entered the Blue Parlour and looked around the room, open-mouthed.

Looking up, he gazed at the twinkling chandeliers. A slight breeze moved them, setting them tinkling and sending rainbows dancing on the ceiling.

'Cor, Tom. I never knew we had a room like this in The George. It's the best parlour, ain't it?'

'It is, Billy. Sit down,' Tom said, pulling out one of the blue upholstered chairs.

Billy carefully sat on the finest chair he had ever seen.

'Tell me, what did you find out?' Tom asked sitting opposite him.

'Well, Tom, it's like this. I followed the sailor cove like yer asked. He went to a house in Poland Street; number ten, it was. Now, I happen to know a lad works in number thirty-three. I goes to him an' I asks him if he knows who lives at number ten. "No," he says, but he says he's sweet on a girl at number twelve. So, I gets him to go with me, to talk to her. Anyways, she knows all o' them as lives there in number ten. So, I asks her, I says, "do you know anythin of a seafarin' cove visitin' there?" And she says, "No, but there's a Captain Crenshaw lives there." So, I thinks to meself, that's who Tom wants to know about. Was I right?'

Tom, his patience taxed, was grateful when Billy came to the end of his story.

'You were absolutely right, Billy. Thank you. You've earned your money. Here,' Tom said, handing

Billy another half-crown.

Billy beamed a crooked smile.

'Thank you, Tom. If there's any other little messages you want doin', you only 'ave ter ask.'

'I'll bear that in mind, Billy,' Tom said. He was about to dismiss the lad when curiosity took the better of him.

'Where's your mother and father, Billy?' Tom asked.

'They died three year ago, Tom,' Billy replied, a mournful look coming to his eyes.

'How did you come to be working here?'

'A friend o' me da's knows Gem. He asked Gem if I could come here till somethin' else turned up.'

Sympathy for the boy filled Tom. Billy's story was similar to his own.

'I see,' Tom said gruffly and paused, frowning.

Suddenly Tom rose from his seat.

'Right, Billy, I have a lot of work to do. Thank you again,' he said.

Billy followed Tom to the door, where the two exchanged a nod. Billy, smiling his crooked smile again, continued down the hallway toward the stairs, jingling his new-found wealth in his pocket all the way.

Tom sighed.

Poor lad. Even though he went all around the houses in the telling, he did an excellent job in finding out what I wanted to know, he thought, and smiled.

So, Jimmy went straight to Crenshaw and told him everything, I'll be bound, just as I wanted him to, and Crenshaw will go straight to the authorities.

Tom chuckled to himself.

'Ha! It's all coming together.

Tom glanced at his pocket watch and realised time was getting on. He must set off for Blackwall.

Leaving The George, Tom hailed a cab and gave directions to Blackwall Reach. From there he directed the driver to his dry dock. Upon arrival, Tom alighted and paid the jarvey the fare.

The cab drove away leaving Tom standing outside the door. He had given Peter Marriot the key so he rapped on the door. It was a while before a tall, tattooed, barrel-chested bald man opened it.

'Tom!' the giant exclaimed pulling him into the vast space of the dock, closing the door behind him.

Many years before, when Bear awaited execution in a Spanish jail, Tom had helped him to escape. From then on Bear had treated Tom as a brother.

'Bear Mowbray! It's good to see you, lad. It's good to see you,' Tom said, extending his hand.

Grinning widely, Bear firmly grasped Tom's hand, and used it to pull him into a hearty hug, applying a few thunderous slaps to his back.

Letting him go, Bear called an echoing ring around the dock.

'Look, me lads, here's Tom!'

Heads popped up from inside *Eagle*. Several men climbed down from the top of the mast while others crawled out from the sides of the ship. They all cheered a greeting as they gathered around Tom.

Tom held up a hand to quiet the delighted throng. Over the last of the din, his voice rose.

'Quiet, me Boys. Quiet. Don't you know we're trying not to attract attention?'

The men, still exultant, quelled their noise to a murmur. They came to Tom, one or two at a time, to shake his hand or slap him on the back or embrace him like Bear had.

Peter Marriot pushed his way through the crowd.

'A few more than I expected turned up, Tom. When they heard your story, they all wanted to help you. I reckon she'll be good and seaworthy by Thursday, with time to spare.

'That's marvellous, Peter. We can launch her late Wednesday, and set sail on the ebb tide on Thursday.

Have you asked Pedro whether he will come with us in *Nautilus*?'

'I did, Tom. He said he will. Oh, but this is good, isn't it? All the old crew together like before.'

'It is, Peter. It is,' Tom said, wrapping an arm around his old shipmate's shoulder.

'But I didn't come here just to engage in a social gathering. We have work to do,' Tom said, stripping off his hat and coat and rolling up his sleeves.

He turned to the stairs beside *Eagle*. Scaling them two at a time he arrived at the ship's bulwark. Swinging himself over it, he jumped down and landed, both feet at once, on her deck. As he heard the familiar resonance of his boots on ship's wood, his heart filled with pure joy.

Having worked with the men for several hours, Tom saw that everything progressed well and decided to return to The George. He bade his shipmates farewell and left to walk to a main thoroughfare to find a cab.

On his way back to The George, Tom sat in the Hackney, listening to the clip-clop of the horse's hooves, and brooding on his schemes. It had cost him a great deal of money to continue building *Eagle* after Fulton had died. The idea of using the craft to aid in rescuing Napoleon had sparked in him his old sense of adventure. In the past, he had enjoyed evading those who tried to capture him. It gave him great pleasure to thwart excise men, runners and patrolmen alike. To frustrate the Government itself, by freeing their most prominent prisoner, would be a joy. Sacrificing her was not something he liked doing. However, when it was all over, he might be able to recover possession of her.

Arriving at The George, Tom went in through the scullery entrance and straight up the staff stairs to Nancy's room. He undressed, got into bed and waited for her. He knew she and Betty would be tidying the taproom in readiness for the morning. She would be a while yet.

Tom was beginning to doze when Nancy arrived with the glow of her candle lighting the way. She put the candle in its holder down on the dresser and turned towards the bed.

Seeing Tom's form there, she sighed, not sure whether she was glad he was there, or not. She was angry with him, because he wouldn't tell her. At the back of her mind was the chance he might not come back, and she didn't want that.

Reaching out a hand Tom caught her skirt and pulled her towards him. Nancy sat beside him on the bed.

Tom came fully awake.

'Nancy-love,' Tom said, his voice a husky growl.

Nancy wanted him as much as he wanted her. But she also wanted the answers he had promised to give her.

It took all her will for her to rise from the bed and look down at him.

Tom pulled himself up to lean on his elbow.

'Nancy? What ails you?'

Nancy swallowed.

'You said you'd tell me what you're getting into. I promise I won't try to persuade you out of it, just tell me what it is.'

Tom hauled himself up into a sitting position. The candlelight lent a glow to his skin as he ran his fingers through his hair.

Tom let his breath out on a long sigh.

'All right … I'll tell you,' he said, hesitating a moment to gather his thoughts.

'The French have a plan to rescue Napoleon from St Helena and sail with him to his brother, Joseph, in America.'

Nancy sat down heavily on the bed. She hadn't dreamed his enterprise would be something so enormous. This thing carried real danger. She felt a tingle of fear for him run through her.

Tom leant forward and took her hand.

'You know about Jimmy Young overhearing Corbeau and me discussing a plan.'

Nancy nodded.

That was the day he came back to me, she thought.

'You know he went with his captain to the authorities and told them.'

Nancy nodded again.

'I have a scheme to overcome their meddling. I'll run *Eagle* aground in the Thames, and when they question me, I'll spin them a yarn while Corbeau and the French escape. On the Sunday after, I'll sail *Nautilus,* disguised as a steam yacht, down the Thames at slack tide. I judge that to be at five in the morning on that day. *Nautilus* will meet up with Corbeau in the Straits of Dover. From there we will make our way to Plymouth. Eight or nine weeks later we will be on St Helena.'

Nancy sat very still while Tom spoke. She looked at him, hardly crediting what she was hearing.

'How will they get Napoleon off St Helena?' she asked, her voice flat.

'They have a double, a man who is the very image of Napoleon. He is willing to take the General's place,' Tom explained.

Nancy swallowed.

'Oh, of course,' she said. *As easy as that,* she thought cynically.

She was almost afraid to move, thinking of the consequences if they discovered him.

'Tom, do you realise, if you're caught they'll probably hang you?'

Tom gave a quiet laugh.

'I won't get caught. I have it all planned, and I'll be several steps ahead of the authorities. Just as I've always been,' he said.

Tom pushed aside the covers and rose from the bed.

He began to undress her. She made no protest as he helped her step out of her dress. He smiled at her, his eyes tender as he put his hands up to undo her hair.

He sensed her unease.

'Are you afraid for me, Nancy?'

'Yes, I am,' she said and hesitated.

'This enterprise of yours is much more dangerous than I thought, Tom,' she said at last. 'How long will you be gone?'

'About four or five months. And then I'll come back rich.'

An urgent need for her came over him.

'Enough of this, Nancy-love. Come,' he said.

Turning to the dresser, he blew out the candle. His hands found Nancy in the dark. Pulling her into his arms, he kissed her gently. Deepening the kiss, he moved his hands down her back.

He pulled her gently onto the bed.

She lay in his arms, wishing she had not insisted on being told what he was doing.

As he positioned himself to make love to her, she dismissed her misgivings welcoming his caresses and his lovemaking with heightened ardour.

Her need for him satisfied, on the brink of sleep she thought, *he is so sure he'll succeed; how can I not believe it too?*

On Monday morning, Tom woke as Nancy was brushing her hair. He swung himself out of the bed and came to stand near her as she wound her hair up in a knot on the top of her head.

'Nancy, I need to talk to you,' he said.

'What about, Tom?' she asked, turning towards him.

Tom caught her hand and put it to his lips.

'I know I can trust you not to say a word of what I told you last night. But even if someone comes to you saying I sent them, don't believe them, and don't say a word about what I'm doing. Trust no one, Nancy, do you hear?' he said, his eyes more serious than she had ever seen them.

'All right, Tom. I won't even tell Betty,' she said, putting her arms around his neck.

'That's my girl,' Tom said and kissed the tip of her nose.

'How long before you go?' Nancy asked and turned to the mirror once more.

'I hope to set sail in *Nautilus* on Sunday. I want to be down at Plymouth, and away as soon as I can.'

He caught her shoulders and turned her towards him. His face dark and serious, he looked deeply into her eyes.

'Listen, Nancy, I'm telling everyone I'm going to Ireland to claim a legacy. That's where you must say I have gone if anyone asks. Before I go, I shall spend a few days going here and there around London spreading that story, telling them I will invite them to a celebration when I come back. Promise me you won't tell anyone where I've really gone.'

'Of course, I won't tell anyone, Tom. You can count on me.'

She stepped back from him, smoothing her apron.

'But now I have to go and get on with my work. It's a coaching day.'

As Nancy made to go, Tom caught her hand.

'Ah, Nancy. One more thing. Could you or Betty bring me some food in the Blue Parlour? I have a lot more work to do, and I don't want to get caught up with things in the taproom.'

'I will, Tom. I'll bring something there right away. I won't have time later,' she said.

Going to the door, Nancy stopped. Turning back, she kissed her fingers and smiled at him before she left. Tom stared at the door for a while after she had gone and he sighed.

While working on his charts in the Blue Parlour, Tom

heard the bustle of breakfast down below him in the dining rooms. He heard the coaches taking off and still he continued working. In the late afternoon, he sat back in his chair, having done as much as he could. He would calculate fresh courses on the voyage as conditions dictated.

Tom had acquired a sturdy box in which to store his maps and charts. Carefully rolling them up, he put them in the box and locked it. Leaving the Blue Parlour, Tom carried the box to Nancy's room where he pushed it under the bed. With a sigh of relief, he descended to the kitchen and went to the taproom

A rowdy group of men sat in the bow window to the left of the door, a fug of smoke from their pipes surrounding them. The smell of the many breakfasts cooked earlier in the kitchen still lingered in the air.

Tom barely noticed any of it as he sat in his usual seat, musing on his night with Nancy. It was a good night. They had never been closer. Lifting his head, Tom looked around the room for her.

And there she was, coming towards him with his tankard of ale. She set it before him, and laid a gentle arm about his neck.

Putting his hand up he held hers for a long tender moment.

Coming back to earth, Tom looked around the taproom.

'Where's Jimmy?' he asked.

'He's sitting by the fire as usual,' Nancy replied, shifting her chin in his direction.

'Right. Bring over a tankard for him please, Nancy,' Tom said.

Nancy stroked his neck then moved away.

Tom watched her go, thinking on their future and how good it would be.

Looking towards the fire, he saw Jimmy tucked away in the corner.

'Good day to you, Jimmy. A word if you please,'

Tom called.

Jimmy had finished his ale and was contemplating whether to order another. He hastily got up, hoping perhaps Tom would buy him one and scurried to where Tom sat.

'What have you done about gathering a crew for me?' Tom asked as Jimmy took the seat opposite him.

Nancy returned with Jimmy's ale, which she placed before him. Jimmy looked up at her with a smile.

Nancy moved away swiftly, fearing she would betray her scorn for him.

Jimmy turned to Tom.

'I put the word out, Cap'n. I got five men in readiness, and they're askin' around too. I should have the lot by tomorrow, Cap'n Sir.'

'Well done, Jimmy. Do you know where Blackwall Reach is?'

'I do, Cap'n.'

'Good. My ship, *Eagle* is moored there. We sail on Thursday. You and your men must come here on Tuesday afternoon at about three o'clock. I'll give them instructions then,' Tom explained.

'I'm lookin' forward to it, Cap'n,' Jimmy said and took a long swallow of his ale.

'Eh… Jimmy. You haven't discussed our conversation with anyone, have you? About being on a government mission?'

'O' course not, Cap'n. I know when to keep me mouth shut,' Jimmy said with a huge wink.

Lying little git, Tom thought.

'Good,' Tom said again with a smile that didn't reach his eyes. 'I'll see you Tomorrow.'

Tom rose and went to the bar where Nancy was pulling four tankards of ale. She took them to the rowdy men and returned to stand by Tom.

He leant down to speak quietly in her ear.

'I'm away to Blackwall, Nancy. I don't know when I'll be back. If anyone asks for me, tell them to come back tomorrow,' he said.

'I will, Tom,' she replied, looking at him with a warm expression in her eyes.

Tom flicking her chin with his finger, grinned at her and left.

CHAPTER FOURTEEN

After working through Monday night with his old shipmates, Tom was satisfied that *Eagle* was ready to sail. With the launch planned for Thursday, Tom instructed Peter Marriot how to flood the dock and float his ship.

'None of you must be aboard *Eagle* when she is launched. The crew will consist of the men Jimmy Young recruited. I don't want them to see the interior of *Eagle*. I want all the hatches battened down so they can't go below.'

'I gather you don't want them to know *Eagle* is not a normal ship,' Peter said.

'No, I do not,' Tom replied.

'Won't they be suspicious when they can't stow their gear?'

Tom shook his head.

'You must take their ditty bags and chests and stow them somewhere in the dry dock. They will not be parted from their possessions for long enough to kick up a barney about it.'

'But...'

Tom held up a hand.

'I will make sure they get everything back.'

'You read my mind,' Peter said.

'Yes Peter,' Tom said with a grin, and continued.

'I will meet them in The George this afternoon, and direct them to report here the following morning at nine o'clock. Will you wait for them at the entrance to the dock?'

'I will, Tom. But do they know your intention? Do they know you mean to run her aground?'

'No, they do not. If they knew of my plans they would not man the ship,' Tom replied.

Peter looked sidelong at Tom. He had always known him as a fair-minded man.

'Tom, these men are honest, are they not?'

'They are as honest as any sailor in the British Navy. What are you getting at, Peter?' Tom asked.

'It seems wrong to lead them into the arms of the authorities when they have done nothing wrong, Tom.'

'It's because they are innocent and know nothing of my plans that I have hired them,' Tom explained.

'But, they may be arrested,' Peter said, baffled by Tom's seeming unconcern for the men.

'We will all be arrested, Peter,' Tom said, his eyes twinkling, his mouth hiding a smile.

'And this does not bother you?' Peter asked raising a quizzical eyebrow.

'No, Peter, because the Port Authorities, and anyone else who makes accusations, will not have a shred of evidence to say our voyage is unlawful.'

Still perplexed, Peter shook his head, his mouth stiff.

Tom understood Peter's doubts.

'Listen, Peter. I have my story ready. I shall tell them that a Frenchman approached me to hire my submarine. But when I discovered what he wanted it for, I decided to run it aground in case they decided to take it anyway. And no one can prove otherwise,' Tom explained.

'And if the authorities hunt down your Frenchmen? What then?' Peter asked, his puzzled frown deepening.

Tom laughed as he reached for his jacket.

'You forget, Peter. The Frenchmen sail today. They will be gone and will not be found.'

'So, the unsuspecting sailors will avoid trouble?'

'Indeed they will. And what is more, I intend to pay them well to compensate them for their trouble,' Tom said.

Peter's expression cleared as he watched Tom don his jacket and hat.

'You haven't changed, Tom. You always did cover all eventualities.'

'And that is why they rarely caught me,' Tom said, with a smile.

Tom's expression shifted to seriousness as he slid a greatcoat over his jacket.

'When will *Nautilus* be ready?'

'Oliver and Pedro are working on it. Once *Eagle* is out of the way, we will all take a hand. It should be the perfect example of a small yacht by Sunday,' Peter replied.

'Excellent,' Tom said. 'Now I must go. I want to see *La Miséricorde* set sail.'

'Is that wise, Tom? What if you're recognised?' Peter said, a worried look returning to his eyes.

Tom waved a nonchalant hand around his head.

'Note the high collar on my coat. See the wide brim of my hat and the length and bulk of my greatcoat. I borrowed them from a giant. I will not be recognised,' Tom replied and made for the door.

The tide in the Thames was high, the early morning air bracing.

Tom knew *La Miséricorde* would sail within the hour to take advantage of high tide. The early morning air was bracing; he knew a brisk walk would clear his head.

As a pale-yellow Sun streaked the grey clouds in the East, Tom's heart filled with a sense of well-being. London was a different place in the dawning light. The streets were comparatively clean. Few people were about. The high water in the Thames blanketed the unpleasant stench given off by the mud at low tide.

After walking for half-an-hour, Tom arrived near the London Dock in time to see the French ship making sail. No matter how many times Tom observed the sight of sails unfurl and belly, he was always filled with a sense of exhilaration.

He stood on the dock watching *La Miséricorde* manoeuvre downstream, making for the estuary. He thought he saw Babineaux standing on the poop deck at the taffrail. Tom had to quell the desire to raise his hand to him in farewell.

Tom sighed. He could see no reason why the authorities would stop Corbeau and his crew. The first part of his plan was going well.

He set off towards London Bridge and crossed into Southwark. Walking along Borough High street, it was not long before he arrived at The George.

Entering through the rear, Tom passed through the scullery and into the kitchen.

Nancy was kneeling on the floor setting a fire in the range.

She turned when she heard the scullery door open.

'Tom! Where have you been all night?' she asked as she rose and removed her begrimed calico apron wiping her hands on it.

'Working with my old crew to ready *Eagle* for her launch on Thursday. We laboured all night. When we finished, I went to watch Corbeau's ship set sail.'

Nancy took his arm and led him towards a chair by the table,

His eyes felt gritty, his head was light, and his muscles ached. He sank into the chair.

'You must be exhausted,' she said.

'I am. I shall go up to bed right away,' he said, making to rise from the chair.

'Sit there a minute, Tom. I'll get you some small beer,' Nancy said. She patted his shoulder as she moved around him to go to the taproom.

Moments later she came back with a tankard and handed it to Tom.

'Thank you, Nancy,' Tom said as he accepted it. 'I'm parched.'

He downed the small beer in one go. After the last drop was gone, he lowered the tankard and puffed his cheeks in a long, hard breath.

'I needed that,' he said and rose from his seat.

'Whoo! I must go to bed. I can hardly stand.'

With a great yawn, he stretched.

'Go then, Tom. Do you want me to wake you?'

Tom yawned again.

'What time is it now?'

'About half-past six,' Nancy replied.

'Wake me at one o'clock, please, Nancy-love,' he said.

He leant down to kiss her softly on the cheek before staggering out of the kitchen and up the stairs.

At one o'clock Nancy, entered her room to wake Tom. She carried a flagon of water and a cup on a tray, which she placed on the table by the bed.

Tom lay on his back, one arm flung above his head, his hair in disorder curling on his forehead. In repose, his face was attractive with his high cheekbones, his long chiselled nose, and full lips above his strong chin. Considering he was no longer a young man, he looked decidedly handsome. As Nancy gazed at him sleeping, she smiled.

'I love you, Tom Johnson,' she whispered.

Leaning forward, she smoothed the hair from his forehead and kissed it.

'Wake up, Tom.'

Bleary-eyed, he was slow to come to.

'What time is it?' he mumbled.

'It's one o'clock. You asked me to wake you,' she said.

Tom sat up. He rested his elbows on his knees. holding his head in his hands, he cleared his throat.

Nancy poured water into the cup and handed it to Tom. He raised his head from his hands.

She was careful to be sure he had a firm grip on the cup before releasing her hold.

'What day is it?' Tom asked.

'Tuesday,' Nancy replied.

Blinking, Tom lifted the cup to his lips and gulped

the water. Yawning, he held the cup out for more.

Nancy poured more water for him. and laid a hand on his shoulder.

Tom patted her hand and took a mouthful of water.

'Ohh, that was a day-and-a-half,' he said, feeling the stubble on his chin.

'It must have been, Tom. You were walking like a drunk when you came in.'

'Ah, I can rest today. All I have to do is meet Jimmy's crewmen and give them instructions for Thursday,' he said as he pulled back the covers and swung his legs out of the bed.

Nancy gave him a thoughtful look.

'Are you all right, Tom?'

'Oh, I will be once I've cleaned myself up a bit,' Tom said as he put the cup down on the table.

Nancy gave him a swift kiss.

'I must go, Tom. I have work to do. I'll give you your dinner when you come down,' Nancy said and hurried away to the kitchen.

Half-an-hour later, Tom appeared in the kitchen. Freshly washed with Nancy's soap, he smelled good. Shaved, wearing a clean suit of clothes with a snowy neckcloth, he looked like a different man from the one that had staggered up the stairs earlier that morning.

'Who is this handsome gentleman in my kitchen?' Nancy said, beaming at him.

'Why, madam,' Tom said, executing a gentrified bow, 'Do you not recognise your own fiancé?'

Nancy laughed.

'Go to the taproom, Tom, and I'll bring you your food,' she said, giving him a little push in the right direction.

Tom smiled as he passed through the brocade curtain at the kitchen entrance. Looking around the tap room, he took his usual seat. The tavern was unusually full for the time of day. Tom reached into a pocket for his watch.

'Quarter-to-two,' he murmured to himself.

Jimmy Young slid into the seat opposite him.

'The boys are all here, Cap'n,' he said, leaning towards Tom.

'What! Where?'

'Look about you, Cap'n,' Jimmy said waving his hand around.

That accounts for the number of people here today, Tom thought.

'I didn't tell you to bring them to the taproom, Young.'

Tom reined in his temper.

No point in making a fuss. They're here now, he thought.

'Take them up to the Blue Parlour,' Tom said, fishing the key out of his pocket and handing it to Jimmy.

'I'll be with you in about ten minutes. Tell them to touch nothing, do you hear?'

'Aye-aye, Cap'n,' Jimmy said with a wink.

He got up. Jerking his chin towards the door, he walked out. The sailors rose as one. The air filled with the noise of scrabbling feet and mumbled murmurs. They bunched up at the door and left the bar to follow Jimmy.

Tom noticed the two government men seated in their usual place beside the bar.

Ah, no harm done. Those two seeing the men here will progress my plans. If I let it slip that Eagle *will sail on Thursday, it's certain the authorities will keep an eye out for her.*

Nancy came to his table and put a plate of beef stew and a plate of bread before him.

Tom was hungry. He inhaled the steam rising from the plate of welcome food.

'Thanks, Nancy,' he said and reached for his spoon.

Nancy moved away to fetch ale. When she returned,

Tom spoke to her in a raised voice so that the two covert men could hear.

'You didn't tell me Jimmy Young was already here with his sailor boys. I have to give them their instructions for Thursday. We'll be catching the tide at Blackwall Reach at about ten o'clock to sail down the Thames to the estuary.'

Nancy frowned at Tom. She was about to comment when Tom softly pinched her arm and swivelled his eyes in the direction of the government men.

Nancy shifted slightly and gave Tom a small nod of understanding before returning to the kitchen.

Tom broke his bread into his stew and began to eat his dinner.

It's a good job I moved the maps and charts. Tom reflected. *I wouldn't want Jimmy Young's men to go sniffing around them.*

Tom pushed back the empty stew plate as he rose from the table.

The government men watched Tom follow the same route taken by Jimmy and his companions. Sweet lifted his chin at Brooking who gave him a sage nod.

Tom climbed the stairs to the Blue Parlour. Opening the door, he found fifteen men sitting about in groups drinking Sack from the expensive crystal glasses they had discovered in the sideboard. Tom let his eyes wander over the men who laughed and joked with each other, oblivious of Tom's displeasure. In two long strides, Tom was on Jimmy. Gripping his arm, Tom raised him from his seat and marched him to the end of the room.

'I thought I told you not to touch anything, Young?' he said in an under voice.

Jimmy's face took on a sheepish expression.

'You know what sailors are like, Cap'n. They can sniff out grog like bloodhounds.'

Tom's eyes narrowed as he sucked air through his

teeth.

'I would not have thought Sack would be to their taste.'

Jimmy smiled, glancing at the men.

'Them lad's 'ud drink anything to make 'em feel good.'

Tom held Jimmy's eyes in an angry gaze. Letting go of his anger with a sigh, he decided the transgression was not worth complaining about with a critical mission in progress. He satisfied himself with a tightened grip and a shake on Jimmy's arm before he released it.

'Call the men to attention,' Tom growled.

Jimmy cleared his throat and called as loud as he could over the din of the liquor swilling sailors.

'Attention, men! The Cap'n wants a word.'

The sailors rose and moved forward. Standing stiffly to attention, they faced Tom.

Tom took a moment to pass his eyes over the group.

The men before him were obviously British Naval men, going by their neat appearance. Tom continued to look them over as he began.

'First, men, I should inform you that I cannot tell you our destination until I receive my sealed orders on Thursday. I can only tell you it will be a long voyage. Therefore, today you must gather together whatever you need with you on such a voyage. You will pack your ditty bags and sea boxes and take them to Blackwall Reach tomorrow. My man will meet you there and show you where *Eagle* lies. You may leave your possessions in his charge. He will see that your gear is safely stowed away. On Thursday morning, at nine o'clock, you will present yourselves again at Blackwall Reach. Once on board the ship, Young will appoint you to your posts. Our first port of call will be Chatham Dockyard. You may go now, men. Make sure you are at Blackwall Reach in good time on Thursday. That will be all. Dismissed,' Tom proclaimed.

The sailors relaxed and looked at each other. They had anticipated more. They broke into small groups, muttering among themselves, and gradually left the room.

Jimmy stayed beside Tom. Cap in hand he looked up at him, uncertain what to do next.

'Is there anything else you want me to do, Cap'n?'

'Yes, Jimmy. Make sure they all turn up. Once they are aboard, give each man whatever task best suits his ability. Can you do that?'

'I certainly can, Cap'n. But I still don't know what cargo we carry,' Jimmy said, shuffling his feet.

'No, Jimmy. You are right. We do not. We will know when I receive my orders,' Tom said, holding out his hand.

'The key, if you please.'

Jimmy took the key from his pocket and placed it on Tom's palm.

'I'm sorry about the grog, Cap'n,' he said.

'It wasn't grog, Jimmy. It was Sack. Very expensive Sack. I hope you and they enjoyed it,' Tom replied.

Jimmy missed the sarcasm.

'Oh, aye, Cap'n. We did. A bit syrupy, but still, it went down well,' Jimmy said with a big grin.

Jimmy's grin faded at sight of Tom's thunderous expression. Coughing in discomfort, Jimmy decided it was time to leave.

'I'll be off then, Cap'n. I'll see ya tomorrow,' he said.

Scuttling to the door, he was off before Tom could say more.

Tom assessed the meeting that had just taken place. His previous attitude toward Jimmy had been one of antagonism. But today, seeing him among his peers, Jimmy seemed a simple, efficient soul. He had done the right thing, as he saw it, letting the government know about what he saw as treason. In a way, others would see him as some kind of hero.

Agh, Tom Johnson, you're getting soft in your old age, he told himself.

Remembering Jimmy's larger scheme, he scowled.

Be damned to him! He was willing to send me to the gallows.

Leaving the Blue Parlour, Tom paused to lock the door. Making his way back to the taproom, he checked his watch. It was five o'clock. He could spend this evening putting into practice his plan of spreading the word about his legacy and his impending voyage to Ireland.

But Tom was restless with anticipation. He did not feel like putting on a play of sociability. Looking about the full taproom, he saw Nancy, busy serving customers. He knew lying with her would ease his tension, but it would be hours before she was free to be with him. Killing time had never been Tom's forte. He knew if he sat waiting for her, he would drink too much and he needed a clear head.

He moved to where she stood at the bar and gently touched her arm.

'Nancy,' Tom murmured.

Nancy looked up at him, smiling.

'It's busy today Tom. What is it?'

'I wanted to tell you, I've got to go out. I'll see you tonight.'

Nancy looked into his eyes, dark with tenderness for her. Her breath caught. Her heart skipped.

'Yes, Tom. Tonight,' she softly promised.

Tom brushed Nancy's cheek with the back of his fingers, not caring who was watching. Smiling warmly, he turned toward the door and walked out of The George.

Tom made his way to London Bridge. He leant on the parapet, watching ships moving along the water. From his vantage point, Tom looked down the Thames, imagining in his mind's eye the place where he planned to run *Eagle* aground. Perhaps when he returned in about four months' time, he could beg the government to allow him to take possession of her again. At least he would still have *Nautilus*.

Lost in his thoughts, he started when a hand touched his arm.

'Tom Johnson?'

Tom frowned and stiffened as he regarded the man next to him.

'Who wants to know?'

'Andrew Craddock. It's been a long time since I saw you.'

'Andrew? Damn it, I thought you were dead. I heard you were run over by a coach,' Tom said, shaking the man's outstretched hand.

'I was. Fortunately, I survived, with only a stiff hip to tell the tale,' Andrew explained. 'I heard you were working for the Navy.'

'I was. But no longer,' Tom replied.

'I am on my way to an assignation at the *Cheese.* Walk with me to the inn. When my business is concluded, we may talk of old times,' Andrew suggested.

'Indeed, I will, Andrew. Your invitation is timely. I have several hours to kill and wondered how I would do it,' Tom replied.

The two men set off across the bridge and within twenty minutes, arrived at Fleet Street. Turning down Wine Office Court, they came to the *Cheese* and entered the inn. Candles lit the place day and night as there were no windows to let in natural light.

Andrew glanced around the room until he saw the person he had come to meet.

'Ah, there is Mr Gilchrist. Let me introduce you, Tom,' Andrew said, guiding him towards a man sitting on his own at the back of the room.

Gilchrist's face was pale, yet handsome. Well-dressed, his hair was cut in a fashionably unruly style. His shirt points were high, his neckcloth intricate.

'Good evening, Mr Gilchrist. I trust you are well?' Andrew said.

Gilchrist nodded, glancing at Tom, and shooting a questioning look at Andrew.

'And you, Mr Craddock?' Gilchrist responded.

'Thank you, yes. Allow me to introduce my friend, Tom Johnson, whom I met just now on London Bridge. I have not seen him in—how many years is it, Tom?'

'It must be over ten years. I am pleased to meet you, Mr Gilchrist,' Tom said with a nod.

Gilchrist picked up a document case lying on the floor beside him. Opening it, he took out a sheaf of papers and handed them to Andrew.

'My latest contribution to your *Gentlemen's Magazine*, Mr Craddock,' he said as he rose.

'I hope you will excuse me. I have a dinner engagement. I trust you will let me know whether you approve my treatise?'

'It goes without saying, Mr Gilchrist,' Andrew replied.

Gilchrist turned to Tom.

'Forgive me, Mr Johnson. Perhaps some other time we may converse together?'

'I look forward to it, Mr Gilchrist,' Tom replied.

Tom was glad the man was leaving, feeling sure he would be out of his depth with him. With relief, Tom slid into the seat Gilchrist had vacated.

'You are still in the printing line, Andrew?'

'I am. It is a lucrative business. I have a finger in many pies, from erudite treatises, such as Gilchrist supplies, to scurrilous pamphlets for those with a taste for scandal.'

A serving maid came to their table. Tall, willowy, with flowing blond curls and an ample bosom on show, she flashed a smile at Tom.

'What is your pleasure, Gentlemen?' she asked.

'Brandy, if you please Molly. Will you join me, Tom?'

I might as well start spreading my word Tom thought.

'I cannot, Andrew. I have come into a legacy and am about to go to Ireland to claim it; therefore, I have much to attend to and must keep a clear head,' Tom replied mendaciously and turned to Molly. There was a time when Tom would have shown her his appreciation. But, in his opinion, the creature could not hold a candle to Nancy.

'Tea, if you please, my dear,' he requested with only a hint of a smile.

'Now, I've seen everything. Tom Johnson, refusing a drink,' Andrew growled and laughed.

'But tell me of this legacy,' he said.

Tom made up a fantastic and complicated story.

'And you may publish that, if you wish, Andrew,' Tom said, hoping he would.

'Indeed I might,' Andrew said, raising his glass.

For the next couple of hours, they talked of old times when Andrew, chasing material for his scandalous pamphlets, had mixed with disreputable characters, Tom amongst them. Tom's adventures had always fascinated him. It was he who had publicised the legend that no prison could hold Tom.

Craddock continued drinking his brandy, becoming increasingly mellow as time passed. His eyes glittered as he leant close to Tom.

'I have heard a strange rumour, Tom. I wonder whether you know of it? I was told it by a Naval Officer.'

Andrew leant in closer, putting his finger to his lips.

'Shhhh,' he said, moving his eyes about, to make sure no one could hear.

'He said there would soon be an attempt to rescue Napoleon from St Helena.'

Tom swallowed. Dark fog filled him as he held Andrew's gaze. He let a slow smile creep across his face. Sitting back in his chair, he allowed a soft, deep chuckle to become louder.

'You jest, Andrew,' Tom said, still forcing a chuckle. 'I have met men who sail on the supply ships bound for St Helena. They tell me the place is so heavily guarded it is impossible to penetrate it. The Navy patrol the waters continually and the military presence is about two-thousand strong.'

'Nevertheless, Tom, the man who told me says the Admiralty is on high alert. If you hear anything, I would be grateful for the information. I would pay you, of course,' Andrew said.

He fumbled in his waistcoat pocket for his card case. Opening it, he took out a card and gave it to Tom.

Tom took it, putting it in his own pocket.

'I will bear it in mind,' Tom said, keeping a tight hold on his rising alarm.

He took out his pocket watch.

'Well, well, nine o'clock. I must go,' Tom said, pushing back his chair. He stood beside Andrew a moment, placing a hand on his shoulder.

'I have enjoyed our meeting, Andrew. If I hear anything I will be in touch,' he said as he turned to leave the *Cheese* with a carefully measured step.

Tom retraced his steps, thinking all the while about Andrew's disclosure.

There's bound to be rumours. You can't keep a thing like an attempt to rescue Napoleon quiet. Forewarned is forearmed. I needn't fret. I have everything covered.

When Tom arrived back at The George, only a few customers remained. He saw Nancy, busy gathering empty glasses and tankards. She smiled at sight of him. He walked to where she stood and looked down into her eyes.

'Do you want a drink, Tom?' she asked.

Tom bent his head to whisper in her ear.

'No, Nancy, I want you. I will wait for you in your

room.'

Nancy patted his cheek, her face glowing, her eyes sparkling.

'I won't be long,' she said, smiling.

CHAPTER FIFTEEN

Tom Spent the whole of Wednesday helping his comrades readying *Eagle* for sailing.

He heard Jimmy's shipmates delivering their belongings, which were taken from them at the door. Tom had given Pedro and Oliver the task of stowing them away under lock and key.

Five men, experts in carpentry, worked on *Nautilus.* By the end of the day, her transformation had progressed apace. She stood beside *Eagle* in a smaller well. With one side of her metal hulk clad in wood, her masts raising towards the roof, she presented a pleasing sight. When they had completed their work, no one could suspect her true status.

'She makes a pretty little yacht. I think she needs a new name,' Tom said, letting his eyes wander over the "yacht".

'What about *Last Venture?*' Peter suggested.

'Excellent, Peter, for this is indeed my last venture. I will sail again, but never with illegal intent. I promised Nancy,' Tom said with a smile.

Peter's eyebrows rose.

'Nancy?'

'The woman I mean to marry,' Tom murmured.

Peter chuckled.

'You? Marry? Why, I thought it impossible for a woman to capture you, Tom.'

'So did I. Yet it is so. With the money acquired from our voyage, I need not step over the line again. I do believe I may become what they call "a good catch"'.

Late in the evening, Tom returned to The George, exhausted but content that things were going well at Blackwall.

On Thursday morning, he took a cab back to Blackwall

Reach, arriving at nine-thirty. On entering the dry dock, Tom saw *Eagle* was no longer there. He walked to the other end of the dock where the river flowed at high tide. At the sight of *Eagle* afloat, Tom breathed a sigh of satisfaction. Jimmy was on deck, barking orders to the crew as they darted around making the ship ready to sail.

Peter hurried down the gangplank to greet Tom.

'A fine day for it, Tom,' Peter said as he stood beside Tom, watching with him. 'I must say, Jimmy Young is a born Master's mate. He knows how to direct men.'

Tom gave a harsh laugh. 'A pity his voyage will be a short one.'

Peter was still dubious about Tom's use of Jimmy's men. However, he kept quiet on the subject. He knew Tom to be a fair man and trusted they would come to no real harm.

Hearing the familiar *"kree-ah...kree-ah...kree-ah..."* of seagulls circling overhead, Tom looked up. Puffy white clouds wafted by in a bright blue sky, blown by a fresh breeze; perfect sailing weather.

Jimmy's eyes twinkled as he saw Tom on the dock. He descended the gangplank to greet him.

'Good-mornin', Cap'n,' he said, touching his forehead. 'She's ready when you are, Sir. Shall I tell the men to make sail?'

'Yes, if you please, Young,' Tom said and turned to Peter, his hand outstretched.

'Wish us luck, Peter.'

'I do, Tom,' Peter said shaking Tom's hand.

After Tom followed Jimmy up the gangplank, Tom's friends removed it and stood to watch *Eagle* leave.

At Jimmy's loud call of 'Make sail,' the crew hurried into action.

They scrambled up the ratlines to unfurl the sails. Tom was much impressed with their efficiency. They had, obviously, all worked together before.

Tom looked up from the poop deck at the unfurling sails, and felt great satisfaction. The second phase of his plan was underway.

'Weigh anchor,' Tom called, and within a short while, *Eagle* moved farther into the river. A little way along Blackwall Reach, a rowing boat came out to them from the shore carrying the pilot and his apprentice. Jimmy's sailors let a rope ladder down over the side, and the two climbed aboard.

'Good morning, Captain,' the pilot called with a nod as Tom approached him. The apprentice said nothing but touched his cap. Tom watched them as they made their way to the bridge. There was something not quite right about the apprentice. He seemed older than he should be and had a sullen look about him. Tom put the idea to the back of his mind as he followed them to the bridge.

Although Tom was an excellent pilot himself, his licence had lapsed. This circumstance tied in nicely with his plans as he could not be blamed for any error.

Most pilots needed no charts; they knew the river well. Nevertheless, when passing through unstable areas—such as the place where Tom had chosen for *Eagle* to run aground—they consulted the most up to date charts. He had asked Peter Marriot to find a pilot with little experience, whom Tom was sure would check the chart as they approached Woolwich.

True to Tom's expectations, Tom saw the man move to the chart and correct his course accordingly.

As the ship approached the spot where Tom had seen the ship run aground, he held his breath.

Any minute now, he repeated several times to himself.

And sure enough, the ship shuddered, water lashing around the bows as she came to a halt.

Before the Crew had time to think, Tom took control.

'Furl the jib. Lower the main. Drop anchor,' Tom roared.

The crew leapt into action. Having performed what Tom required, they began furling the other sails.

Tom moved swiftly to the bridge and ascended the stairs. Much as he hated to do it, he had to upbraid the pilot.

'What in hell's name are you about, you incompetent cur?' Tom shouted.

'I don't know what happened, Captain. I followed the chart meticulously 'cos I know this stretch of water is treacherous if you can't keep to the middle of the channel.'

Tom went to the desk on which the chart was laid out.

'I copied this chart myself,' he said and then assumed an expression of surprise.

Turning to the pilot, Tom put a hand on his shoulder.

'I apologise, Mr Gibson. It is my mistake. There must have been an error on the chart I copied.'

The pilot's assistant stepped forward. Tom remembered his gut feeling about him.

'Leave us please, Mr Gibson,' the apprentice pilot said.

With a deep frown and glancing from Tom to the other man, Mr Gibson left the bridge.

'Now, Captain Johnson, allow me to inform you that I am Lieutenant Meiklejohn of His Majesty's Navy. I will come straight to the point. We have been observing you for some time. It has come to our attention that you and a group of Frenchmen have hatched a plot to rescue Bonaparte from St Helena.'

'Ah,' Tom uttered, smiling as he looked Meiklejohn in the eye.

'The situation is a little complicated, Lieutenant. But I assure you, I am no traitor.'

'Do not attempt to explain yourself to me, Johnson.

You and your crew are under arrest. Even now two launches are pulling alongside to remove all of you from this ship. You may save your explanations for those who are waiting to interrogate you.'

As he spoke, another officer in uniform arrived on the bridge.

'All right, Meiklejohn, step aside, I will take command,' he said and roughly grabbed Tom's arm.

'Come with me, Johnson,' he growled.

As Tom came down the steps from the bridge, he saw four Marines guarding seven of the sailors as they descended a ladder leading down to one of two launches. Each launch held six oarsmen. Jimmy stood to one side with a man wearing a captain's uniform.

Tom didn't look at Jimmy as he passed him.

'Well done, Jimmy,' he heard the Captain say.

'A pleasure, Captain Crenshaw,' Jimmy replied.

At first, the sailors in the launches protested loudly at being arrested, having done nothing wrong. The threat of Naval punishment, which was severe in the extreme, quelled their objections. Disgruntled, they reluctantly contented themselves with murmuring and giving their guards dour looks.

The officer who arrested Tom kept him in the stern of the launch, apart from the men.

As they pulled off, Tom saw the rest of the sailors climb into the other launch followed by Jimmy and his captain.

The oarsmen rowed farther downstream towards The Royal Arsenal at Woolwich.

Arriving at Ship Stairs, the Marines ordered the sailors from both launches to disembark. From the stairs, they were marched along Half Moon Passage at the end of which stood a long, covered cart. The four Marines manacled each man and hustled them up a set of steps placed at the back of the cart. They then drove it from the area of the Royal Arsenal through Woolwich, eventually arriving at the Admiralty buildings in Whitehall.

They kept Tom in the stern of the launch until the sailors were out of sight, as they thought he might incite them to escape. The officer who arrested Tom climbed out first followed by Tom and two more men, Marine Sergeant Daniels, and Marine Redmond.

When they had climbed the steps up from the river, Daniels produced a set of manacles.

'Hands behind your back,' Daniels ordered Tom.

'Is that necessary?' Tom said, keeping his temper, and looking mildly put out.

The officer faced Tom.

'Your reputation goes before you, Johnson. You are known as a person adept at giving your captors the slip,' the officer said.

He turned to Daniels.

'Put the manacles on him, Sergeant Daniels.'

'My dear… Ah, I didn't catch your name, Sir,' Tom said.

'I didn't give it. It is Albany, Commander Albany. Put your hands behind your back.'

Tom sighed and did what Albany told him.

Daniels applied the manacles to Tom's wrists and gave him a push.

Tom, with a hurt expression, turned to Daniels.

'My good man, there is no need to treat me like a criminal, for, although they accuse me—of what I do not know—I am innocent.'

'Just move along,' Daniels said, adding with a cynical snarl, 'if you please.'

Tom shrugged, smiled resignedly and, following Albany, climbed the path along Half Moon Passage where a coach awaited them. Marine Redmond opened the coach door and let down the steps to allow Captain Albany to climb in. The two Marines caught Tom by his upper arms and shoved him up the coach steps. Tom managed to keep his balance and sat opposite the Captain. Daniels sat next to Tom. Redmond folded the steps, shut the door, and climbed up beside the driver.

As the coach drove off, Tom shifted his arms into a more comfortable position and gave Albany a hard look.

'You're making a mistake, you know. I am guiltless of any crime.'

Albany sneered.

'I know nothing of your guilt or innocence. They sent me to detain you. That is all that concerns me. It is not I to whom you need plead your case. It is the men at the Admiralty you must convince,' Albany said and turned his gaze to the window.

Tom realised he was wasting his time with the contemptuous fop. He leant back and, making himself as comfortable as he could, he closed his eyes and went over his plans again in his mind.

I must present myself to them in a quiet, reserved manner, amenable, above all placating, he thought, smiling to himself. *In fact, the exact opposite of who I really am.*

CHAPTER SIXTEEN

The Admiralty building was a long drive from Woolwich. Tom dozed fitfully and woke with a jolt when the coach came to a halt. In the Admiralty building's courtyard, Marine Redmond swung himself down from his seat beside the driver to join Sergeant Daniels as he stepped out of the coach. The two caught Tom by the arms again and pulled him out of the door. They kept hold of their prisoner as they waited for Commander Albany to alight.

With a glance of disdain at Tom, Albany silently walked toward the building. Marine Redmond and Sergeant Daniels propelled Tom along in Albany's wake.

Inside, the men marched Tom down a long corridor, lined with office doors. Towards the end of the corridor, Albany stopped outside a door to his right. He knocked and waited for the call of 'Enter' before twisting the knob.

'Good morning Admiral Buckley. I have detained Johnson as you requested, Sir.'

Albany opened the door further and turned to the Sergeant and the Marine.

'Bring the prisoner in,' he commanded.

Before they could grab him again, Tom walked into the room.

Daniels and Redmond followed.

'That will be all. Wait outside,' Albany told them. The two stood to attention, saluted, and made to leave.

A grey-haired man behind a large, highly-polished desk, raised his chin.

Although his voice was soft, it held the unmistakable tone of command.

'A moment. Before you go, remove the prisoner's manacles,' he said.

Daniels stepped back into the room. He took a key

from his pocket and freed Tom.

Massaging his wrists, Tom smiled at Daniels.

'Thank you,' Tom said.

'Huh,' Daniels growled and joined Marine Redmond outside the door.

Albany closed the door and went to stand beside Tom.

Having sufficiently rubbed his wrists, Tom adjusted his cuffs while turning towards Albany. With a twist to his mouth, he looked Albany up and down before facing the man behind the desk.

'Whom do I have the honour of addressing, Sir?' Tom asked.

'I am Sir Joseph Buckley, Admiral of the Blue.'

'I am honoured to make your acquaintance, Admiral,' Tom said with an elegant inclination of his head.

'And you are Tom Johnson, a man with a chequered past, I am told. I have heard of you, Mr Johnson. You were pardoned and employed as a pilot and navigator with the Navy for over six years. What has led you to turn traitor?' Admiral Buckley asked, tilting his head, an expression of interested enquiry on his face.

Tom shook his head.

'I am not a traitor, Sir. In fact, I have thwarted a treacherous plot,' Tom explained.

Albany snorted.

Buckley shot him a disapproving look.

'You are accused of plotting Bonaparte's escape. If that is not treachery, I do not know what is,' Buckley said, his chin raised.

'On the contrary, Sir. I was engaged in foiling the attempt when I was arrested.'

'This is nonsense, Admiral. If his ship had not gone aground, he would, no doubt, have been on his way to join his accomplices,' Albany snarled.

Buckley held up his hand.

'A moment, Commander Albany,' he said turning

his head to look at Tom.

'You intrigue me, Johnson. Explain, if you please.'

'Admiral, it is true that there is a plot to aid Bonaparte to escape,' Tom began.

'Ha! So, you admit it!' Albany crowed.

'Let Mr Johnson speak, if you please, Albany. Continue, Mr Johnson,' the Admiral said, leaning back in his chair.

'Thank you, Sir,' Tom replied, giving Albany a narrow-eyed stare.

Tom straightened his posture and gave a small cough before he began.

'About two weeks ago, Sir, a Frenchman approached me. He said he heard I owned a submarine and wanted to hire it. He offered me a great deal of money; naturally, I agreed. Some days later, I discovered he wanted my ship to sail to St Helena and use it in a rescue attempt. Of course, the idea appalled me, and I was not sure what to do. I thought if I were to refuse them the use of my ship, they might take it from me. I, therefore, continued to ready her and accepted the money they offered me. At the same time, I hatched a plan to foil them. I asked a sailor, Able Seaman James Young, who was staying at The George Inn, whether he could gather together a crew to man my ship and he agreed.'

'Why did you choose him?' the Admiral asked.

'Because I believed him to be a loyal servant of the Crown, Sir. However, fearing loose lips among the crew, I did not immediately tell them of the French plot. I thought they did not need to know until the day we sailed, if at all.'

'Your plan was scuppered when you ran aground, though, Johnson, was it not?' Albany said.

Tom laughed softly.

'No, Commander Albany, it was not. The ship running aground was the crux of my plan. I knew it would take some time to right the ship after she hit

159

bottom, and she would attract a lot of notice. I felt sure the French, in such circumstances, would give up the idea of using my submarine.'

'How did you accomplish your plan for her to run aground?' The Admiral asked.

'My pilot's licence was not current; therefore, I could not guide the ship myself. Knowing the unstable nature of the river's silt, I drew up a chart with the wrong information. The pilot followed my misinformation, and the ship foundered.'

Tom glanced at Albany, who obviously didn't believe a word.

The Admiral tapped his fingers on his desk as he digested Tom's explanation. Tom watched him, recognising the man's shrewdness, giving nothing away.

Buckley pursed his lips and shifted his position. He gave Tom a piercing look.

'Why did you not come to us for aid in foiling them, Johnson?'

'I did not know whom to trust, Sir,' Tom replied. 'Also, I became aware of two suspicious characters in The George watching my every move. On one occasion, one of them followed me. I thought the French might have sent them. If they saw me contacting the authorities, I might have been in danger.'

'And what of Able Seaman James Young? He informed us that he overheard you plotting with the Frenchmen,' the admiral said, raising an eyebrow.

Before Tom could speak, the Admiral turned to Albany.

'Commander Albany, go and fetch Able Seaman Young.'

Albany nodded and left the room.

Tom was tempted to explain further but decided to say nothing and let matters with Jimmy take their course.

An awkward silence ensued.

Buckley busied himself with taking snuff.

Tom stood before the Admiral, his feet planted apart, hands behind his back, his stance relaxed, his mind in tension.

I must be careful, now. I must make sure to counter whatever Jimmy says. I have my story straight. I have answers for whatever he says. There's nothing to be concerned about.

Tom allowed his eyes to wander around the room. Apart from the large desk with the Admiral's chair behind it, the office contained little furniture, only two other chairs, a cabinet, and bookshelves covering one wall. The other wall, of aquamarine stucco, was hung with a number of paintings of past Naval heroes. Tom recognised a portrait of Nelson. The others were unknown to him. However, with nothing else to do, Tom made a business of studying them with exaggerated concentration.

After an interminable few minutes, filled only by the sound of a ticking clock and the crackle of the fire in the grate, the door opened to allow Jimmy to enter, accompanied by Captain Crenshaw, followed by Albany.

Tom glanced at them.

Jimmy averted his eyes.

Crenshaw gave Tom a curt nod.

'Able Seaman James Young, as you requested, Admiral Buckley, accompanied by Post Captain Richard Crenshaw,' Albany announced.

'Thank you, Albany,' Buckley said.

The Admiral observed each man before him in turn. Lastly, he regarded Captain Crenshaw

'Why are you here, Captain?'

Captain Crenshaw inclined his head deferentially in the Admiral's direction.

'Able Seaman Young is somewhat nervous, Admiral. I am here to provide moral support,' Crenshaw replied.

'Just so. Let us proceed,' the Admiral said, turning to Jimmy.

'Able Seaman Young, you came to the Admiralty to report what you construed to be a treasonous plot, hatched by Mr Johnson. Will you please elucidate?'

Jimmy looked blank. With furtive eyes, he turned to Crenshaw.

'Tell what you heard in The George, Jimmy,' Crenshaw encouraged.

'Oh, right, yes, well, it were like this. There I was in The George on me own, suppin' a tankard of ale, when I hears this Frenchie talking and me ears pricked up. "What's a Frenchie doin' in the middle o' London?" I asked meself. So, I goes to sit nearer to him, and the man he were talkin' to—that were Tom Johnson, Sir—and I overhears the Frenchie tellin Johnson he were plannin' to ship Boney off of St Helener an' Johnson were advising him how to do it.'

The Admiral sat very still. His lips tight, his eyes narrowed. He looked first at Jimmy then moved his eyes to Tom.

'Hmm,' he said, rubbing his chin with finger and thumb.

He pursed his lips, tilted his chin, and addressed Tom.

'What have you to say to that, Mr Johnson?'

'It's true, Sir,' Tom said, pausing for effect.

Tom allowed the atmosphere to intensify before he continued.

'That was the second interview with the Frenchman. On the first occasion, he did not mention Bonaparte. I have already explained this.'

'Hmm,' the Admiral said again. 'Continue, Young.'

Jimmy gave Tom a questioning look before he spoke.

'I weren't sure what to do, Sir, so I went and told Captain Crenshaw and he brung me here to the Admiralty. We bumped into this high up cove…'

'Earl St Vincent, Sir,' Crenshaw supplied.

The Admiral's eyebrows flew up. He decided not to complicate the issue and made no remark.

'Go on, Young.'

'Well, the long and the short of it is, I told his secretary what I'd seen and heard, and he said to keep watchin' Johnson and report anything suspicious to Captain Crenshaw.'

Jimmy moved forward a step and winked at the Admiral.

'And I think he set two men to spy on Johnson 'cos there was these two leery-lookin' coves sitting in The George every day after that.'

The Admiral stiffened a little at this information.

That ties in with the two men Johnson mentioned, he reflected.

He turned to Tom.

'Where are the Frenchmen now?'

'They rented a house; number fifty-two, Aldeburgh Street. They are probably there,' Tom said.

Admiral Buckley shifted his chin at Albany, who nodded and left the room.

The Marines entered.

'You,' Buckley ordered, addressing Daniels, 'Take Johnson to my anteroom and lock him in.'

Daniels took Tom's arm in a rough grasp and marched him out of the room.

Buckley pulled a sheet of paper towards him. Dipping his quill, he hurriedly wrote a note, blotted, and folded the paper, and handed it to Marine Redmond.

'Go to my secretary's office and give him this,' he directed. 'Take Captain Crenshaw and Able Seaman Young with you.'

He smiled at Crenshaw.

'Captain Crenshaw, I am sorry to inconvenience you, but would you mind waiting? I am not sure whether we will have further need of you, but I would

163

ask you to stay until this business is completed.'

'Of course, Admiral Buckley. Come, Jimmy,' Crenshaw said before following Redmond out of the room.

Admiral Buckley rose from his seat, straightened his waistcoat, and blew out a breath. He went to a cabinet to retrieve a glass and a bottle of whiskey from it. Placing the glass on his desk, he filled it with a generous measure.

The Admiral walked to a window at the side of his desk.

Gazing first at the ornamental fountain splashing at the centre of the quadrangle opposite his window, he allowed his gaze to wander around the three sides of the roofed colonnade.

Black suited clerks and uniformed officers moved along the pavements. Some hurried individually, while others walked together in leisurely conversation.

Buckley watched them as he sipped his whiskey and mused on Johnson's case. He could not be sure of Johnson's innocence. The only evidence against him was the word of a simple sailor who could easily have misinterpreted what he heard and saw.

Johnson is a rogue, Buckley mused. *But he has a plausible explanation for everything.*

Do I take Young's word and recommend a man be tried for treason based on a possible misconception? On the other hand, perhaps these two men may have been government agents, watching Johnson. If that is so, they should be able to verify much of what Johnson says.

Buckley resolved to wait and see what the raid on the house in Aldeburgh Street uncovered before he came to a decision.

Finishing his whiskey, the Admiral sat back at his desk. He took up a volume of the *Quarterly Review* and leafed through the pages until he found an article to hold his interest.

"*Curiosities of Literature,* by J D'Israeli, Esq."

Within the hour, Albany returned accompanied by Daniels.

With a smug expression, Albany stood before Admiral Buckley.

'Well, Commander Albany, what did you find?'

'Nothing, Sir. The house was empty.'

'It had been occupied recently, though, Sir,' Daniels intervened.

Albany gave Daniels a hard stare and was about to admonish him when the Admiral addressed the sergeant.

'Was there anything to point to the occupants being French?' The Admiral asked.

'We found papers and books written in French. I think the Frenchmen were there, Sir, but have now gone.'

A sharp knock on the office door interrupted the report. Albany moved to the door and admitted Marine Redmond who stepped forward and handed a folded paper to the Admiral.

Buckley took the note from him, unfolded it and began to read.

Sir,

I have made enquiries regarding the two men you suggested were agents stationed in The George *to observe Mr Johnson. I can confirm that this was the case. Further, they have reported that they found no evidence to suggest that Mr Johnson is involved in anything deemed to be illegal or treasonous.*

Your obedient servant

Appleby.

Post scriptum,

Earl St Vincent suggests Able Seaman James Young should be rewarded for his loyalty, even though he was mistaken. He may present himself at the bursar's office to sign for his remuneration.

Buckley smiled, refolded the note and placed it before him on the desk. Linking his fingers over the top of the folded paper, he raised his head.

'Fetch Mr Johnson here, Sergeant Daniels,' he said.

Daniels left the room for the admiral's anteroom. Having locked the door on Tom, he now released him and, gripping Tom's arm firmly, escorted him to the Admiral.

Daniels pushed Tom into position in front of the admiral before letting his arm go.

Buckley regarded Tom for a moment before he spoke.

'It seems, Mr Johnson, that the two men you found observing you in The George were, in fact, government agents. They have reported that your activities did not suggest anything treasonous. You are free to go.'

Tom's face broke into a broad grin.

'Thank you, Admiral. I knew truth would triumph in the end.'

Tom turned to Albany, whose thunderous expression spoke volumes.

'Good day to you, Commander Albany,' Tom said and leant towards him.

'Better luck next time,' he murmured.

Tom turned. He straightened his shoulders and, with a spring in his step, he strode from the room.

When Tom had gone, the Admiral turned to Albany.

'Thank you for your assistance, Commander. You and the Marines may go.'

Albany saluted, turned, and left the room with Redmond and Daniels.

Admiral Buckley beckoned Captain Crenshaw to his desk and proffered his secretary's note.

'Read the postscript, Captain.'

Crenshaw frowned and took the note from the Admiral's hand.

When Crenshaw had finished reading it, he laughed out loud.

Buckley suppressed a smile. 'Accompany Young to the bursar's office if you please, Captain.'

'With pleasure, Admiral Buckley, Sir. Come, Jimmy,' Crenshaw said, leaving with a bewildered Jimmy following him.

The room was empty. Buckley smiled and chuckled to himself. *An interesting morning,* he thought and, picking up his *Quarterly Review*, he continued reading.

When Jimmy and Crenshaw had collected Jimmy's reward of ten gold sovereigns, they made their way to The Admiralty courtyard, where they found Tom waiting for them.

Jimmy recoiled at sight of him when Tom stepped forward.

'It's all right, Jimmy. I bear you no grudge. You did what you thought was right. I have something for you and the crew,' Tom said producing a small leather pouch from his pocket.

'I made enquiries. They have released the crewmen. This bag holds thirty-two gold sovereigns to compensate them for their efforts and inconvenience. I trust you to give two sovereigns to each of them and keep two for yourself. They may pick up their gear from Blackwall as soon as they like.'

Jimmy's eyes were round as saucers beneath eyebrows half-way up his forehead. His mouth fell open.

'Thank you, Cap'n Johnson. Oh, Lord, I'm real sorry for what I nearly did to you. No hard feelin's?'

Fervently hoping he would never come across Able Seaman Jimmy Young again, Tom lied.

'No hard feelings.'

CHAPTER SEVENTEEN

Tom left The Admiralty with a profound sense of relief. His plan had succeeded. He was free to continue with Corbeau and sail to St Helena, assist in replacing Napoleon with Laroche and return home a rich man.

Sounds easy when said quickly, Tom thought, with a soft laugh.

He walked along Whitehall and hailed an approaching Hackney.

'The George, Southwark,' Tom directed and climbed in.

The first thing he must do was see Nancy. After that, he would visit Peter at Blackwall Reach to arrange for sailing at dawn on Sunday.

Not quite everything stopped on the day of rest, but at five o'clock in the morning, he had a good chance of not being observed. Later most people would be at Church. With a good wind, he would rendezvous with *La Miséricorde* then sail the channel and set off from Plymouth for St Helena.

He sat back in his seat with a sigh, absentmindedly looking out of the window as he gathered his thoughts.

So far so good. All I need now is make myself as conspicuous as possible for the next couple of days, and tell everyone I meet that I'm going to Ireland. If Craddock does print my story, it will add credence to the tale.

Arriving outside The George, Tom alighted from the cab and paid the driver. He stood outside the door for a moment, debating whether to go in from there, or from the scullery entrance. He chose the latter and went around the back of the inn.

Entering the kitchen from the scullery, he saw Billy.

'Morning, Billy. Where's Nancy?' he asked.

'She's in the taproom. Will I fetch her for you?'

'Yes please, Billy. But just tell her she's wanted in

the kitchen. Don't tell her I'm here. I want to surprise her.'

Billy gave him a cheeky grin.

'Right y'are, Tom,' Billy said before darting off.

Tom stood to one side of the curtain in the doorway.

In a moment, Nancy came in and looked around the kitchen. Seeing no one there, she tutted in annoyance and turned to go. Tom stepped forward.

'Hello, Nancy,' he said smiling.

Nancy's eyes widened.

'Tom!' she exclaimed, and threw herself into his arms, kissing every inch of his face.

Tom held her close and kissed her deeply.

Her hands moved over him as if to make sure he was really there.

'I take it you're pleased to see me,' he said as he loosened his grip on her.

'I didn't think you'd get away with it, Tom. I thought you'd be in prison by now. It went well, then?' she said, trying to catch her breath.

'Without any hitch. My plan worked. I answered all their questions and explained everything away. I think, perhaps, the Admiral knew I was up to something. But there was no evidence. So, I'm free, Nancy-love,' he said, catching her in his arms again and dancing around the kitchen with her.

'Ah, stop, stop, Tom,' Nancy cried, laughing. 'I've got to get back to work. Come out and have some ale.'

'A good idea, Nancy. I'm parched. Being arrested is thirsty work.'

Tom went into the tap room before her and moved to his seat. Running his fingers over his initials he smiled.

Nancy went to the bar and took down Tom's tankard. She found a clean cloth and rubbed the pewter to a dull shine.

Betty came to the bar from the other side of the room where she had waited patiently for the three

169

gentlemen there to find enough coins in their pockets to pay for the ale they ordered.

'You look a bit more cheerful, Nancy,' she remarked, seeing the high colour in Nancy's cheeks.

'Yes, I am, Betty. Look,' Nancy said, raising Tom's tankard.

Betty frowned and took the tankard from Nancy's hand. As she looked at it, her frown deepened.

'It's Tom's,' she said, mystified.

'Yes, Betty. It's Tom's, and I am about to fill it,' Nancy said, taking the tankard from Betty.

'He's back?' Betty asked.

Betty knew Tom had gone somewhere. When she asked where he had gone, Nancy told her he had sworn her to secrecy. But Betty had noted the tension in Nancy and knew there might be danger involved.

Nancy's smiling face shone with happiness. She nodded and lifted her chin towards where Tom sat. Going to his table, she set his tankard beside him before sitting opposite him.

'I can't stay long, Nancy-love, I have to go to Blackwall to see Peter. But I'll be back tonight. I only came here to tell you everything went well.'

'I'm glad you did, Tom,' Nancy said.

'I'll be leaving at dawn on Sunday,' he said and took a swig of ale.

'I know, Tom,' Nancy said.

'I'll be gone about five months.'

'I know, Tom, you told me.'

'I just want to make sure you do know. I think getting over today's business was the worst bit. Once at our destination, it will be plain sailing, and then I'll be home, and we'll be married.'

'Yes, Tom,' Nancy said and gave him a big smile.

Tom caught Nancy's hand and gave it a squeeze.

He stood up and drained his tankard.

'I've got to go, Sweetheart. I'll see you tonight,' he said, leaning over to kiss her. Straightening, he stood a moment looking at her. She smiled up at him, and he nodded before he turned towards the door and left.

On leaving the taproom, Tom made his way to the stable yard.

'Is Jed about?' Tom asked the nearest ostler.

'Last time I saw him he were in the hayloft,' the man replied pointing across the yard to a half-timbered building.

'Thanks,' Tom said and wandered over to the hay loft which stood above the stables.

At the front of the upper floor, Tom saw Jed forking hay down to a groom below.

'Ho, Jed,' Tom called up to him. 'Can I speak with you?'

Floating particles from the hay formed a halo around Jed's large head as he peered over the floor of the loft, his face red from his exertions. Dust liberally covered his brown hair. He wore a course, grey shirt, a leather waistcoat over it, his sleeves rolled up.

'Oh, it's you, Tom. I'll be with you now,' he answered.

He hefted another bale of hay down to a groom before going to the front of the loft where wide double-doors stood open. A beam, attached to the roof of the loft, jutted out over the stable yard.

A rope ran through the block and tackle attached to the beam. A hook on the loft wall held the end of the rope. Jed released the rope from the hook, took it in a firm grip and swung down to the yard below, landing a few feet from Tom.

'What can I do for you, Tom?'

Tom was over six feet tall and strong, with broad, well-muscled, shoulders. A good man to have on your side.

Jed was more than a head taller. The muscles of his shoulders and arms bulged fit to burst his shirt. He dwarfed Tom.

'I need a disguise, Jed. Can I borrow your hat and your greatcoat again?'

Jed grinned.

'You're up to something, Tom. I can smell it,' Jed said, digging Tom in the ribs.

Tom put a hand on Jed's arm.

'I am. I'll tell you about it when it's over. In the meantime, …'

'You want my hat and coat. I'll go and fetch them. When can I have them back?'

'In a couple of hours. But before you go, Jed, can I borrow a horse?'

'Anything else?' Jed asked.

'No, that's all,' Tom said, chuckling.

Jed nodded and made off, stopping on the way to have a word with the ostler about the horse.

As Jed returned from his room with the coat and hat, the ostler led out a large black stallion, his coat shining, his head tossing.

'That's a magnificent bit of blood to be in a coaching inn,' Tom said, running his hand down the horse's neck.

'It ain't a coach horse or a hiring horse. It belongs to a gentleman who will be here to collect him on Monday. Reckon the poor beast will be glad of some exercise,' Jed said, with a wry grin.

'Reckon he will,' Tom said as he put on the coat and hat, turning the collar up.

'What's his name?'

'I heard the gentleman call him Thunder,' the ostler said.

'Thunder, eh?' Tom said, mounting, and gripping the reins.

'I'll be back within two hours, Jed, and thank you,' Tom said, pulling the hat down low on his forehead.

'You're welcome, Tom,' Jed said, giving Thunder a hefty slap on his rump.

Thunder sidled, shaking his head. Tom leant

forward to stroke his neck and make crooning noises near his ear. He gave the horse's sides a firm dig with his heels. Thunder took off at a smart trot as Tom lifted an arm high in a farewell salute.

Next to sailing, Tom enjoyed a good gallop. He wished he could go for a gallop now, but on the streets of London, speed was impossible. Still, he hadn't been on a decent horse in a long while. He enjoyed the ride.

Crossing London Bridge, Tom followed the route he had taken earlier when he had gone to Blackwall Reach with Corbeau and Mollien. He sat erect in the saddle shoulders back to make himself look bigger, hoping no one would recognise him.

Arriving at the gate to the dry dock, he dismounted and knocked on the door.

After a short while, Peter came to the door. On seeing Tom, his face broke into a smile.

'Tom! You succeeded!' he exclaimed holding the door wide.

Tom led the horse into the gloom, while Peter closed the door behind him.

'Did you doubt I would, Peter? How's the work on *Nautilus* progressing?' Tom asked as he tethered the horse to a ring in the wall.

'Come and see,' Peter said.

Tom removed the coat and hat.

'Did they put you under lock and key?' Peter asked as they moved to where *Nautilus* lay.

'Na,' Tom replied. 'The closest they came was manacles on my wrists for a short while, and twenty minutes in a locked room. They knew something was going on but my story held good, so they let me go. I'm not out of the woods yet. I'm probably being watched.'

'Hence the big coat and hat, again, and the horse too, this time,' Peter said.

'Yes. I intend going about London over the next days as if nothing has happened. If there are people watching me, I shall lead them a merry dance,' Tom said and stopped in his tracks when he saw *Nautilus.*

'She looks good, doesn't she?' Peter said.

'She looked well yesterday. She's even better now,' Tom said, looking at the finished cladding.

He climbed the steps to the top of her bulwarks. Hiking his legs over, he jumped down on her deck. Tom had not had time before to give the wooden cladding a full inspection. Now he found it was made of thin slats laid along the inside and out, held together with a line of beading at the top and painted to look robust. Pedro had suggested the wood should be easy to remove when the time came for the submarine to lose her disguise.

'If you inspect the panels, you will see they are attached to thin cables held fast to the deck. With a twist of these pegs, we may easily remove and replace them when needed. Pedro and I know how to do that, so you need not be involved in it,' Peter explained.

Tom ran his hand over the cladding, feeling a small protrusion here and there.

'Remarkable,' Tom said. 'When I first saw what you were doing I thought perhaps the cladding would not stand up to a long sea voyage. But if it is removable, we need only have it in place when necessary.'

'That was Pedro's thinking,' Peter said.

'It will be ready by Sunday?' Tom asked.

'Easily. We want to spend Saturday practising removing and replacing it, just to make sure there are no difficulties.'

'Where will you store it when it's not fixed in place?'

'Ah. We were hoping we could keep it on *La Miséricorde.* Do you think the Frenchies will oblige?'

'They have no choice,' Tom said, giving Peter a cynical smile before climbing over the bulwark and onto the steps. Peter followed him, and they went back to where Tom had tethered the horse.

'Everything seems to be going well, Peter. If you have a problem, send word to Nancy at The George. All being well, I'll see you here at five o'clock on Sunday morning,' Tom said putting on the coat and hat again.

'One more thing, someone will come to you with my gear. Will you stow it for me?'

'Who will come?'

'You will know them when they say, "Ned sent me",' Tom replied.

'Ned?' Peter questioned. 'You mean Ned Marlow?'

'Yes. My things are with him.'

'Oh,' Peter said, surprised. 'I have not heard that name in many a year,' he said as he opened the door and held it while Tom led the horse outside.

'Oh, he's still around,' Tom said as he mounted.

'Till Sunday, Peter,' he called pressing his heels against the horse's flank, and, with a tip of his hat, he rode away, back to The George, to give Jed back his coat and hat and the gentleman's horse.

For the rest of the day and late into the evening, Tom spent his time visiting old haunts. He made sure he encountered old acquaintances and enemies alike. Today he was everyone's friend. He boasted about his legacy and how he was going to Ireland to claim it. He bought them drinks, smoked a pipe or two with them, played cards, and made sure the inns he called at would not forget the night Tom Johnson visited.

As the evening wore on, Tom checked his watch.

Nine thirty. This must be my last drink; otherwise I won't be able to see a hole in a ladder, he thought.

'Drink up, lads, for I must go,' Tom said.

A cacophony of protest met him.

Tom held up his hand.

'I have a woman waiting for me.'

Much ribald laughter and crude comments met his

words.

Tom caught the serving girl's eye, and she came to his side.

'One more round for my friends,' he said, putting several coins in her hand.

While the men were sorting out whose drinks were what, Tom slipped away.

Just as Nancy and Betty were gathering up the empty pots and tankards, Tom entered The George. He had managed to stay relatively sober but was exhausted. He sat in his seat to wait for Nancy and quickly fell asleep with his head resting on the back of the settle.

The girls finished their work, and Betty went off to bed.

Nancy went to Tom's side. Knowing why he had spent the night on the town, she quelled her irritation.

'Tom, wake up. You can't sleep here,' she said, shaking his arm.

Tom woke with a jolt.

'Sorry, Nancy-love. I had a busy day,' he said rising and stretching his muscles before following her into the kitchen.

Nancy took a candle from a cupboard and lit it. Catching Tom's hand, she led him to the stairs.

CHAPTER EIGHTEEN

Friday morning dawned bright and fair. Tom decided to borrow the black stallion again for his journey. He was going to Chiswick, to visit the place he called home when he wasn't away sailing. Ned Marlow owned a large riverside house, Mirabilis.

He had captained the first smuggler's ship on which Tom sailed.

Retired now, Ned lived on the ground floor of the house, Toms rooms being on an upper floor.

As his horse trotted along the quiet roads of Chiswick, Tom compared its peaceful atmosphere to the bustle of London. At home in either location, he wondered what Nancy would think of living outside the capital.

Tom arrived at Mirabilis and walked his horse to the stables at the side of the house. A groom came to take his bridle.

'Good morning, Mr Tom,' he said.

'Good morning, Will. Fine day.'

'Aye,' Will said and led the horse into the stable.

Tom's feet crunched on the gravel path as he walked to the front of the house and rapped on the polished brass knocker.

Chivers, Ned's Butler, opened the door. He had been with Ned since the old days, serving as his steward when at sea. Behind his dour exterior was a man dedicated to his master, and to Tom.

'Mr Tom, we have been wondering when we would see you next. Are you well?' Chivers asked, greeting Tom with a huge smile.

Tom felt honoured. Smiling was something Chivers didn't often do.

'Yes, Chivers, I'm well. Is Ned at home?'

'He is in the drawing room, Sir. Allow me to announce you.'

'That's all right. I know my way,' Tom said, striding off to the back of the house.

Tom entered the drawing room. The décor and furnishings exhibited the latest style, as did the rest of the house. Looking about the elegant room, Tom thought no one was there. Then he caught sight of a tall figure standing on the veranda, dressed soberly in expensive clothes, as befitted a gentleman.

Ned's neighbours—who knew him as "Mr Edward"—looked upon him as a most respectable person. No one would have recognised him as the free trader who had taken Tom under his wing at the age of twelve and had taught him all he knew.

Ned smoked a cheroot as he looked out over the lawn to the Thames running past the garden.

'Good Morning, Ned,' Tom said, moving to stand next to him.

'Tom, my boy, where have you been? Engaged in something interesting?'

'Yes, Ned, very interesting. I'm about to sail to the South Atlantic on a mission. Mum's the word, though. I've been arrested once already in connection with this venture. I don't want that again.'

'Well, well, my boy. And I thought you were ready to settle down,' Ned said with a chuckle.

'Ah. That's another thing. When I come back, I'm going to be married. This venture will gain me forty thousand pounds. I'll be nearly as wealthy as you.'

'Hmm,' Ned said. 'You'll need more than that to pull alongside me.'

'Ah, but Ned, you accumulated your fortune over years of indulging in illicit activities. Perhaps, if I live to be your age, I too will have amassed as much,' Tom said.

Ned laughed.

'Yes, perhaps. But tell me, who is this lady you are about to espouse?'

'Her name is Nancy, and she's a serving maid at

The George,' Tom said.

Ned gave Tom a sceptical look.

'Well, she's a bit more than that,' Tom said, seeing the look. 'She runs the place. The owner is infirm.'

'Have you known her long, Tom?' Ned asked gently, wondering whether the woman knew that Tom was not exactly poor.

'Years. We're recently reacquainted,' Tom replied.

Ned's face still portrayed reserve.

'Ned, don't look disapproving. I never loved a woman in my life before. And I know she loves me. She's willing to wait for me until I come back. That won't be for four or five months …'

Ned interrupted.

'I am not disapproving, Tom, I am concerned for you. I would not want you deceived.'

'Ned, it's me you're talking to, you know,' Tom said, his eyes twinkling.

'True. I have never known you deceived by anyone. Yet with women, sometimes things work differently.'

'You are right, Ned, in general. When I return, I will bring her to you, and you may judge for yourself,' Tom said, not for a moment lacking faith in Nancy.

Ned bowed in gracious assent.

'And to what do I owe the pleasure of your company today, Tom?'

'Two reasons. One is to inform you I will be absent for about four or five months, depending on conditions in the Atlantic. The other, to pack my things for the voyage,' Tom said, watching Ned go to a sideboard.

Several decanters stood beside a tray holding expensive cut-glass snifters. Ned poured two generous measures of brandy and took one to Tom.

'To your health and your success, Tom,' Ned said, holding his glass up in salute.

Tom raised his glass to Ned before sipping the brandy.

'You will take luncheon with me, Tom?' Ned asked.

'Indeed, I will, Ned. Thank you.'

'You may tell me something of your venture while we eat,' Ned suggested as he pulled the bell cord beside the white marble fireplace. 'I know it is not wise to disclose all of your plans, even to me, Tom. However, you may give me a flavour of your forthcoming exploits, will you not?'

Chivers quietly entered the room.

'You rang, Mr Edward?' he asked.

'Tom is staying for luncheon. See to it if you please, Chivers,' Ned replied.

Chivers bowed and silently retreated.

Over Luncheon, Tom disclosed that his dealings were with Frenchmen. He told Ned of the submarine, but not its use.

'*Nautilus* is lying in the dry dock at Blackwall Reach. The lads are disguising her as a yacht. I wonder, Ned, whether you could send someone to carry my gear there? I think I am watched. I have put it about that I am going on a trip to Ireland. I feel it would seem strange to someone watching me if they observe me and my luggage arriving at Blackwall,' Tom said.

'Of course, Tom. Lay your things out on your bed. I will see to it they are packed and brought to Blackwall.'

'Ah, thanks, Ned,' Tom said, relieved of a niggling inconvenience.

'Who is going with you, Tom?' Ned asked as he sipped his wine from a crystal glass.

Tom proceeded to tell Ned about the men from the old days who had rallied around to help him. Peter Marriot, Bear, Pedro, Oliver and the rest.

'Ah, how I wish I could see them all again. I am comfortable here, and too old to indulge in my past occupation. But sometimes I miss the old days and all our comrades,' Ned said, the germ of an idea forming in his mind. *Might it be possible to deliver Tom's baggage to Blackwall Reach myself?* he mused.

After finishing their luncheon, the weather being

fine, Tom and Ned went to the veranda. From there they strolled down the lawn to the river in companionable conversation while smoking cheroots.

'Do you remember when I first met you, Tom?' Ned asked.

'Huh. Like yesterday.'

Tom took a puff on his cheroot before he continued.

'I was dodging a runner who accused me of picking a fop's pocket. I was in the middle of talking my way out of it when you stepped in and said I was known to you. I have often wondered why you did that, Ned.'

Ned paused before he spoke.

'I saw in you a kindred spirit, Tom. Like you, I came to crime at an early age. When my family fell on hard times, my conscience did not hinder me in my pursuit of crime, since it was criminality that parted my father from his wealth.'

'But you are well educated, Sir. Surely you might have made a living by honest means? I, on the other hand, could hardly read, until you took charge of me.'

Ned gave a slow nod.

'It is true, Tom. Yet you had intelligence enough to outwit the plodding representatives of the law. Oh, but you were a reckless Lad!' Ned said, placing a paternal hand on Tom's shoulder.

'You must know I look on you as my own son,' he added.

'Thank you, Sir,' Tom said, somewhat overcome.

To cover his unaccustomed emotion, Tom took out his pocket watch.

'I must leave shortly, Ned. I shall go to my room now and lay out the things I want to take with me.'

'So soon? Will you not lie here tonight?'

'I would like nothing better, Ned. However, for the sake of those watching me, I mean to make myself conspicuous. As I told you, I have said I am going to Ireland. My story is that I have come into money and am going there to claim it.'

'I hope your ruse will work. Good luck to you, Tom,' Ned said.

Tom returned to the drawing room, dressed in a plain, dark grey worsted coat, beneath it, a black waistcoat, of unostentatious, yet fashionable cut. His shirt points were lower than fashion dictated – for comfort's sake – with a black cravat tied in a soft bow. As he was riding, he wore breeches, also in dark grey. A pair of high, soft, black leather boots completed his outfit.

'I've laid out my clothes and my gear as you suggested, Ned. Thank you for luncheon and for the pleasure of your company, my dear friend. I will go now,' Tom said, extending his hand.

Ned pulled Tom into a swift embrace, patting Tom's back. Before he let him go, Ned spoke softly in Tom's ear.

'Be careful of the French, Tom. They are a treacherous bunch. I rather hope Boney will fare well when you remove him from St Helena.'

Tom stood back from Ned, his eyes wide in disbelief.

'I never mentioned him, Ned. How did you know?'

'I keep my ear to the ground, my boy. I have heard rumours of a rescue attempt. Why else would Frenchmen employ you and *Nautilus* to sail with them on the Atlantic?'

'You're still as sharp as ever you were, Ned,' Tom replied and chuckled.

Ned responded with a grin.

'I have had your horse made ready for you, Tom. Will has him at the front gate. Goodbye now, my boy, and good luck to you,' Ned said.

'Thank you, Ned. I will come to you on my return,' Tom replied.

In the hall, Chivers opened the door and bowed to him as Tom left the house.

A feeling of contentment filled Tom as he mounted

his horse.

Tom arrived back in London in the late afternoon. He took the horse to the stables in The George, gave him into the charge of an ostler and made his way to the taproom.

Nancy's eyes opened wide at seeing Tom dressed in fine clothes. She wondered where he had been.

'Hello, Tom. Why are you dressed like a gent?' she asked regarding him from his soft leather boots to his black cravat.

'I'm going out again tonight, Nancy. This time to be seen in select circles. I know a few men of quality. I shall proclaim my legacy and my new-found wealth and make assignations with them for when I return. It's all part of my strategy, Nancy-love. I told you, the more people I tell I am going to Ireland, the less likely I am to be missed.'

'When will you be back?' Nancy asked.

'About the same time as last night, Nancy, around ten o'clock,' he replied.

'And will you go out again tomorrow?'

'For a little while but I'll be back early. I want to spend the evening with you. Can you spare the time? Can Betty see to the taproom? Maybe you could get Molly to help.'

Nancy chuckled.

'I hoped you'd say that, Tom. I've already seen to it.'

Tom spent the rest of Friday in assembly rooms, gambling dens, and boxing establishments, finding he knew more people in the social set than he had thought. It rapidly became known by all that the reformed smuggler, Tom Johnson, was soon to be rich. The *Haut Ton* liked nothing better than a colourful character. Now that he had money, he became even more appealing.

Arriving back at The George, he went straight up to Nancy's room where he was careful to hang his trousers, waistcoat and coat over a chair before he climbed into her bed.

He was asleep when Nancy entered the room an hour later. She didn't wake him, knowing they would spend the whole of the following evening together.

CHAPTER NINETEEN

Tom woke late on Saturday morning and lay still, enjoying the pleasure of a comfortable bed.

Who knows when I will sleep in anything so snug in the months to come, he thought.

Sleeping arrangements on shipboard were cramped and stuffy. A crew member usually slept in a hammock, with an allowance of but fourteen inches' space for himself. Officers slept in cots, several to a small cabin. Important people like Count Mollien would be given a larger cabin, sometimes sharing with one other. Only the Captain lived in solitary ease.

I wonder in which category they'll put me? Tom reflected.

A week before, Tom had taken a gown from Nancy's cupboard and given it to Betty.

'I want you to take this to a dressmaker. It will serve as a pattern. Ask her to make up a new gown for Nancy in the latest fashion, no expense spared. Can you also buy shoes and stockings for her?' he said and gave Betty a small bag of coins.

'Of course, I can, Tom,' Betty said, but gave him a quizzical look. 'You are very good to buy Nancy fine clothes, Tom. However, I can't help but wonder, when will she get the chance to wear them?'

Tom smiled and tapped the side of his nose.

'I will tell you something Betty, but you must say nothing to Nancy. I intend to take her to Vauxhall Gardens on the Saturday before I sail.'

Betty's face lit up as she gasped.

'Tom! She will love it. We have heard such tales about Vauxhall Gardens. We had thought of going there, just to look around, like. But we have heard it isn't safe for girls alone at night.'

'You're right, Betty. Only women of easy virtue go

there alone. You and Nancy aren't like that. Perhaps, when I come back, I will take you both.'

'Would you, Tom? That'd be lovely! We'd be safe with you,' Betty said, excited at the prospect. She hurried off with the gown under her arm before Nancy caught sight of it.

Tom put on the clothes he had worn the day before. When dressed, he descended to the kitchen and was pleased to find Betty on her own. Taking her arm, he drew her into the scullery.

'Did you get the gown, Betty?'

'Yes, Tom. I have it in my room,' she said her eyes alive with pleasure in the shared secret.

'Thank you, Betty. I can't wait to see her in it,' Tom said before making his way to the taproom.

Going through the curtain, he saw Nancy talking to a man sitting by the door. Tom caught her eye, and she came to him.

'Good morning, Tom,' Nancy said. 'Do you intend to do more of your wandering this morning?'

'Yes, Nancy-love. But I'll be back at about six to take you out,' Tom replied.

Nancy smiled, her eyes shining.

'Where are we going, Tom?'

'It's a surprise,' Tom said, moving to his usual seat.

Nancy smiled again and followed him. 'Do you want breakfast?'

'Yes please, Nancy-love.'

Nancy left him but was back soon with a dish of kedgeree.

'That's a bit fancy for The George,' Tom remarked.

'Mr Scarlett, the owner, bought Gem a little book of recipes and he's trying them out,' Nancy said.

Tom tasted an experimental spoonful. He nodded to Nancy.

'This is good!' he said in surprise.

Nancy smiled her appreciation.

Tom set down his spoon and grasped Nancy's hand.

'I'll be off as soon as I've finished this Nancy-love, so I'll say goodbye to you now. I'll see you at six.'

'Right you are, Tom,' Nancy replied nodding, a huge smile on her face.

After leaving The George, Tom spent most of Saturday walking about the city. He visited markets, chop houses, shops, taverns, and coffee houses, spreading the news of his good fortune.

At four in the afternoon, he went to Schweitzer and Davidson, located in Cork Street, a tailor of the highest reputation.

Tom had visited them the week before. When he entered the shop, Mr Davidson, a tall, thin man with a pale complexion and lank hair, stepped forward to greet him. Seeing Tom in his working man's clothes, he looked askance down his long nose.

'The tradesmen's entrance is at the back,' he said with a derisory sniff.

When necessary, Tom could take on the persona of a gentleman, as he did now.

'My good man,' Tom drawled in a cultured accent. 'If you treat all your new clients as you are treating me now, I would imagine you will soon be out of business. Lord Wellington himself recommended you to me. I shall certainly upbraid him for suggesting I visit you. Good day to you.'

Tom turned and made for the door.

Mr Davidson took a swift step forward, raising a hand.

'Ah, Sir, do not be too hasty. I will be glad to have you measured for whatever you require.'

I imagined you might, Tom thought.

Tom returned and stood before the man, one eyebrow raised, a hand on his hip.

'Well?' he said.

'Forgive me, Sir, but you must admit, your present

garb is a little… eh… basic,' Davidson said regarding Tom with a jaundiced eye.

'Just so,' Tom said looking down at his clothes. 'What I want is a complete set of evening wear. Is it possible to have them by next Saturday?'

'It is rather short notice, Sir. But for a friend of the Duke, I will make it possible,' Davidson said.

He went to a door at the back of the shop and opened it.

'Forward, please, Mr Mudgely.'

A fussy little man with receding hair, spectacles balanced on the end of his nose, and one of the new measuring tapes around his neck, hurried into the shop. He stopped short at the sight before him.

'Oh, dear me,' he said, stepping back a little.

'Mr… eh?' Mr Davidson turned enquiring eyes on Tom.

'Johnson,' Tom supplied. 'Thomas Aloysius Johnson.'

'Ah yes. Mudgely, Mr Johnson requires evening dress by Saturday week. Measure him if you please.'

He turned to Tom.

'When will you be returning for a fitting, Mr Johnson?'

'I must decline, Sir. My current business precludes such a visit. I am sure you can accomplish all you need today,' Tom said with his best upper-crust, insincere smile.

Mr Mudgely ushered him away to the room at the back of the shop. He did, indeed, make do with measuring every relevant inch of Tom's anatomy and promised he would do his best without a further visit.

So it was that, on Saturday afternoon, Tom, carrying a valise, paid another visit to Cork Street. He thought perhaps he should have gone a day earlier, but he had stipulated Saturday, therefore, Saturday it must be. He hoped his clothes were ready and that they were of a good fit.

When Tom entered the shop wearing his decent

clothes, it pleased Mr Davidson to see him looking more respectable than the last time he visited.

'Ah, Mr Johnson. Your evening dress is ready for you. Please step this way,' he said, leading Tom into Mr Mudgely's domain.

Mr Mudgely led Tom to a large cubicle, curtained off with black velvet drapery. Inside there stood a burgundy-upholstered chair, to the side of it, a full-length oval mirror, on the wall a brass rail.

'When you have removed your clothes, Mr Johnson, please put on the trousers so I may make sure they fit,' he said, laying the new black trousers over the chair, and drawing the curtain discreetly as he left.

Tom removed his clothes and hung them on the rail.

After some minutes, Mudgely's voice sounded outside the curtain.

'May I enter, Mr Johnson?'

Tom pulled back the curtain.

Mudgely stood back to regard Tom.

The trousers were fashionably tight and showed off Tom's muscular thighs.

'Please, turn around, Sir.'

Tom obeyed.

'Perfect, Sir. You have an excellent physique, if I may say so. Does Sir have an evening shirt?'

'Ah… no…' Tom replied.

'Very well, Sir,' Mudgely said with a stiff smile. 'I can supply one.'

Mudgely returned moments later with a dazzling white lawn shirt. He held it out for Tom's approval.

Tom took it and put it on.

'I took the liberty of bringing cravats, too,' Mudgely said extending his arm over which he had draped six cravats of varying shades from pure white to a gentle cream.

'Cream is a fashionable colour for cravats this season, Sir,'

Tying a cravat was something Ned had taught Tom

189

to do. So adept was he, Tom could do it in the dark. He picked up one of pale ivory and deftly folded it before tying it intricately around his neck, finishing with a soft bow.

Mudgely was impressed.

Tom tucked the shirt into his trousers as Mudgely came forward with his waistcoat and coat.

Standing before a mirror in his new clothes, Tom hardly recognised himself. On occasion, he had worn evening dress before, but never anything quite so grand.

The collar of his shirt was fashionably high. His white figured-silk waistcoat was short, just reaching to his waist. The black coat fitted so snugly that Mudgely had to hold it for Tom as he eased himself into it. It too had a high collar. The waist was cut a little higher than his waistcoat which showed beneath it. His coattails hung down to the back of his knee. Mudgely had also suggested fashionably flimsy pumps. Tom declined these for a pair of soft leather shoes in a plain style.

Over all this, Tom wore a greatcoat that came down below the knee and had three short capes at the shoulders. Mudgely also supplied Tom with a black silk-covered, curly brimmed top hat.

'Thank you, Mr Mudgely. It is perfect,' Tom said.

He picked up the valise he had brought with him. Removing a leather purse from it, he was about to pack the clothes he had hung on the rail when Mr Mudgely stepped forward and took the valise from him.

'Allow me, Sir,' he said.

Tom opened the door of Mr Mudgely's room, emerging into the shop in all his splendour.

'Mr Davidson, I am about to leave the country for some months. I am sure you would prefer me to settle my account with you now, rather than await my return,' he said, holding the purse in his hand.

Mr Davidson went to his desk, wrote a figure on a card and handed it to Tom. Tom took the required sum from the purse and placed the coins on Mr Davidson's desk. Davidson bowed graciously and scooped the money into a drawer at the side of the desk.

Mr Mudgely came from his room and handed Tom his valise.

'A pleasure doing business with you, gentlemen,' Tom said, tipping his top hat before he left the shop.

Heads turned when Tom entered The George, many doing a double-take when they saw that the "gentleman" was Tom.

Tom spotted Betty serving tankards of ale to a group of men. As she turned from them to walk towards the bar, he stood in her way.

'Excuse me, Sir,' she said as she attempted to pass him.

'Betty, is Nancy ready?' Tom asked.

'Oh … my goodness … Tom, I didn't recognise you. Nancy's waiting for you in the little parlour. She didn't want to come into the taproom dressed as she is,' Betty said, leading the way through the door to the passage which led to the stairs to the Gallery.

'She looks ever so beautiful, Tom,' Betty said, opening the door.

Nancy turned towards the door as it opened. Instead of a serving maid, there stood before him a beauty to put any high society lady to shame.

A small fillet of pearls encircled her curls, piled high on her head. Ringlets fell softly on her neck at the back. The gown was of amber taffeta, in a simple, elegant design. The low, square neckline enhanced her voluptuous bosom. The high waist, decorated with a darker amber satin sash, complimented the little puff sleeves, trimmed with a matching satin cuff. The plain straight skirt fell smoothly from the high waist. More satin ribbon ran in three bands above the hem. Matching satin slippers peeped from beneath the skirt. Betty had painted Nancy's face with subtle colour, enhancing her dark eyes.

The sight of her took Tom's breath away.

'By God, Nancy,' he exclaimed, 'You're beautiful.'

Nancy was equally surprised at how sophisticated Tom looked.

'Thank you, Tom. I swear, you're the handsomest man I've ever seen,' she said.

Tom laughed. He reached for the brown velvet cloak resting on a nearby chair and draped it around Nancy's shoulders. Turning her around, he gazed at her. His eyes held a look of wonder, which made Nancy's heart stop.

'I love you, Tom' she said, her cream-gloved hand reaching to caress his cheek.

For once Tom Johnson was speechless. He smiled and led her to the door; opening it he stood back.

'Your carriage awaits, Ma'am,' he said with a bow and a flourish of his hand.

Outside in the inn yard, a footman handed Nancy into a magnificent, shining, black coach. Lined all over inside with squabbed green velvet, Nancy had never been in anything so grand. She sank back into the cushioned seats sure she must be dreaming. Tom climbed in and sat beside her. He took her hand in his and kissed her fingers one by one, his eyes shining in the twilight.

He kept hold of her hand as they sat in silence.

The coach travelled through the darkening streets as lamplighters ignited the gas in the street lights.

Nancy smoothed her gown and adjusted the skirt so it wouldn't crease.

'Thank you for my gown, Tom,' Nancy murmured.

Tom lifted her hand to his lips.

'Where are we going?' she whispered.

'I told you, it's a surprise,' Tom replied.

'Oh no, Tom, please tell me,' Nancy pleaded, gripping his arm.

'Oh, all right,' Tom said, deciding not to tease her.

'I've booked a box in Vauxhall Gardens where we'll have supper. After that, we'll watch the entertainment, see the fireworks and listen to the music. After that, we'll return to The George and … well, I think you know the rest.'

As he spoke, Nancy's eyes became more and more round. Her heart beat faster and when she could speak it was almost a whisper.

'I have always wanted to go to Vauxhall Gardens. Oh, thank you, Tom.'

She flung her arms around his neck, and kissed him.

Arriving at Vauxhall Gardens, as their coach stood before the gates, a groom opened the door, and Tom stepped out. He gave Nancy his hand and helped her down. The coach moved off as Tom paid the entrance fee.

Thousands of glass-covered lamps illuminated the tree-lined walks. Tom and Nancy joined the promenading throng.

Tom had booked a supper box for seven o'clock. He caught a waiter's eye; the young man hurried over to him. Tom handed him his ticket. The waiter read it.

'Follow me, please, Sir,' he said and led them to a box overlooking the entertainment area.

Music floated in the air, played by the Orchestra mounted on a stage supported by high pillars. In front of the orchestra, men and women danced to the music.

Nancy watched it all, mesmerised.

'Come, Nancy,' Tom said as the waiter held the door to the box open for them.

Although the table within the box was large, it was set only for two.

Before seating them, the waiter took Nancy's cloak and Tom's greatcoat. He handed Tom a card.

'Would you like to choose your wine, Sir?' he asked.

Tom waved the card away.

'We will have Champagne if you please,' Tom said.

'Very good, Sir. I will return with your supper presently, Sir, Madam,' he said and left them.

'Oh my, Tom. Champagne!' Nancy said.

A small amount was held at The George for those who occasionally ordered it for celebrations. Someone had left a little in the bottom of a bottle. Nancy had tasted it but had never had a whole glass to herself.

They watched the world go by as they waited for the supper to arrive.

'There's a great mixture of people here, Tom. Some of them are very grand indeed, and some are, well, just like us,' Nancy remarked.

'Yes, Nancy. Provided they pay the entrance fee, everyone is welcome,' Tom said. 'Because three princes of Wales have frequented this place, it's acceptable to the *haut ton.* On the other hand, there are many harlots plying their trade.'

Nancy gave him an uncertain glance. She looked more closely at the crowds going past and saw women she would have frowned upon had they entered The George. One dark beauty stood out among the rest.

'Look, Tom, that dark girl there, she's lovely. The woman with her is not of the same class at all. She can't be her Mamma?'

'Who knows, Nancy. Only women of low degree come here on their own. She is probably her chaperone,' Tom said. *Or her procuress,* he thought.

'I am a woman of low degree, Tom, even though I don't look like it tonight,' Nancy said, a sad note in her voice.

'Indeed, you are not, Nancy Mason. You are more of a lady than many I have met,' Tom declared, a crease between his eyebrows.

'I am a servant, Tom,' she said in a small voice.

'And I am a thief,' he answered. 'Tonight, we are part of the gentry. When I come back, I will be richer than all of them.'

The waiter, accompanied by two others, entered the

box to place covered dishes on the table. Vauxhall was famed for its thinly carved cold meats. Tonight, fresh salads accompanied it, followed by pastries and cakes.

The waiter deftly popped the cork from the champagne and poured it for them.

The speed and efficiency of the well-trained waiters serving them impressed Nancy.

When they left, Tom lifted his glass.

'To you, Nancy-love,' he said.

'To you, Tom,' Nancy said, and they clinked their glasses.

As they ate their supper, both mused on their situation.

The buzzing atmosphere of the place filled Nancy with excitement. The thought of Tom being rich and her married to him was almost incomprehensible. But then, she didn't mind whether they were rich or poor. As long as they were together, it didn't matter.

Tom had been unsure whether to expose Nancy to the varied Vauxhall society. He thought she might be overwhelmed. Yet he had given her the gown and she, like him, had risen above her birth and looked and behaved like a lady. Tonight, she shone with a brilliance that lay hidden in her menial occupation.

Unlike him, Nancy was honest. But, like him, she was self-reliant.

They spoke little as they ate their meal, entertained by the music, the dancers and the people passing by their box.

Tom resisted the temptation to run his hand across his mouth when he had finished eating. Instead, he used his napkin.

'Nancy,' he said.

She turned her bright, delighted face to him.

'Yes, Tom?'

'Will you walk with me?'

'Yes, Tom, I will,' she said.

She had read the program, which she found lying on

the table. Madame Saqui, the tightrope walker, had caught her eye.

'But I don't want to miss the entertainment,' she said and pressed her lips together in a smile.

'We have half an hour before it starts,' Tom said.

Nancy rose and linked her arm in his.

They left their box and moved along the main avenue, brightly lit by the glass-covered lamps.

'Have you been here a lot, Tom?' she asked.

'Yes, when I was young and sowing my wild oats. It's years since last I was here.'

They strolled for a while up and down the walkways, until Tom pulled her into a secluded spot to kiss her.

'What was that for?' Nancy asked, smoothing her gown.

Tom laughed. 'It's tradition here to ah—pay court to your partner,' Tom said.

'Oh, well, Tom, we must not break with tradition,' she said and reaching up, she kissed him and laughed with him.

As they strolled back towards the entertainment spot, the sound of loud organ music spread over the gardens, heralding the beginning of the programme.

They took their seats before a covered stage, the strains of *Sweet Lass of Richmond Hill* filled the air, sung by a voluptuous, statuesque soprano.

To Nancy's delight, many other entertainers came to the stage till her head spun in amazement. Her favourites were the ballet dancers.

At last came the highlight of the evening: Madame Saqui, the tightrope walker.

Dressed in a Columbine costume, with feathers in her hair, her legs encased in white tights, she stood before the audience, scanning them with a majestic sweep of her head.

Captivated, they watched her ride a white pony to a mast set at the end of one of the walkways. Madame

Saqui slipped from the pony to sit on a trapeze. Two men raised her to the top of the high mast with a hoist. At the top, she alighted on to a platform, to which the tightrope was attached. The audience gasped, as she took her place on the rope.

With graceful movements of her arms, she started to move slowly along the tightrope, elegantly placing one foot before the other. The audience gasped and shrieked as she stood on one leg, the other she stretched slowly to the side. The noise of the audience grew louder when she began moving more quickly down the rope. Most spectacular of all, fireworks began exploding around her as she descended faster and faster.

Transfixed, Nancy furiously clapped her hands in excitement, oohing and aahing with the rest of the crowd.

Madame Saqui concluded her descent by jumping off the rope. Poised and smiling, she raised an arm in the air and bowed several times to her adoring, roaring audience.

Nancy, breathless with excitement, turned to Tom.

'Wasn't that magnificent, Tom? Have you ever seen anything like it?'

'Well, yes, I have, but not so spectacularly done,' Tom teased, making light of the woman's breath-taking feat.

'Sailors move about in the rigging of a ship all the time. But there are no fireworks unless you count the occasional boom of a ship's gun.'

'Oh, you, Tom Johnson,' Nancy said, playfully hitting his arm.

Although some of the crowd stayed behind, many, like Tom and Nancy, had come only for supper and for the entertainment. They went to their box to retrieve her cloak and his great coat. The waiter stood outside holding them and helped them put them on.

Tom took the man to one side and spoke quietly to him, putting something in his hand.

'Come, Nancy,' he said and led her away from the path the rest of the crowd took.

They emerged just beside the gates where their coach awaited them.

A footman handed them into the coach, which took off swiftly to escape the inevitable rush.

'How did you manage that, Tom?' Nancy asked.

'I bribed the waiter,' Tom replied with a mischievous grin.

They arrived back at The George after ten o'clock.

'I must find Betty and tell her all about it,' Nancy said, making to go to the taproom.

Tom caught her arm.

'You can tell her tomorrow, Nancy. I want you with me now,' Tom said, his eyes dark, his voice gruff.

Nancy's body tingled with anticipation. She looked up at Tom's face and swallowed.

'Do you, Tom? Well, come with me,' she said, taking his hand and leading him towards the patron's rooms.

'Where are you taking me, Nancy?'

'Ah, it is my turn to surprise *you*, Tom,' she said as she took a key from her reticule to open the door.

The room was the best in the inn. Nancy had booked it when she knew this would be her last night with Tom.

The furniture and décor of the room matched the blue parlour, from the curtains and carpet to the light blue painted walls. A huge bed stood in the middle. The heavy curtains at the window were partly open. Cool moonlight crept through them to bath the room in faint light, vying with the flickering yellow flames of the fire in the grate.

Nancy, standing before the fire, smiled at Tom. She seemed to glow.

He moved towards her, savouring her beauty. Turning her around, he undid the laces at the back of her gown, then tugged at the sleeves until he freed her from them. The stiff taffeta swished as the gown fell to the floor. Next, Tom removed the pins from her hair. It flowed around her in a cascade of shining darkness. Nancy stood still as Tom removed her underwear until she stood naked before him. Tom stepped back from her, gazing on her loveliness.

'Damn me, Nancy, but you are a splendid woman,' he murmured.

Tom picked her up in his arms and carried her to the bed, laying her down gently. He lit the candle on the nightstand then swiftly removed his own clothes before he joined her.

'When we make love in my room, Tom, we do very well in the dark. Why did you light the candle?' Nancy asked.

'Tonight, my Nancy, I want to make memories to take away with me. I want to savour every moment, every smile, every touch, every caress,' he replied, running his hands over her curves.

They had made love many times over the past weeks as their relationship grew. Tonight was the culmination, the crescendo to their long symphony of sensation. They moved as one, knowing each other's bodies as intimately as their own. Knowing how to deliver pleasure and ecstasy, they rode together on a tide of loving sensuousness, rising slowly till the climax came, landing them together on the shores of satiation.

They breathed deep, shuddering breaths, looking into each other's eyes, both trying not to think of their parting. Tom turned over on his back and gathered Nancy to him.

Beneath the covers they slept, soft and warm in each other's arms.

Tom woke in near darkness. The moon had set. The candle had gone out. The faint, red glow of the dying embers in the fireplace the only light.

Tom slid from the bed. He lit a candle on the mantel shelf. Searching the floor for his waistcoat, he found it and pulled his watch from the pocket. It was three thirty.

Wondering whether Nancy had the presence of mind to bring his clothes from her room, he opened the armoire to find them neatly placed within.

'Good girl,' he said under his breath when he saw the box, filled with his maps and charts, on the floor of the armoire.

He found the washstand and hastily dipped a sponge in the basin, covered it with soap and scrubbed his body with it. Then he quickly dressed in his warm, serviceable clothes. Picking up his evening wear, he placed them over a chair then he turned to look at Nancy.

'Time to say goodbye,' he mumbled to himself as he went to her.

'Nancy-love,' he said, stroking her cheek.

Nancy moaned and turned over.

Tom shook her shoulder. She opened her eyes and turned towards him.

'Tom,' she murmured and stretched an arm in his direction.

'Nancy-love, it's time for me to go.'

Nancy had dreaded this moment for days. She didn't want to make it difficult for him.

'Kiss me, then, Tom,' she said holding her arms open to him.

He leant forward and held her close. They didn't rush the long slow kiss that must last them for months.

Rising from the bed, 'I'll be back before you know it, my Nancy,' Tom said.

Picking up his box, without looking at her, he left.

Outside the room, he swallowed hard.

Inside the room, Nancy buried her face in the pillow and sobbed.

After leaving Nancy, Tom made his way to the stables, saddled the black stallion and rode along Borough High Street. Once more he crossed London Bridge on his way to Blackwall Reach.

The time was four-thirty when Tom arrived at his destination. He dismounted and knocked at the door. While he waited, he wondered who owned the grand coach, which stood in the yard at the front of the dry dock.

Peter opened the door. He smiled when he saw Tom and flung it wide for him to enter.

'The lads are all out by the river. We launched *Nautilus* an hour ago. She's ready to sail. Come, Tom. There is someone here you will be pleased to see.'

Tom led the horse into the building, unstrapped his box from his saddle and followed Peter through the empty dry dock to the mooring where his little ship stood at anchor. The lads were in a bunch, laughing and talking, pleased with their work.

'Here's Tom,' someone called as he approached the group.

The men parted to reveal Ned standing in their midst.

'Ned! What do you here?' Tom exclaimed as he walked forward to shake Ned's hand.

'I came to deliver your luggage, Tom, and to meet with my old shipmates again,' Ned replied with a satisfied grin.

'So, it is your coach that stands outside,' Tom said.

'Yes. Devilish early hour, though. But I wanted to wish you bon voyage.'

Peter took Tom's box from him.

'I've stowed your gear on *Nautilus*, Tom. I'll put this with it. I think we're about ready to cast off now,' he said.

'Right, Peter. You and Pedro get aboard,' Tom said before turning to Ned.

'Well, then, Ned. I appreciate your coming all this

way. I shall say au revoir, and see you in five months or so.'

'I look forward to it, Tom. And to meeting your fiancée,' Ned replied. He clapped Tom on the back and shook his hand.

Tom nodded and was about to follow Peter, and Pedro onto *Nautilus* when he remembered the horse. He caught sight of Jake and put a hand on his shoulder.

'Jake, lad, will you do something for me? Will you take my horse back to The George?'

'Right y'are Tom,' Jake said with a huge grin.

'Thanks,' Tom said and followed Peter up the gangplank

Pedro went below to manage the steam engine. Tom gave Ned and the rest of the lads on shore a final wave before he went below. Tom intended to stay out of sight while the little "steamboat" moved along the river.

After all his preparation, he didn't want to chance recognition if he stood on the deck of *Nautilus* while sailing in the Thames. He would wait until they were well out into the Thames estuary before venturing on deck.

Below deck, there was nothing for Tom to do, as the other two men had the voyage under control. Tom looked about for somewhere to sleep. He noticed his box fixed on a shelf above his head. Going to the cabin next to the boiler room, he saw four hammocks stowed in a net He fished out one of these and suspended it from hooks in the wall provided for that purpose.

He slung himself into it and lay with his hands behind his head. He thought about meeting the Frenchmen again. He thought about sailing along the channel taking care to avoid notice as they passed the Naval base at Portsmouth.

It was while he thought of Nancy that a feeling of contentment stole over him, and he drifted off to sleep.

CHAPTER TWENTY

Tom felt a hand shaking his shoulder.

Peter's voice penetrated Tom's foggy mind.

'Tom, come on lad. Wake up.'

'Uh. What?' Tom mumbled as his consciousness rose from the depths of a deep sleep.

Peter's grip on him prevented his falling from the hammock as he tried to sit up.

'Peter?'

Tom yawned, squinting as he looked about. He blinked a few times and yawned again.

'Ah, good Lord, I'm on *Nautilus.* Where are we?' Tom said, rubbing his eyes.

Peter chuckled.

'Well, now, let me see. We passed Whitstable all right. A couple of ships sailed by. Didn't take much notice of us. I felt like putting in at Herne Bay; I knew a girl there once, or was that Reculver? Anyway, we passed both of those and Westgate.'

Tom scratched his head. He frowned as he listened to Peter.

'Thank you for the details, Peter. Where are we now?'

'Heading towards Margate,' Peter replied.

Fully awake, Tom calculated the time.

'Good God, man, I've been asleep for hours. Why didn't you wake me?' he said as he swung his legs over the edge of the hammock.

Peter surmised Tom had spent the night with his woman. He smiled.

'I reckoned you needed the sleep.'

Inwardly, Tom smiled, too, as he thought of Nancy.

'You're probably right. I didn't get much sleep last night.'

Tom slid out of the hammock and began to search for his boots.

'How is she handling?' he asked.

Peter found the boots under the hammock. He pulled them out and handed them to Tom.

'She's handling well, and she's fast. Don't know what she'll be like under sail – or underwater for that matter,' Peter said.

Tom took his boots from Peter.

'Thanks,' he said and pulled them on.

'I'm starving, Peter. Is there any food?'

'Just bread and cold mutton, or cheese. And there's small beer to drink.'

The two men made their way to the main cabin where a little table and two seats folded down from the wall. Another chair stood by a stack of chests holding supplies. Peter went to one of the chests and took out the food wrapped in a napkin. He handed it to Tom with a square wooden plate and a knife.

'Don't eat it all. We have to make it last till we meet up with *La Miséricord.*'

Tom carved meat from the joint. He cut two slices of bread and placed the mutton between them while Peter poured the small beer into a conical pewter mug.

When he had finished eating, Tom made his way up on deck.

The day was overcast with a grey mist hovering away to the east.

'Looks like rain,' Tom observed.

'Wind's south-easterly. We might miss it,' Peter replied.

Nautilus passed Margate. She rounded the headland and kept well away from the land as she passed Broadstairs, Sandwich Bay and Deal, heading for the Straights of Dover where she would rendezvous with *La Miséricord.*

Only half of the forty sailors on *La Miséricord* were French. The rest were South American, mostly from Argentina. From time to time, one or other of them glanced astern, trying to catch a glimpse of the little craft they awaited.

Corbeau's navigator, Yves Gosselin, kept his eye on the map Tom had supplied detailing the sandbars around the Straights of Dover. He identified the rendezvous point and told *La Miséricorde's* Captain, Isaac Joubert, he should drop anchor.

Corbeau stood on the bridge next to Joubert who held a telescope to his eye, scouring the skyline for a sight of *Nautilus.*

'I see something, Monsieur,' he said, lowering the telescope.

'Is it *Nautilus*?' Corbeau asked.

'Perhaps. It's hard to tell. It has no sails, so it could be,' Joubert replied.

Raising the telescope again, he watched the small craft as it neared.

'She is moving fast. The craft is steam-driven you say? The size of a small yacht?'

'That is how it was described to me,' Corbeau replied.

'I cannot be sure, but I think the craft I see could be *Nautilus.* If it is, she has made good time.'

As soon as *Nautilus* pulled alongside *La Miséricord,* they threw a line down and drew a cable across. The crew made the two vessels fast together. When all was secure, a sailor let down a rope ladder which Tom and Peter expertly climbed. Two crewmen helped them over the bulwarks. Pedro stayed on Nautilus.

Standing on the deck of the French ship, Tom looked around. What he saw was a well-appointed, clean vessel. The crew went about their business with quiet efficiency—a good sign in Tom's opinion.

'*Bienvenue á bord*, Monsieur Johnson,' Corbeau said as he came towards Tom with his hand outstretched.

'Thank you, Monsieur,' Tom said, shaking

Corbeau's hand. 'May I introduce to you Mr Peter Marriot? He is responsible for the maps and charts of St Helena and the Atlantic. Peter, this is Monsieur Corbeau, the man who has commissioned us to rescue the Général.'

'Your servant, Sir,' Peter said with a bow.

Corbeau returned the bow and turned to Tom.

'I would not have recognised that little yacht as a submersible vessel. I deduce you have disguised her?'

'Indeed, Monsieur Corbeau. My lads did a good job.'

Thinking Corbeau was not looking his robust self, Tom added,

'Is all well with you, Sir?'

'Thank you, yes,' Corbeau replied with an uncharacteristic sweet smile.

'Will you come to my cabin and take refreshment with me? I wish to verify our position and our route.'

'I'm pleased to leave the deck, Corbeau. Although we are out a good way from land, still I fear being recognised by someone on a passing ship. It would put our whole venture in jeopardy.'

'*Tellement*. Follow me Messieurs,' Corbeau said and led the way below.

Tom was surprised to find Corbeau had a cabin to himself, knowing that only people of great importance warranted the privilege.

Admittedly, it is not spacious, but neither is it cramped, Tom reflected.

The cabin was long but not wide. The bunk took up the wall at one end. A narrow table ran down the middle with three chairs on either side. Against the outer wall, under a porthole, stood a line of chests.

'Pray, be seated, Messieurs,' Corbeau said.

He produced a decanter of brandy, and three glasses from a cupboard under his bunk, followed by a map of the English Channel, or as he called it, *La Manche.*

Corbeau poured the brandy into two glasses. He

passed them to Peter and Tom. Tom noticed, as Corbeau poured his own drink, he gave himself an overly generous measure.

'We are here, are we not, Mr Johnson?' Corbeau asked, taking a gulp of his brandy before placing his finger on a spot on the map.

'Yes, Corbeau. Given that the navigator keeps to the route I advised, we should have no trouble,' Tom replied.

Ever since Tom had sighted *La Miséricorde,* something had troubled him. He decided to voice his concern.

'I see you are flying the Prussian flag. I hope we are not hailed.'

Corbeau finished what was in his glass and poured himself more brandy.

'I thought it better than sailing under a French flag. Although we are no longer at war, suspicion of the French still runs high in England.'

'You should not sail under false colours, Monsieur. It is the mark of a pirate. However, you are right; they are less likely to stop you this way. Once we leave British waters, I recommend you run up the French Ensign,' Tom suggested. 'Now, we must be careful when sailing near Portsmouth. It is a large Naval base. There will be British ships about. We must stay far out in the channel to avoid them. Again, I charted a route so we should have no trouble,' Tom said.

A knock sounded at the door.

Corbeau rose from his seat and moved with a dignified step to open it.

'Ah, Adrien, my boy, join us. Mr Johnson, you know. This other Gentleman is Mr Peter Marriot.'

Babineaux, with his usual impeccable politeness, bowed elegantly to Tom and Peter.

'Welcome Mr Johnson; your servant Mr Marriot,' he said, taking a seat next to Tom.

Corbeau took another glass from the cupboard and

slid it in Babineaux's direction. Before passing the decanter to him, he poured more brandy into his own glass.

'Thank you, Paul,' Babineaux said and turned to Tom.

'I was looking at your *Nautilus,* Mr Johnson. How will you submerge her? She resembles *Eagle* not at all,' he remarked, as he poured brandy for himself.

Tom grinned. 'She is covered in wooden cladding,' Tom explained before turning to Corbeau.

'Which reminds me, Corbeau, when we remove it, may I store it on your ship? There is not room on *Nautilus.*'

'Of course,' Corbeau said, raising his glass before taking another swallow.

'I hate to impose, Monsieur, but may I store my baggage, too?' Tom asked.

'Yes, you may, Mr Johnson. Mr Marriot, you may do the same,' Corbeau said, smiling at Peter.

He's far more genial than he used to be, Tom mused, looking thoughtfully at Corbeau.

'What about the other man?' Corbeau asked.

'Someone must stay on *Nautilus* to make sure all is well. Peter, or I, will relieve him every four hours, and we will take it in turn to sleep there. I hope that meets with your approval, Corbeau,' Tom said.

'Of course, Mr Johnson. And all three of you must take your meals on *La Miséricord,*' Corbeau said.

'Thank you, Sir. You are kind to suggest it,' Tom said, wondering what had happened to Corbeau to make him so amicable.

'I take it you must stay permanently on *Nautilus* once we reach St Helena,' Babineaux said. 'Will the other gentlemen stay with you, Monsieur?'

'Only Pedro. Peter will act as an envoy from the Naval Office. We thought he might smooth the way for you when you disembark.'

'Ah, Mr Johnson, we will have at least eight weeks

to hone our plans, Come Monsieur, I am sure you are hungry. Let us all partake of dinner,' Corbeau suggested.

'Gladly, Corbeau. And I may reacquaint myself with Count Mollien,' Tom said, mischief gleaming in his eye.

Babineaux stifled a chuckle and gave Tom a sidelong look.

Tom could not resist commenting on Corbeau's genial mood.

While Corbeau pored over the map with Peter, Tom spoke to Babineaux in a low voice.

'What has come over your cousin, Babineaux? What a contrast to the man whom I came to know.'

'But, Mr Johnson, the answer is simple. My cousin is suffering from *mal de mere*. He has discovered that brandy steadies him. Alcohol always puts him in a good mood. *Et voila*! You receive a sociable welcome,' Babineaux whispered and stifled another chuckle.

On their way to the great cabin, where they were to dine, Peter turned to Tom.

'I did not look forward to living with the Frenchmen for eight weeks together, on a cramped ship, Tom. You didn't paint too rosy a picture of the men with whom we are in association. Now, having met them, I find my misgivings dissipating. Corbeau and Babineaux seem to be pleasant company.'

'Oh, Babineaux has always been so,' Tom replied. 'He is a gracious and astute young man. Corbeau, I am told, is drunk.'

'Oh,' Peter murmured.

'But you haven't met Count Mollien yet,' Tom said. 'I doubt very much if any amount of booze could change his overbearing attitude.'

The day was drawing to a close as they passed Portsmouth. No British ships came near them, and by morning, they had passed Plymouth, too.

The following morning, much to Tom's relief, when they judged themselves outside British waters, they lowered the Prussian Ensign to replace it with that of the French.

At last, they were truly on their way.

CHAPTER TWENTY ONE

La Miséricorde made good headway as she sailed south on the Atlantic Ocean.

Up early every morning, Tom took a walk around the deck of *La Miséricord,* stopping to lean on the bulwark and view the dawn. Tom liked to watch the sun rise over the sea. He could tell what the day would be like by the colour of the sky, the shape of the clouds and the direction of the wind.

Not being part of the crew, Tom had little to do. He found it hard to fill his day. He would have spent time with Peter Marriot. But Peter was busy forging sets of documents to present to the authorities on St Helena.

Much of his time Tom spent reading or conversing over meals. He devoted several hours each afternoon teaching Laroche English—for although Napoleon's English was not great, he could converse in it. Laroche had no English at all. Suspicions would arise when "Napoleon" lost all knowledge of the language. So, Tom had stepped into the breach.

Laroche spoke French with a Corsican accent (as did Napoleon). Laroche also spoke Italian and his native Corsu. Knowing several languages gave him a good ear. He was a quick study, and Tom took pleasure in teaching him.

'He is an intelligent man. We are fortunate that your cousin, Henri, found him,' Tom remarked to Babineaux.

Sharing a cabin with Babineaux, he and Tom had become good friends. More familiarity with Corbeau and Mollien gave Tom understanding. He became more tolerant of them, bearing their company with ease and empathy.

Tom had spent a great deal of his time thinking about their plans. On the surface, the schemes were good. The more Tom pondered on them, however, the more holes he could see that needed addressing. In their cabin one evening, Tom brought the subject up with Babineaux.

'I have been thinking about our arrival on St Helena, Babineaux,' Tom said, 'and there are several things that need reviewing.'

Babineaux looked up from the book he was reading.

Tom continued.

'The first is a small point. I think it best if Renoudin does not accompany the party visiting the Général. The fewer people there, the better.'

'I, too, have been thinking about that, Tom. Renoudin himself is nervous about leaving the ship, let alone accompanying us. I will speak to Paul on the matter. You said your first point. What else have you thought of?' Babineaux said.

'Several things. The next concerns the time after you and the Général leave Geranium Valley. You must get away as soon as possible, agreed?' Tom said.

'Of course,' Babineaux said.

'At the same time, Mollien and Corbeau will return to Longwood house with Laroche dressed as Napoleon.'

'Yes. We discussed that,' Babineaux said, wondering why they were going over old ground.

'There is a problem. Five leave. Three return,' Tom said.

Babineaux gasped when he understood what Tom meant.

'Ah yes, of course! I shall not return with them and neither will Laroche. They must account for our absence. How did we not see this before?'

'It is a common mistake. When People become wrapped up in the main idea, attention to detail is lost. I think the only way to account for your absence is to say you and Laroche returned to the ship.'

'Yes. But, why would we?' Babineaux rubbed his chin as he thought. An idea struck him. He snapped his fingers and pointed. 'Perhaps we could say I had an accident!'

'Yes. That would work. Again, you need more detail. I could make suggestions. However, it is better if you and Corbeau discuss this as it is you who will act it out. Just remember, it is important that you are ready to adapt your strategy. Nothing is ever how we think it will be. You must plan for a multitude of scenarios.'

'You are right, Tom. Thank you for your advice,' Babineaux said.

'There is something else.'

Babineaux lifted his chin.

'Laroche does not know the servants or any of the staff at Longwood. Neither does he know the layout of the house or the land. To quell any suspicion, you must account for Laroche's loss of memory.'

'Hmm, yet another obvious difficulty we did not think about. How do you manage to see all angles as you do, Tom?'

'Practice, Adrien,' Tom said, grinning.

Babineaux gave an amused grunt and knit his brows in thought. He nodded slowly as an idea formed in his mind.

'Ah, I have it. "Napoleon" must have a seizure or a fall where he hits his head. He must then say he has lost his memory. It is a crude ploy, I know. But unless we can think of something better, we must use it.'

'Well thought, my friend,' Tom said and put on his coat to go on deck.

The following morning Babineaux went to Corbeau's cabin. He told him of his conversation with Tom.

'Tom is right, Adrien. We have made broad plans and now need to look at the details.

Over the next week, they went over everything together. Finally, they were content that they had all situations covered.

Sometime later, Tom and Adrien were in the salon

of *La Miséricorde* going over their plans as they pored over maps and charts. The two men were now on first name terms.

The escape plan involved moving north from Longwood house (Napoleon's residence). Babineaux and Napoleon would traverse the rocky terrain to the top of the cliff. From there Babineaux would lower Napoleon over the cliff in a boatswain's chair. Indignity aside, at a time before the escape, it would require someone, probably Tom, to climb to the top of the cliff with a rope and spikes. He would then hammer the spikes into the rock and assemble the tackle with which to lower the Général.

'I think it is a cumbersome idea. Far too much could go wrong, not to mention dragging Bonaparte over exceedingly rough terrain. Surely, we can think of something more elegant, Adrien?' Tom said.

Babineaux frowned. Not taking in what Tom said, he returned his gaze to the northern part of the map.

Tom's eyes followed the path Babineaux's finger traced. He shook his head.

'You know I am in favour of hiding in plain sight. It has always worked for me in the past.'

'Hmm?' Babineaux murmured.

Tom studied the map, concentration drawing his brows together.

'Perhaps overland might be a better plan,' Tom said.

Leaning over Babineaux's shoulder, he stabbed at a place on the map to the south of the island.

'Look. What is this place?'

Babineaux moved his finger from north to south.

'That is Sandy Bay. There are manned fortifications along that stretch of the coast. It would not be safe.'

Tom grinned mischievously.

'I wager it would. Look. Here are the fortifications. Over here to the west of them, there is a horse-shoe shaped beach and beyond that, multiple coves. The soldiery would be hard put to keep constant guard on them all. This large one, for example, look how the cliff dips down. Why, it could have been carved purposely as a safe harbour for *Nautilus*. She could not be seen from the fortifications.'

'Well, Tom, you have been a smuggler. You must know more about concealing tactics than I do. It sounds risky. Yet it might work.'

Tom put a hand on Babineaux's shoulder.

'Listen, Adrien. The walk from Longwood to Sandy Bay, depending on how fast one walks, will take, at most, four hours. I am of a mind that Napoleon would far prefer a long walk to clambering over rocks and dangling precariously over the edge of a cliff,' Tom said.

Another thought came to his mind.

'Before leaving Longwood, the General will swap clothes with Laroche. He will also wear Laroche's beard and wig. Although this aide—Atherton was it you said?'

Babineaux nodded.

'Although an astute man, he will not see Laroche and Napoleon together so cannot compare them. With that in mind, I doubt whether anyone you met along the way to Sandy Bay would look twice at Napoleon.'

'Hmm,' Babineaux said, 'He would be hiding in plain sight, which you constantly advocate, Tom. And you think I should accompany him to show him the way to Sandy Bay and to your vessel?'

'Yes, Adrien!' Tom said, pleased Babineaux began seeing eye to eye with him.

When they told the rest of the party of the plan, there was much objection.

'What if the Général *is* recognised? We would all be under suspicion. They might even execute us,' Mollien objected.

'Babineaux and the Général will dress simply. They will look like servants or farmers. Why would the guard take notice of such people?' Tom said.

Another idea came to Tom.

'Something else, if we can find out when the guard changes at Longwood, Babineaux and Napoleon could pass them at such time, when their concentration is lax.'

Corbeau nodded, seeing the sense in it.

'How will Adrien know where to take the Général?' Mollien asked.

'Adrien will follow the map. Pedro and I will keep a constant lookout. I will meet them and guide them to *Nautilus*,' Tom said, keeping a rein on his rising irritation.

'You will be seen,' Mollien objected.

'Yes, probably. However, if we act as if we are comrades meeting and stopping to converse, if we act naturally, all will be well,' Tom said.

'How can you know that?' Mollien challenged.

Peter raised a finger. 'May I speak?' he asked.

'What is it you wish to say, Mr Marriot?' Corbeau asked.

'Just this,' Peter said. 'I have known Tom for over fifteen years. Of his many enterprises, I will name but a few. He has organised smuggling expeditions, prison breaks and one or two abductions. I have never known a strategy of his to fail. I think his plan is far less dangerous than the original proposed.'

Mollien and Corbeau looked at each other.

'There is something else, Messieurs,' Tom said.

'And what is that,' Mollien asked, hauteur in every pore.

'The routine on St Helena is tedious. Although there have been rumours of escape bids, nothing has ever been attempted. The soldiers are bored. Boredom breeds laxity.'

Tom paused to let his words sink in.

'The British soldiers will not be watchful. Why would they suspect anything untoward when Napoleon will be, in effect, safe at Longwood?'

Corbeau needed no more persuasion. He nodded.

And so it was that the original plan was turned upside down.

CHAPTER TWENTY TWO

La Miséricorde with *Nautilus* tethered abaft, sat still in the water, waiting for the first light of dawn. The navigator had calculated the position of St Helena. But on a moonless night, the chance of attaining their mark was slim. They might arrive on a rocky coast, or overshoot their landing altogether. Correcting such mistakes was not an option. They could not afford to lose time or gain notice.

La Miséricorde's ultimate destination was the port of Jamestown, in the north of the island. Before arriving there, the plan was to deposit *Nautilus* at Sandy Bay, to the south of the island and almost the only place where the land did not meet the sea in a vertical cliff.

At the first appearance of the rising sun creeping over the horizon, they saw the dark silhouette of St Helena to the west.

La Miséricorde skirted the island, on the eastern side, far from the land so as not to be seen. They arrived in Sandy Bay just as the light began seeping into the grey clouds, tinting them with the colours of dawn.

Tom appeared on deck wearing a warm, old-fashioned frock coat over a woollen waistcoat and coarse homespun shirt, a black neckcloth tied at his throat. Knee breeches, high boots, and a tricorn hat completed the ensemble. No one would have taken a second glance at him.

Mollien and Corbeau watched as Tom prepared to climb down to *Nautilus.*

Babineaux smiled as he shook Tom's hand.

'I will see you and the Général here in Sandy Bay in a day or two, Tom,' he said.

'You will, Adrien,' Tom said and laughing turned to Peter.

'Ha! It's like old times, Peter.'

Peter took Tom's arm.

'Good luck to you, Lad,' he said and patted his back.

'Thanks,' Tom said.

The cladding had long been removed from the sides of *Nautilus* and was now stored on *La Miséricorde.* Pedro had previously boarded *Nautilus* to make checks to be sure she was ready for the journey.

Tom swung his leg over the bulwark and climbed down a rope ladder from *La Miséricorde* onto the deck of the *Nautilus*, where Pedro stood waiting for him and greeted Tom with a grin.

They released the tethers, which tied *Nautilus* to the French ship.

Pedro, followed by Tom, immediately went below to prepare the submarine to sink beneath the waves.

Mollien and Corbeau moved to the bulwark.

Everyone on *La Miséricorde* stood to look over the bulwark, waiting in the gathering light for *Nautilus* to submerge.

Several minutes passed.

'Look, she's sinking!' Corbeau cried.

Inch by inch they watched the water rise up the sides of the little vessel.

'I did not think it would take so long,' Corbeau remarked.

'She takes on water at a slow rate so that it is evenly dispersed within her tanks,' Peter explained.

At last, only the periscope was visible. It moved forward towards Sandy Bay and soon was lost to sight.

The crew returned to their duties.

Corbeau and Mollien went below with the incredulous Laroche.

Adrien and Peter stayed gazing at the spot where *Nautilus* had disappeared.

'No turning back now, Babineaux,' Peter said.

From Sandy Bay, *La Miséricorde* sailed west, then sailed northwards far enough such that she appeared to be arriving at Jamestown from the north. Those on land, seeing her approach from there would never suspect she had been at Sandy Bay.

Their arrival at the port, sailing under the French Ensign, put the platoon, on guard duty that morning, in some confusion. They had no foreknowledge of a French ship arriving. Usually, a foreign vessel would send word well in advance of their plan to put in at St Helena.

In his excitement at the possibilities of battle, Sergeant Morgan burst into Captain Stapleton's office. Suddenly aware he had forgotten to knock, Morgan, his face red, stood to attention and saluted.

'Captain, there's an unknown French craft approaching.'

Captain Stapleton looked up from his four-month-old *Times* newspaper.

'Is she flying the French Ensign?'

'Yes, Sir. What shall we do, Sir?'

'Allow her to dock, Morgan, but keep the platoon at the ready. Request Lieutenant Northover to stand by to ride to Plantation House in case hostilities ensue.'

Stapleton rose from his seat, adjusted his neckcloth, and straightened his jacket. As he came around his desk, Morgan opened the door for him.

Stapleton walked the short distance to the quay and watched *La Miséricorde*. Having sailed into the harbour, she proceeded to dock.

Once dockers had erected a gangplank, Peter Marriot stood at the top. Dignified, he wore a sober suit of dark grey, a white neckcloth at his throat, a tricorn hat in his hand. He surveyed the platoon below. Catching sight of an officer, he descended.

'You must be Captain Stapleton,' he said with a pleasant smile. 'May I introduce myself? I am Sir Peter Marriot, sent to accompany Count Mollien, Colonel

Corbeau, and Capitaine Babineaux. They wish to visit Napoleon Bonaparte. I have in my possession the necessary papers to verify their cordial intent.'

Before leaving England, Peter had sought out his many contacts. He asked them to provide him with the proper legal wording for a person visiting St Helena, wishing an audience with the ex-Emperor. Peter also requested they supply him with the correct paper so that his forgeries would look authentic.

'Greetings, Sir Peter. I am sorry to say we were not expecting you,' Captain Stapleton said, regarding Peter with a frown.

Peter's eyes opened wide.

'Ah, Captain Stapleton, that is not possible. Some months ago, I myself watched Admiral Wainwright sign letters informing you of our proposed visit. I would have thought they would be with you by now. How vexatious.'

Stapleton said nothing. He heard Sergeant Morgan clear his throat. Stapleton knew Morgan was itching to take Marriot into charge along with the two gentlemen (Mollien and Corbeau) standing at the top of the gangplank, and anyone else who attempted to land. Stapleton gave Morgan a hard look, shook his head, and turned his gaze back to Peter.

Peter put a hand to his face and rubbed his jaw.

'Perhaps you could take a look at our papers, Sir? I am sure you will find them in perfect order.'

Adrien Babineaux appeared at the top of the gangplank. He paused to survey the sights below before descending at a leisurely pace.

Morgan stiffened at sight of him.

Stapleton's dark expression lifted.

Babineaux provided Stapleton with his most charming smile.

'Good morning, Captain. We meet again. How is your wife?' he asked.

'She is well, Monsieur Babineaux. Thank you for

your enquiry,' Stapleton replied with a slight bow.

'I am gratified to hear it,' Babineaux said, pausing to look from Peter to Stapleton.

'Is there a problem?'

'There seems to be, Monsieur Babineaux. We have not received prior notice of your arrival.'

'*Quelle domage,* Captain. But surely our papers will tell you we mean no harm. We simply wish to visit the Général, just as I did a few months ago,' Babineaux said, turning to Peter.

'Sir Peter, I believe you have our papers in your possession. Maybe you should give them to Captain Stapleton.'

Stapleton took in a sharp breath and shook his head.

'I am sorry, Monsieur Babineaux. In the circumstances, with or without papers, I do not have the authority to allow you to disembark. We must put the matter before The Governor, Sir Hudson Lowe, for his approval. My hands are tied,' Stapleton said.

Morgan, unable to contain his hostility towards the French any longer, stepped forward.

'Shall I put them under arrest, Captain,' he growled.

Stapleton let out an impatient breath.

'No, Morgan, you will not. Where is Lieutenant Northover?'

'When you saw the ship, Sir, you instructed me to ask him to hold himself in readiness in case you needed him to ride to Plantation house and …'

Stapleton broke in on him.

'Just so. Have him come here, Morgan.'

Morgan looked around and seeing Private Scrope standing behind the Captain, beckoned to him.

'Go and tell Lieutenant Northover he's wanted on the dock,' he said.

Scrope saluted, turned on his heel, and marched away.

Reaching into his inner pocket, Peter retrieved the papers.

'Should I give you these now, Captain?' Peter said, holding up the papers verifying those wishing to visit Napoleon.

With the proper wording and the paper supplied by his friends, Peter spent much time on the voyage producing papers which were, if possible, even more authentic looking than originals.

He handed them to Stapleton.

Morgan's face fell. Seeing the—forged—Foreign Office red wax seals, complete with traditional red tape, he believed they were genuine.

Lieutenant Northover arrived. Youthful, with coltish long legs and a restless gait, his fine, straight, shoulder-length blond hair blew about him in the breeze. His blue eyes took on an eager shine as he contemplated the possibility of interesting affairs alleviating the boredom of his mundane posting.

'You sent for me, Captain?' he said, coming to a halt, and saluting before Stapleton.

'Yes, Northover. Take these to Plantation House,' Stapleton said, handing the sealed papers to him. 'Explain that an unexpected French ship has docked. The passengers wish to visit Bonaparte and have supplied these papers from London validating their permission to do so.'

Northover nodded and clicked his heels. He took the papers from Stapleton and put them in a pouch which hung by his side from his belt.

'Very good, Captain. My horse is saddled and ready. I will go at once.'

Northover strode off in the direction of the stables.

'Well, Captain Stapleton. What are we to do now?' Babineaux asked.

'I am sorry to say, Monsieur, you must stay on your ship until we have word from Plantation House.'

Peter had warned Mollien, Corbeau and Babineaux that this might happen. He had told them under no circumstances were they to object to their treatment but simply do as they were told.

'You will inform us when this matter is resolved, Captain?' Peter asked.

'Of course, Sir Peter. Meanwhile, I must place a guard on your ship. A mere formality, you understand,' Stapleton said.

'I understand perfectly, Captain. We shall await the decision with patience. Everything must be above board when dealing with your prisoner. I hear there have been several plots to perform his escape. Naturally, I would not lend myself to such a scheme. However, it is necessary for you to be vigilant and trust no one.'

Peter bowed and returned to the ship followed by Babineaux. When they were safely on board, the dockers removed the gangplank.

Sir Hudson Low had taken his time in reading the papers. Meanwhile, Northover took himself off to the kitchen where he begged the cook for a bite to eat.

'With all this pother going on, Mrs Borden, I didn't eat any breakfast,' he said, giving her a doleful look.

She had met Everard Northover when he first arrived on St Helena. Not knowing his way about, and looking for the entrance to the house, Everard had stumbled into the kitchen courtyard. He became entangled in the washing. Much of it had fallen to the ground. The noise of the laundress berating him had caught Mrs Borden's attention.

Seeing the gangly lad trying to extricate himself from his embarrassing situation, she had taken pity on him. Drawing him into her kitchen and seeing how young and awkward he was, she had taken him under her wing.

'If you're not too grand to sit in my kitchen, Lieutenant, I'll dish you up some chicken pie and fresh vegetables,' she said fetching a plate and filling it with a sizable portion.

'You know I am never too grand for your kitchen, Ma'am. Thank you,' he said tucking into the meal with gusto.

As the bottom of his plate began to show, Mrs Borden delivered another helping to the lieutenant. Mouth full, he could utter no more than a mumble of gratitude and smile his thanks at her.

Just as he had scooped up the last spoonful, he heard his name shouted from the hallway.

Northover rose from his seat in such a state of confusion, he knocked over his chair. He hastily righted it and gave Mrs Borden a smile and a thank you. Wiping his mouth with his handkerchief he dashed out of the kitchen, and followed the direction of the voice.

'Ah, there you are, Northover. Where have you been?' Sir Gordon Atherton asked.

'Nowhere in particular, Sir. I was waiting for Sir Hudson to finish with the papers I delivered to him.'

'Come along then, man. He has given them back to me. Where is your horse?'

'In the stables, Sir,'

'Then hurry up and get it. I will wait for you at the front of the house.'

When Atherton learnt of an unexpected French ship arriving at the port, he bristled with suspicion. Having seen their papers, signed and sealed by a person in London who was known to him, he had lost interest and reverted to his usual indifference.

It was late in the afternoon when Lieutenant Northover returned to the port accompanied by the oily Sir Gordon Atherton.

They had ridden in silence. Northover too much in awe of the high and mighty aide to Sir Hudson Lowe to speak without being spoken to; Atherton too bored to bother talking to the gauche, young lieutenant.

Arriving at the dock, Atherton dismounted.

'You need not return with me, Northover,' he said, and made his way to Stapleton's office.

Without knocking Atherton entered and found the captain asleep with a newspaper over his face.

'Good afternoon, Captain Stapleton,' Atherton's voice boomed, a sarcastic smirk on his face.

Unhurried, Stapleton rustled the paper from his face and looked to see who had disturbed him.

'Ah, Sir Gordon. Good afternoon. Do you bring me word of what I am to do with the Frenchmen?'

'I do, Captain. Their papers are in impeccable order. Sir Hudson has given his permission for them to visit Bonaparte. I am to accompany them, as I did Babineaux. I shall be here tomorrow at ten o'clock. Please inform them to that effect.'

Captain Stapleton disliked Atherton's high-flown attitude. But he was in no mood to take umbrage—he rarely was—and merely smiled.

'Thank you for informing me, Sir Gordon. I shall notify the French straight away. Until tomorrow, then,' he said, rising from his seat.

Captain Stapleton went to the door. He opened it for Atherton, who, having placed the papers on the Captain's desk, left without delay.

Northover had taken his horse to the stables. He was on his way to his room in the Barracks when he saw Atherton leave. Interested in the outcome of the situation regarding the Frenchmen's visit to Napoleon, Northover went to Stapleton's office.

When the young lieutenant knocked, Stapleton was by the fire, in the act of lighting his pipe.

'Enter,' Stapleton said and was surprised when Northover came in.

'Excuse me, Sir. May I ask whether the Frenchmen will be allowed to visit Bonaparte?'

Stapleton took several puffs on his pipe to get it going before he replied.

'Yes, Northover. They may go,' he said and took his seat behind his desk.

Thinking about going to the French to give them the news, he was loth to leave his warm office and brave the chilly wind on the dock. He decided Northover could do it.

'Would you be so good as to tell the dockers to replace the gangplank? You may then deliver these papers to the French and inform them of the good news.'

Northover smiled. He was curious about the French. He had been on St Helena for five months. And although he had accompanied others to the Longwood estate, he had never come near it, so had not met any Frenchmen.

'It will be a pleasure, Sir,' he said.

'Ah, you had better warn them, they must not leave the ship until tomorrow. Place a guard at the bottom of the gangplank, if you please.'

'I will, Sir,' Northover said, overjoyed at having something interesting to do.

As he came out of Stapleton's office, he caught sight Sergeant Shenfield.

'Sergeant. The French have permission to stay. Order the dockers to replace the gangplank, and appoint two men to stand guard. None of them may disembark until tomorrow.'

'Very good, Sir,' the sergeant said.

While Northover waited to board *La Miséricorde,* he inwardly rehearsed how he would tell the French they had permission to visit Napoleon. With a jolt, he realised he knew very little French and hoped they understood English.

CHAPTER TWENTY THREE

A crewmember spread the word on board *La Miséricorde* when he saw the dockers restoring the gangplank. The brooding silence and occasional strained conversation as they waited for news, gave way and tension eased.

Northover stood by as he waited for the dockers to finish, his coattails flapping in the breeze. As soon as the gangplank was in place, Peter watched as Northover's long legs carried him to the top in quick time.

Peter greeted him warmly.

'Good afternoon, Lieutenant. I hope you bring me good news.'

'Yes, Sir,' Northover said, grinning. 'You are Sir Peter Marriot, are you not?'

'I am. And you are Lieutenant Northover,' Peter replied.

Weighing up the lieutenant's bright, unguarded countenance, Peter concluded he was a young, innocent, and very inexperienced.

'Yes, Sir. I am sent to inform you that Sir Hudson Lowe found your papers in order and gives permission for you to visit... er... Ex-Emperor, Général Napoleon Bonaparte,' he said.

Northover had inwardly debated how he should refer to Boney. He chose to use all the titles he knew and wished he had not.

Oh, Lord, he thought. *How awkward that sounded.*

Having taken a great deal of care in creating the papers, Peter knew they would pass muster. He smiled.

'That is indeed good news, Lieutenant,' Peter said, shaking Northover's hand. 'We are about to dine. Will you join us, Sir?'

Everard blushed. He spluttered, wondering what he should do. The idea appealed to him, but there was no one to ask whether he might accept the invitation.

'Oh, I…'

Peter misunderstood the young lieutenant's hesitation.

'I assure you, Frenchmen are not the ogres popular opinion paints them to be,' Peter said, leading Northover towards the great cabin at the bow of the ship.

Northover's flush deepened.

'I do not look upon the French as ogres. Why, even now we are no longer at war.'

He glanced down at the dock. The guards were not yet in place. No one was around to censure him. He came to a decision.

'Thank you, Sir Peter. I will accept your invitation,' he said, breaking into his leggy stride beside Peter.

All eyes turned towards the door when Peter entered with the English lieutenant in tow. Conversation stopped. Corbeau and Mollien exchanged looks, Laroche shrunk in his seat to appear as inconspicuous as possible, and Babineaux regarded Northover with interest.

Northover, oblivious of their scrutiny, glanced around the cabin. He had never seen such luxury on a ship. The polished wood of the great cabin gleamed. Candles flickered in ornate sconces fixed to the walls. Crystal pendants hung above them, sparkling in the candlelight. A long table, set with lustrous white crockery, silver cutlery, and cut glass, sat athwart the ship.

Characteristic of all ships, the windows sloped at an angle following the line of the side of the vessel. Drawn across the windows, curtains matching the upholstery created a charming atmosphere.

Peter addressed the group.

'Gentlemen, may I present to you, Lieutenant Northover…Ah, I am sorry, Sir, I do not know your first name.

Northover's deep blush coloured his cheeks again. He coughed.

'Everard. Lieutenant Everard Northover,' he said with several bows to the men sitting around the table.

Nods and mumbled greetings met him.

'Lieutenant Northover has brought us good news, Messieurs,' Peter explained.

A more active murmur followed this disclosure.

'Would you like to tell them, Lieutenant?' Peter asked.

The men leant forward a little in their chairs. A charged silence fell.

'Oh, yes, well,' Everard said, feeling important. He cleared his throat before he began.

'Sir Hudson Low has given permission for you to visit… the Général.'

That sounds better, he thought.

Enthusiastic French exclamation rippled through the room, accompanied by the ring of cut glassware as Mollien, Corbeau and Renoudin tapped their glasses with their spoons. The pleasure among the French brought a smile to Northover's face.

'When are we to go?' Babineaux asked above the din.

'Sir Gordon Atherton will accompany you from here at ten o'clock tomorrow morning,' Northover replied.

Babineaux relayed this news in French.

'Tomorrow at ten we are to meet Sir Gordon Atherton—the unpleasant creature of whom I told you. He will accompany us.'

'He was suspicious of you, Adrien, was he not?' Corbeau said. 'We must be careful not to raise his suspicions again.'

Babineaux nodded and turned to Northover.

'You will join us for dinner, Sir?'

Peter put a hand on Babineaux's shoulder.

'I have already invited him, Adrien.'

Babineaux smiled and rose. He pulled out the chair next to him.

'You had better sit by me, Sir. I speak English, so we may converse. I am Adrien Babineaux,' he said, holding out his hand.

Northover shook hands and slid into the offered seat; Babineaux resumed his.

'Do you accompany us tomorrow, Sir?' Babineaux asked.

'I do not know. Perhaps; It depends on Sir Gordon,' Northover replied.

Babineaux made a wry face.

'Ah, yes, Sir Gordon Atherton. I met him when I was here some months ago,' Babineaux said. 'He accompanied me to Longwood then.'

Northover turned to Babineaux, frowning a little.

'I have not had much contact with him,' he said. 'I find him somewhat menacing.'

While they spoke, a servant placed a cover before Northover, consisting of three plates, of various sizes, numerous knives, forks, and spoons, and glasses for each course, to hold the appropriate wine. The servant bowed and filled Northover's glass.

Northover had never tasted French cuisine. He recognised the taste of turbot, chicken, beef, and lamb in the intricately prepared dishes, cooked in ways unknown to him. The courses kept coming. Northover ate everything set before him.

Throughout the meal, Babineaux kept Northover supplied with wine. Unused to consuming large amounts of alcohol, the more he drank, the looser Northover's tongue became. Babineaux saw his chance to discover the times of the watches and which parts of St Helena were well guarded and which were not.

In the course of innocent conversation, about their respective families, about ships, and about his duties on the island, Northover revealed a great deal concerning the Army's movements and schedules.

The meal ended. The servants cleared the covers. They placed decanters of port, whisky, brandy, and Madeira on the table before retiring. The men were left to their private discussions while drinking and smoking cheroots.

After helping him to a generous measure of brandy, Babineaux offered Northover a cheroot.

Eyelids drooping, Northover gave Babineaux a lazy, inebriated smile. He had never smoked but, inhibition flown to the winds, he accepted.

Northover coughed violently after inexpertly inhaling the smoke. Fearing he would vomit, Babineaux quickly propelled him from the cabin and onto the deck, steering him towards the bulwark. There, sure enough, Northover and his unfamiliar French cuisine parted company.

Babineaux felt a pang of guilt. It was he who had deliberately made Northover drunk. Although it had paid dividends in information, Babineaux felt sorry for taking advantage of the youth.

In the near darkness, Northover groaned as a chill wind blew his hair about. Babineaux put a hand to Northover's forehead. It was cold and clammy.

He can't be much older than eighteen or nineteen, Babineaux pondered. *As I'm not allowed off the ship, I can't escort him home. Even if I could, I don't know where his quarters are.*

A sailor on watch came to his aid.

'Do you need help, Capitaine Babineaux?' he asked.

'I do, Masson. Will you help me get him to my cabin? I fear this is my fault for giving the lad too much wine.'

'It might be the first time he gets drunk, Capitaine, but I doubt it will be the last,' Masson said with a grin.

He took one of Northover's arms and draped it over his own shoulder.

'Up you come, *mon garçon,*' he said.

Babineaux took the other arm, and between them,

he, and Masson manoeuvred Northover below deck. Northover, with his limp long legs and arms, and lolling head, impeded their progress. Finally, they came to Babineaux's cabin. Inside they deposited Northover on Babineaux's cot.

Checking the pitcher on the washstand, Babineaux found it was empty.

'Will you fetch me a pitcher of water, if you please, Masson?' Babineaux asked.

The sailor nodded and left. While he was gone, Babineaux, with some difficulty, pulled off Northover's boots.

Masson returned moments later with the pitcher.

'Anything else, Monsieur?' he enquired.

'Yes, Masson. Will you wake me at five? The lieutenant must get back to his barracks before anyone notices he is gone. Will you also bring me a carafe of water. The poor lad will need it.'

'I will, Monsieur. But for now, I must go back on watch.'

'Merci, Masson,' Babineaux called after him as he left the cabin.

Babineaux sat Northover up and removed his jacket and waistcoat. After laying him back down, he put them on the one chair in the cabin.

'At least you didn't get vomit on your clothes,' he said to the prone Northover.

Babineaux poured water into the basin on the washstand. He dipped a washcloth in it and carefully wiped Northover's face. Wringing out the cloth, he folded it and placed it on the lad's forehead.

After caring as best he could for Northover, Babineaux stood and inhaled deeply. Considering where he might sleep, now that Northover occupied his bed, he decided on Tom's cot. The two men shared a cabin; Tom was now on *Nautilus,* so his place was free.

After a final check on Northover who had either passed out or was in a deep sleep, Adrien returned to the grand cabin.

'Where's Northover?' Peter asked when Babineaux appeared.

'He's asleep in my cabin. I plied him with a little too much wine. He's dead drunk. But it was worth it. He talked without inhibition. I learnt much about how they run this island, when the watches change, and such. I feel somewhat ashamed of myself for taking advantage of the youth. But, as you English say, needs must.'

The following morning, Masson, true to his word, came to Babineaux's cabin at five a.m. to wake him.

'Capitaine Babineaux,' he said, leaning close to his ear.

Babineaux roused the moment Masson touched his shoulder. Swinging his legs out of the cot, he stretched his arms and yawned.

'Thank you, Masson,' Babineaux said.

'I have put the carafe of water on the table, Sir,' Masson said. He nodded towards Northover

'Do you think he will need help, Monsieur?' he asked.

'I don't think anyone will be able to help him, Masson,' Babineaux said with a rueful smile.

Masson chuckled, touched his forehead with two knuckles and left as the ship's bell rang out the next watch.

Babineaux poured a cup of water from the carafe. He shook Northover's arm several times before the lad opened a bloodshot eye.

Northover sat up. Moaning, he held his forehead. He smacked his lips and moved his tongue, which seemed too big for his mouth.

'What am I doing here?' he asked.

'You drank too much last night, Everard,' Babineaux informed him, handing him the glass of water.

Everard took the glass and drank greedily from it. Babineaux poured another, which went the same way. The lieutenant looked around the room recognising nothing.

'Where exactly am I. And where are my clothes?'

'You are in my cabin aboard *La Miséricorde.* Your clothes are over there on the chair, your boots are beside them,' Babineaux told him, remembering the times in his youth when he had woken in just such a state.

'Good Lord! I am on first duty. What time is it?'

'Several minutes after five o'clock. May I suggest you make haste and dress? You must hurry before anyone realises you spent the night here.'

Northover rose quickly from the cot and gasped.

'Oh, my head.'

'Do not mind your head,' Babineaux said, holding his waistcoat out to him. 'Put this on.'

Northover obeyed.

Babineaux picked up Northover's jacket.

'Now, put this on.'

Northover obeyed again. He took his coat from Babineaux and, with difficulty put his arms into the sleeves. The buttons were too much for him. Babineaux came to his aid, doing up the waistcoat and the jacket. Northover groaned as he bent forward to ease his feet into his boots.

Babineaux stood back to inspect him. Apart from his dishevelled hair and pale face, he didn't look too bad. Babineaux led Northover up on deck.

The two men were greeted by a dense, grey, swathing fog covering the morning. The rising sun filtered through it, tingeing it with a yellow hue.

'Will you be alright, Everard?' Babineaux asked.

'I hope so. I've never been drunk before,' Northover said, swaying slightly at the top of the gangplank.

Pangs of conscience intruded on Babineaux. He took the lieutenant's arm and led him down to the dock.

'Drink plenty of water, and you'll soon be all right,' Babineaux advised as Northover took his first shaky steps along the dock.

Babineaux watched Northover walk unsteadily out of sight into the fog and hoped he would get to the barracks before they discovered his absence.

At ten o'clock Count Mollien, Colonel Corbeau, and Captain Babineaux stood at the bottom of the gangplank to wait for Sir Gordon Atherton. Christophe Laroche stood behind them wearing his wig, false beard, and his large hat and greatcoat.

The fog had cleared somewhat. But visibility was low.

They heard the clop-clop of horse's hooves approaching. Sir Gordon moved through the fog, leading two horses, followed by Lieutenant Northover leading two more. He looked pale and grave, sitting remarkably stiff and straight in his saddle.

'Good morning, gentlemen,' Sir Gordon called, looking about him. 'Perhaps it is *not* good with all this fog; a pity we must travel in it. Mayhap it will lift, but I doubt it.'

Northover dismounted and led his two horses to the men. Laroche and Corbeau mounted. Northover took the other two bridles from Sir Gordon and brought them to Babineaux and Count Mollien, standing by as they mounted.

Sir Gordon watched the group with unconcern, making no effort to assist.

'I shall lead the way, gentlemen. Northover will take up the rear. I suggest you keep together between us. We don't want any of you to get lost,' Sir Gordon said before spurring his horse.

Babineaux, still a little worried about Northover, watched him mount and took up a position next to him, behind the others.

The group rode at a cautious trot. The fog was

lifting a little. Babineaux recognised the road he had travelled before. The lush green of summer gently gave way to autumn's influence. The leaves, now dripping in the fog, day by day were slowly changing colour.

'How are you feeling, Everard?' Babineaux asked.

'A little better than I did. Although riding is not improving my condition,' came Northover's doleful reply.

Babineaux laughed.

'You are probably vowing never to drink again.'

'I am,' Northover said, with a rueful grin.

'But you will. It's a matter of knowing how to pace yourself and not drinking too much all at once,' Babineaux advised. 'You arrived at your barracks in time?'

'Yes. But no sooner had I lain down then I must get up again. The fog seems heavier again here,' he said.

'Yes,' Babineaux agreed.

They rode on in silence, watching their way with care. As they went, Babineaux, with happy anticipation, contemplated seeing Napoleon again. Northover broke in on his reflections.

'Why are you visiting Napoleon?'

It took Babineaux a moment's thought before he decided what best to say.

'Count Mollien is devoted to him,' he explained. 'After he heard the great man was suffering from low spirits, he decided a visit from him might give the Général heart.'

A somewhat lame reason, Babineaux thought and was glad Sir Gordon had not asked the question. Northover simply made conversation. The same question coming from Sir Gordon's lips would have had purpose. He would not have been so easily fobbed off.

Northover shook his head.

'I do not know how anyone can give him heart when there is no hope of his ever leaving St Helena,' he said.

This statement gave Babineaux pause.

Northover sounds sympathetic to Napoleon's plight.

'Have you met the Général, Everard?'

Northover shook his head.

'I have seen him at a distance, but never met with him. Shall I meet him today do you think?'

'Possibly,' Babineaux said. 'Although we have requested a private meeting with him. The Général likes to go with his visitors to Geranium Valley.'

'Oh,' Northover said.

Babineaux detected disappointment in Northover's manner.

'Would you like to meet him?'

Northover brightened.

'Yes. It would be an experience to recount to my grandchildren,' he said with a chuckle.

They continued through a wooded area until they emerged from the trees and saw Longwood House on a rise before them. As they approached, it seemed to float up out of the thinning fog.

Just as he had done when escorting Babineaux on his last visit, Sir Gordon said he would amuse himself elsewhere while he waited for them. He intended visiting his mistress again.

'I shall return at two o'clock to escort you back. I hope you will have finished your business with Bonaparte by then.'

Hearing this statement, Northover walked his horse over to Sir Gordon.

'Sir, if you prefer, I could escort the party back to Jamestown.'

'Hmm. Could you indeed?' Sir Gordon said, fingering his chin.

If Northover takes the party back, I shall have more time with Selene.

He gave Northover a cold smile.

'Why not?' he said, looking with disdain at the youthful Lieutenant. 'Yes, you may do so, Northover.

238

It's time we put some responsibility on your shoulders.'

'Ha!' he snorted. 'But do not lose them, Sir,' he said, wheeling his horse, 'or there will be the devil to pay,' he bellowed as he galloped off into the fog.

Babineaux gave Corbeau a speaking look. Corbeau raised an eyebrow. He knew Babineaux already had the lad eating out of his hand. The mission would be easier with the inexperienced Northover in charge.

They dismounted at the stables of Longwood House and walked to the front door. As before, The Marquis de Montholon, himself, came out to greet them.

'My dear Babineaux, I am pleased to see you again. They told us only yesterday of your arrival on St Helena, and of your impending visit,' he said, ushering them through the front door into the vestibule.

Babineaux bowed to the Marquis.

'Monseigneur, may I present to you, Count Mollien.'

The count stepped forward making an elegant bow to the Marquis.

Montholon gave back a gracious inclination of his head.

'We have met before, Count Mollien, have we not?'

'Indeed, we have. It is some time ago, however, in happier times,' Mollien replied.

Babineaux moved to Corbeau's side.

'May I also present my cousin, Colonel Paul Corbeau.'

Standing to attention, Corbeau clicked his heels and saluted.

'Your servant, Monseigneur,' he said.

Catching sight of Laroche, Montholon asked.

'And who is this?'

Count Mollien moved forward.

'He is my body servant. I am in poor health and go nowhere without him.'

Montholon looked Laroche up and down, uninterested in one whom he considered beneath notice, a menial creature.

Babineaux inwardly smiled; little did Montholon know. The group had agreed that no one, not even one so close to Napoleon as Montholon, should know that Laroche was to take the General's place.

Having been promised an introduction to Napoleon, Northover had followed them into the house. He stood at the edge of the group. Babineaux had almost forgotten him. Catching sight of him at last, he beckoned Northover forward.

'Excuse me, Monseigneur. This gentleman, who knows not a word of French, is desirous of an introduction to the Général. Would it be possible?' Babineaux asked.

'The Général is in his library. He is looking forward to meeting with you. I am sure he will allow an introduction to one who should be his enemy and seems not to be. Follow me if you please.'

The five men followed Montholon through the Salon and the dining room, stopping outside the heavy wooden door to the library.

Montholon knocked.

Familiar to most of the group, Napoleon's voice bade them enter.

They filed into the room as Napoleon turned from the window and his contemplation of the garden.

At sight of Babineaux, the Général smiled.

'Adrien, my dear boy. You said you would return. I hope you bring me good news.'

Adrien moved forward and, as on his last visit, he bowed his knee and kissed Napoleon's hand. Rising, he spoke quietly.

'I do bring good news, mon Général. However, before we discuss anything, we have an English officer with us who has expressed a desire for an introduction to you.'

'*Mon Dieu.* How remarkable,' Napoleon said.

The Général looked at the men in the room.

Northover's red uniform jacket stood out. When Babineaux beckoned to Northover, the Général saw the officer move forward.

Napoleon spoke in French.

'Someday this man will be an imposing figure; he is so tall. Not yet, however, he is too young. What is his name?'

Babineaux introduced him.

'Lieutenant Everard Northover, Mon Général.'

Northover bowed his head.

Napoleon made a fair attempt to speak to Northover in English.

'I cordially greet you, young Sir. Welcome in my house. For now, we must leave you. We have business to discuss.'

Northover was quite overcome. That such an important person, albeit currently a prisoner, should speak to him in such a pleasant way amazed him.

'Thank you, your … Majesty,' he said, blushing furiously.

Napoleon gazed at him intently for a moment before smiling broadly.

He turned to Montholon and switched to French.

'If all my enemies were so affable, I could have ruled the world. I like this young man, Montholon. See to it that he is treated well.'

He turned to Babineaux.

'Shall we go to my valley, Babineaux? You may make the introductions to your companions on the way. Although I recognise all but one of them.'

So saying, Napoleon opened the French windows and proceeded onto the terrace, leading the way to the secluded Geranium Valley.

CHAPTER TWENTY FOUR

As *Nautilus* continued moving towards Sandy Bay, Pedro monitored her progress through the periscope.

'I can't see much, Tom, there's not a lot of light,' Pedro said.

Tom watched the depth gauge as he worked the screw that drove the submarine.

'I reckon we might be coming closer to land. The water's becoming shallow. Look east,' Tom suggested.

Pedro moved the periscope around to face east.

'Still can't see much.'

'Right,' Tom said. 'If we can't see the fortifications, they can't see us. I'm going to surface.'

Tom, with his highly skilled and practiced hands on the controls of Nautilus, carefully pumped air into the ballast tanks displacing the water therein, causing the submarine to surface.

'We're rising,' Pedro said, his smile showing his white teeth.

Tom continued guiding *Nautilus* forward as they rose. Before they reached the sand, he stopped the vessel, not wanting her to run aground on the beach. When he was happy with her position, he pulled a lever to drop anchor and moved to undog the hatch that opened onto the deck.

Tom inhaled the fresh, sea air as it flooded into the cabin.

Sandy Bay was a sheltered part of the island. Light waves foamed as they broke on the beach leaving ripples in the sand. Farther up, the fine, dry sand gave way to a line of dark shale.

'We're well in under the cliff, Pedro. There's a cave in front of me. You stay here while I have a look.'

'I'll haul up the chest while you're gone, Tom.'

'Right,' Tom said as he ascended to the deck. He looked into the water lapping along the side of the boat.

Judging it was shallow enough to wade through, he climbed over the bulwarks and let himself down and paddled to the beach. He tramped up the soft stretch of sand until his feet crunched on the shale as he made his way to the cave yawning before him. He paused and tried to peer inside. Smelling of salt and damp seaweed, it was too dark to see what might be there.

Tom went down the beach towards Pedro. Having unloaded the chest that held their equipment, Pedro rummaged through it.

He looked up as Tom approached.

'What's in the cave?'

'It's too dark. I can't see.'

Pedro unearthed a lantern from the chest and held it up.

'Good man, Pedro. Put it back in the chest, and we'll carry it to the mouth of the cave.'

Tom reached down to grasp a rope handle at one side of the chest. Pedro took hold of the other. Together they walked back towards the mouth of the cave.

Pedro opened the chest and took out the lantern again. He fished his tinderbox from his pocket, struck the flint, made fire, and lit the candle in the lantern. Tom took it and walked into the cave. Pedro followed.

'Ah,' Tom said, looking at the solid wall to his right. 'I hoped a passage might run towards the garrison. There might have been an opening from which we could observe the fortifications.'

Tom moved deeper into the cave.

'Look, Pedro, it slopes downwards to the left,' Tom said. 'And I can hear water rushing.'

Tom followed the sound of the water. The passage narrowed, and he found himself on a ledge. He held the lantern high. The source of the sound of rushing water came from a swiftly flowing stream beneath the ledge. Kneeling, Tom dipped a cupped hand into the stream. Carefully lifting his hand to his mouth, Tom tasted sweet water. He rose and moved back to where Pedro stood.

'Well, if we are here for any length of time, we won't go thirsty. There's a fine stream at the bottom of the slope.'

'That's good to know, Tom. But I hope we're not here for long. The quicker we get away, the less likely we'll be caught.'

'Na,' Tom said. 'Our people will probably be at Longwood tomorrow. Babineaux will lead Napoleon here as soon as he may. I reckon they'll be here late tomorrow afternoon.'

Pedro glanced at him, wondering on what he based his assumption. 'You seem very sure, Tom.'

'It's what was agreed, Pedro. If nothing untoward happens to stop them, Babineaux will make sure things run to plan.'

Pedro's reservations stilled when he thought of all the schemes Tom had devised. They had always run to plan, sometimes missing danger by a hair's breadth, but missing it all the same.

Tom carefully retrieved his prized telescope from the chest. Holding it securely in one hand, he reached back into the chest for the tripod that went with it. Securing the telescope to the swivel at the top of the tripod, Tom left the cave and climbed the rocks to the right in search of level terrain.

A ridge of rocks to the right of them led down to the sea. These screened Tom, Pedro, and *Nautilus* from the garrison.

With a breeze whipping his hair about his head, Tom safely secured the tripod. Turning the telescope in the right direction, Tom knelt and looked through the eyepiece. To his great satisfaction, Tom clearly saw the fortifications and the men guarding them.

'Yes!' he said in triumph.

Climbing down the dark, volcanic rocks, he called softly, 'Come up here, Pedro.'

Pedro climbed up, curious to see what Tom was

doing.

'Look,' Tom said.

Pedro put his eye to the telescope.

'Ha, Tom,' he said, as he straightened up. 'it's an excellent telescope.'

'It should be,' Tom said, 'It cost me a fortune.'

'And this is a well sheltered spot so you won't be seen.'

'Right. I can reconnoitre the land surrounding the fortifications and see when Babineaux comes in sight with our disguised General. Nothing much will happen until tomorrow. However, if any of the soldiers take it into their heads to wander this way, we must launch *Nautilus* immediately and submerge.'

'Ah, we can't have that,' Pedro said. 'We'll have to keep watch.'

'Yes. We will take turns. Two hours on and two off. I will take first watch.'

'I'll go back and prepare us a bite to eat, Tom.'

'Good idea, Pedro,' Tom said, peering through the periscope.

Pedro headed down to the beach. Moments later he came back carrying a metal pitcher. He made his way to the cave to collect water from the stream.

Tom scrutinised the fortifications.

Sandy Bay, unguarded, was an ideal spot for invasion.

Hurriedly built by the authorities when they knew Napoleon would be exiled on St Helena, the construction was not as solid as it might be. The Twenty-foot walls, with crenalllated parapets, ran parallel to the beach. Made of dark stone, hewn from the surrounding rocks, several bastions stood at intervals along the walls. Atop the bastions, Tom saw cannon pointing towards the sea.

Tom viewed the soldiers on watch, pacing the walls. He saw laxity in their bearing. Their observation of the surrounding area lacked motive. They stood in conversation before they passed each other. With such improper surveillance, Tom felt easy. He also noted the buildings above them on higher ground and surmised they must be barracks, while others looked as if they might house administrative staff.

Tom swung the telescope towards the sea and saw local men sauntering along the horseshoe-shaped stretch of sand, gathering seaweed from the shore. Tom knew that in some places around the world, seaweed was used as food. He had eaten it himself and liked its unusual taste.

After about half-an-hour, Pedro gave a low whistle. He climbed the rocks carrying a canvas bag, from which he produced two hunks of bread, a little past its prime, wrapped in a napkin. Another napkin contained salt pork and sliced onions. Two pewter mugs and a stoppered flask containing hot tea put the finishing touch to the plain meal.

Both were hungry and tucked into the food eagerly.

Tom took a gulp of his tea. He looked up at Pedro.

'This tea tastes good, Pedro.'

'It's the water, Tom. I took it from your stream.'

'Hmm,' Tom said and carried on eating.

After the meal, Tom went up to keep watch again. Pedro went back to *Nautilus*.

Two hours later, Pedro, sat at ease on the beach, smoking his pipe, dreamily gazing out to sea. The vast blue sky darkened as the sun began to set, casting deep shadows beneath the rocks. The tide would soon turn, leaving their craft deeper in the water.

Tom climbed down to the beach.

'Your watch, Pedro.' Tom said.

Pedro knocked out his pipe on the heel of his boot.

'Right you are, Tom,' he said and stood up.

'They changed the guard about half an hour ago. As far as I can see, there are only two of them for the night. Lax they may be, but we cannot afford to go off watch. Chances are if we do they'll descend on us. I don't want to take the risk. We must be sharp and vigilant.'

'Aye,' Pedro said and made his way up to the telescope.

CHAPTER TWENTY FIVE

On the way to Geranium Valley, Babineaux introduced Napoleon to Corbeau.

'May I present my Cousin, Colonel Corbeau, Mon Général. It is he who organised our original plan for your escape.'

Corbeau inclined his head.

'It would please me to take the credit, Monseigneur. However, without Tom Johnson, this meeting would never have taken place,' Corbeau said.

'Tom Johnson?' Napoleon questioned.

'The Englishman whom I recruited, Mon Général. He owns the submarine in which you will travel to our ship. He has led a chequered past. Once a smuggler, recently a pilot and navigator for the British Navy, his expertise has been invaluable.'

'I look forward to meeting such a character. But tell me, have we met before, Colonel? Your face is familiar,' Napoleon said a hand on Corbeau's shoulder.

'Yes, Mon Général. The last time was at our victory at Heliopolis.'

'Indeed,' Napoleon said.

Babineaux made to continue with the introductions and turned to Mollien.

Napoleon put up a hand. 'I need no introduction to my finance minister. I am pleased to see you Count Mollien,' Napoleon said, pausing in his tracks to embrace him.

Released from the embrace, Mollien was overcome.

'I am overjoyed at seeing you once more, Mon Général.'

Stepping aside, he paused to wipe a tear from his eye.

Walking beside Babineaux, Napoleon lowered his voice.

'Adrien, who is this other person?'

Babineaux gave Napoleon a sly look.

'I will save his introduction until we are safely in the valley, Monseigneur.'

Napoleon lifted an eyebrow.

'*Vraiment*?' he said and continued with his four visitors to the valley.

On reaching it, he led them straight to the large willow tree with its overhanging branches. She had not yet shed her leaves.

'We are safe here away from prying eyes,' Napoleon said as Babineaux held back the branches for Mollien and Corbeau to move beneath the tree. Napoleon followed.

Laroche hesitated.

'Come, Christophe. This is the moment we have all been waiting for,' Babineaux said.

'I know, Adrien. But I feel anxious,' Laroche replied.

'It's too late to turn back now, Christophe. Come.'

Babineaux took his arm and led him beneath the branches before letting them down.

Napoleon looked at the four men before him. An expectant silence stilled the atmosphere.

'If I may make so bold, Monseigneur, perhaps you should be seated,' Babineaux said.

A puzzled frown crossed Napoleon's face. With a lift of his chin, he went to the bench near the tree trunk and sat.

'Remove your disguise, Laroche,' Babineaux said.

Laroche moved back from the group. First, he took off his greatcoat. Next, he removed his hat.

Napoleon watched, impassive, until Laroche removed the wig from his head and the beard from his face.

Napoleon looked at him, astounded. He leant back in the seat with his hands on his knees.

'*Mon Dieu*!' he uttered, staring at Laroche. He glanced at the other three men.

'He is my very image! Where did you find him?' he asked.

Corbeau stepped forward.

'My brother Henri met him in Ajaccio, in Corsica, Monseigneur. He saw the likeness and brought him to me in England.'

'Ajaccio is where I was born, Corbeau—perhaps we are related,' he said, making a wry face. 'This man, is he willing to take my place?'

'He is, Mon Général. He is most enthusiastic about it. Are you not, Laroche?'

Laroche came to stand in front of Napoleon. To everyone's surprise, he went down on one knee.

'My life has been one of drudgery, Monseigneur. I will admit, to live as you live would be happiness to me,' Laroche said, looking Napoleon in the eye. 'I never was a soldier, Monseigneur. I never served you. But I am willing to serve you now. My hope is that they will not discover me before you are far away from St Helena.'

Napoleon rose. He looked around at the other three men, then down at Laroche, his eyes dark with emotion.

Corbeau and Mollien caught a glimpse of the emperor they knew; his towering presence obliterating all else.

Catching Laroche's arm, Napoleon lifted him up to stand before him. He put his hand on Laroche's shoulder.

'And my hope, Laroche, is that they never find out and you may live as me in comfort for a long time.'

Laroche favoured Napoleon with a wide smile.

'We are of one mind, Monseigneur.'

Napoleon's laughter lightened the mood as he turned to Babineaux.

'Do you think he can pull it off, Adrien?'

'I do, Mon Général. On the voyage here, we have all schooled him. We taught him to speak and walk like you, your mannerisms, and your dislikes, as well as your preferences. Tom Johnson taught him English. Christoph is an intelligent man and learnt well. Fortunately, he is literate and is looking forward to studying your books.'

'All that remains now Mon Général,' Corbeau said, 'is for you to change clothes with him.'

'And what will happen after that?' Napoleon asked.

'After that, Monseigneur, Laroche will become you and will go back to Longwood with Count Mollien and Colonel Corbeau. You and I shall journey to Sandy Bay to meet Tom Johnson with his submarine,' Babineaux explained.

'Will you not be missed, Adrien?' Napoleon asked.

'We worked out a strategy to take care of that. Fate has been kind, however, Monseigneur. If we were dealing with Sir Gordon, things would be different. Instead, that young Lieutenant to whom I introduced you, is to escort our party to the ship. He is an innocent. Corbeau will spin a tale of how Laroche and I went back to the ship ahead of the others. I doubt he will question it,' Babineaux explained.

'I see,' Napoleon said as he removed his jacket and waistcoat. Laroche did the same.

Napoleon picked up Laroche's waistcoat and scrutinised it.

'There was a time this would have drowned me,' Napoleon said as he put it on and did up the buttons. 'It fits well, but is far from my usual style,' he said, looking down at himself. 'I believe that is all to the good.'

He took off his boots and breeches, passing the breeches to Laroche who passed his trousers to Napoleon.

Napoleon put his boots on again.

'I am pleased to see Laroche's boots are a replica of my own. We will not need to exchange them. A long walk in someone else's boots would not be wise,'

Napoleon said.

'Tom Johnson was of the same opinion, Monseigneur. May I help you with the wig?' Babineaux said.

Napoleon stood still while Babineaux pulled the wig into place, adjusting it with a tweak here and there. He produced a small pot of glue and a brush. After applying the glue to the beard, he lifted Napoleon's chin and carefully pressed it into place on Napoleon's face.

Babineaux stood back to regard his handiwork.

'Do not touch the beard, Monseigneur. We must allow a few minutes for the glue to dry,' he said.

Dressed in each other's clothes, the two men stood side by side.

'Remarkable,' Mollien murmured, shaking his head.

'It is hard to tell which is which,' Corbeau said. He paused before speaking again.

'But now, Monseigneur, we must bid you farewell.'

Mollien knelt before Napoleon. Taking his hand, he kissed it before rising. Napoleon embraced him and kissed him on both cheeks, being careful with his beard. Too overcome with emotion to speak, Mollien stood back, tears in his eyes. Corbeau took his place.

'Mon Général. I wish you good fortune,' he said.

He stood to attention, clicked his heels, and saluted. Taking one step back, he bowed his head for several seconds, turned and went to stand next to Mollien.

Laroche, who had been quiet all through the exchanging of clothes, came to stand before Napoleon.

'I hope all goes well with you, Monseigneur,' he said, with a tentative smile.

'*Bon Chance, mon amie, et merci,*' Napoleon replied.

Laroche picked up the greatcoat and helped Napoleon into it. Napoleon pulled the big hat down on his forehead.

Babineaux lifted the branches for Mollien, Corbeau

and Laroche to leave the willow tree.

They had agreed that the three would walk farther up the valley before turning back and making their way to Longwood House. This would give Napoleon and Babineaux a little more time to get away.

Babineaux gave a heavy sigh.

Napoleon faced him.

'Well, Babineaux, does my beard and long hair suit me?' Napoleon asked.

'It is a good disguise, Mon... ah no, I must not call you by your name. You are now Christophe Laroche.'

Babineaux's clothes were appropriate for visiting Napoleon. They were not appropriate for a labourer going about his business. He began undressing.

Removing his coat, he turned it inside out. The lining was of plain woollen material. From his pocket, he took a battered old hat and placed it on his head, then took off his boots and trousers. He turned the trousers inside out to reveal work worn breeches. He pulled the bottoms of the trousers up inside the breeches and put them on. When he had put on his boots, he went to the stream and smeared them with mud.

'Now, "Laroche", we are ready to go,' he said.

Napoleon laughed softly as they left the willow tree together and set out on the road south.

'How far is Sandy Bay from here, Adrien?'

'It is about five miles, Monseigneur...pardon me... "Christophe",' Babineaux replied.

'That *should* take about two hours. I am not in good condition, Adrien, so it may take a little longer. Nevertheless, I am happy to walk. The original plan whereby they would lower me on a rope over a cliff to a beach was not to my liking.'

Babineaux grinned.

'Tom Johnson thought you would prefer to walk.'

'Hmm, I am curious to meet this Tom Johnson,' Napoleon said.

Napoleon was right. Of late, he took little exercise. After walking for half an hour, he needed rest.

'Stop, Adrien. I am out of breath,' he called.

'Rest here on the grass at the roadside, Christophe. I have a canteen of water. Are you thirsty?' Babineaux asked, all solicitude for his charge.

Napoleon lowered himself onto the grass.

'Yes, I am, Adrien. Thank you,' he said as he took Babineaux's canteen.

'I wonder how Corbeau and Mollien are faring with the real Laroche?' Napoleon mused, after taking a long pull on the canteen.

'Corbeau is probably enjoying it. Mollien will be hiding behind his dignity,' Babineaux replied.

'How will they explain Laroche's inability to recognise my staff?'

'We decided you would receive a blow to the head, which momentarily affected your memory,' Babineaux explained.

'Another of Tom Johnson's ideas?'

'No, Christophe; it was mine,' Babineaux said with satisfaction.

They continued along the road, frequently stopping for rest.

Our journey will take much longer at this rate, Babineaux reflected.

He had thought of asking one of the carts, which passed them, whether they would take them up. But he could not, for although his English was excellent, his French accent would give him away in a moment.

Babineaux noticed Napoleon's drawn face. Red patches on each cheek stood out against his pallor. His need to stop increased. His rests became longer.

I hope he does not become ill on the road. We could not ask anyone for assistance.

'I am sure you are finding me a burden, Adrien,' Napoleon said when next they stopped.

'No, Christophe. Take your time. Providing we arrive before nightfall, all will be well,' Babineaux said, trying to look cheerful.

Rising from his place under a tree, Napoleon looked squarely at Babineaux.

'Let me tell you, this, Adrien. Although my body betrays me, my mind does not. My heart is stout, and I am determined to carry on. So, my young friend, do not despair. We will get there before nightfall.'

In the face of Napoleon's determination, Babineaux took heart as they started walking again.

The next time Babineaux looked at the map to calculate the distance left to go, his spirits rose. The fortifications were less than a mile farther. Sandy Bay lay south of them.

Babineaux itched to stride out. He curbed his inclination and continued plodding alongside Napoleon.

At last, they saw the fortifications in the distance. Babineaux kept up a steady stream of instructions as they approached them.

'We must be careful here, Christophe. Slow your pace. Amble like a man out for a stroll. We must pass the fortifications and walk along the strand. Slowly now, we must take our time so Tom will notice us and come to meet us.'

Tom and Pedro had taken it in turns through the night to keep watch on the guards at the fortifications. While one watched, the other returned to *Nautilus* to sleep. It was a cold night. However, the wind had died down.

Tom was on watch as the sun came up. From his perch on the rocks, he looked out to sea and could not distinguish where the sea ended, and the sky began. Fog drifted towards the land. Soon Tom could not see the fortifications. His heart sank. He hoped the fog would lift as the day progressed. If Napoleon and Babineaux should come while visibility was bad, he would have difficulty in seeing them. He had brought a blanket with him to ward off the cold. Removing the telescope from the tripod, Tom wrapped it in the blanket and secured it with a rope.

He picked his way to *Nautilus* and climbed inside. Pedro was asleep in his hammock. Tom was loath to wake him, but he was tired himself and needed sleep. He must have his wits about him.

Tom went to the jug on the table and filled his mug with the sweet water from the stream.

If I could find a way to put this in barrels and ship it to England, I could make a fortune, he thought.

Having refreshed himself with the water, he went to Pedro's side.

Tom tugged on Pedro's foot.

'Wake up, Lad,' Tom said.

Instantly Pedro was awake.

'My turn on watch, Tom?'

'Aye, but there's fog. I couldn't see a thing. But then, neither can the garrison,' Tom said and threw himself into the hammock vacated by Pedro.

'Keep watch from the deck, lad. But if the fog lifts, go back up and watch from the rocks.'

'Right,' Pedro said and, wrapping a muffler around his neck, he went on deck.

Tom fell asleep before new thoughts could take root.

The day passed with Tom and Pedro watching in turns for Babineaux and Napoleon. To Tom's relief, by mid-morning, the fog had thinned to a light mist. By mid-afternoon, it had dispersed, and Tom re-erected the telescope on the tripod. He and Pedro resumed their watch on the fort, turn and turn about.

Tom lay on his back in the sand, under the shelter of the rock. He looked at the grey, rain-laden clouds out to sea. He had never been a patient man. Waiting for something to happen had always irked him. He found if he distracted his thoughts, it helped to control his frustration. Nancy drifted into his mind. He entertained the thought of her for a while but decided she was *too* much of a distraction. Instead, he began counting the seagulls flying above him.

And then, at last, Tom heard Pedro's low whistle. He was on his feet at once, rushing to where Pedro sat by the telescope.

'Do you think that's them, Tom?' Pedro asked when Tom came up to him.

Tom took Pedro's place and looked into the eye piece.

He gave a deep-throated laugh.

'Yeah, Pedro. That's them,' Tom said.

He pulled his hat down and buttoned up his greatcoat as he made for the beach.

Strolling along the curve of the shore, hands in his pockets, he stopped now and again, to shuffle his feet in the sand or look out at the clouds ranging towards the land; once he bent to examine a shell.

Babineaux and Napoleon arrived at Sandy Bay. Wandering past the fortifications and onto the beach they sauntered along at a slow pace.

Babineaux caught Napoleon's arm.

'There's Tom,' he whispered.

Napoleon looked up and saw a tall man in a large greatcoat moving slowly towards them.

Napoleon stopped, his whole body taut and alert with expectation.

'The figure is far away. Are you sure, Adrien?' Napoleon asked.

'Yes, Christophe, I am sure,' Babineaux said, smiling to himself.

He did not think he had ever been so glad to see anyone in his life.

'Don't hurry, Mon Général. Let it appear we meet by accident.'

Tom rose from his scrutiny of the shell as

Babineaux and Napoleon approached.

Perhaps the soldiers observed them with curious interest, perhaps not. Nevertheless, Babineaux acted out a scene with Tom.

Stepping forward, Babineaux made a great play of greeting Tom like a long-lost brother. He embraced him and slapped him on the back. Tom joined in the drama gesticulating in the direction from which he had come.

Babineaux brought Napoleon forward. Tom shook Napoleon's hand. Putting a hand on each of their shoulders, Tom made as if to invite them to walk with him. The three wandered away towards the jutting rocks. Tom and Adrien helped Napoleon to climb over them. They were now hidden from the garrison's sight. Once safe, their anxiety subsided.

'Mon Général, may I present Tom Johnson to you?' Babineaux said.

Tom greeted the Général with a civil inclination of his head.

'I am pleased to meet you at last Mr Johnson,' Napoleon said putting out his hand.

'I'm pleased to meet you, Sir,' Tom said as he shook the general's hand.

'What are we to do now?' Napoleon asked.

'I will show you and Babineaux onto *Nautilus*. Come, Sir. Come, Adrien,' Tom said. Taking Napoleon's arm, he led him across the beach and down to the submarine while Babineaux followed.

Napoleon paused at sight of *Nautilus*.

'So, this is your submarine, Mr Johnson? She is bigger than I supposed,' he said as he moved forward again.

'*Eagle* is even bigger. We had to sacrifice her when the authorities almost discovered us. Then again, *Nautilus*, being smaller is easier to hide,' Tom said.

They reached the water's edge. The tide was out. The sea was less than a foot deep as the three men waded to the side of the ship.

Tom and Babineaux aided Napoleon over the low bulwarks. When Tom took up the hatch, Babineaux helped Napoleon to climb down the steep ladder into the cabin.

Napoleon looked around him. Vaguely he noticed the sparseness that confronted him, and the hammock hanging to one side. He caught himself wondering how long he would be here.

Seeing a chair by the small table, with a grateful sigh, he dropped onto it.

'You are exhausted, Sir. Let me give you some water,' Tom said.

He felt sorry for Napoleon, who looked as if he would collapse. Despite his disdainful attitude towards figures in authority, Tom could not help but treat Napoleon with compassion and respect. He took a pewter mug and gave the weary man a drink.

Napoleon accepted it gratefully.

'You are tired, Sir,' Tom said.

'I am, Mr Johnson. It was a long walk.'

'You should rest, Sir.'

'Ah, Mr Johnson, do not concern yourself. I do not complain. I have been on campaign in far worse conditions than this.'

'Have you ever slept in a hammock, Sir?' Tom asked.

'Yes, Mr Johnson. It was a while ago, but I have.'

'Then, come with me, Sir, and take your rest.'

Tom ushered Napoleon to the small cabin next door and set up a fresh hammock for him.

Napoleon removed his coat, his hat, his wig, and his beard, handing them to Tom.

Sitting on the edge of the hammock, he swung himself into it.

Tom placed Napoleon's things on top of a chest. Retrieving a blanket from another chest, he turned to Napoleon.

'You won't be travelling in these conditions for

long, Sir,' he said, draping the blanket over the tired man. Once we reach *La Miséricorde,* you will find her comfort more to your taste.'

'Thank you, Mr Johnson,' Napoleon said. With a sigh, he closed his eyes.

Tom slipped from the cabin.

It was some time before the tension lifted from Napoleon's mind, enabling him to enter a deep sleep.

On returning to the larger cabin, Tom found Babineaux waiting for him.

'When do we leave, Tom?' he asked.

'We must wait a few hours for high tide. We cannot safely submerge until then. I shall go now and tell Pedro that you and Napoleon are here.'

'Will Pedro not join us?'

'No. We must continue keeping watch to make sure no soldiers come this way. I will not bring the telescope down until just before we leave. I cannot risk our being caught now.'

Tom went on deck. Babineaux heard his footsteps above him, and a splash as Tom jumped from the deck into the water.

Although the walk had not exhausted him as much as it had Napoleon, Babineaux felt a wave of lassitude wash over him. He looked at the hammock hanging nearby.

Why not, he thought and lay in it. He was soon asleep.

The tide came in. Tom and Pedro packed the telescope and tripod in the chest and carried it down the beach to *Nautilus.* Pedro swam out to her first. He threw a line to Tom who attached it to the chest and swam with it to the submarine.

Once in the cabin, they changed their clothes before addressing their task of submerging *Nautilus.*

When Babineaux awoke, they were underwater, an hour on their way to the spot where they hoped to rendezvous with *La Miséricorde.*

CHAPTER TWENTY SIX

After the party had left for Geranium Valley, Lieutenant Northover amused himself by walking in the grounds of Longwood House.

On one occasion, when Sir Gordon escorted a couple to visit Napoleon, Northover had gone with them. But Sir Gordon had confined him to remaining on guard with the horses outside the perimeter of the grounds.

Without Sir Gordon there to restrict him, Northover took advantage of his freedom to wander where he liked. He found an exceptionally fine, well-kept garden to the rear of the house. While inspecting it, Northover came upon a Chinese gardener, busy hoeing weeds. He wore typical oriental attire: a green smock with a mandarin collar and wide sleeves with matching loose trousers. A pigtail hung down his back, and a brimless round hat sat on the back of his head. When he saw Northover, he stopped to stare at him.

'This garden is beautiful,' Northover remarked. 'Are you responsible for its upkeep?' Before he answered, the man leant on his hoe and scrutinised the British officer, a suspicious look in his eye. He hadn't seen this one before.

'No, Sir. It's the General's garden,' the gardener said and bowed deeply. 'He whiles his time away looking after it. I see to all the jobs that don't amuse him.'

Northover smiled.

The gardener bowed again.

'If you go a little farther in that direction,' he said, pointing north, 'You'll come to a lawn with trees around it. The Général often walks there.'

'Thank you,' Northover said and went to inspect the gardener's suggestion.

It was indeed pleasant. The sheltering trees

protected it from the wind.

Northover walked about admiring the place. Farther along, he came to a glade where the sun, shining through the trees, cast dapples on the ground. Birds sang and insects hummed as they went from flower to flower, the scent of them, planted nearby, hung in the air. All the elements of a tranquil spot.

Northover sat beneath a tree, his back against the trunk, drinking in the "joys of nature" and thinking of home.

Not having fully recovered from his hangover, he yawned. His eyelids drooped, and he fell asleep.

When a bird flew by shrieking an alarm call, Northover woke with a start.

He took out his watch. Two hours had gone by since the party had set out.

He jumped up.

Oh, Lord! I hope they have not yet returned, he thought as he set off at a run in the direction of the house.

With great relief, he saw they were not there. Red in the face and out of breath, he sat on the veranda to compose himself.

Corbeau and Mollien left the willow in company with Laroche dressed as Napoleon. As agreed, they spent time wandering around the grounds to give Napoleon and Babineaux more time to get away. After walking for half an hour, they judged that by the time they returned to Longwood House, the two would have had the chance to have left the estate. Turning, they made their way to the path leading back to Longwood House.

From the veranda, Northover caught sight of three men returning.

Three of them? Where are the other two? He thought, remembering Sir Gordon's shout of, "Do not lose any of them." as he rode away.

Curious, Northover went to meet them.

'Where are they?' Northover asked Corbeau when they met.

'Who?' Corbeau inquired.

'Your cousin Babineaux and the servant, Laroche,' Northover said.

'Why, they left a while ago. Did you not see Laroche?' Corbeau asked.

'No, I have been looking around the estate. Why did you separate?'

Corbeau and Mollien put their plan into action.

'It was extremely unfortunate. While we were walking in the valley, Babineaux caught his foot in a rabbit hole and fell. We are not sure whether he broke a bone, but he could not walk. Laroche came back here and ordered a cart be brought to draw Babineaux back to the ship.'

'Where is Laroche now?' Northover asked.

'He went with Babineaux to see to his comfort. A servant from the house drove the cart,' Corbeau said.

'I see. Well then. We should now return to your ship, too,' Northover said.

'Yes, we shall. Give us a moment to say our farewells to the Général, if you please.'

'Of course. You must. Come to the stables when you are ready.'

I hope I am not in trouble again, Northover thought as he went towards the stables.

Corbeau and Mollien escorted "Napoleon" into the house.

The next part of the plan went into action. Inside the house, "Napoleon" began staggering, holding his head. Clutching the drooping form, Corbeau and Mollien made a lot of noise.

Montholon came to investigate. His face turned pale as he rushed forward to help.

'Ah, Mon Général, what has happened?' he cried, filled with concern for his master.

'He fell and hit his head. We had great difficulty

getting him back. We almost had to carry him,' Corbeau explained.

Other members of Napoleon's staff and servants came rushing to see what caused such a commotion.

'Where is Doctor Antommarchi?' Montholon demanded.

'I believe he is sleeping in his room,' a servant said.

'Fetch him at once,' Montholon cried.

The servant rushed off to wake him.

While the staff fussed over "Napoleon", Mollien and Corbeau rose from beside the fallen "Général". With such a crush of people surrounding him, no one noticed as the two quietly retreated to the veranda. From there they went to the stables.

Northover had ordered the stable hands to saddle their horses. Seated on his horse, impatience making him cross, Northover did not show his usual courtesy when the two men arrived.

'What kept you so long?' he asked.

'Napoleon collapsed,' Corbeau said.

Northover gasped.

'Is he all right?'

'Ah, he is prone to the occasional fit of weakness. He will soon recover,' Corbeau said.

'Oh. Well, please mount, gentlemen. I am charged with escorting you to your ship,' Northover said.

The cause of his impatience gone, Northover's usual friendly manner returned. As they rode to Jamestown, he pointed out areas of interest to Mollien and Corbeau who were far too preoccupied with thoughts of Napoleon to take much notice.

Northover assumed their lack of response was due to their worry about Napoleon's health. He decided not to intrude on them further with his interesting information. They rode in silence until they approached Jamestown.

'Will you be returning to France from here, Gentlemen?' he asked.

'Yes, we will,' Corbeau replied.

A helpful thought came to Northover's mind.

'You must be worried about the General. If you wish, I could send you reports about his wellbeing.'

Corbeau and Mollien glanced at each other. Information regarding the success or failure of the substitution of Laroche for Napoleon would be welcome.

'Would you not bring suspicion down upon yourself if you corresponded with us, Lieutenant?' Mollien asked.

'Not at all, Sir. There is no restriction on my correspondence, and they do not scrutinise my letters. They are too busy monitoring Napoleon to waste time on me, a lowly British Officer'.

'You might correspond with Babineaux, Lieutenant,' Corbeau suggested.

'I will, Sir. Can you furnish me with his direction?'

'I will ask him to give you his card when we go on board,' Corbeau said.

By this time, they had reached the dock.

Mollien and Corbeau dismounted and handed their bridles to Northover.

'Might I bid Captain Babineaux a safe journey? He can then give me his card himself,' Northover said.

Knowing Babineaux was not on the ship, Corbeau dissuaded Northover.

'It is probably best if no one observes you coming on board, Lieutenant. I will fetch him for you,' Corbeau said and walked up the gangplank followed by Mollien.

In a few moments, Corbeau returned and came back down the gangplank.

'I am sorry, Lieutenant Northover. Babineaux has indeed broken his leg and cannot come to you. He sends his card to you, and his best regards. He says when he comes to visit Napoleon again, he will be sure to look for you.'

'Thank you, Sir,' Northover said, disappointed, but

taking the card from Corbeau.

'My pleasure, Sir. *Au revoir,* Lieutenant. You have been of great help to us,' Corbeau said.

'Goodbye, Monsieur Corbeau,' Northover said.

Leading the horses out of the way, he stepped back to allow the dockers to remove the gangplank.

Northover watched as the crew weighed anchor. He stayed while the sailors readied the ship. Exhilaration filled him as he watched the sails fill and belly. The crew manned the sheets, positioning the sails to catch the wind.

The ship moved slowly from the dock and turned. She sailed farther away as the outgoing tide took her in its grip.

Northover waited a long time on the dock, watching her.

The horses in his charge stamped and pawed the ground, reminding him he had duties to perform.

Lieutenant Northover could not understand why he felt such a sense of loss as *La Miséricorde* left Jamestown, heading for the open sea.

CHAPTER TWENTY SEVEN

Nautilus, submerged, moved out of Sandy Bay. Moving West, she skirted the Island and then headed North of St Helena. A while into the journey, Tom emptied the ballast tanks and the vessel surfaced. Still visible in the distance, St Helena loomed to the south.

Going on deck, Tom and Pedro hoisted up the masts and set the sails.

If observed from the island the submarine would appear to be a distant fishing boat, barely worthy of notice.

After scanning the horizon, he turned to Pedro.

'Not a ship in sight, Pedro. We are safe from the British patrols,' he said.

'For now, Tom,' Pedro said. 'Babineaux told me they saw a frigate and two brigs while they were in port. But I doubt they would take notice of a vessel so small as *Nautilus*.'

'I would rather not take the chance. We must get out of here as soon as we may. First, I must take bearings,' Tom said and, having retrieved his telescope from the chest, while St Helena was still visible, Tom noted the position of several points on the island. From this information he could calculate his position.

When he had finished taking his bearings, Tom went below to plot a course for the rendezvous point with *La Miséricorde*. He went to a locker and took out his marine chronometer. Precious to him because it was an expensive piece of equipment, it was also precious because Ned had given it to him as a present when The Navy appointed Tom as Navigator.

In the cabin, Babineaux felt the craft surface and heard Tom and Pedro go on deck. As *Nautilus* began to move forward on the waves, Babineaux wondered how much longer it would be before they would rendezvous with

La Miséricorde.

Babineaux went from the main cabin to the small cabin astern to make sure Napoleon still slept. He walked back through the main cabin to the bridge to find Tom standing over a map on his sloped desk.

Hearing Babineaux enter, Tom stood up straight. He placed his hands on his lower back and stretched.

'Do I disturb you, Tom?' Babineaux asked.

'No, Adrien, not at all. Come in. I have calculated our position and am about to set a course for the rendezvous.'

Babineaux leant forward and looked at the spot Tom had marked on the map.

'How long will it take to get there?'

'It is difficult to say. If the winds hold, a matter of about three hours. The sky is clear, so even after dark, navigation is possible,' Tom explained.

Babineaux had some knowledge in the use of Tom's instruments, having plotted routes when he was in the army. But his skills were nothing compared to Tom's.

'Come on deck with me, Adrien. I must relieve Pedro. I am not a cook. He is, and I am hungry.'

Opening the hatch in the roof of the bridge, Tom climbed up to the deck. Babineaux followed.

The wind, steady and cold, was behind them. Babineaux, wearing his makeshift coat, felt it slash him like a sword. Sea spray swept over the bulwarks, hitting him in the face.

'She's sailing well, Tom, and the wind is fair,' Pedro said to Tom, acknowledging Babineaux with a nod.

'It might be fair, Pedro, but it is exceedingly cold. I think I will go below again,' Babineaux said, eyeing Tom and Pedro's warm clothing.

'You can help Pedro cook, Adrien,' Tom said, glancing at Pedro.

'Agh, I wish you'd learn to cook, Tom,' Pedro said, disappearing below with Babineaux.

Pedro was not a proficient cook. However, he knew how to heat the food. He also knew how to add spices to a dish to make it more palatable. More importantly, Pedro knew about scurvy and served pickled vegetables and fruit with his meals.

They stored all their supplies in chests stacked in a corner of the main cabin. Two barrels stood beside the chests, one holding salted meat, the other the pickles.

When the food was ready, Pedro put two spoons and two square dishes of unidentifiable meat stew on the table.

'Either Tom or I must be on deck, Adrien. I do not like eating alone. So, come, eat with me.'

'I am pleased to share your company, Pedro,' Babineaux said, taking a seat at the small table.

Pedro was about to sit when a thought came to him.

'Should we wake the Général?' he asked.

'No, he needs his sleep. I will look in on him when we have eaten.'

Although the food did not look appetising, to Babineaux's surprise, it tasted good. He ate it with relish.

'Have you served the Général for long, Captain?' Pedro asked.

'I have. I was in the Horse Grenadiers of the Imperial Guard. As the name suggests, we guarded the emperor. Our common love and respect for him created a comradery between us. Ah, Pedro. I miss those days,' Babineaux said, nostalgia blurring the horrors of war.

'Was Colonel Corbeau in the same regiment?' Pedro asked.

'He was. We are disbanded now, though. But what of you? Have you always worked for Tom?'

'In the old smuggling days, I did, yes. You say you shared comradery; so did Tom's crew. We all came to help when we heard of this voyage.'

'What did you do when Tom left off smuggling?'

'Me and the rest of us, we joined the Navy, and

went straight, like Tom. Plenty of work for a sailor in wartime. Not so much now though,' Pedro said with a rueful smile.

When they finished their food, Pedro returned to the deck to relieve Tom.

Babineaux went to see whether Napoleon had woken.

'Ah, Mon Général, I trust you feel refreshed after your rest,' Babineaux said, seeing Napoleon balanced on the side of the hammock.

'I do, Adrien. And now I am hungry. I believe I smell ragout,' he said, rising to his feet.

Babineaux pursed his lips, shaking his head.

'You smell food, Monseigneur, but it is a far cry from ragout. However, it tastes better than it looks, and will fill your stomach.'

Babineaux held the door for Napoleon to pass into the main cabin. They ducked their head as they passed through the low door.

Going to a chair, Napoleon sat at the table.

'Where is Tom Johnson?' he asked. 'I must speak with him.'

'He is on deck, keeping the ship on course. I must speak with him, too. I suspect we have the same subject in mind,' Babineaux said.

He went to a shelf where a pot sat on a gimbal. Babineaux ladled stew onto a dish.

'About his payment?' Napoleon said.

'Yes, Mon Général. Corbeau gave him money for his expenses but was vague when discussing the full amount. Forty thousand was mentioned, but he would not fully commit until you were safely off St Helena.'

Babineaux placed the dish on the table before Napoleon.

'Indeed, he wrote as much in the letters you brought to me. I agreed and instructed him in my reply. Do you think Johnson would join our cause, Adrien?'

Babineaux took a spoon from a box and placed it by

270

the dish. He shook his head and gave a low laugh.

'Oh, ho-ho. No, Monsieur. He told me once he owes allegiance to no one but himself, not even to the British Government. Nevertheless, I am certain he has no hostility towards you, or towards the French in general. He has helped our cause because we pay him to do so. Do not misunderstand me; I like the man. But he is a rogue.'

Pulling out his chair, he sat back down to finish his food.

'A rogue to whom I owe much, Adrien. I am of a mind to reward him handsomely—a lot more than forty thousand. What say you?'

'Yes. I agree. Without him, our venture could not have come about.'

Tom entered the cabin and found Babineaux and Napoleon eating. He picked up a dish and went to the pot.

'May I join you, Messieurs?' he asked.

'Of course, Tom,' Babineaux replied. 'Maritime ragout is on the menu.'

Tom chuckled and ladled Pedro's concoction into the dish. Taking a spoon from the box, Tom moved to the table and sat opposite Napoleon.

'We wish to speak with you, Tom,' Babineaux said.

'Hmm?' Tom said, his mouth full.

'We are entirely indebted to you, Mr Johnson,' Napoleon began. 'I wondered whether you would throw in your lot with us? Although I am not sure where I shall go, I mean to continue my mission to bring my principles to the world, ruling people fairly, with integrity, justice, and compassion for honest and honourable people. Those who oppress others and hinder my aims, I will overcome,' Napoleon said, a spark to his eye and fervent passion in his voice.

Tom swallowed his food.

'Noble sentiments, Sir. Liberté. Égalité. Fraternité,' he said and raised another spoonful to his mouth.

271

'Adrien thinks you would not wish to be part of my enterprise, Tom.'

Chewing his food, Tom said nothing. He sipped at the glass of water beside him before he answered.

'No, Sir. Adrien is right. I do not take any interest in politics. I would not lend myself to revolutionary uprisings or governing people. I have seen too much corruption. Too many men wish only for power so they may line their pockets and appear important. They want to place themselves above their fellow man. I want no part of that.'

'And yet you are helping me to escape,' Napoleon said.

Tom took a breath and looked intently at the once mighty Napoleon.

'I believe your ambitions are noble, Sir. The overthrow of the oppressive aristocracy in France was supposed to rid your country of tyrants. It did not. It removed oppressors to make way for other self-aggrandising despots. You brought order to that chaos. You were successful there,' Tom said.

Napoleon accepted Tom's approval as his due since he believed in the rightness of his cause.

Tom hadn't finished.

'But then you spread your wings abroad, Sir. Not content with ruling France, you went on campaign to impose your governance far and wide. What did your ambitious crusades accomplish?'

Tom paused for effect.

'Nothing but the spilt blood of war. Death and poverty reigned for lowly people everywhere you planted your foot.'

Tom leant forward, eye to eye with Napoleon.

'Do you think you can accomplish a better outcome in the countries of America?'

Tom breathed heavily, fire in his belly as he paused before his next words.

'I doubt it,' he uttered gruffly.

Tom strove to gain control of his rising passion before he continued.

'Sir, I must tell you, I was born into poverty. Orphaned at an early age, I lived on my wits. Anything I have gained I earned by my own endeavour.

'I have watched those in power grind the last drop of blood from the poor, then criticise and punish them when they became indigent. I have no love for hierarchy.

'Why do I help you, you ask? And I answer: because I see some good in you. You are the successful Général who won many glorious victories. But then you craved power and adulation. Perchance you may accomplish your original high ideals in the countries in this part of the world. Some have overthrown their governments, just as France did. Can you bear to lead them to peace without courting fame?'

No one had ever spoken to Napoleon in this way. He listened to Tom's speech with his chin raised, his mouth a thin line, his eyes dark and brooding.

A tense, pregnant silence blanketed the cabin. Babineaux dared not speak as the two formidable characters held each other's gaze.

Have I gone too far? Tom wondered.

The stormy look left Tom's eyes. His shoulders relaxed. He almost smiled.

'I am sorry if I speak out of turn, Sir. I do not mean to insult you. I merely speak my mind. Thank you for complementing me by asking me to join you, Sir, but the answer is no.'

Napoleon looked down at the table for a moment. Lifting his head to face Tom, the Général spoke.

'I may not have suffered the hardships you describe, Mr Johnson. But I experienced hardship just the same. My native land is Corsica, as you may notice from my accent.

'The year after I was born, Corsica came under French rule. As the nation was perishing, I was born.

273

Thirty thousand Frenchmen were vomited on to our shores, drowning the throne of liberty in waves of blood. Such was the odious sight which was the first to strike me. I am no stranger to oppression. When Corsica revolted, I was there.

'I was educated in France, and graduated from a military academy, yet I fought against the French. Later I returned to the army and fought against royalists. When the revolutionary regime became corrupt, I fought against them too. I never asked for adulation. It was thrust upon me. However, having tasted power, I used it to advance France's rule—France's rule, not mine, Mr Johnson. I believe I have done more good than harm in France. My reward is abandonment by the country I love and delivery into the hands of my enemies.'

Babineaux watched the two strong men from either end of the social scale.

Tom, quick-witted, with an abundance of self-taught knowledge. A villain, yes, but men looked up to him.

Napoleon, well-educated, equally quick of mind, capable of ruling nations.

He felt he had to speak.

'Mr Johnson, I served under my Général when I was with the Grenadiers. He never acted towards his fighting men as someone far above them. He treated us with respect. We all loved and revered him.

'His staff were a different matter. They acted in the way you describe, lusting for power and recognition. This man before you did not. Yes, he accepted their adulation. He was the one person who deserved it. You do not know him as I do.'

Tom studied Babineaux, knowing him to be a man of integrity. He had wisdom beyond his years in dealing with people. Never would he have behaved in the high-flown manner Mollien adopted. And Tom liked him for it.

Thinking further, Tom frowned. He knew that in

times of war, hatred for the enemy was encouraged. Now he realised that British propaganda coloured his view of Napoleon

A different silence came upon them as Tom and Napoleon evaluated each other.

It could be that Napoleon is the one exception to the rule where men in power are concerned, Tom reflected.

Napoleon knew Tom Johnson for someone with values of his own; a rebel against the status quo. Although not formally educated, he exhibited sharp intelligence. Had he not collaborated with Fulton in the building of the vessel on which they now travelled? Had not Johnson masterminded the plot to set him free? Coupled with this, Babineaux had said he regarded Tom as a born leader of men. He reported that Tom's comrades thought highly of him.

Babineaux made his own evaluation of Tom and Napoleon.

Poles apart, yet much alike, was his conclusion.

Napoleon leant back in his seat, one hand resting on his portly stomach.

'Ah,' he breathed. 'Perhaps my time has passed. I do not know. Nevertheless, acquainted as I am with revolution, I may be of some service to the American lands.'

'And if such is not the case, Sir, what will you do?' Tom asked.

'I do not know, Mr Johnson. We have made many plans; explored different avenues. My brother, Joseph, sits in comfort in America—making the bullets for me to fire, I think. I love him, but he never showed much spark.'

Napoleon lowered his head as he thought of his brother.

'How different things might be had they allowed me to go to him in America instead of incarcerating me on St Helena.'

Napoleon gave a rueful smile and a gentle laugh.

'Agh, perhaps I have outstayed my welcome on the world's stage,' Napoleon said as he looked at Tom. 'You ask me, Mr Johnson, what I shall do if my services are not required. I have never been one to sit contemplating. I must be doing. Perhaps I should channel my energies into managing a plantation somewhere.'

Tom raised an eyebrow.

'I understand your predicament, Sir. I am also a man who "must be doing" as you put it. I am about to marry when I return to England. But I shall not be still. I mean to acquire an estate, and hope the running of it will keep me occupied. I promised my Nancy there would be no more ventures for me.'

'Then my proposition will not go amiss, Mr Johnson,' Napoleon said. 'I mean to reward you well for releasing me from captivity.'

Tom's face illuminated in surprise. He leant back and glanced from Napoleon to Babineaux and back.

'Thank you, Sir,' he said and laughed.

Napoleon felt the need to explain further.

'When France sold Louisiana to the Americans, the deal was brokered by Barings Bank in London. The letter which Adrien brought back from me to Count Mollien in London instructed him to contact Barings. Once I am safe, Mollien will furnish you with papers which you must present to them on your return. Half-a-million in gold awaits you there.'

Tom's voice rose an octave.

'How much?' he asked, not believing his ears.

'Half-a-million. Is it enough?'

'Enough? Enough, he says! Napoleon, never in my wildest dreams did I contemplate so much money. Forty thousand was what Mollien mentioned. Why, I could buy a whole county for half a million,' Tom said.

Unable to keep still Tom rose from his seat to pace three steps in one direction and then in the other in the small space of the cabin.

Napoleon smiled and nodded to Babineaux who chuckled at the sight of Tom, always calm in the face of danger but unsettled at the thought of such a windfall.

CHAPTER TWENTY EIGHT

Tom stood on the forecastle of *Nautilus* with his telescope to his eye. She was nearing her destination, and Tom was eager to get his first glance of *La Miséricorde*.

Pedro watched as Tom swept the horizon for the hundredth time; back and forth, back and forth. Then Pedro saw him stiffen and swing the telescope back to where he had looked a moment before.

He turned to Pedro, his face beaming.

'I see a ship, Lad, Tom said.

Pedro hardly dared breathe as Tom looked through the telescope again.

'I can't tell whether it is her or not. She's about the right size.'

'Will I go below and tell them?' Pedro asked.

'Not yet,' Tom said. 'We'll wait until we're sure. If it's not, we might need to submerge. I'll keep watching.'

Pedro stood as still as he could, holding onto a rope to steady himself. Tom continued to watch the ship in the distance.

Tom took his eye from the telescope.

'I think it's her,' he speculated as he wiped spray from the lens. He put it to his eye again.

'Yes! I see the French Ensign. It has to be *La Miséricorde*. You can go below to tell them now, Pedro.'

Within moments of Pedro's disappearance below deck, Napoleon, Babineaux and Pedro came to stand beside Tom.

The biting wind was as cold as ever. Babineaux had wrapped himself in a blanket to ward off its penetrating chill. Napoleon was glad of Laroche's heavy, warm greatcoat.

La Miséricorde sailed close hauled into the wind,

moving swiftly towards *Nautilus.*

Anticipation built as the distance between the two vessels decreased. Tom waited until he could see the men on the deck of the other ship before he hailed them.

'Ahoy, *La Miséricorde,*' he roared.

A distant cheer from the larger vessel greeted him in reply.

Tom watched as the men at the stern of *La Miséricorde* prepared to throw down ropes attached to cables towards *Nautilus*. Others had already let down a rope ladder.

When they were close enough, Pedro caught the ropes and hauled the cables over to tether *Nautilus* to *La Miséricorde.*

Tom caught the rope ladder.

'Come, Sir,' Tom said to Napoleon and held the ladder taut for him to climb. Babineaux ascended next. Tom went to help Pedro fasten off the cables tethering the ships.

'Well, Pedro, we made it,' Tom said.

'Aye, Tom,' Pedro said and went ahead of Tom up the ladder. Tom made sure *Nautilus* was secure before he followed.

As Napoleon boarded *La Miséricorde,* his first sight was of the crew standing in a row facing him. As his feet touched the deck, they stood to attention. With a loud stamp, they saluted him.

Napoleon took his hat off, held it to his chest and bowed his head to them.

Corbeau and Mollien, filled with emotion, stepped forward and knelt before him, as did Renoudin.

Before they could speak, Napoleon said, 'Get up. Get up. I do not deserve such homage. And yet, I thank you for it,' a mixture of sorrow and happiness in his voice.

The three men stood and, along with Babineaux, led Napoleon towards the great cabin.

He went with them but looked around before he entered.

'Where is Tom Johnson?' he asked.

They turned to look at Tom.

Taken off guard, Tom stared back at them, unsure of what he should do.

'I am here, Sir,' he said.

'Well, do not stand there, Mr Johnson; we have matters to discuss,' Napoleon said and stepped back to let Tom enter first.

In the luxuriously appointed cabin, Babineaux led Napoleon to the head of the table.

Tom waited until they all took their seats before he sat down.

'Messieurs, particularly you, Mr Johnson, I must express my thanks for your efforts in effecting my rescue,' Napoleon said.

Count Mollien rose.

'On behalf of us all, Mon Général, I thank you and welcome you aboard *La Miséricorde.*'

Napoleon acknowledged Mollien's words with a tilt of his chin.

'Thank you, Nicolas. I will come straight to the point. I want to know what plans you have made for the future. But first I want to know how Mr Johnson is to return to England, for I do not believe he wants to go with us.'

'May I speak?' Babineaux asked.

'You may, Adrien. What have you to say?' Napoleon enquired.

Babineaux hadn't consulted anyone about the arrangements he had made for Tom. He looked around at the men sitting at the table, hoping they would approve what he had done.

'I put much thought into the matter and have arranged a solution. Before we left London, I made inquiries regarding trading ships heading for Ascension Island. I found one, called *Spirit of Enterprise,* and paid a visit to her captain. I informed him that in about eight or nine weeks we needed a ship to pick up three passengers from Ascension Island and give them passage to England.'

Babineaux looked at Tom.

'I assumed Mr Marriot and Pedro would want to return to England, too.'

Tom nodded. 'You assumed correctly, Monsieur.'

Babineaux continued.

'I asked Mr Leonard, the ship's Captain, to delay his return and await the passengers. I paid him two hundred gold guineas to do so. I promised that on the safe return of the men to England, he would receive a further three hundred guineas.'

Babineaux lifted his chin as his eyes wandered over the group to see whether they approved. Mollien's face showed disapproval. He rose from his chair, his attitude typically haughty.

'Captain Babineaux, do you not realise that for *La Miséricorde* to deposit Messieurs Johnson, Marriot and the Spaniard on Ascension Island, she must sail farther from our destination? Such manoeuvres will add weeks to our journey,' Mollien proclaimed.

Tom could see guarded amusement in Napoleon's eyes as he regarded Mollien.

'What is our destination, Nicolas?' Napoleon asked, his voice ominously quiet.

Mollien favoured Napoleon with a deferential bow of his head.

'Argentina, Mon Général.'

'Hmm,' Napoleon said.

He moved his gaze over Mollien, finally looking him in the eye.

'When did you decide on Argentina?'

'We discussed it on the voyage, Mon Général,' Mollien said, his face reddening.

Napoleon's brows knit with displeasure.

'I would prefer to be present when such decisions

are made, Nicolas. We may discuss this later.'

He turned to Babineaux.

'I approve your arrangements, Adrien. Nothing would have been accomplished without Mr Johnson. We owe it to him to see him safely on his way home.'

Tom could have laughed out loud. Napoleon had put the imperious Mollien in his place as no other could. His opinion of Napoleon went up yet another notch. He schooled his face to seriousness as he turned to the great man.

'Thank you, Sir.'

Tom cleared his throat.

Napoleon raised his eyes to look at him.

'What is it, Mr Johnson,' he asked.

'There is the matter of *Nautilus*, Sir.'

'Be easy, Tom,' Babineaux said. 'I informed Captain Leonard of the need to tow a yacht. He has agreed.'

'Good,' Tom said, with a nod in Babineaux's direction.

Napoleon swept his gaze over the men.

'Is there anything else?' he asked.

Corbeau rose.

'I propose we put aside further discussion until tomorrow. Mon Général, with your permission, we will partake of dinner.'

'Excellent, Paul. I admit I am hungry,' Napoleon said.

With a charming smile and a twinkle in his eye, he looked at Tom.

'With no disrespect to you, Mr Johnson, the food I consumed on *Nautilus* left a lot to be desired,' he said.

'While they are dressing the table, Messieurs, I think Babineaux, Mr Johnson and I should change out of these damnable clothes.'

He rose. A general scraping of chairs sounded as the rest of the company rose, too. The three men left the room to change; the others returned to their cabins to allow the servants to prepare the room. The servants took more care than usual, as did the cook and kitchen staff. They knew they must present a meal fit for an emperor.

At that time of year, the prevailing south-easterly winds on the South Atlantic Sea were fair. On her course toward Ascension Island, which the navigator calculated to last not more than a week, *La Miséricorde* sailed at a good speed.

Tom, now released from responsibility, took pleasure in wandering on deck. Loving the sea, he felt exhilarated and at peace, moods often at odds. But in Tom, the two emotions combined in a sense of contentment.

Tom held Napoleon's attention throughout the week as they wandered on deck together.

He had never met anyone like Tom, once a thief and a smuggler. Tom was a man with little respect for law, yet a man who could command loyalty from other men, and who exhibited similar attitudes to life as Napoleon himself.

'I will miss our conversations when you are gone, Mr Johnson. You have no idea how refreshing it is to speak to a man on equal terms as I do with you. Although we follow disparate paths, we have similar ideals. I am glad to have known you, but I doubt we will meet again,' Napoleon said during one of their frequent strolls around the deck.

Tom was aware of the compliment Napoleon paid him and was touched by it.

'I am pleased to have met you, too, Sir. It's a rare Englishman who can say he has known Napoleon. You are the only man I have met who, although he inspires respect and honour from those he commands, does not take advantage of his position. I believe what you have is called "the common touch".'

The day before they sighted land, Babineaux spoke to Tom in their cabin.

'Over these past months, Tom, I have come to regard you as a friend. I wonder whether we shall ever meet again?'

Tom smiled. He had become fond of the quiet, self-assured young man.

'Fate has a way of throwing people together, does it not, Adrien? Throughout my life, I have gathered many loyal friends. But I never thought I would befriend a Frenchman.'

Babineaux laughed.

'Nor I an Englishman. Or a rogue like you, Tom.'

Tom gave a mock scowl, then laughed and slapped Adrien on the back.

'We should not lose contact, Adrien. But I am not much of a writer of letters. I believe you are. I shall give you a friend's address in Chiswick, Ned Marlow; I stay with him at times. He is the nearest thing I have to a father. If you ever have cause to visit England, you may write to him, and he will direct you to me.'

'I would like that, Tom,' Babineaux replied.

Immediately he retrieved his portmanteau from on top of a chest and took his diary from it. He opened it on the table and, dipping his quill, sat poised to write.

Amused by Babineaux's typical efficiency, Tom dictated Ned's address.

'If ever you need my help again, Adrien, you know now how to contact me.'

Babineaux smiled as he replaced his pen in the inkstand.

'I doubt I will ever again set foot on French soil,' Tom continued. 'In case I do, you must give me your direction, too.'

Babineaux put his diary back in the portmanteau and withdrew a card. He handed it to Tom.

'This is my father's house in St Valery. It is my home.'

Tom took the card and read it.

'I know St Valery. It is not far from Dieppe.'

'Ah, Dieppe. You would know Dieppe, Tom, from your smuggling days, I think,' Babineaux said with a chuckle.

Tom nodded, tapped his nose, and gave a soft laugh.

'Aye,' he said, his eyes shining.

Tom knew the location of Ascension Island. Each morning, he stood on the forecastle with his telescope and scanned the horizon. Some mornings, Peter stood with him.

'Barring the wind changing, Peter, we should meet up with the *Spirit of Enterprise* sometime tomorrow.'

'And be back home in a couple of months,' Peter said.

Tom stood back and shut his telescope. With a steadying hand on a rope, he turned to Peter.

'It's been quite a venture, has it not Peter?'

'Indeed, it has, Tom. And we cannot speak of it. We'd be imprisoned, if not executed, if the government heard of it.'

Tom laughed. He refused to entertain the prospect of such things.

'You know, Peter, I'm of a mind to contact old Andrew Craddock.'

'Andrew Craddock? I don't think I know him, Tom, do I?' Peter asked.

'Yes, you do. He's a printer. You must know him. He gathers writings for *The Gentlemen's Magazine.* He also prints pamphlets. I promised him if I came across any scandalous material, I would contact him.'

Peter looked at Tom in amazement. He could not believe that Tom would be so reckless.

'Ah, Tom! How can you think to publish what we have done?'

'I do not mean to tell the whole, Peter. Just a hint in a question among a cluster of other tit-bits of scandal.

Only those involved would understand it.'

'You enjoy sailing close to the wind, Tom. Really you do.'

The following day they sighted the *Spirit of Enterprise* anchored just off the coast of Ascension Island. As Tom regarded the ship, he noted the shape of her stern and knew it would be an easy thing to tether *Nautilus* abaft.

Pedro came to stand beside Tom.

'I will not be coming with you, Tom. I have decided to stay on *La Miséricorde,*' he said.

Tom looked at him in surprise.

'Are you sure, Pedro? It's a big step, leaving your home.'

'England is not my home, Tom. I was born in España. My parents are dead. I have relatives in Buenos Aires, whom I have not seen in many years. I look forward to meeting them again.'

'I do not wish to put obstacles in your way, Pedro. I just hope you are not making a bad decision. How will you earn your living?'

'Thank you for your concern, Tom. I have already spoken to the captain. He will take me on whenever I wish to join his crew. I feel at home on this ship. Many of the crew are from Argentina.'

'I hear there is unrest in Argentina. They do not want Spanish rule. Different factions want to take over. You might be in the middle of an uprising.'

Pedro shrugged. He had been part of Tom's crew in their smuggling days. When Tom went straight, Pedro had joined the Navy. Now, with the country no longer at war, as with many sailors, he found it hard to find work. Tom's venture had filled him with excitement. Now it was over, he could not face going back to inevitable poverty. Argentina held out a hope to him.

'I believe in Argentina's independence. If I am not killed in the conflict, I'll be proud to be part of it.'

Tom did not try to dissuade him further. Pedro was younger than he. Tom recognised his need to be part of something. Not that Tom had ever felt that need, but he understood those who did.

'Good luck to you, then Pedro,' Tom said.

'And to you, Tom,' Pedro replied, holding a hand out to him.

Tom shook Pedro's hand and pulled him into an embrace. When they stepped apart, Pedro put two knuckles to his forehead, in salute to Tom, then turned, and walk away.

Tom watched him go with a feeling of regret.

With a jolt, he remembered his intention of rewarding all those who had helped him. He left the bulwark and went in search of Babineaux.

He was in their cabin, reading a book.

'Adrien, I have a favour to ask of you,' Tom said.

'What is it, Tom?' Babineaux said, setting the book aside.

'It's about Pedro. He is not returning to England. I want him to have his share of my reward. Can you help me?'

Babineaux glanced at Tom, frowning. His frown cleared as he grasped what must be done.

'Yes, Tom. It is easy. You must write a promissory note to me for the amount you wish him to receive. I will pay him out of my own funds, and when I return home, I will take the note to my bank, who will present it to yours. *Et voila* I am reimbursed,' Babineaux said with a wave of his hand.

'You make it all sound so simple, Adrien. Thank you. You must tell me what to write, and I will do it now,' Tom said.

Captain Leonard sent a jolly boat to *La Miséricorde* to pick up Tom, Peter, and their luggage.

'Before we depart, Peter, we must bid Napoleon and his entourage farewell,' Tom said.

'Of course, we must,' Peter replied.

They set off across the deck in the direction of the great cabin.

Before they reached it, Napoleon came onto the deck with Corbeau, Mollien, and Renoudin.

Renoudin came forward first to silently shake Tom's hand.

Corbeau was next. He did not shake his hand but embraced Tom.

'I bid you a safe journey, Mr Johnson,' he said, and added, 'If ever I have need of someone to carry out another clandestine enterprise, Tom, I shall call on you.'

Tom inclined his head.

'I am at your disposal, Corbeau,' Tom said, further venturing, 'as long as you pay me.'

Corbeau suppressed a laugh at Tom's audacious words.

Mollien stepped forward. To Tom's surprise, he was smiling.

'We are much indebted to you, Mr Johnson. I thank you for all you have done,' he said.

'I am pleased to have been of service to you Monseigneur,' Tom replied.

Tom looked about for Napoleon. The man for whom they had planned the venture stood apart from his men, watching the scene, in silent contemplation.

Tom moved to stand before him. Napoleon and Tom regarded each other with understanding in their eyes. Over the past month, a rapport had built between them. Napoleon, as was his habit, kissed Tom on both cheeks and held him at arms' length.

'Au revoir, Tom Johnson. Our meeting has been eventful, the outcome magnificent. I believe I owe you my life, for I am sure I would have died within a year if not rescued from St Helena. Good luck to you, Tom, and may God go with you.'

'Thank you, Your Imperial Majesty,' Tom said, and

bowed deeply to him.

Napoleon's eyes widened at being addressed in this manner by Tom, whom he knew was averse to paying homage to authority.

Tom took a step back and gave Napoleon a curt nod. His footsteps sounded on the deck as he walked confidently to join Peter by the opening in the Bulwark where a ladder led down to the waiting Jollyboat.

Napoleon, still reeling with surprise, watched Tom Johnson disappear down the ladder and out of his life.

Tom and Peter stood on the deck of the *Spirit of Enterprise* and watched *La Miséricorde* sail south. Their ship took to the north on the long journey to England.

Thoughts of Nancy filled Tom's mind. This time he did not dismiss them. He indulged in them with pleasure.

CHAPTER TWENTY NINE

Tom Johnson walked across London Bridge and made his way to Borough High Street, to visit The George in Southwark once more.

Whenever Tom returned from a voyage, the difference between the smells and noises and the feel of the city and of the sea always struck him.

On board ship, a symphony of sounds surrounded him. The wind whistling in the rigging, the flap of the sails, the waves lapping against the hull and the creaking of the ship moving through the swell of the ocean. He was never sure whether it was like a slap or a rough kiss when spray stung his face with its salty fishiness. Together, the ship the ocean and the wind became part of him.

Now, the city's sounds and aromas welcomed him. Street sellers voices as they plied their wares, the clip-clop and jingling harness of the horses drawing carts and coaches, their wheels rumbling over the cobbles. The close, warm mixture of smells from the city was also part of him. She held a vibrant buzz. Much of it was unpleasant to someone not used to it as Tom was. He had spent his childhood here. It had fashioned his senses.

The sea was a wonder when first he met her, so vast and dangerous in her power, fresh alive and exhilarating. She was like a lover. In contrast, the city was his mother.

At this time of day, mid-morning, the press of people going about their business along the pavements made Tom's progress difficult.

His thoughts were all of seeing Nancy again, of hugging and kissing her after his long absence. How she would look, eyes big and bright when he told her of his windfall.

He came to The George and looked up from the

courtyard at its galleries. It seemed cleaner than it had been before.

When Tom entered the tap room, he could not believe his eyes. He thought he had come to the wrong building. The place had changed out of all recognition. The settles, including the one he liked to think of as his own, were no longer there, replaced by benches on either side of long tables, a chair at either end. Gone was the inglenook fireplace, where Jimmy Young had sat eavesdropping. In its place, a shiny steel grate stood on the hearth, framed by a surround of carved sandstone, a new mantelpiece above it. A door replaced the brocade curtain that had divided the taproom from the kitchen.

The walls, once a nondescript-bluish hue, were whitewashed. Instead of sawdust-covered boards, the floor sported new granite paving slabs. Of the large barrels with the plank atop them, serving as a bar, and of the shelves behind, there was no sign. A newly-built, polished bar stood beside the kitchen door. No longer did the taproom smell of sawdust, spilt beer and tobacco smoke. Instead, the room smelt of paint, beeswax polish and of potpourri, pots of which stood on the mantle shelf above the fire, their scent wafting through the room.

Under the windows and in quiet corners of the room new tables and chairs replaced the old battered ones. To Tom's way of thinking, the old furniture had a familiar homely feel about it. The new was stark and uninviting.

A serving maid stood behind the bar polishing tankards and glasses. Another stood in front of it; her eyes alert as she watched the few customers conversing in low tones.

Tom looked past the girls, his eyes searching for Nancy. He took several purposeful steps towards the kitchen.

The maid from in front of the bar was quick to spot Tom as a new customer and moved towards him.

'Good afternoon, Sir. What is your pleasure?' she said, barring Tom's way.

'My pleasure is to know what has happened to this place,' Tom said, in a none too friendly manner.

'We have had changes, Sir,' the girl said, purposely holding on to her pleasant smile.

'Where's Nancy?'

'She's gone, Sir.'

Tom's eyes opened wide. He raised his voice.

'Gone? Gone where?'

The girl glowered at him, disliking his demanding attitude. She raised her chin and looked him in the eye.

'I don't know, Sir,' she said following the words with a dismissive shrug.

Tom's eyes blazed into hers.

She pursed her lips, slowly blinked her eyes and averted her gaze from Tom's.

Her discourteous unconcern infuriated Tom so much he caught her by the arm.

'Confound it, girl. You *must* know.'

The maid looked at Tom's hand and then at his face.

Tom, aware that he had stepped over the mark, let go.

'Where's Betty?' he asked in a quieter voice.

'She's gone, too, Sir. The new owner sent all the old staff away.'

Tom, baffled, raised his voice again.

'New owner? What happened to the old one?'

'He died, Sir,' she said, adopting a false, melancholy expression.

Tom lifted his chin and looked down his nose at her.

'Oh, aye?' he grunted. 'So, who's the new owner?'

'I think he's a relative of the old one. But I'm not sure,' she said.

Her pale blue eyes took on an innocent air. They opened wide as a thought struck her.

'Oh, but he kept Billy on—do you know Billy? He was the cook's assistant. He's a pot-boy now.'

A hopeful light shone in Tom's mind.

'Where is he?'

'He's washing the tankards. Do you want me to fetch him?'

'No, I'll go to him myself. Is the scullery in the same place?'

'Yes, Sir, it is, but we don't allow patrons in the back,' she said, sidling towards the door to block his way.

Tom snorted and narrowed his eyes.

The maid raised a hand. 'I'll fetch him for you,' she said. Avoiding further discussion, she moved towards the kitchen door.

At the door, she remembered her duty and turned back to face Tom.

'Would you like a tankard of ale while you wait, Sir?' she said, her simpering nasal voice grating on Tom's ears.

He was in a mind to throttle her, but curbed his temper and nodded.

'Yes, if you please,' Tom grunted.

The maid flicked her chin towards Tom as she passed the girl behind the bar. She disappeared into the kitchen as the other girl, who had watched the scene before her with dispassionate unconcern, put down her cloth. She took her time to choose a tankard and filled it from a barrel beneath the bar. Picking up her cloth again, she wiped a dribble from the side of the tankard.

Tom missed his old seat. Looking around, he decided to sit on a chair at the end of a table, his back to the fire, near where the settle used to be. From there he could observe the entire taproom. Not that there was much to observe. With the familiar old décor, The George had lost its atmosphere and most of its regulars.

The bar-girl came over to him with his tankard of ale. Tom noticed her clothes were the same as the other girl's. A white mop cap trimmed with lace sat on her head, covering her hair. She wore a white apron, also trimmed with lace, over a royal blue gown which buttoned up to the neck. Long sleeves, puffed at the top covered her arms.

Betty and Nancy had always worn their own style of clothes. They were both attractive and made the most of their appearance.

Tom found nothing to attract him in the two new girls; they weren't even pleasant. All trace of friendliness buried beneath a façade of efficiency.

The girl put his tankard before him, positioning it neatly.

'Can I get you anything else, Sir?'

'No. Not unless you can tell me where Nancy has gone,' he snapped.

'I heard Miss Langton explaining things to you, Sir. We don't know where any of the old staff are now, apart from Billy.'

Miss Langton returned with Billy. His eyes widened with pleasure at sight of Tom.

'Tom! You're back!' he said at the top of his voice.

'Sit down, Billy. Maybe you can tell me what's happened to…'

Miss Langton interrupted.

'Staff aren't allowed to sit with patrons, Sir.'

The possible loss of Nancy driving him to distraction, Tom lost his usual grip on his patience.

'Oh, for the love of God, woman, will you stow it? I want to know where my Nancy is. She's my fiancée. Billy, do you know where she is?'

Billy gave Miss Langton a sheepish look before he answered Tom.

'I sorta do, Tom. She went off with this man in a carriage, her and Betty.'

'What?' Tom shouted. He stood up and took Billy by the shoulders, about to question him further.

'We don't tolerate loud voices here, Sir. You must leave,' Miss Langton said, her hands folded in front of her, her back stiff, her eyes frosty.

'Oh, be damned to you, woman,' Tom growled. 'Come, Billy, you can tell me on the way to the coffee house.'

Tom strode towards the door, hauling Billy behind him by the arm.

'I'll lose me place, Tom,' Billy wailed.

Tom let go of Billy's arm. He turned towards the two girls, glaring at them.

'I'll give you a place, Billy. I need someone to run errands for me,' he said.

Swinging the heavy door open so that it banged on the newly-whitewashed wall, he held it and waited for the boy to go out.

As they left The George, Billy almost tripped over his feet, trying to keep up with Tom.

'What about me things, Tom?' Billy piped at Tom's back.

'I'll buy new things for you,' Tom called over his shoulder.

They were almost at St Saviour's church before Tom stopped and took Billy by the shoulders again.

'Where is she, Billy. Tell me,' he said, his eyes boring into Billy's.

'I told ya, Tom. She went off with a man in a carriage,' Billy said, the corners of his mouth pulled down.

'Who was the man?' Tom asked looming over him.

'I dunno. He came to The George a couple o' times afore it got took over. And then, on the last day, he came again an' took Nancy and Betty away,' Billy said, sniffing as he dragged his nose along his sleeve.

'God damn it,' Tom snarled. Straightening, he took his hands from Billy's shoulders, looking around him for inspiration.

His gaze fell on Billy again.

'Who is the new owner, Billy?' he asked, not holding out much hope that Billy would know.

'His name's Joseph Scarlett. I didn't like the look of

'im. Long streak he is, putting on airs an' graces and tryin' to talk posh, which I knows he never is. If I...ow!'

Billy yelped as Tom took his arm in a fierce grip.

'How can I get hold of him, Billy?'

'Let go me arm an' I'll tell ya,' Billy said.

Tom let go.

Billy cradled his arm and glared at Tom.

'Agh, I'm sorry Billy. Please, tell me what you know,' Tom said, ashamed at having taken out his frustration on Billy.

'Scarlett comes once a month to make sure the place is runnin' right and to collect the takin's,' Billy said.

'Tah', Tom spluttered, his lip curling.

Looking at Billy's worried face, Tom adjusted Billy's jacket and put a hand on his shoulder. Trying to be calm, he spoke to Billy in a milder tone.

'Can you think of anyone else who might know where Nancy is?'

Billy rubbed his forehead and wrinkled his nose.

'Gem *might* know. I saw 'im sayin' gubbye to Nancy afore she got into the coach with the man. 'Ere, Tom, did ya mean it when ya said you'd take me on?'

'Yes. You'll have to clean yourself up, though; you're very grubby. Where can I find Gem?'

'He went next door to work for them as owns the *White Hart*.'

'God's teeth, you young varmint! Why didn't you tell me that before?' Tom snarled and trod off, back the way he had come.

'Ya never arsked,' Billy said to Tom's retreating back before he ran after him.

With long, purposeful strides, Tom retraced his steps. He passed The George and waited at the door to the *White Hart* for Billy to catch up with him.

'Is there a back door, Billy?' Tom asked.

'Acourse, there is. Come on,' Billy said.

He dodged down a narrow alley between two

buildings. It led to the stable yard of the *White Hart*. Billy went to a door to the side of the stables and pushed it open. He turned to make sure Tom followed, then disappeared into a musty-smelling, gloomy passage leading to the kitchen.

The smells, the noise and the bustle, reminded Tom of The George on a coaching day. Gem was busy at the range. Tom's thoughts turned to Nancy again. It was on a coaching day he had asked her to marry him.

'How do, Gem,' Billy said.

Gem turned his head. Seeing Billy, he straightened.

'What are you doin' here, Billy?'

'Tom wants to know where Nancy is,' Billy said, indicating Tom with his thumb.

Gem caught sight of Tom. He handed his cooking fork to another man, wiped his hands on his apron and held out his hand to Tom.

'Well, I'm blessed. Tom Johnson.'

Tom shook Gem's hand.

'Do you know where Nancy is, Gem?'

Gem scratched his head.

'Well, I know she went off with a man, Tom. But I'm damned if I know who he was.'

'What did he look like?' Tom asked, becoming frustrated.

'He was in a coach, and it was dark. I couldn't see his face. But judging by his clothes, he was gentry. Sorry I can't give you any more, Tom,' Gem said.

'Ah, don't apologise, Gem. Thank you anyway. Come, Billy,' Tom said.

They left the hot, busy kitchen where Gem shouted, 'get on with it' to the staff, who had stopped to listen.

Back in Borough High Street, Tom looked down at the scruffy boy standing next to him. Billy looked up at Tom.

'What now, then, Tom?' he asked.

'Well, I'm not going all over London with you looking like that. On the rare occasions you wash, where do you go?'

'I sluices meself under the pump in the inn yard every Sunday.'

'Right. Go back to the *White Hart* and clean yourself up. Here's five shillings. Go and buy yourself something to eat, then buy some decent clothes. Be as quick as you can—without skimping on the washing— and meet me in *The Hambro Coffee House* in Water Lane when you're done,' Tom said and strode off along Borough High Street to buy himself breakfast.

After finishing his breakfast, Tom sat reading a newspaper and drinking coffee. He couldn't take in what he read, and he found the coffee tasteless.

Someone came to stand beside him. Tom looked up. It was Billy, although Tom didn't recognise him at first. Under his close-fitting short, brown jacket, Billy wore a white shirt with a round collar, trimmed with a ruffle. The buttoned cuff of his dark grey twill breeches met white woollen stockings coming up to his knees. Laced black ankle boots completed the picture. He carried a new cap in his hand. He had beaten his hair into submission, and his face shone with cleanness. The only recognisable thing about him was his crooked smile.

'How do, Tom. Here's your change,' Billy said, beaming at him and holding out his hand with several coins on his palm.

'Keep it, Billy,' Tom said, amazed at the transformation.

'Thanks, Tom,' Billy breathed as he swiftly put the coins in his pocket.

'How good are you at calling a cab?' Tom asked.

'Reckon I'm better at it now I looks respectable. Where do ya want to go?' Billy asked.

'Rathbone Place,' Tom said.

'Right y'are,' Billy said and dashed off.

Moments later he opened the coffee shop door.

'It's here, Tom,' he called.

Tom went to the door. Outside, he got into the waiting cab.

'Fifty-five Rathbone Place, please Jarvey,' Tom said and leant back in his seat.

Billy hesitated on the pavement.

'Well, don't just stand there. Get in,' Tom ordered.

Billy looked excited. He had never ridden in a coach or a cab before. He climbed in and sat next to Tom.

On the way, Tom thought about the boy next to him.

He's not much older than I was when Ned took me in. He's an orphan, too. I wonder whether I'm balancing the books by taking Billy on? Although he talks too much, he's not a stupid lad; he's quite intelligent.

Tom's thoughts turned to Nancy and her whereabouts.

Where the hell is she? Why didn't she leave a message with someone?

Billy interrupted his reflections.

'Why are we goin' to Rathbone Place, Tom?'

'I want to see what Peter makes of this,' Tom said.

'Who's Peter?'

'A friend.'

'What d'ya think this friend can do, Tom?' Billy asked.

'I don't know, Billy; but two heads are better than one,' Tom replied.

The cab pulled up at Rathbone Place.

'Go and knock on the door, Billy,' Tom said as he got out of the cab.

Billy jumped from the cab onto the pavement. He walked cautiously up the steps and reached a hand up to the lion's head knocker while Tom went to pay the driver.

Billy flipped the knocker twice and stood back, hoping Tom would join him before anyone came to the door.

Tom reached the door as Nate, the apprentice who had opened it to Tom the last time, opened it again today.

He recognised Tom and smiled.

'Good morning, Mr Johnson. Mr Marriot is in; you can go straight up, Sir.'

'Thank you, Nate. Come, Billy,' Tom said.

Billy's eyes followed Nate (not much older than himself) who had gone back to his printing work. Billy stuck his head around the door and saw the lad pick up a shallow box and put pieces of lead into it. Mystified Billy wandered into the room.

'Billy!' Tom called.

Billy beat a hasty retreat. He reached the top of the stairs as Tom knocked on Peter's door.

'Tom! Welcome, I didn't expect to see you so soon,' Peter said when he opened the door.

'I didn't expect it either, Peter,' Tom said, entering Peter's room.

He looked around for Billy who was standing inside the door, peering around the room.

'Go and sit over there out of the way, Billy,' Tom said.

Billy perched himself on the chair Tom indicated.

Peter could see there was something wrong.

'Tom, you look worried. What's the matter?' he asked.

'I can't find Nancy,' Tom blurted out. 'She's not at The George. The only thing I know is that she went off in a coach with a man. Gem said he looked like gentry.'

'Have you asked around?' Peter said.

'No, not yet. I don't know where to start,' Tom answered and began to pace the room.

Pausing in his pacing, he looked at Peter, a concerned expression in his eyes.

'We were going to be married, Peter.'

'Yes, I know, Tom. Sit down. Let's think this through,' Peter said.

Tom told Peter about The George having a new owner and the changes made.

'Would the new owner know where Nancy went?' Peter asked.

'He might. But he only visits The George once a month, and they haven't got his address.'

'You should go to Chiswick and see Ned. He's got more connections than the King. He even mixes with gentry these days. He could probably find her for you, Tom,' Peter suggested.

'Good Lord, Peter! Why didn't I think of that? I promised to visit him on my return!'

Peter lifted his mobile eyebrow and smiled.

'Ahhh!' Tom breathed in relief, his gloomy expression clearing.

'Yes,' he said, 'That's a good idea, Peter. I'll do that; I'll do it right away.'

'You can borrow my coach, Tom. Do you want me to go with you?'

'Yes, Peter; if you wouldn't mind. We can put our heads together on the way,' Tom said.

'If you still can't find her, I can have some leaflets printed asking whether anyone's seen her, and offering a reward for information,' Peter suggested.

'I'd rather not do that. We'd have all the scroungers in creation saying they found her and claiming the reward. We might do that as a last resort, though,' Tom said.

'I'll go down and tell them in the stables to ready my carriage,' Peter said, making for the door.

Billy had listened to the men's conversation with interest. He jumped up.

'I can do that for you, Mr Peter. Tom's hired me to do errands. Might as well earn me keep. Where's the stables, Sir?' he asked.

Peter raised an eyebrow as he glanced at Tom, then faced Billy.

'Downstairs, along the passage and out through the

back door,' Peter said.

Billy nodded and was off. They heard him clattering down the stairs and then, in the distance, a door banged.

'Who is he, Tom?' Peter asked.

'He's me, twenty or so years ago, Peter.'

Peter gave Tom a questioning look.

'I was about his age when Ned found me. Billy is an orphan. He was the cook's assistant when The George was taken over. They kept him on as a pot-boy. But I have the impression they give him all the dirty jobs to do. He may be a bit rough and raw, but he has quick understanding.'

Within five minutes Billy was back.

'They're wheelin' the coach out and getting' the horses ready, Sir,' Billy said.

'I must pack a portmanteau and...'

'You get your stuff out, Sir, an I'll pack it for you,' Billy said, eager to impress Tom with his efficiency.

Half an hour later found Tom and Peter in the coach, bowling along towards Chiswick. Billy, to his great delight, sat up next to the driver, chatting to him and learning all he could about driving a team.

When they arrived at Mirabilis House, Billy jumped down to open the coach door. Tom and Peter alighted.

'Kit Coachman wants to know where's the stables,' Billy asked Tom.

'Tell him to drive to the left of the house. He will see them at the back,' Tom said, before climbing the steps to the front door.

Peter followed him.

Tom knocked. He stood back from the door, pulling at his waistcoat, and adjusting his neckcloth.

When Chivers opened the door, he was surprised to find Tom there.

'We didn't expect you home so soon, Mr Tom. I hope you had a pleasant voyage, Sir,' he said, holding the door wide.

'Thank you, Chivers, I did,' Tom said, as he entered the hall. Chivers took their hats and turned to put them on the French mahogany marble-topped console table.

'Will you please tell Ned I am here with a guest, Chivers.'

Chivers nodded graciously and walked with dignity to the back of the house.

'I hope Ned doesn't mind us descending on him without notice, Tom,' Peter said, feeling uncomfortable as he looked about at the opulence of the house.

'Who? Ned?' Tom asked and laughed. 'Ned is never put out by such things. He will be pleased by the diversion. I just hope he can help me,' Tom said.

When Chivers told his master of Tom's visit, Ned Marlow hurried into the hall to greet him.

'Well, well, Tom. How are you, my boy?' he said, putting a hand on Tom's shoulder.

'I'm well, Ned. But I need your help.'

'Oh?' Ned said. 'Come in and be comfortable while you tell me what you want me to do for you.'

He led the way to the drawing room at the back of the house. The French doors to the veranda stood open. From there, Ned had been watching the river go by, just as Tom had found him on his last visit.

Chivers was in the room arranging glasses and a decanter on a tray. He placed this on a table next to two couches arranged at right angles to a magnificent marble fireplace.

'I assume you will stay for dinner, both of you?' Ned asked.

'Yes, if you please, Ned,' Tom answered.

'Advise the cook, Chivers,' Ned instructed.

With his customary dignity, Chivers bowed and left the room.

'Ned, you remember my friend, Peter Marriot,' Tom said.

'Of course, I do, the ex-riding officer.' Ned said, pouring brandy into the glasses on the tray.

'Yes, Sir, until Tom showed me the error of my ways,' Peter said accepting the glass that Ned handed to him.

'Peter forged the papers we used on our recent enterprise, Ned,' Tom said, picking up a glass for himself.

'You must have been an invaluable asset to Tom, Mr Marriot. Do sit,' Ned said indicating a couch.

Peter smiled and took a seat.

Tom joined him on the couch. 'Yes, he was,' he said and raised his glass in salute to Peter.

Ned sat opposite Tom and Peter. He turned his famous impenetrable stare on Tom.

'Tell me, what do you want of me, Tom?'

Tom cleared his throat.

'You remember when I came here before I went to St Helena?'

'I do. And a very pleasant visit it was,' Ned replied.

'And do you remember I told you I was engaged to be married?'

'Yes. To a serving maid from The George, as I recall,' Ned said, a light coming to his eye.

'Well, Ned, I went to The George today, and she wasn't there. No one knows where she is. The only thing I know is that she went somewhere with a gentrified man in a coach.'

Ned glanced down at his sleeve and flicked a speck of dust from the cuff.

'Indeed?' he said, unmoved.

'I thought maybe you could help me find her,' Tom said, puzzled by Ned's lack of response.

Without a word, Ned went to sit behind a desk near the window. He took a sheet of paper and, dipping a quill in the inkwell, he began to write.

Tom and Peter looked at each other, baffled by Ned's unconcerned behaviour.

Ned shook sand on the note, folded it and wrote something on the outside.

He went to the bell cord beside the fireplace and pulled it.

Chivers appeared.

'Give that to my visitors, please, Chivers,' he said, handing him the note.

Chivers took it, bowed, and left.

'What was all that about?' Tom asked, annoyed that Ned did not seem to grasp the enormity of Nancy's disappearance.

'All in good time, Tom. You were saying?'

'I was telling you that my fiancée has disappeared, and I was asking for your help in finding her,' Tom said, tight-lipped.

Ned tutted.

'Now, now, Tom. There is no need to fly into a miff. I will help you. But you must have patience.'

Chivers came back into the room.

'Dinner is served, Mr Edward,' he said as he held the door open.

'You delivered the note?' Ned asked.

'I did, Sir.'

'Is all in place,' Ned said.

'It is, Sir,' Chivers replied.

Ned smiled. 'Come, gentlemen. I, for one, have an appetite,' he said.

He sauntered into the hall and up the stairs to the dining room without a backward glance.

'I don't understand this, Peter. Is he playing games with me or what?' Tom said, ascending the stairs beside Peter.

'From what I remember of him, Tom, he's a wily old cove. I think he's got something up his sleeve,' Peter said, viewing with interest the impressive, ornate, black iron banisters and the sweeping curve of the wide staircase, carpeted in dark red.

'Oh yeah? What?' Tom said, his frustration mounting.

They came to the top of the stairs, and entered the

dining room.

Tom stopped short.

A woman stood by the fireplace. Slowly she turned to face him.

'Nancy!'

'Hello, Tom,' she said, giving him a radiant smile.

She wore a deep-blue silk gown, made in the latest high-waisted fashion, with a low neckline, puff sleeves, and trimmed with silver lace. Her dark hair tumbled over her shoulders; her eyes shone.

Tom, in a daze, moved towards her and gazed into her eyes.

'I thought I'd lost you,' he murmured as he took her hands in his and brought them to his lips.

'Betty's here too, Tom,' Nancy said looking towards the window.

Tom glanced in Betty's direction.

'So she is,' Tom said, returning his eyes to feast on Nancy.

Betty had watched the reunion with tears in her eyes.

Peter watched Betty with admiration in his.

Betty wore a jonquil-yellow muslin gown, similar to Nancy's, with a high waist and puff sleeves. A green ribbon wove through her golden curls.

Ned went to her and drew her arm through his.

'Betty, my dear, as Tom is otherwise occupied, may I introduce you to Mr Peter Marriot, Tom's long-standing friend.'

Betty nodded to Peter, her eyes twinkling.

'Peter, this is Nancy's cousin, Betty,' Ned said.

'I know, Ned. We've met before when I visited The George. I'm pleased to see you again, Betty.'

'I'm pleased to see you, too, Mr Marriot. You were dressed as a government official last time. You looked very important.'

Delicious aromas filled the room as Ned's servants arrived carrying trays packed with covered silver dishes.

They had set the table for five with shining silver cutlery, sparkling cut glass, and gilt Coalport china.

'Put the dishes on the table. We shall serve ourselves,' Ned said.

The servants, supervised by Chivers, deposited the dishes on the table and left.

Before Chivers could go, Tom called him.

'Chivers, do you know the whereabouts of my errand boy, Billy?'

'I do, Mr Tom. He is in the kitchen. The Cook says he looks half-starved, so she is feeding him,' Chivers said in solemn tones.

Tom laughed.

'Keep an eye on him, Chivers. He's a good lad, but he's inquisitive. I wouldn't want his curiosity to lead him into trouble.'

Chivers bowed and with his slow gait, left the dining room.

Tom's delight at seeing Nancy was so great, it had put all else from his mind. He turned to Ned.

'Tell me, Ned, how has this come about? How is it that Nancy and Betty are here?'

Ned smiled and led them to the table.

'Let us be comfortable first, Tom, then I shall explain everything.'

Tom was used to Ned's habit of keeping people in suspense. With difficulty, he stifled his curiosity and followed Ned.

Ned's place was at the head of the table, with Nancy to his right, and Betty to his left. Tom sat next to Nancy and Peter next to Betty.

Before he took his seat, Ned filled their glasses with good white wine.

'We shall celebrate with champagne at the end of the meal,' he said as he took his seat.

While they passed the dishes of rare and luscious food around the table, Nancy turned to Tom.

'Billy's here, Tom?' she asked.

'Yes, Nancy-love. I'll tell you about it later. For now, I want to know how you got here,' Tom said looking at Ned.

'How did it happen, Ned?' he asked, hoping Ned would not prolong the suspense.

Ned took pity on him. He put down his knife and fork and took a sip of wine before launching into the tale.

'After you sailed, I decided to meet this girl of yours. I went to The George and introduced myself to Nancy. I was pleasantly surprised. She is a lovely girl and not at all what I expected. When I told her I had watched you go, I saw tears in her eyes. I invited her to come to Chiswick, but she refused, saying she couldn't leave her post. I told her where I live and said if she needed anything while you were away, she had only to send me a note, and I would come to her.'

Ned looked about at his listeners and took another sip of wine before continuing.

'Some weeks later, I received a message from Nancy telling me she was about to be turned out of her position. I travelled to London to see what I could do. She told me the owner of The George had died, and his nephew had inherited. He had new bold ideas on how to run the place. Nancy overheard him say he wanted all new staff and was about to let the current employees go.'

'The base born son of a jade,' Tom muttered.

'Quite,' Ned said and resumed.

'I suggested Nancy came to live with me until your return, Tom. She agreed, and on the last day of her employment, I went in my carriage to fetch her. Nancy didn't want to see Betty struggling to find another position, so she asked me whether she could come too. And I agreed.'

After telling his story, Ned sat back in his chair, a satisfied smile lighting his eyes.

Tom frowned and turned to Nancy.

'But, Nancy-love, why didn't you leave a message to tell me where you were?' Tom asked.

'I did, Tom. I asked that "miss prim," Nora Langton to say I was with Ned,' Nancy said.

'What a lying trollop! She said she didn't know where you were,' Tom said, wishing he could strangle "miss prim".

'Well, you've found me now, Tom. That's all that matters. Oh, but it's good to see you,' she said, catching hold of his hand.

After dinner when they rose from the table, the servants came to clear it.

Tom and Nancy went to stand by the window. The pleasing view of the twinkling lights on the barges moving along the Thames did not draw Tom's eyes. With one arm around her waist and the other holding her hand against his chest, he couldn't take his eyes off his Nancy. Neither could Nancy tear her eyes away from his as Tom told her of his adventures.

Betty sat next to Peter on the couch listening to him recount the same exploits on St Helena and their journey home. Ned noticed she watched Peter with rapt attention. He also noticed Peter glancing down at her with a bright spark in his eye each time he caught her gaze.

Ned knew the rules of etiquette required the ladies to leave the men to their port in the dining room and retire to the drawing room after dinner. He was sure the other four knew it too.

To hell with etiquette, he thought and carried on enjoying their most pleasant company.

Later that night, when everyone had gone to bed, Tom stole into Nancy's room.

'Are you awake, Nancy-love?' he whispered.

'Of course I am,' Nancy said.

'Why of course?'

'I was waiting for you, Tom. I knew you'd come to me,' she said and opened her arms to him.

THE END

AFTERWARD

Three weeks after being reunited, when the banns had been read, Tom and Nancy were married in St Nicholas Church, Chiswick.

Betty was Nancy's maid of honour.

Peter was Tom's groomsman.

(Tom and Nancy speculated on their being married, soon, too.)

Ned gave Nancy away.

Billy acted as usher—and an excellent job he made of it.

Tom wrote to Babineaux who, to Tom's great surprise, arrived in Chiswick in time to see Tom marry his Nancy.

Peter contacted all of Tom's old shipmates and cronies; some Tom hadn't seen for years. They all attended the wedding, and were there at the reception afterwards in Mirabilis House.

Three months later, a letter arrived for Tom from Corbeau, informing him that Napoleon had decided to hang up his sword and live incognito in French Guiana.

With the letter were the papers for Barings Bank, entitling Tom to draw on an account which held half a million guineas.

With his vast fortune, Tom bought a sailing ship and employed his friends as his crew.

He also bought a large estate in Sussex.

As the years went by, Billy grew up to be a fine young man.

Tom, following in Ned's footsteps, regarded Billy as his son.

One day, Tom called Billy to him and handed him his well-worn diary.

'Listen, my boy,' Tom said. 'If anyone got wind of

the things I've written in here, they'd hang me. You must keep this safe 'til after I'm gone, then publish it.

'I'll die happy knowing others will hear of my submarine and how I met Napoleon.'

And Billy must have carried out Tom's wishes, otherwise, how would we know his story?

BIBLIOGRAPHY

Brian Unwin *Terrible Exile* (IB Tauris 2010)

Emilio Ocampo *The Emperor's Last Campaign* (University of Alabama Press 2009)

Alan J Guy *The Road to Waterloo (*Alan Sutton Publishing Ltd 1990)

Philip J Haythornthwaite *The Napoleonic source book* (Guild Publishing 1990)

A.E. Richardson & A.E. Eberlein *The English Inn Past and Present* (Fleetway Press, Ltd. 1925)

Dean King *Harbours and High Seas* (Henry Holt and Co. 1996)

Donald Macintyre *The Adventure of Sail* (Ferndale 1979)